Mike Will

The Secret Channel

THOROGOOD

Thorogood Publishing Ltd
10-12 Rivington Street
London EC2A 3DU
Telephone: 020 7749 4748
Fax: 020 7729 6110
Email: info@thorogoodpublishing.co.uk
Web: www.thorogoodpublishing.co.uk

A CIP catalogue record for this book is available
from the British Library.

ISBN 1 85418 612 4
        978-185418 612-6

Book designed and typeset in the UK by Driftdesign

Printed in the UK by Ashford Colour Press

Dedication

================

This book is respectfully dedicated to the people of the Isles of Scilly – especially those from Tresco – and to all the servicemen and women, British and French, of the many covert flotillas who courageously kept open secret channels between England and France during the Second World War.

Mention should also be made of the extreme sacrifice during that conflict of the Dorrien-Smith family – the proprietors of Tresco island – who lost three sons, killed on active service.

Author's note

==================

The story is based upon the fact that such a covert flotilla operated between Tresco island and Brittany, delivering and bringing back secret agents together with vital intelligence about German troop dispositions and coastal defences.

HMS Godolphin is pure imagination, included to provide the Tresco flotilla with a focal point and context for its shore-based activities.

Certain names have been inspired by the names of real people, but the characters are figments of my imagination — based upon Service experience. Any similarity between them and persons living or dead is purely coincidental.

Contents

==============

Principal characters

===============================

In order of seniority of rank.

Character:	Referred to as:
Rear Admiral Hembury	
Director of Coastal Forces Operations	*Admiral, The Admiral*
Captain Mansell	
Officer commanding HMS Godolphin	*The Commanding Officer*
Commander Rawlings	
Operations Director, HMS Godolphin	*Operations Director*
Capitaine de Vaisseau, Jean-Pierre	*Jean-François (Resistance*
Duhamel	*code name)*
Lieutenant Commander Enever	
Senior Naval Intelligence Officer	*Commander, SNIO*
Lieutenant Richard Tremayne	
Central figure in the story, an RNVR	*Boat Commander, Boat*
Officer, recently transferred to	*Captain, Skipper, Flotilla*
Coastal Special Forces	*Captain/Commander*
Sub-Lieutenant David Willoughby-	
Brown, Tremayne's First Lieutenant	*First Lieutenant,*
(i.e. second-in-command)	*Number One, Sub, WB*

Second Officer Emma Fraser
Wren Intelligence Officer, serving
on Lieutenant Commander Enever's
staff, on HMS Godolphin   *Intelligence Officer, IO*

Petty Officer Bill Irvine
Tremayne's Coxswain   *Cox'n, 'Swain, PO*

The Isles of Scilly

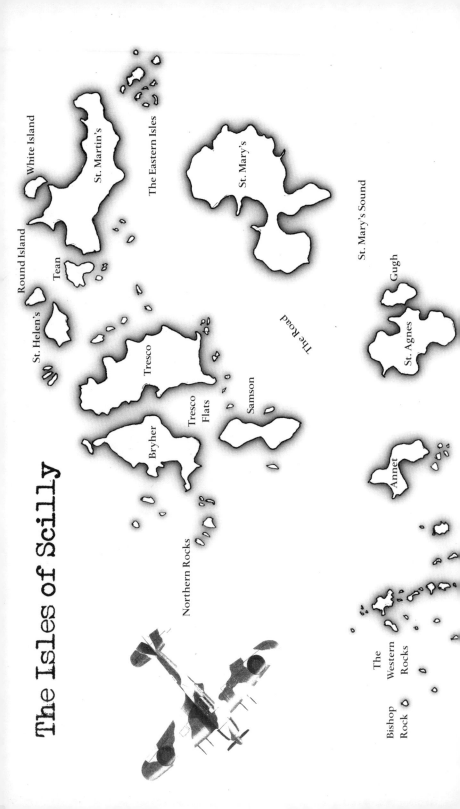

Tresco island

One

This remote and beautiful place

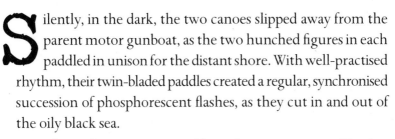

S ilently, in the dark, the two canoes slipped away from the parent motor gunboat, as the two hunched figures in each paddled in unison for the distant shore. With well-practised rhythm, their twin-bladed paddles created a regular, synchronised succession of phosphorescent flashes, as they cut in and out of the oily black sea.

"There's the answering signal from the reception party, Number One." Tremayne spoke quietly, little above a whisper, to his First Lieutenant. "Three white flashes, followed by a green one."

The night sky was already just beginning to lighten. The previously invisible outline of the Brittany coast started to take shape as an indistinct, but emerging, darker mass, as the first signs of the early spring dawn gradually began to appear in the black sky. The relatively calm sea was similarly dark, swelling and subsiding gently like slowly moving, glistening black treacle. Through their binoculars, the eyes of the two anxious young naval officers on the MGB's cramped armoured bridge, strained to follow the phosphorescent wake of the disappearing canoes as they steadily made their way, under cover of darkness, to the dangerous rock-strewn beach some five hundred yards away.

Tremayne suddenly became conscious of their proximity to the shore, as the gentle evening breeze carried the characteristic, yet indistinct, smells of the land mass across his vessel. For a moment, he thought about how often people become aware of the smell of the sea when on the coast and yet so rarely experience the reverse effect on their senses. A quick, instinctive glance at the luminous face of his watch brought him back to their immediate reality and the need to leave the area as quickly as possible.

Within a matter of minutes now, MGB 1315 would start to become visible to any keen-eyed sentry, awake in the German blockhouse at Pen Enez and, all-too-quickly, be a sitting duck for the adjacent battery of 88mm anti-aircraft guns, sited in their adapted role as coastal defence weapons.

The thought of those long, menacing barrels and the devastating impact of their flat trajectory, high-velocity shells on his vulnerable boat, sent a shiver down Tremayne's back as he slowly lowered his binoculars. The mounting tension was evident on the bridge and among those at action stations, on deck, manning the MGB's weapons and compulsively checking their guns' cocking mechanisms for the umpteenth time.

"Thank God there's no moon, Number One, but it's high time we took our leave. We'll make our move now. If we're seen, it could mean trouble for our recent guests. It wouldn't take a genius to work out why we're standing off, so close inshore." Turning to the other silent, duffel-coated figure beside him on the bridge, Tremayne, in hushed voice, gave the order to return to base.

"Take her home, Cox'n. Gently does it. Run her quietly at first until we've cleared Le Libenter, then lively as she goes, if you please, back to New Grimsby."

"Aye aye, sir. Course set for 0-four nine," Petty Officer Bill Irvine's clipped response, quiet though it was, immediately confirmed his East Belfast origins.

A stocky, strongly built man of forty-one, Bill Irvine had progressed from boy's service to able seaman through the course of the Great War. He had served in Admiral Beatty's *Lion* at Jutland and had been a contemporary of boy Jack Cornwell who, at sixteen years of age, had been awarded a posthumous Victoria Cross for gallantry in that costly, but inconclusive engagement against the German High Seas Fleet twenty-five years ago.

As he eased the brass-trimmed wooden wheel round the final five degrees to starboard and the boat's engines throbbed into life, Irvine glanced briefly at Lieutenant Richard Tremayne, RNVR, the youthful, but already battle-experienced skipper of their motor gunboat.

The dimmed glow of the masked light on the chart table emphasised the shadows of the lines of pain etched around his young captain's eyes and mouth. Though more than a year had passed since that fateful air raid on Plymouth, Irvine knew that the grief and heartache of Tremayne's terrible loss remained with him.

As a regular, who had completed a twenty-two-year engagement and who had then, within months of leaving the service, re-joined the Navy on the outbreak of war, Petty Officer Irvine viewed many RNVR officers with a disregard bordering on derision.

'*Really Never Very Ready*' was how many of the regulars interpreted the initials and Irvine had recently expressed the commonly-shared view, with customary forthrightness, to his fellow long-serving, regular petty officer colleagues:

"Bloody amateurs, most of 'em. Gentlemen playing at being naval officers. And some of 'em don't even qualify as gentlemen these days, so they don't. God help us, one even came straight to the Andrew from being a second-hand car salesman. Wouldn't know a Fairmile from a bloody Ford, so he wouldn't."

This skipper was different, mused Irvine – very different. He was 'pusser' and he was professional. He had quickly established a balance, Irvine felt, between maintaining naval discipline and the automatic expectations of a commanding officer while, at the same time, showing the level of concern and personal interest in his crew so necessary in such a small, close command as an MGB. He both looked and sounded the part but – most important of all, felt Irvine – he acted the part, day-to-day, both on board and ashore. The crew liked him and, above all, they respected him for the competent leader that undoubtedly he was. More understated than obvious, in his approach to the role of boat captain, Tremayne exuded a quiet, personal authority and aura of capability which created confidence amongst the members of his crew.

In a vessel of that size, there was little personal space and even less privacy. Typically, two or three officers and fourteen petty officers and ratings would be thrown together for hours on end – often in the harshest of conditions – and soaked to the skin. Many MGBs and motor torpedo boats (MTBs) – including the earlier Fairmiles – were notoriously wet boats in rough seas and Tremayne's vessel was no exception.

In action, mutual trust and support were critical, and there was no substitute for total reliability – and no excuse for a lack of it – in a crew where interdependence is vital to survival. Being able to rely on others and depend upon their ability – and readiness – to take the right action, at the right time, could be a matter of life and death, for officers and men alike, in the tight-knit community of a motor gunboat crew.

Richard Tremayne, at twenty-six, was mature beyond his years – despite the engaging boyishness, which only a few had been lucky enough to see, especially during the last thirteen months.

In his two and a half years as a naval officer, since his enlistment in September 1939, Tremayne had already seen active service in several theatres of war. He had served under Captain D, Philip Vian, in *HMS Cossack* during the *Altmark* incident in Sognefiord, Norway; manning a Lewis gun when the gunner was injured in the brief firefight with the German crew. Subsequently, he had seen repeated action, while still a Sub-Lieutenant, on convoy escort duty in the Western Approaches – the U-boats' sickeningly profitable Atlantic hunting grounds. There he had served as a Junior Gunnery Officer on board the modified Grimsby class anti-submarine corvettes, HM ships *Fleetwood* and her sister-ship *Portree*.

In command of *Portree*'s anti-aircraft guns, Tremayne's leadership, initiative and devotion to duty should, many believed, have earned him a DSC, but through lack of eyewitness verification of his contribution in fighting off two Focke-Wulf Condors, the coveted blue and white ribbon had eluded him on that occasion.

Twice mentioned in despatches, in anti-submarine and anti-aircraft engagements in the Atlantic, Tremayne's professional credentials and personal courage were already established beyond doubt.

In Bill Irvine's eyes, his young skipper's credibility also stemmed from his calm authority in an emergency and his consistent commitment to his word.

"If our skipper says he'll do something, then he'll do it, so he will," announced Irvine one night at dinner in the petty officers' mess. In what is one of the closest clubs in the world, where acceptance is invariably earned the hard way and rarely given freely – to superiors or colleagues alike – that was praise indeed.

Sub-Lieutenant David Willoughby-Brown, Tremayne's Number One, a twenty-two-year-old RNVR officer was, in Petty Officer Irvine's sceptical view, "still wet behind the ears – but there's nothing wrong with him that a gelignite suppository wouldn't cure. Green as grass so he is, but he's right enough and the skipper will soon lick him into shape."

On their first memorable encounter – which had rapidly become part of the petty officers' mess folklore at the flotilla base – the fresh-faced reservist officer introduced himself with proffered hand to the grizzled Coxswain with the words: "Willoughby-Brown. How do you do, PO?" A stranger to reverence, if not protocol, Bill Irvine saluted, gripped the outstretched hand and, parodying the young officer's double-barrelled name, muttered in reply: "Well-I'll-be-buggered," giving his response theatrical timing for full impact before adding, "Petty Officer Irvine, sir – Coxswain."

Ever since that first meeting, Willoughby-Brown had regarded the older man with something approaching undisguised awe and the hushed, guarded respect that the innocent often give to the worldly and supremely confident. He was well aware, too, that the Coxswain took great delight in exaggerating his Shankhill Road accent and vocabulary to a level that was quite incomprehensible to his young English ears. "Quare an' thran" and "great craic" were terms as divorced from the King's English to Willoughby-Brown as would be Lithuanian, or Cantonese.

Willoughby-Brown's family traditions were rooted, over generations, in the Light Cavalry and so the Royal Navy, its people and its customs, were still a source of both amazement and mystery to the very recently commissioned officer – "the young lad" – as Irvine generally referred to him.

Tremayne, however, was quick to sense the potential in his new First Lieutenant and showed Willoughby-Brown both patience and consideration, as he took the younger man under his wing, to develop his experience and confidence as second-in-command. Willoughby-Brown had the enthusiasm, as well as the inexperience of youth, and he was anxious to learn all he could and keen to be a success as First Lieutenant.

Already, Tremayne had seen in Willoughby-Brown both a ready, perceptive sense of humour and flashes of insight that revealed a degree of acuity, rare among such junior officers.

Willoughby-Brown – or WB as his fellow officers quickly dubbed him – was a language graduate who hailed from Sussex and who had obtained a first class honours degree in French and German at Durham University. He spoke both languages fluently, including several dialects, which was the reason for his secondment to Rear Admiral Hembury's so-called and newly created 'secret flotillas'.

The appointment of an officer of Flag Rank as Director of Coastal Forces Operations was welcomed by those who had been pushing for units capable of making the Strategic Operations Executive's (SOE) plans for clandestine warfare on the Continent of Europe a reality.

Operating under cover out of Tresco in the Isles of Scilly – twenty-five miles west of Land's End – the Admiral had assembled a small, but motley collection of MTBs, MGBs, fast motor launches and various fishing vessels, whose role involved covert operations along the coasts of northern and western France, but especially Brittany.

"Now we need to go on the offensive and begin hitting the enemy hard," he had told officers and ship's company at his first, memorable meeting with them at Tresco:

"Churchill has demanded that we 'set Europe ablaze', so let's start doing just that. Our small coastal craft and our role are not the stuff of major set-piece battles. We're going to become 'hit-hard-and-run-fast' specialists – and we've got to become bloody good at that. We have a major part to play in undercover warfare on mainland France – particularly around their naval bases along the coast of Brittany. Our role will be to 'out-guile' the Abwehr – who are not to be underestimated. We're now going to take the war to the enemy. Your 'secret channel' will be from here to Brittany, gentlemen."

Hembury was both something of a visionary and an opportunist, ready to exploit any possibility of his flotilla hitting and hurting the enemy in his own backyard. Already he could see – and was preparing plans to develop his ideas – how the role of the Tresco flotilla could be progressively exploited and expanded, as officers and ship's company gained in both competence and confidence, through increasing operational experience and the necessary specialist training in the arts of sabotage and subterfuge.

Earlier passive reconnaissance missions had progressively given way to the active insertion and extraction of agents, at various points along the coast, to support – and give impetus to – both espionage and sabotage against German naval and military installations in Brittany. Already, it was recognised that the endgame was the eventual invasion and re-occupation of Europe and that intelligence gathering in preparation for that longer-term objective was vital.

Hembury's intention was to raise his game with clandestine operations, but he recognised that in doing so, there were likely to be some very costly lessons to be learned. There were, he knew, no easy routes to gaining the experience and capability critical to success in this form of covert warfare.

Along with carefully vetted and selected officers, ship's company and specialist support personnel picked, variously, for their language skills, intimate knowledge of the Brittany coast and in-shore navigation skills, Admiral Hembury had recruited several French naval personnel, including those fluent in the Breton language.

"I'll get the talent we need for this job anywhere that I can find it," Hembury had declared, as he accepted his appointment from the Director of Naval Intelligence at the Admiralty. "All I ask sir is that, at times, you will be prepared to put the telescope to your blind eye, as it were…"

Gathering both the people – and the vessels – that he needed for increasingly dangerous and sophisticated clandestine operations had forced Hembury to employ levels of subterfuge and skulduggery that would make many a Balkan politician blush – and had certainly given his chief many a sleepless night.

Despite the recent daring and success of the Bruneval and St Nazaire raids, some members of both the War Cabinet and higher echelons of the Admiralty still regarded unconventional units and special service operations with scepticism and suspicion. Added to that were the self-defeating battles and frustrating lack of necessary collaboration between the SOE and British official Secret Intelligence Services – the SIS.

Beyond the direct intervention and personal initiatives of Churchill and Mountbatten, there was still much ignorance and many bureaucratic blocks to creating – and financing – the mobilised resources and talent for organised clandestine warfare.

As a consequence, Admiral Hembury had been forced to persuade, threaten, cajole and manipulate, as appropriate, in order to assemble his flotillas of small boats and specialists. Much-needed stores, equipment and weaponry were begged, borrowed and stolen to equip the flotillas, using levels of guile – and bare-faced audacity – that even the most hardened victualling and supplies officers had neither experienced before, nor ever imagined were possible.

Similarly, Hembury had short-circuited and circumvented RN drafting procedures to recruit the officers and ratings that he so desperately needed.

In senior naval circles, at Queen Anne's Mansions, he had earned the nicknames "The Artful Dodger" and "The Body Snatcher" – which both made him, privately, very proud. They not only appealed to his own wry sense of humour, but also reflected the measure of success that he had achieved in cutting through unnecessary service bureaucracy and red tape.

Because of their similarity in profile to German E-boats, especially in conditions of poor light, Hembury had concentrated on acquiring as many Fairmile Class C boats as he could – in both MTB and MGB format. It was one of the latter craft, one hundred-and-ten feet long and weighing in at over seventy tons, that Lieutenant Richard Tremayne commanded.

In addition to the three Fairmiles, which were inclined to be top heavy when fully loaded and tended to roll alarmingly in heavy seas, Hembury had also acquired for the Tresco flotilla, two Vosper MTBs and one Camper and Nicholson MGB, as his most powerful and heavily armed boat. Three Breton fishing boats, brought over by their defecting crews from Concarneau and Roscoff, together with two British Power Boat harbour motor launches, completed the flotilla operating out of New Grimsby harbour on Tresco. Flotillas of similar makeup had been established on the River Helford in Cornwall, at the Royal Naval bases at Plymouth and Dartmouth, and along the Channel and East Anglian coasts round to Lowestoft.

What lent uniqueness to the Tresco flotilla were the relative remoteness of its idyllic location; the absence of a large, major, traditional naval base – apart from a few vestiges of the former Royal Naval Air Service base remaining since the First World War; and the presence of several French naval personnel, familiar with Brittany and the Breton fishing industry.

This departure from Royal Navy traditions was to prove crucial to the success of covert operations, in a theatre of war still dominated by the Luftwaffe and the Kriegsmarine. The flotilla motto '*Labore et ingenio*' was freely translated by officers and ratings alike as '*By brute force and low cunning*', in recognition of the Machiavellian tactics adopted by Admiral Hembury to equip his Special Forces for their demanding and increasingly perilous role.

Two and a half miles off the jagged north-west coast of Brittany, with L'Aber Wrac'h now well behind them, MGB 1315 increased speed to her maximum twenty-seven knots.

The three Hall-Scott supercharged petrol engines, with their combined thrust of 2,700 horse-power, lifted the MGB's bow clear, exposing the black anti-fouling paint on her lower hull as she surged forward at full throttle. Her course was north-west by north for the island of Tresco and her anchorage there at Braiden Rock in New Grimsby Sound. Tremayne felt the sudden increase of speed transmitted through the boat's hull and the now vibrating wooden decking beneath his feet on the floor of the bridge.

Built by A. M. Dickie and Sons, of Bangor, North Wales, MGB 1315 possessed a range of five hundred miles, at a constant twelve knots, and carried 1,800 gallons of high octane fuel – 'a potential flaming coffin – so she is', was Irvine's laconic description of her.

Commissioning trials confirmed that she was capable of a maximum speed of twenty-eight knots but, to her 'Chief', Engineer Petty Officer Alastair Duncan, she was a surrogate child on whom he lavished constant loving care, within his central domain of the permanently gleaming engine room with its constant, familiar smell of warm oil and high grade petrol. During a recent refit, to equip her for her new, clandestine role with Naval Special Forces, she had been given dual steering – one wheel in the small, but well laid out wheelhouse, immediately forrard of her bridge, and the other – which Irvine now steered her by – in the armoured upper bridge itself.

Along with the Coxswain, the bridge was now occupied by Tremayne, the First Lieutenant and Leading Seaman 'Brummie' Nicholls. The latter three were each slowly sweeping the gradually emerging horizon with binoculars, on the lookout for marauding E-boats and destroyers, travelling to and from their bases in and around Brest.

Another major danger of the early dawn were predatory Junkers Ju88s patrolling the area, searching for British submarines and light coastal craft, themselves out on speculative seek-and-kill missions, as they sought vulnerable, unescorted German merchantmen, or slow-moving armed trawlers. Heavily armed and fast, the versatile, powerful Ju88s were a feared hazard, both at sea and on the land.

The course steered for Tresco took MGB 1315 across the Germans' coastal convoy route and there were often rich pickings to be had for fast, well-armed hit-and-run MGBs and MTBs close to the Brittany coast. Closed up at defence stations, the duty watch was on the lookout for both possible prey as well as potential threats – the natural role and lot of the hunter.

As Tremayne warmed his numbed hands in his duffel coat pockets, his fingers found – and held – the small silver photo frame with her photograph. Turning aside from the others, her name – Diana – silently crossed his lips as the desperate feeling of her loss engulfed him, which it so often still did. The picture had been with him every day since the bombers had so suddenly and brutally taken her from him on that terrible night in Plymouth. Tremayne had come to dread the silent, lonely watches in the dark, when his thoughts – and his heart – inevitably turned to her.

He was suddenly jolted out of his very private and painful reverie by a noisy, sing-song, adenoidal Midlands voice: "Gentlemen, a cup of kye, steamin' 'ot and luvly. Not yo', Nicholls, yo' idle bastard – yo' can get yer own bleedin' cocoa."

"Thank you Watkins, that's a real life-saver and very welcome at this time of the morning." Tremayne and the First Lieutenant gratefully took the steaming mugs of hot, glutinous, pussers-issue drinking chocolate – known throughout the Royal Navy as 'kye'.

As Willoughby-Brown sipped the boiling brew he looked quizzically at Leading Seaman Nicholls. "Don't worry yerself about 'im, sir. Me an' 'im's real oppos. 'Pablo' Watkins an' me was at the Austin at Longbridge together, before we joined the Andrew in '37 an' we've stuck together ever since. Just yo' see, sir, Pablo'll come creeping back up in a couple of shakes, mekking out 'es doin' me a favour, with a mug, all for meself."

Moments later, true to Nicholls' prediction, Able Seaman 'Pablo' Watkins appeared on the bridge. "Ere yer are, yo' idle sod. Your ol' lady would kill me if I didn't give yo' a mug of kye on a night like this," he said, with mock solemnity, as he handed the mug of hot chocolate to a grinning Nicholls. "I didn't ferget yo' neither, PO," added Watkins, passing another mug to the Coxswain of his 'torpedo propellant', as Tremayne called it.

"It would be more than your life's worth, so it would," said Irvine as he reached for the proffered mug, with just the hint of a smile softening his normally craggy face.

" 'Ot breakfasts ready in an hour, sir," Watkins said, addressing Tremayne.

"Thank you, Watkins. We'll all look forward to that. Carry on please."

"Aye aye, sir." With a broad wink at Nicholls, his fellow Brummie, Watkins disappeared below in the direction of the boat's cramped galley, with its precarious paraffin cooker and the limited facilities which never seemed to daunt the redoubtable AB.

"Well Number One. I wonder just what sort of culinary miracle Watkins has in store for us. This night's work has made me ravenous

— I'll be ready for anything Watkins throws at us by then."

"Absolutely, sir. But why ever do they call him 'Pablo'? Do you know, sir?"

"Haven't a clue, Number One — do you know Cox'n?" inquired Tremayne, turning to Irvine.

"Yes sir. When they were in Panama together, on a goodwill visit in '38, Watkins bought himself a Mexican sombrero on a run ashore, so he did, and insisted on wearing it at every opportunity. It was Nicholls there who dubbed him 'Pablo' and the name has stuck ever since. Isn't that right, Brummie?" he said, addressing Nicholls, who was still searching the sea and sky to starboard with his binoculars.

"Right, 'Swain," came the laconic reply, without any interruption of his continuing visual sweep of the horizon.

Any further light-hearted conversation was abruptly cut dead by Irvine's urgent call to Tremayne. "Sir. Aircraft, bearing red five-o. Two of 'em sir — both twin-engine jobs."

Speaking into the voice tubes, Tremayne called "action stations" and pressed the klaxon alarm button. "All guns bring to bear, red five-o. Stand by to fire."

Almost as one, the two-pounder, the twin Vickers and the Oerlikons traversed round to the indicated line of sight.

He quickly swung round to Irvine. "Thank you, Cox'n. Well spotted. Stand by to zigzag, on command. Maintain maximum revolutions."

"Aye aye, sir." Petty Officer Irvine gripped the wheel, straining his eyes to follow the flight of the now rapidly approaching aircraft.

"Stand by, all guns. Gun crews — MARK YOUR TARGET!"

Tremayne's strong, clear command focused everyone's attention on the two planes coming in fast, at around one hundred feet above sea level – the right height to make aerial torpedo attacks and to rake a vessel with devastating close-range cannon fire.

The two planes were now down to just above mast height, their engines shattering the still dawn air and whipping up the surface of the otherwise calm sea. To those on the bridge and the crews manning the guns, the next few nerve-straining seconds felt like an eternity, with everything seemingly happening in unnatural, agonising slow motion. Tense fingers nervously curled around triggers and thumbs hovered in urgent anticipation over firing buttons as gun muzzles were zeroed-in on the two menacing, fast approaching aircraft...

"Hold your fire. ALL GUNS – HOLD YOUR FIRE – they're ours." Tremayne's urgent order cut through the tension like a knife, as the two dark Beaufighters roared low overhead, waggling their wings in a salute of recognition.

"Good luck lads," muttered Irvine, as he stared over his shoulder at the disappearing aircraft.

"They must be looking for early morning prey, Number One. With that concentration of weaponry up forrard, they'll make a mess of most things smaller than a cruiser," said Tremayne, following their departure through his binoculars.

MGB 1315 continued her course for home, with the shivering gun crews and watchkeepers maintaining action stations in the cold, damp dawn, as the freezing spray of her bow wave cascaded over her deck. Chances were that their next visitors might not be Beaufighters.

"Number One, make sure everyone has kye, with a tot of rum – make it 'neaters' please," called Tremayne, seeing the forrard two-pounder gun-captain blowing into his freezing hands, while his colleague, the gun-layer, repeatedly jumped up and down to fight off the light, but bitter early morning wind that penetrated the thickest jersey and duffel coat.

"Aye aye, sir," replied Willoughby-Brown, as he moved to leave the bridge to initiate the distribution of that potent, but cheering concoction, for the shivering watchkeepers.

His return to the bridge some ten minutes later, was greeted by a plaintive, catarrhal wail, which rose from the boat's tiny galley:

"There is no snow in Snowhill,

Way down in Summer Lane

But when it's winter time in the Argentine,

It's summer in Summer L—a—n—e."

'Pablo' Watkins was in nostalgic mood, obviously homesick and singing about his beloved Brummagem as he prepared the watchkeepers' breakfasts.

"Should have been drowned at birth, so he should," muttered Irvine to no one in particular, his eyes fixed on the emerging horizon dividing sea and sky into two featureless shades of grey.

At which point Tremayne, pre-empting the start of any more verses of the mournful dirge, called down to the galley: "Watkins – any sign of that breakfast you've been threatening us with?"

"Aye, aye sir. It'll be with yo' in two shakes – brown sauce an' all, sir."

Tremayne smiled broadly as Willoughby-Brown winced, one

refined eyebrow raised in horror, at the mention of brown sauce. True to his word, Able Seaman Watkins duly appeared with a tray loaded with bacon, fried eggs, sausages, fried bread and beans – and mugs of hot fresh coffee, laced with pusser's rum.

"Watkins, you're a genius," said Tremayne. "Even the First Lieutenant will forgive your dreadful singing for a breakfast like that."

"Thank you sir, an' there's more brown sauce, should anyone want some!" he added, with a wink to Nicholls.

"Savoy Grill – eat your heart out," enthused Willoughby-Brown, as he speared one of the rapidly vanishing sausages.

"Here 'Swain, Nicholls, tuck in," called Tremayne, "before the First Lieutenant eats us out of house and home."

The atmosphere on the bridge and among duty gun crews was transformed by Watkins' breakfast which was, as Tremayne said, "a bloody gastronomic miracle."

Even the dour Coxswain was moved to exclaim that Watkins' culinary efforts were the closest he'd been to a genuine "Ulster fry" since he'd left Belfast.

About ninety minutes later, with MGB 1315 still at maximum revolutions, crashing through the 'white horses', Irvine called out: "Isles of Scilly dead ahead, sir, so they are. St Mary's to starboard and St Agnes and Annet islands to port."

"Right, Number One," called Tremayne, "duty watch to stand down from action stations and resume defence stations."

As they drew nearer, the sinister Western Rocks – which had seen many a ship founder on their terrible, jagged teeth over the centuries – gradually took eerie shape in the early morning light.

Tremayne began to identify them for the young First Lieutenant. "That's Melledgan, Number One, and then, further to port, you can see Gorregan, Daisy and Rosevean. Another mile further out, you can see Bishop Rock and the Crebinicks. Get to know them well. They are as dangerous as hell, but your life may depend upon your ability to play hide-and-seek with our friends, the E-boats, among these rocks, if they decide to try their hit-and-run tactics over this way."

Willoughby-Brown nodded silently, impressed by the mysterious, awesome-looking rocks, as is everyone who sees them for the first time.

"As far as we know, the Germans are completely unaware of our flotilla and its activities. But, if they ever do get wind of our clandestine operations, they'll come searching, in force, with aircraft, U-boats and most certainly fast, well-armed surface-craft. Some of these small off-islands and rocks are full of useful nooks and crannies to skulk in," said Tremayne, as he continued to name them for Willoughby-Brown.

"Thank you sir, I'd welcome the chance to spend time with the new crew when they start training in earnest and find my way round all these islands. I gather there are over a hundred of them, including the large rocks. It'll be quite a challenge, sir."

"So be it, Number One. We're all so new but, after three months here as a founder member of Admiral Hembury's flotilla, I'm considered an old hand. Last night's insertion of the four agents by canoe into Brittany was, in fact, my first real operation with Coastal Special Forces." Tremayne paused to check his bearings, as MGB 1315 began to clear the remaining Western Rocks, heading north, passing close to St Agnes and Gugh.

"We all have a hell of a lot to learn, and this is certainly no job for amateurs and untrained enthusiasts – too much is at stake. Speak with Jock Donaldson, Number One. He's the regular RN lieutenant responsible for all training activities within the flotilla. We shall, in any case, be undergoing training as a complete crew, to prepare us for the next series of big operations."

Within a short time, the MGB entered St Mary's Sound, passing under the forbidding presence of Star Castle, the impressive looking Elizabethan stone fortress atop Garrison Hill on the western edge of St Mary's island.

Then, at reduced revolutions, carefully negotiating the shallow, remarkably clear emerald waters between, first, Samson and Tresco, then the island of Bryher and New Grimsby, they finally arrived off Braiden Rock, their anchorage in New Grimsby Sound, at 09.50 hours.

With hands mustered on deck, fore and aft, for entering harbour routine, MGB 1315 looked trim and purposeful and drew admiring looks from the shore as, under Irvine's experienced hands, she glided towards her mooring.

After three months at Tresco, Tremayne had formed a deep affection for what he called "this remote and beautiful place". As they dropped anchor, he looked at what had now become something of a familiar, homecoming sight in New Grimsby Sound – the reassuring, solid stone structure known as Cromwell's Castle, dating from the mid-seventeenth century, that silent, grey guardian of the channel between Tresco and her smaller island neighbour, Bryher. His greatest sadness was that Diana had not lived to see him posted to this incomparably beautiful island, and that he was unable to share its ever-changing colours and moods with her.

In the little time that he had between routine patrol work, operational conferences, planning meetings and training in the highly specialised arts of clandestine warfare, Tremayne regularly walked the islands of Tresco, Bryher and nearby St Martin's and St Agnes, alone with his thoughts and his at times overwhelming, but always private, grief.

Each island was unique, with its own very special, distinctive beauty and scent-laden atmosphere, and he longed to tell Diana just how lovely they each were and how much their compelling charm was beginning to mean to him.

Almost invariably when walking the islands, Tremayne was accompanied by Bertie, his two-year-old black Labrador. Far greater on mettle and character than pure pedigree, Bertie had already proved to be a devoted and caring companion for one so young. He quickly sensed – and responded to – the changes in Tremayne's moods as, periodically, the finality of his loss swept over him as they walked together. Bertie would often briefly nuzzle Tremayne's hand and, as his master turned to him, look intently at him with his honest, gentle brown eyes showing mute concern beyond his tender years. The subtle bonds that can develop in the relationship between human beings and their dogs were proving to be a blessing to Tremayne, particularly the unconditional affection and sensitive, supportive companionship that only a dog, or a saint, are capable of giving.

Walking along the magnificent empty beaches, or tramping

over the heather and ling-covered hills, he would try to relieve the desperate pain of his wife's death by having imaginary conversations with her, until he returned to the officers' mess at HMS Godolphin, the flotilla's HQ and operations base.

Situated about half a mile from the Braiden Rock anchorage, HMS Godolphin occupied the site of a former anti-submarine seaplane base of the Royal Naval Air Service in the First World War, and telltale remains of the previous occupants and their equipment were a silent reminder of Tresco's role in that other war, which was supposed to end all wars.

It was located quite close to the ancient ruins of Tresco Abbey and the adjacent magnificent tropical gardens, overlooking the southern end of Bryher and the uninhabited island of Samson, with its characteristic twin humps of North Hill and South Hill. Surrounded by such dramatic and captivating scenery, it was sometimes difficult to imagine that there was a war on and that he was part of it. Stationed at Devonport or Portsmouth, Tremayne reflected, meant that the Navy and, therefore the war, were ever present and impossible to escape from. Here, in Tresco, away from the base, there was a sense of tranquillity and timelessness that provided regular, if temporary, respite from duty and the ever present threat of attack, when out on the open sea or close to the enemy coast.

Under Tremayne's supervision and the Coxswain's experienced hands, MGB 1315 secured and made fast alongside the big, rakish Camper and Nicholson MGB 1501. Leaning nonchalantly against the forrard six-pounder, her skipper, Hermann Fischer, a tall, blond, young South African RNVR lieutenant, called out to Tremayne: "Hello there, Richard. How's that poor man's E-boat of yours? When *are* you transferring to the Kriegsmarine?"

Richard Tremayne grinned back at Fischer. "With a name like yours, you should be the prime candidate for the next Korvettenkapitän's vacancy! Anyway, *we* can play the furtive lurker to perfection, with our deceptive profile and Number One's impeccable colloquial Plattdeutsch! Remember our motto, Hermann – we're the 'low cunning bit', so we'll leave the 'brute force' to you and that amphibious removal van of yours!"

The banter ended in loud laughter, as Tremayne went below with his First Lieutenant to conduct captain's rounds, before all but the two duty watchkeepers went ashore for a second breakfast, some much-needed sleep and then the daily routines so typical of the highly regulated life of a Royal Navy 'stone frigate' such as HMS Godolphin.

Tremayne looked around at the cosmopolitan flotilla of coastal boats and small craft anchored off Braiden Rock as he scrambled ashore onto the rocky, makeshift jetty.

Apart from the two MGBs, a Fairmile Type C motor torpedo boat lay off Hangman's Island, at low tide a promontory jutting out from Bryher across the Sound from Braiden Rock. Close to her, riding at anchor, were three fishing vessels – known to the island's local population as the 'mystery boats'. Intended for undercover work in broad daylight, these boats were being transformed from regulation RN grey vessels to bright and garishly painted fishing boats, in colours so beloved of the Breton fishermen.

About a dozen seamen were busy applying blue, brown and

white paint to the hulls and upper works, under the critical eyes of two Breton RNVR officers. Mixed in with the vivid colours were iron filings from Godolphin's workshops. A clever but necessary addition to the paint, these created a worn, distressed finish which produced an appropriately weathered appearance to the fishing boats.

In such a guise and skippered by French naval officers, or with similarly Breton-speaking Frenchmen as first lieutenant, these vessels were being prepared for clandestine insertion and extraction assignments, to transport intelligence agents back and forth between Tresco and Brittany.

All the French officers had been given RNVR commissions, together with British naval uniforms – complete with appropriate VR rank insignia. All, too, had been given the option of British identities to provide them, and their families in France, with some protection – albeit limited – in case of capture and subsequent interrogation. If caught, their fate would most certainly be brutal torture followed by execution by firing squad, were they to be identified as Frenchmen serving in covert British operations in their native country.

Able to take their place among the fishing fleets off the coast of Brittany, it was intended that these boats should escape all but close inspection. Modifications to their hulls and engines meant that they could sail at top speed from Braiden Rock, leaving at around 01.00 hours and seemingly drift into and mingle with the fishing fleets coming out of the many coastal ports of Brittany in the early morning.

Outside the traditional Breton fishing areas – or, when alone and free from observation, within them – these vessels could open their throttles and make around thirty knots or more with their cleverly re-engineered underwater hulls and up-rated engines.

On sea-trials, one RNVR officer had almost given the game away, inadvertently, when he had taken on the challenge of a destroyer, coming out of St Mary's harbour, and eventually outpaced her when she was making thirty-one knots. Needless to say, the reprimand he received from the consequent Admiralty Board of Inquiry was monumental, memorable – and painful, in the extreme, for him.

Names and pennant numbers of Breton ports of origin painted on the hulls, along with the regulation tricolour currently demanded by German naval authorities of the OKM – the Oberkommando der Marine – meant that they were able to sail very close to, or even directly into, the drop-off and pick-up points to be used for various agents. The Bretons amongst the French naval officers at HMS Godolphin maintained close links with agents in Brittany who kept them informed of changing recognition codes and signals that the Germans forced the fishermen to use to confirm their identity.

With summer coming and less hours of darkness, it was felt that the MGBs and MTBs would have a decreasing role in covert operations and so would hand over, progressively, to the heavily adapted, but generally very lightly armed fishing boats.

Specialist Wren officers and French nationals from "Y" Service, were providing "crash" immersion courses in French and Breton for officers and ratings alike. Because of the similarities between Welsh and the Breton language, a proportion of Welsh-speakers had been recruited amongst the ratings and petty officers.

They had already become adept at remembering the names of key locations along the coasts of Britanny and could pronounce them with sufficient Celtic lilt and confidence to fool any German and most French people – other than Bretons.

Led to believe that they were making Breton-style fisherman's clothes as spare dry clothing for sailors rescued from torpedoed vessels in the Channel, one small clothing company in Cornwall was busy producing smocks and trousers, in blue canvas, for Admiral Hembury's deliberately, but cheerfully vague Supplies and Victualling Officer. Once in Godolphin's victualling stores, the new sets of clothing were repeatedly washed and scrubbed to give them a suitably well-used appearance.

Following the rocky, narrow and heather-bounded coastal path from Braiden Rock, Tremayne and Willoughby-Brown made their way together to New Grimsby harbour and then on to Godolphin for debriefing of their night's activities off Pen Enez and their disembarkation of the four French agents.

"The Senior Naval Intelligence Officer here is Lieutenant Commander John Enever – he'll most likely conduct the debriefing," said Tremayne. "He's a charming chap who genuinely qualifies for the description – 'a gentleman'. You'll like him, I'm certain, Number One," added Tremayne, as they passed the saluting Royal Marine sentry on their way into the naval base and to hut 101, the debriefing centre.

Deliberately, Admiral Hembury and Captain Mansell, the officer commanding HMS Godolphin, had insisted on a universally low-key approach, to preserve the carefully fostered anonymity of the Tresco base. Outwardly, Godolphin appeared as a small unit consisting of old, ramshackle buildings, ostensibly there to provide a base for local defence and coastal patrols.

Accordingly, numbers identified buildings and deceptively innocuous notices belied their true function.

John Enever's debriefing centre, hut 101, which doubled as an intended interrogation centre, was labelled 'Victualling Stores'. All other signs gave the impression, to the outside world, of a small, but conventional and local temporary naval base, hastily constructed and put together for the duration of the war.

"As you're about to discover, Number One, Lieutenant Commander Enever is no 'Jack Dusty'. In fact, he's much more like a university professor," said Tremayne as they entered the anteroom of the corrugated iron Nissen hut.

"Good morning, gentlemen – please seize a pew," beamed Enever, in response to the salutes from Tremayne and his First Lieutenant. As Tremayne had predicted to WB, the Senior Naval Intelligence Officer had an empty and unlit pipe clenched firmly between his teeth.

Tremayne's overriding impression of the interior of hut 101 was that it was more reminiscent of a university lecturers' common room, than a centre set aside for activities which included some of the less attractive aspects of intelligence work – particularly interrogation. Even Enever's SOE warning notice, an alternative to the more usual *"Careless talk costs lives"* and *"Be like Dad – keep Mum"*, had a deceptively non-threatening, incongruous, almost 'classical' flavour: *"Silence is of the Gods... only monkeys chatter"*. Enever's apparently benign – rather academic – style added to the seemingly harmless and innocuous ambience of the centre. This no doubt deliberate stratagem was to pay off handsomely, as it soon transpired, in both the selection of people for intelligence roles – especially as agents – and in the uncovering of dangerous double agents.

Despite his own pivotal role and his high referential power-base, not only at Tresco but also within British Naval Intelligence and the wider arena of SOE and SIS, Enever tended to be informal to the point of egalitarianism. He seemingly abandoned rank – or mention of it – whenever he could, with the result that many people easily took him into their confidence and told him things that an autocratic, more status-conscious officer would never hear about.

"Jenny, please rustle up a couple of mugs of your magnificent tea for these gentlemen – they've had a busy and tiring night," said Enever to the young communications branch Wren, who appeared in response to the 'buzzer' on his ancient, leather-topped walnut desk.

"Please also bring some tea for Second Officer Fraser and Sub-Lieutenant Tabarly, Jenny. They'll be joining us for the debriefing," Enever added, turning to Tremayne.

"Emma Fraser is on Admiral Hembury's staff as an Intelligence Officer and is one of my immediate colleagues. Daniel Tabarly is from Brittany. He slipped out of Roscoff one evening in a local fishing boat – one of those you may have seen being repainted – and made his way over here some six months ago," said Enever. "You'll find them both very committed to what we're doing here and easy to work with," he added.

"Come in," called Enever, in response to the knock on his

door, as Tremayne and his First Lieutenant rose to greet the very attractive chestnut-haired Wren officer and her shy-looking, serious young Breton colleague.

"Richard, WB, let me introduce Emma Fraser and Daniel Tabarly." Enever smiled, taking the unlit pipe from his mouth, and waved his gathering visitors towards the assortment of vacant chairs around a large mahogany boardroom table which – like the walnut George II desk – was "rescued" anonymously in one of Admiral Hembury's many "seek and filch" operations.

"Emma and Daniel are both absolutely vital to our work at Tresco, and I'm delighted to have them on board," he said, smiling benignly at the two young officers.

"Richard here is one of our "star" Coastal Forces officers with a great deal of experience gained in the Atlantic, hunting U-boats and fighting off the Luftwaffe, while WB is an outstanding linguist – not only fluent in French and German but also, so I hear, a master of several dialects in both languages."

Having graciously introduced people to one another, Enever turned to Tremayne:

"Right, Richard, take us through the events of last night as they relate to the four agents that you dropped off Pen Enez. We need your first-hand account of the operation, up to the point where you left them in order to return to Tresco."

Tremayne, taking in each person sitting round the table, recounted, in detail, how the four – all Frenchmen – had assembled and checked their weapons and their radios, intently studied their maps, and spent most of their time on board the MGB huddled in conversation together.

"From their conversation, sir, that I overheard, they spoke a good deal about routines and agreed procedures. They also talked about the people they were going to meet, and mentioned the names 'Jean-François', 'Muguette' and 'Louis'. Beyond this, I didn't really hear much more of their discussion, sir." Enever removed his empty pipe, placing it in the large ceramic ashtray in front of him, as he listened attentively to Tremayne.

"Just after embarking in the two canvas folboats, they signalled the shore and received the expected reply within seconds – three white flashes, followed by one green one."

Second Officer Fraser's steady, intelligent blue eyes studied Tremayne's face and controlled gestures, as he reviewed the agents' preparation and disembarkation.

"We were in place, to get them to their RV, with about five minutes to spare and we followed them through our binoculars, tracking the phosphorescence of their paddles and canoe stern-wakes towards the shoreline as far as we could," continued Tremayne.

"Were you able to see them make actual contact with the reception party?" asked Emma Fraser.

"No, that was impossible because of the darkness, and the shore was about five hundred yards away. Why do you ask?" queried Tremayne.

Lieutenant Commander Enever, looking uncharacteristically serious, cut in: "Because Richard, we have received no message from them since, and they have not replied to our attempted radio contacts at 06.00, 07.00 and, again, at 08.00 hours this morning. Sub-Lieutenant Tabarly, who worked with them on the setting-up of their mission and who knows their contacts personally, is convinced that the operation has been "blown." Daniel, over to you, please," added Enever, looking earnestly at the young Breton, who wore the single wavy gold stripe of a RNVR Sub-Lieutenant on his uniform sleeve.

"Thank you, sir. Gentlemen, can you remember how long after the three white flashes, before you saw the green one?" asked Tabarly, turning to Richard Tremayne and his First Lieutenant.

"Hmm, good question, I would have said a consistent gap of about one second, between each of all four flashes," replied Tremayne, looking towards Willoughby-Brown for confirmation. Emma Fraser suddenly gave an anxious look towards Enever at Tremayne's response.

"Number One, what do you recall of the signal we saw on shore?"

"I agree, sir," said Willoughby-Brown. "All four appeared in pretty rapid succession."

"Aha", muttered Tarbarly. "But you see, there should be a delay of five seconds after the three white flashes, before they show the green light. The green one means 'all is OK, come on', and we use a red one if everything is not OK."

"Someone's slipped up somewhere sir," said Tremayne to Enever. "We were simply given the colour code and sequence, but no mention whatsoever of a time lag before the green light. What is more, as I recall events, the canoeists didn't appear to query the response from shore either and responded immediately."

Willoughby-Brown nodded, affirming Tremayne's reply. Again, Enever and Emma Fraser exchanged anxious glances.

"You *could* be right, Richard — someone *may* have forgotten to communicate the correct signal to all of us — me included," responded Enever. "We only learned of the intended delay between the last white flash and the green one through Daniel's radio contact with another agent today." Enever looked very concerned as he added, "But, equally, it could have been a deliberate omission and that's something Daniel, Emma and I need to pursue as a matter of urgency."

"Daniel made contact at 08.15hours today by radio with Jean-François, one of our principal agents of the Confrèrie de Saint Michel, which is the most important and effective Free French intelligence network in Brittany. The result was negative.

The four we dropped were due to contact Jean-François within thirty minutes of landing. Just before this meeting, Daniel again contacted Jean-François who, almost six hours later, had still heard nothing from the four," confirmed Enever.

"Presumably, you heard nothing unusual on shore — shouting or gunfire, for example — before you left the area and started back?" asked Emma, turning to Richard Tremayne.

"No. Nothing at all. It was completely quiet. We were closed up at action stations and obviously maintaining strict silence and would have heard any significant noise at that time of night, especially since it would have been carried over water to us. We would not have heard normal conversation at five hundred yards but shots, or shouting, we would most certainly have been aware of. The sea was calm and the night was quite still, with only the gentlest breeze. As we left the area," added Tremayne, "we kept watch on the shore, both from the bridge and from the after

Oerlikon position, in case Jerry woke up. We still neither heard, nor saw, anything untoward."

"We must find out what has happened, as quickly as possible," said Enever, "and establish just how far the Confrèrie – and our role in supporting it – may have been compromised. Daniel will maintain contact with Jean-François and Muguette, an agent who has infiltrated the OKM HQ in Brest," added Enever.

"You're our most experienced small boat skipper," said Enever, addressing Tremayne. "What we find out from our contacts will determine what action we take next, so it looks, Richard, as if you and your crew will need to go back to L'Aber Wrac'h within the next twenty-four hours. We must get Daniel ashore there – and extract him," said Enever, amid laughter, "once he's met with Muguette and Jean-François and obtained an up-to-date picture."

Turning to Tremayne and Willoughby-Brown, Enever added, "Richard, WB – you must be exhausted. Get some much-needed shut-eye, but stand by for a probable briefing at 21.00 hours."

Emma smiled as they left: "It was good to meet you both. I look forward to working with you again."

Following Lieutenant Commander Enever's debriefing, Tremayne returned to his quarters and quickly fell into a deep sleep. Confusing, seemingly inexplicable dreams began to disturb and disrupt the welcome peace that sleep should normally bring. At one point, Diana emerged, smiling, with outstretched arms, as she beckoned him to go to her. Then, as he eagerly approached her, in response to her laughing eyes, her image faded before him and vanished, just as quickly as she had appeared.

Anguish and panic at her disappearance caused him to call

out, sharply, in his troubled sleep, and he awoke to find an anxious Bertie, with a paw on each of his shoulders, licking his face and squeaking with obvious relief and pleasure, as Tremayne woke up and reached up to pat his dog's neck and ruffle his fur.

"Sorry old fellow – just a bad dream," murmured Tremayne, as he struggled to put the nightmare behind him and come to terms with reality and the need for the daily acknowledgement, yet again, of Diana's untimely death.

"Time for supper, Bertie: let's see what we've got in the locker for you tonight." Tremayne knew that both sanity and his salvation, as a person with a future, lay very much in his ability to involve himself with routines and activities of the moment, however mundane. He was coming to recognise the therapy of routine and the life saving value of regular immersion in simple details and regular procedures. They were fast becoming his link to daily sanity.

"Take each day as it comes, Richard. Concentrate on the detail of those things that have to be done, hour by hour," *Portree*'s navigator, Lieutenant Bill Mitchell, had told Tremayne. "Time may be a healer, but you've got to cope with – and get through – minutes, hours and days; not years, at the moment. That will come later."

Mitchell and Tremayne had become close friends during their time together on convoy escort duty in the Atlantic. Tremayne had found the older man to be an emotional sheet anchor during the unbearable early weeks and months following Diana's death. Mitchell's completely honest caring and concern, together with his sane, balanced perspective, had helped Tremayne to make at least some sense of what had happened, and how he might survive the desolation of his loss.

It had been Mitchell who had first put the idea into Tremayne's head of a transfer to Special Operations.

"You have an intimate knowledge of the coastal water around Brittany from your university sailing days, Richard, and your French is pretty good, by most standards," Mitchell had told him.

"What's more, you won't have the same long periods of sea time, steaming back and forth across the Atlantic, with time on your hands, to reflect and fret. Instead, you'll have far greater variety, a lot of new challenges and much more to keep your mind occupied than you have maintaining station, for days on end, with slow-moving convoys. In a nutshell, Richard, you'll have a hell of a lot more to fill your life with than you have in your present role, and that's what you need more than anything else right now."

Tremayne had been grateful for Mitchell's genuine warmth and support, and he missed the navigator when he transferred to Scilly.

Shortly after Tremayne left *HMS Portree* to join Admiral Hembury's Tresco flotilla, she was torpedoed by a U-boat she was hunting off the south-west coast of Ireland and sunk by gunfire, when the submarine surfaced to finish her off. She was lost with almost all hands, apart from some picked up out of the water by the U-boat but, to Tremayne's distress, Mitchell was not listed among the handful of survivors.

It seemed to him that getting close to people was an experience that was destined to end in pain and heartache.

Tremayne cut short his own thoughts as he routinely

looked at his watch. It was 19.30 hours. Bertie's intervention had pre-empted his wake-up call – or "shake" as it is universally known in the Navy, by twenty minutes.

He shaved, showered and dressed with minutes to spare, before the knock on his door and discreet cough announced the arrival of the duty watch leading hand.

"Good evening, sir. Your shake, sir. It's 19.50 hours and 'ere's a cuppa tea for you, sir. 'Swain said to put a drop of 'neaters' in it, sir. It's a bit parky tonight out there an' 'e thought a spot of pusser's rum might 'elp keep the cold out, sir."

Tremayne looked at the amiable, gangling figure of Leading Seaman 'Lofty' Towers, a veteran of the Narvick campaign and now captain of MGB 1315's after twin Oerlikons.

"Thank you, Towers – just what the doctor ordered. That'll set me up nicely. Is the First Lieutenant awake?" asked Tremayne. "Yes sir an' 'e said to tell you that 'e'd be 'ere in a few minutes, sir. There's 'am an' eggs an' enough coffee to float the *Renown* in the wardroom when you're ready, sir, so steward tells me."

"Thank you. That will be more than welcome. We'll all need a good lining in our stomachs before tonight's tangle with the elements – and possibly Jerry. Have duty crews had their supper?"

"They 'ave, sir, an' duty boats are being fully victualled, ready for the off, right now, sir. Commander Rawlings 'as been seein' to that, sir."

Shortly after Towers left the wardroom, Willoughby-Brown arrived and tapped politely on Tremayne's cabin door.

"Good evening, Number One. Come in – I hope you slept well. Supper awaits us, so the duty killick tells me. Let's grab a bite to eat and get our thoughts together, before we meet up with Lieutenant Commander Enever and his team."

Their route to the officers' mess took them past the First World War seaplane hangar, which now served as the ratings' NAAFI canteen and bar – that unashamedly anti-gourmet institution, yet source of salvation for many a soldier, sailor and airman.

The raucous singing was in full flow, as the two officers approached the building:

"You've got to walk up, walk up, see the tattooed lady,

See the tattooed lady at the fair

In went the lads and gave a mighty cheer,

'Cos tattooed on her arse was every town in Lancashire."

"Hmm, in good heart – and in good voice, too, sir," said Willoughby-Brown, with one dramatically elevated eyebrow.

"Just listen to the rest, Number One. This is 'Jolly Jack' at his choral best," laughed Tremayne.

Peering in through the open window, they saw Able Seaman 'Pablo' Watkins conducting the sing-song, standing on a table, waving his sombrero in time to the music:

"There was Oldham, Bolton and Ashton-under-Lyne

The coalfields of Wigan were doing mighty fine"

At this point, the forty or so voices rose to a deafening crescendo, as Watkins beamed at his 'choir' with his sombrero pointed heavenwards:

"Till some dirty bootneck shouted "don't go down the mine"

At the Rawtenstall a-n-n-u-a l f-a-i-r."

"Heavens. Half of Tresco must have heard that," said the First Lieutenant, with what Tremayne was coming to recognise as a characteristic wince of mock dismay.

"Half of Cornwall too, no doubt, Number One. But thank God. We're most probably going to need something of that spirit and camaraderie before the night's out," said Tremayne, as they entered the spartan, makeshift wardroom for supper together.

At 21.00 hours, they began their briefing with the Senior Intelligence Officer, Second Officer Emma Fraser and Sub-Lieutenant Daniel Tabarly.

They were joined by Commander Julian Rawlings, RN, the Operations Director of the base, who was a career naval officer, typical of the Royal Navy of yesteryear.

Rawlings was a large florid-faced man, of exaggeratedly clipped speech, who frequently added a rather querulous "what?" to his already emphatic, usually judgemental, pronouncements. His principal battle experience had been gained during the First World War, variously, at the battle of the Falklands, the hunt for the cruiser *Emden*, the battle of Jutland and in support of the great St George's Day raid on Zeebrugge by the Royal Marines in 1918. Subsequently, he had served both in Trincomalee in Ceylon and on the China Station.

His time had been spent mainly in cruisers and destroyers and always in the role of an executive officer – his major command being *HMS Worcestershire*, a six-inch gun cruiser based at Hong Kong in the early thirties. His style was to test – and to hector – people and he showed neither patience nor sympathy with those who failed to measure up to his standards and expectations. Something of a martinet, Rawlings was low in tolerance and high on criticism, which made him a difficult and, at times, unpleasant man to deal with. He worked strictly according to the book and possessed neither the imagination nor the flexibility to adapt to circumstances that demanded intelligent initiative, rather than unthinking compliance.

Commander Rawlings was "old school Navy" through and through and, on the lower deck, he was known as 'that Anchor-Faced Bastard' – and frequently something far less charitable. Though he neither understood – nor approved of – much of the work and clandestine role of the Tresco flotilla, he recognised that it was his task to ensure that all operations were given maximum logistics support and back-up to guarantee their success.

Admiral Hembury's unequivocal demands for an efficient, effective and well run unit, 'Naval Party 1798' as it appeared in Admiralty records and returns, were clearly Commander Rawlings' operational priorities and he had been left in no doubt whatsoever, by the Admiral and Captain Mansell, that this was his primary role at HMS Godolphin.

Lieutenant Commander Enever, DSO, made an interesting contrast, reflected Tremayne. He was small by comparison, with deceptively mild grey eyes behind steel-rimmed spectacles and possessed the enviable combination of intensity of intellectual focus with an apparently incongruous, easy-going manner.

He dealt with Commander Rawlings' bluster and bullying by seemingly ignoring it and talking as if the large, more senior officer simply wasn't there. It was an approach to which Commander Rawlings had no answer, but at least he was bright enough to recognise that he and Enever came from – and largely lived in – very different worlds.

In a strangely non-engaging way, the two managed to work well together – principally because of Enever's well-developed art of making soothing noises, while being completely single-minded and ruthlessly committed to his role and the success of whatever assignment was on hand.

As Willoughby-Brown subsequently described the relationship to Tremayne: "It's a curious encounter – rather than a meeting – of minds sir: a matter of the artistic collaborating with the autistic!"

Enever opened the meeting by confirming that there was to be an operation that night, departing from Braiden Rock at 23.00 hours.

The object was to put Tabarly ashore, to make contact with Jean-François, to obtain an up-to-date picture of the fate of the four agents whom Tremayne had taken over, and to determine the extent of compromise of the Confrèrie de Saint Michel.

"We suspect," said Enever, "that Jerry may have cracked the code used in our radio transmissions to the Confrèrie. We must know, as a matter of urgency, if this is true and I want to know how this has happened if, in fact, it is the case. We have organised a fresh RV, close to L'Aber Wrac'h," continued Enever. "Daniel, here, will paddle ashore after being launched from 1315. He will have, as stern paddler, Corporal Kane of the Royal Marines who has been training with a small group of specialist canoeists and frogmen, based over at RM Eastney, in preparation, we believe, for some major clandestine operation. Admiral Hembury managed to secure Kane's release to join us temporarily. Corporal Kane's role is to provide protection for Daniel. In effect, Richard, he will be 'riding shotgun' as it were."

"He's a damn good paddler, an excellent swimmer, as well as a crack-shot with most small arms," cut in Commander Rawlings. "Kane has had battle experience with the Royal Marines on Crete and in Norway, where he won the Military Medal. He will be carrying one of the silent CO_2 pistols, developed by our friends in SOE, for quietly eliminating any sentries who happen to get in the way, what? He's among the best we have for a job like this."

"Thank you, sir," said Tremayne. "At what distance from the shore do we launch the canoe?"

At this point, Enever came back into the discussion: "When you arrive at the RV, Richard, there will be an incoming tide so stand off from shore, as before, at about five hundred yards and make that your point of launching. If all goes according to plan, the tide will not have turned when you begin your return journey. So, if conditions allow, you may need to get in close to help the canoeists who will obviously be paddling back to you against the tide. They will be using what the Royal Marines refer to as a 'Cockle Mk2' which is a substantial, seaworthy canvas and wood canoe, built for carrying-capacity – not speed. It depends on how the tide is running, but they'll be hard-pressed to make more than three knots even in a calm sea and, unfortunately, the 'Met' boys, based at Devonport, have promised us wind and waves tonight."

"Where exactly is the RV, sir?" asked Tremayne. "You referred to a 'fresh RV'. How far is it, for example, from Pen Enez and that battery of 88s?"

Enever turned to Second Officer Fraser: "Emma, the details, please, for Richard."

"Aye, aye sir" – the soft, crystal clear accent of someone born and bred in the Western Highlands was only just discernible. "Gentlemen," she began, "your new RV is contained in sealed orders, which will be given to you at the end of this briefing and which are to be opened once you are underway and clear of Scilly. This may seem rather tiresome drama to you, but we have reason to believe that German counter-intelligence have known in advance much of what we have been doing in Brittany. Since we suspect – but have no real evidence of – the source of any leaks, we are simply being careful and sensible. Using the existing codes, we have radioed Jean-François that the RV is to be off Pen Enez as previously." Emma Fraser almost smiled to herself as she saw the rapt attention with which the others were closely following her.

"As before, the French language was used in the radio transmission. Using totally different codes and frequency we sent a message, in Breton, giving him the real location, which you will find in your sealed orders. One factor we hadn't allowed for in selecting the actual RV is that a trainee Panzer battalion moved into the area two days ago for manoeuvres and gunnery practice. In addition to twenty or so heavy tanks with 76mm weapons, they have several Sturmgeschutzen – large self-propelled guns – which are capable of making a terrible mess of an MGB should a shore-to-ship firefight develop."

"Our forrard pom-pom, which is our heaviest weapon, is going to be about as useful as a pea-shooter against armour like that," said Tremayne. "What are we supposed to do – form a blue-jacket landing party and charge them with bayonets?"

The steady blue eyes gave no hint of a reaction to Tremayne's outburst.

"No, Lieutenant Tremayne," Emma's response was controlled and measured. "You will be accompanied by Lieutenant Fischer in the Camper and Nicholson which, as I'm sure you're aware, mounts a very useful six-pounder, forrard and a 40mm Bofors, aft. His role is to provide the firepower that you lack, in order to give any covering fire necessary to allow you to return with Sub-Lieutenant Tabarly and," she added with a smile, "Corporal Kane. The 'Royals' would never forgive us if we left him behind!"

Tremayne already regretted his tetchy response and the fact that he'd made something of a fool of himself in front of the others. He was very conscious of both Emma Fraser's calm, neutral handling of his ill-tempered rejoinder and also his First Lieutenant's mobile eyebrows which, for once, registered genuine surprise. "Thank you, Emma," said Enever. "Will you now confirm for Richard the recognition signal code that he must use, once at the RV?"

"Aye, aye sir. Your ETA is 04.00 hours. You will make full revolutions for most of the way, but at around five miles short of the RV, we recommend that you reduce speed to minimise engine noise. The new signal, agreed with Jean-François, will be two white flashes, a pause of exactly seven seconds, then the green one. After a further ten seconds, the complete signal will be repeated. Thereafter, if you have not received an identical response from them, you will wait five minutes, then repeat the complete procedure again. If still no response, wait exactly fifteen minutes more, then repeat the two-step signal only. If no answer at this point return to base, maximum revolutions."

"Is that perfectly clear Richard?" asked Enever. "It's quite possible that some young and eager Panzer duty officer may be up and about with his Zeiss binoculars, searching the sea for mermaids, when he suddenly comes across you and young Hermann Fischer hove-to offshore. I don't want any dead heroes, Richard. At the first sign of trouble go about, signal full speed ahead, and the pair of you zigzag like hell and get back to Tresco."

Emma Fraser continued the briefing at this point.

"Two of the other Fairmiles will accompany you for the first fifty miles and then set course for Pen Enez. Their role is both to act as a diversion to concentrate the Germans' attention on them – not you – and also to allay any suspicion that we believe that the Germans may have cracked our codes. If we turn up as announced, we do what they expect us to do, which allows us to regain the initiative in the battle of wits with the Abwehr. Maintain R/T contact with them when out of sight, as well as with Lieutenant Fischer, and agree your RV to meet up to return as a flotilla."

Once again, Enever took over.

"You, Richard, will act as Flotilla Commander. Hermann, of course, will command 1501, while 1316 will be skippered by Lieutenant Mick Taylor." At the word "skippered", Commander Rawlings showed all the signs of incipient apoplexy and a distinct reddening of both ears.

"Taylor has a four-pounder forrard while Sub-Lieutenant

Bower, who will command 1317, has, as you know, a forrard-mounted six-pounder like Fischer. Their role is purely to show the expected presence – and then act as if they were meant to be there. To invest their presence with some significance, the RAF will send in four rocket-firing Beaufighters to "soften up" the coastal batteries. Their attack will precede the Fairmiles' arrival off Pen Enez at 04.00 hours by just three minutes. They will strafe the batteries with both rockets and 20mm cannon fire. As they pull out, so Taylor and Bower will pound the batteries – or what's left of them – at full speed ahead, presenting as small a target as possible to any German gunners still left alive. This diversionary attack – because of its intended ferocity – should, we hope, concentrate Jerry's attention on Pen Enez, as they try to cope with the shambles and chaos that we – and the RAF – expect to create.

"As a result of this diversionary raid, there will inevitably be a lot of both E-boat and Luftwaffe activity in the area, so remain closed up at action stations for at least an hour after you leave your RV. Good luck gentlemen, and a safe return home. Do you have any questions?"

"Only one, sir," replied Tremayne. "Should the Fairmiles get into serious trouble for any reason, can I go to their assistance once I have retrieved Sub-Lieutenant Tabarly and Corporal Kane?"

"Your primary task, Richard, is to get information back to us, which is why this operation is being mounted," answered Enever. "That, quite simply, is my response to your question. Don't do anything that is likely to deny us the answers we must have for future operations in Brittany to succeed."

"Here are your orders, gentlemen," said Emma Fraser, handing Tremayne a large, sealed Admiralty official envelope.

Tremayne took the buff envelope and hesitated, briefly, before he said quietly: "Emma, I apologise about my rudeness – that was unforgivable and quite unjustified."

"Och, dinna fash yerself," she replied, laughingly exaggerating her usual, barely perceptible Scots accent. "Come back safely – both of you."

Tremayne turned to Commander Rawlings, as Enever's Intelligence Team briefing broke up.

"At what time will your ops briefing for boat captains take place, sir?"

"At 22.00 hours, promptly, in the Operations Room – I take it you know where that is, Tremayne. I'll conduct the briefing. It is now 21.55 hours, so look lively there and make sure you're not adrift, what? First Lieutenants to take charge of boats immediately."

"Aye aye, sir." Tremayne bit back any further words that he might regret and winked at Willoughby-Brown.

"Number One, I'll rejoin you as soon as I'm able. In the meantime, I leave 1315 in your capable hands. Carry on please."

Rawlings began his operations briefing at exactly 22.00 hours, labouring the obvious and dwelling on the minutiae of sea-going routines. At times, he appeared to be quoting the most elementary instructions from the Service standard issue *Manual of Seamanship* – the nautical equivalent of the Ten Commandments. His excruciating exploration of the mundane soon had all four boat captains struggling to remain awake.

Hermann Fischer's imaginative doodlings were rich pickings for any psychoanalyst and would have provided scope for the most forensic of Freudian diagnoses. The miniature score card on Fischer's note pad showed that he was also counting the number of times that Rawlings uttered a peremptory "what?"

Fischer acquired his Germanic name from his father, who hailed from Hamburg but who had gone out to South Africa, well before the outbreak of the First World War. There he had met and married a girl from Cape Town who was of English origin. As a consequence, Fischer often appeared to be more British than the British. He had a ready, ribald sense of rather 'black' humour, and he and Tremayne had become close friends in their short time together at HMS Godolphin.

Lieutenant Mick Taylor, RNVR, boat captain of MGB 1316, a likeable, highly intelligent and sensitive, somewhat introverted man, had completely switched off from Rawlings' stupefying monologue and was preoccupied with his own thoughts and the forthcoming operation. A talented musician and an outstanding piano player, Taylor frequently gave the impression that he lived, for much of the time, in a world of his own. He was a man with a dry, engaging sense of humour, and was extremely popular among the younger RNVR officers.

By contrast, Sub-Lieutenant Bob Bower was a lively extrovert and a brilliant mimic. On more than one occasion, he had telephoned the Master-at-Arms Office, the PO's mess and the NAAFI manager, imitating Commander Rawlings and threatening a detailed personal inspection within the hour. The resultant terror and chaos had provided his brother junior officers with a great deal of amusement – usually at the expense of some of the most unpopular and starchiest people at the base.

Apart from being a very adept practical joker, Bower was also a highly competent boat captain and commanded another of the Fairmiles – MGB 1317.

Using the occasion primarily as a vehicle for his status and vanity, Rawlings added little to what Lieutenant Commander Enever and Second Officer Emma Fraser had already given at their briefing. It was, therefore, with considerable relief that the meeting broke up at 22.45 hours and the four RNVR officers left to resume command of their boats.

In a quick, three-minute quayside briefing, Tremayne, as acting Flotilla Commander, emphasised the need not only for clear communication and co-ordinated action, but also for common sense and flexible, intelligent initiative should things not go according to plan.

With his light-hearted professionalism and obvious competence, Tremayne restored the energy level and focused concentration on the task facing the boat captains, which Rawlings' turgid oration had all but killed. His short briefing meeting broke up with laughter and amiable banter, which helped to dispel the inevitable pre-operational tension.

"Follow me, sir – I'm right behind you!" called out the exuberant Fischer through his loudhailer, as Tremayne signalled *'start engines'* then *'slip'* and finally *'half speed ahead'*.

Forming up in line astern, exhausts belching high octane fumes as engines burst noisily into life, the small flotilla moved slowly out of New Grimsby Sound. Picking up speed, they moved purposefully through St Mary's roads, by-passing St Agnes and out into the open sea on a course set for north-west Brittany — and whatever...

Two

Return to L'Aber Wrac'h

O nce clear of the islands, Tremayne ordered *'full speed ahead'* and three sets of Aldis lamps flickered in rapid acknowledgement of MGB 1315's Yeoman of Signals' transmission. Forming up into "diamond" formation, with Tremayne leading and Fischer's Camper and Nicholson directly astern, the tiny flotilla raced sou' south-west at twenty-seven knots, through the ink-black night towards Brittany. At fifteen miles out from Scilly, Tremayne turned to his Yeoman of Signals: "Yeoman, make to all boats: *'Test your weapons please'*."

The lonely silence of the starless night was briefly punctuated by sharp bursts of the Browning and Vickers small calibre machine guns, the crack of Bofors, the rattle of the Oerlikons and the differing thumps of the pom-poms, the four-pounder and the two six-pounders.

"Hmm, sounds as if everything is working, Number One. Let's hope, when push comes to shove, that our rather ridiculous two-pounder doesn't uphold pom-pom tradition and jam at the most critical moment."

Leading Seaman Nicholls, once again sharing the bridge with Tremayne, the First Lieutenant and Petty Officer Irvine, rather self-consciously cleared his throat before venturing: "Excuse me sir, but I think I know how we can stop the pom-pom from jamming."

"Right, Nicholls, you've got my full attention," said Tremayne lowering his binoculars. "How, tell me, do we break this frustrating tradition?"

"Well sir, our kid – my younger brother, that is, sir – works at the BSA where they make Besas, the heavy machine guns they put into a lot of tanks and armoured cars."

"Go on Nicholls please, I'm listening."

"Well sir, at the BSA they had a similar problem with the Besa an' what they do is pour machine oil into the breech an' keep all moving parts well oiled. 'E says to do the same, sir, with our two-pounder. Couldn't we just try it, sir? I told 'im about the jamming an' 'e's sure that oil in the breech would do the same for us, sir."

"Hmm, Nicholls, it sounds like a possible practical solution. Thank you for the suggestion," Tremayne paused. "What do you think, Cox'n?" he asked, turning to the redoubtable Ulsterman at the wheel.

"It's a good, simple idea sir, so it is. But you have to remember, sir, to make sure that the old, burnt oil is cleared out and replaced by fresh clean oil every time the gun is used. In any case, sir, when at sea you'd need to change the oil every week, so you would." Not once did Irvine's eyes leave the gyro compass as he answered Tremayne.

"Thanks, Cox'n. Let's go ahead with Nicholls' idea – it's worth a try. Number One, will you brief Leading Seaman Young, the starboard watch gun-captain of the two-pounder, and then make sure his opposite number on the port watch, Leading Seaman Morrison, also knows the new drill. Take Nicholls with you and start the new procedure with Young immediately please. That two-pounder is our heaviest weapon and if we encounter E-boats – or, for that matter, low-flying enemy aircraft – the last thing we need is a bloody jammed pom-pom. Keep the good ideas coming, Nicholls – so long as they don't include 'splicing the main brace' every day," added Tremayne with a grin.

"Number One, will you please call up Able Seaman Watkins on to the bridge. He can act as temporary lookout while you and Nicholls are up at the forrard gun."

"Aye aye, sir," responded the First Lieutenant and added, somewhat awkwardly, "awfully sorry that I'm not much help with ideas about two-pounders. Apart from firing the Webley .45, that shoulder-breaking Lee-Enfield and the Lanchester during basic training, the only gun I'm really familiar with is the Purdey side-by-side I inherited from my grandfather, sir."

"That's alright Number One," replied Tremayne, suppressing a smile as he noticed the barely perceptible twitch of the Coxswain's face muscles and eyes briefly raised heavenwards. "But if we need to form an assault landing party at anytime, *you* can use the pump-action Remington. It's the only twelve-bore that we carry in our on-board armoury, I'm afraid! Tell me, Number One, on the subject of shot guns, are you any good with the really high birds? They're something I've never been successful with," laughed Tremayne.

"Well sir, as a matter of fact, not bad actually. With a grandfather like mine, sir, I've had rather a lot of practice. With him around in the gun line, it doesn't pay to miss."

"I'll bear that in mind, Number One, if we come under low-level air attack. Jerry will most likely come at us, at high-bird height, so you can man the starboard Vickers!"

As the wind freshened, gusting force six, white caps began to appear on the waves and 1315 started to push her flared bows deeper into them, rising and falling with the increasingly choppy sea. The increasingly relentless motion was evident above and below decks, as crew members strove to retain balance and footing, steadying themselves however and wherever they were able.

Maintaining a maximum speed of twenty-seven knots, the flotilla quickly reached the point of departure where the two Fairmiles, commanded by Taylor and Bower, would take the more southerly sweep to come up off Pen Enez.

Tremayne now knew from his orders he had opened that he and Fischer were to proceed to Pointe de Beg Pol, just east of L'Aber Wrac'h, to disembark Daniel Tabarly and Corporal Kane in their 'cockleshell'.

"Yeoman, make to 1316 and 1317: '*It's time to go our separate ways. Good luck*'."

Within seconds, the flickering Aldis lamps replied.

The Leading Yeoman of Signals reported first: "Signal from 1316, sir: '*You sailors are all the same. You lead a poor girl on and then just dump her*'."

Tremayne roared with laughter. It was the happiest and most at ease that he'd seen him for a long time, thought Irvine.

"Then message from 1317, sir: '*We'll meet again; don't know where, don't know when*'."

"Thank you, Yeo," said the still laughing Tremayne. "I just wish we were using W/T, Number One. I'd love to know what the Jerry radio monitors would make of responses like that." Nodding to the Leading Yeoman of Signals who had joined him on the bridge, Tremayne ordered: "Acknowledge please, Yeoman."

"It would most likely throw the Abwehr into major confusion, sir. They'd probably think it was another secret coded message to the French Resistance and assume that the invasion was imminent!" replied the First Lieutenant who had just rejoined the bridge, together with Nicholls. "Or that we'd parachuted Vera Lynn into France as our latest SOE secret weapon," laughed Tremayne.

"Right, Yeoman, make to 1316 and 1317: '*Take care. Maintain R/T contact. Good hunting*'."

Tremayne and his First Lieutenant followed the churning phosphorescence of the bow waves and then finally the wakes of the two Fairmiles as they both turned to starboard on their new course for Pen Enez.

Tremayne turned to the Leading Yeoman again: "Yeoman, make to 1501 — and I've written it down for you with the First Lieutenant's help: '*Korvettenkapitän. Volldampf voraus*'."

"Let's see what the redoubtable Lieutenant Fischer does with that, Number One!"

The Aldis lamp flickered back, almost instantaneously, from the bridge of the Camper and Nicholson, keeping station astern of Tremayne's boat.

"Signal, sir, from 1501 and I'll spell it sir. It don't make no sense to me, I'm afraid sir," said Leading Yeoman Evans, a serious, rather phlegmatic man from one of those Nottinghamshire mining villages that produce unsung heroes and people who are the very salt of the earth. "'*Zu Befehl Herr Gross Admiral*'."

Once more, Tremayne exploded with laughter. "Thanks for your help, Number One, with our transmission. Lieutenant Fischer obviously approved of that!"

"Beg pardon, sir," said a very perplexed Evans, "what's it all mean, sir?"

"My apologies Yeo," said Tremayne, "I should explain. Lieutenant Fischer is always ribbing us about our Fairmile looking like an E-boat. We pull his leg about his German name. Our signal promoted him to a rank somewhere between lieutenant and lieutenant commander and I ordered him *'full speed ahead'*. Lieutenant Fischer replied *'as ordered'* and promoted me, in turn, to Grand Admiral."

"I see sir, thank you, sir," replied the still very uncertain-looking Evans, whose expression left no doubt that he was convinced that he was under the command of two congenital idiots.

With the duty watch at defence stations, MGB 1315, closely followed by Fischer's powerful Camper and Nicholson, set course, at maximum revolutions, for Pointe de Beg Pol and the rocky north Brittany coast.

Conscious of the drop in temperature and the time underway already, Tremayne turned to the voice tube close by him on the bridge: "Able Seaman Watkins, Captain speaking. Kye for the duty watch please. It's getting cold up here."

"Aye aye sir." The speaking tube lent a strangely disembodied and metallic quality to the human voice.

"Will it be 'neaters' as well, sir"?

"We'll save your 'torpedo propellant' for the return journey, Watkins. We'll most likely *all* be needing it by then."

"Aye aye sir. Kye it is sir."

The muffled, chilled figures on the bridge and manning the weapons instinctively knew that the glutinous nectar was only minutes away as soon as they heard Watkins' inevitable adenoidal wail emanating from the galley. This time, it was the well-known Navy dirge *The Dockyard Church* that assailed their ears:

"Down the aisle walked Matelot Jack
With the organ on 'is back,
Up jumped the organist and 'e said -
Yo' can walz that bastard back, Jack."

Moments later the beaming 'Pablo' Watkins emerged with a battered rum fanny full of hot, steaming kye and a dozen mugs on a lanyard around his neck.

"It's easier this way, sir," he grinned at Tremayne, as he dipped two mugs into the fanny and handed them, full of the hot cocoa, to the Captain and First Lieutenant. Spotting his fellow "townie" on the bridge, with his duffel coat hood up and a scarf covering the lower half of his face, Watkins guffawed, "Bloody 'ell

Brummie, yo' look like bleedin' Eskimo Nell."

Nicholls, deadpan as ever, looked earnestly at Watkins: "Yo' know, Pablo, everyone 'as the right to be ugly, but yo' abuse the privilege."

"The best comic variety act north of the Victoria Palace, Number One – and nearly all done with typical 'Jack' one-liners," laughed Tremayne, as Watkins made his way, complete with kye fanny and mugs to the gun crews. His progress around the deck could be followed in the dark by the roars of laughter that arose, in turn, from the various gun positions.

At 03.30 hours exactly, Tremayne ordered Irvine to reduce speed and the Yeoman to make to 1501 '*half speed ahead*' to reduce engine noise. With the reduction in speed, the previous juddering of maximum revolutions was replaced by a gentle, regular throbbing throughout the MGB.

"Duty watch, keep your eyes open – especially for E-boats. Those predatory bastards could well be skulking anywhere around here on a night like this."

Shortly afterwards, Petty Officer Irvine's sharp eyes saw the indistinct blurred outline of north-west Brittany. "Enemy coast, dead ahead sir."

"Thank you Cox'n. Number One, call up Sub-Lieutenant Tabarly and Corporal Kane to the bridge please."

"Aye aye sir." Less than a minute later, Tabarly and Kane appeared on deck, the latter festooned with Sten gun, grenades, CO_2 pistol, ammunition pouches and a Fairbairn-Sykes commando fighting knife. Tabarly wore a Service Webley at his waist and slung over his shoulder was a Lanchester – a 9mm calibre sub-machine gun almost unique to the Royal Navy and rare among such weapons for its quality finish and capacity to attach a bayonet.

Both had put on camouflage cream and looked, as the First Lieutenant said, "like the devil's own."

"Five hundred yards off shore we'll heave to and launch the canoe. We'll secure it" — Tremayne could not bring himself to call a Royal Marine canoe 'her' — "and rig scrambling nets which you can climb down into your cockleshell. We'll wait one hour as planned. Flash us three short and one long white lights, corporal, with your torch on your return and we will respond identically with a Morse code '*Victor*'.

"If you're not there at the agreed time but return later, lie up as agreed and we'll re-appear in two hours and repeat the signal procedure. If you're not there then, it will be too late and too light to hang around any longer and you will be picked up by one of our Breton 'fishing boats', *Monique*, at 03.00 hours tomorrow. You have a portable radio. Maintain any necessary, but minimal contact, via that. Call sign is '*Tipperary*'; reply is '*Is a long way*'. Any questions, Sub?"

"What happens, sir, if you're spotted before our 05.00 RV with you?"

"If a firefight develops with the Panzers, Lieutenant Fischer and I will put down as much hot metal as we can to keep their heads down before we leave, rapidly," said Tremayne. "We'll keep R/T contact with you but will attempt to pick you up, as agreed earlier, in the event of an 05.00 abort at 06.00 hours. If that is not possible, then plan B will be put into operation and it will be *Monique* that comes for you in just over twenty-four hours. Synchronise watches, gentlemen. It is now 03.35 hours precisely. Corporal, questions?" Tremayne, conscious of the burden that Kane, especially, would be carrying on the operation, addressed the ever-professional Marine NCO.

"No questions, sir, thank you. If things go badly wrong, sir, we can lie up for several days. We will maintain minimum R/T contact, sir. Mr Tabarly and I have checked through our own plans, several times over, while we've been on board, sir. We have enough food, water and most important of all, ammunition, to last us for days. After that we will live off the land if necessary, sir."

"Thank you Corporal." Kane's resourcefulness and imperturbability never failed to impress Tremayne, who quickly turned to Daniel Tabarly, adding: "Sub, as you know, the information you're about to get from Jean François is vital to future operations – especially any likely to take place in the immediate future. Do all that you can, please, to get it to us as quickly as possible. That is critical."

"Of course, sir," replied Tabarly. "One of those agents we sent over yesterday was a school friend of mine. I am as anxious to know what happened as anyone, sir."

Twenty minutes later, at 03.55 hours, the seventeen-foot-long canvas canoe, together with supplies and Corporal Kane's weapons bag, was launched into the breaking waves, secured to the MGB by lines fore and aft.

Tabarly and the Corporal moved off towards the side of the boat. Tremayne and the First Lieutenant shook their hands and wished them Godspeed and good luck.

As the Royal Marine Corporal turned to go, Irvine leant across and grasped his hand and said quietly: "A safe home 'Royal'. Look after yourself, lad."

"Cheers, Cox'n. Keep a tot for me for when I get back. I reckon I'll be needing it."

"Me, too, please Cox'n," grinned Tabarly, "but only if you don't have a good cognac!"

With those brief, but warm farewells, the two made their way along to the scrambling net where a rating, lashed by a waist-line to a stanchion and up to his knees in water, was holding the canoe's wooden cockpit coaming to steady the frail, bobbing craft, while balancing precariously on the bottom rope rung of the net.

Tabarly and the Corporal scrambled down and slid expertly into the canoe. Releasing the two twin-bladed paddles from the deck straps, the two pushed off from the MGB into the choppy sea, as the securing lines were quickly slipped fore and aft.

With a flash of white teeth the Corporal, sitting in the stern seat, grinned as the Coxswain called out: "I hope that the bow paddler didn't have pusser's beans for dinner" – recalling the old SBS maxim: 'Beans for breakfast? Bags I bow paddler!'

Moments later, in response to the canoeist's call-sign challenge, the correct answering flashes came back from the shore to everyone's relief on the bridge.

Tremayne, surprised by the warmth and spontaneity of the normally taciturn, dour Ulsterman, looked at Irvine with undisguised quizzical interest.

Aware that he had unexpectedly shown a side to his personality that he normally kept under tight control and well hidden, the Coxswain rather self-consciously stumbled over his words, as he said: "You see, sir, my eldest brother Jack was a 'Royal', so he was. He was my hero when I was a lad, just out of boy's service. Like Kane there, he was a corporal and he was killed, advancing with the Royal Marines 4th battalion, on the mole at Zeebrugge on St George's Day 1918. It broke our mother's heart, God rest her soul – and mine too sir."

Conscious that in the two months that Irvine had served with him, this was the longest speech he had ever heard his Coxswain utter, Tremayne took the PO's disclosure as a privilege – and a vote of confidence.

"Thank you for telling me that, Cox'n. I appreciate and value what you said. The loss of someone so close to you, especially if they are still young, is very hard to bear as I well know."

"Yes sir, we were all very sorry to learn about your wife sir, begging your pardon."

Tremayne suddenly became aware that – while they were talking – he had unconsciously been holding Diana's photograph, which was still in his duffel coat pocket.

Anxious to break the increasingly heavy and introspective tone of the conversation, Tremayne said – perhaps a little too forced and unnaturally: "Don't let's become too depressed Cox'n, it's not good in our profession. We'll get that scallywag Watkins to organise another wet of kye for the duty watch."

With the First Lieutenant back on the bridge, and Nicholls with his binoculars sweeping both coastline and sea, the irrepressible Watkins appeared once more, minutes later, with a rum fanny full of pusser's kye.

This time his visit was accompanied by complete silence with the enemy coast a little over a quarter of a mile away. All gun crews were now closed up at action stations, and conversations on deck were mere whispers as customary final checks of firing mechanisms took place, more out of instinct than mere drill. Just as off the Brittany coast the night before, the atmosphere was tense as the duty watch officers and ratings alike stood to, at action stations, nervously fingering weapons and binoculars.

As if on cue with Tremayne's closing of his unusually personal conversation with the Coxswain, the distant horizon to the west south-west was suddenly illuminated by a rapid succession of bright flashes, followed by the characteristic "crack" of German 88s. The prolonged sharper rattle of smaller calibre weapons answered almost instantaneously, as Tremayne quickly looked at his watch.

"So, Number One, 03.57 hours – the diversionary attack begins right on schedule. Some of those 88s at least are firing at aircraft, judging by the elevation of the flashes. The Beaufighters must have arrived bang on time. Let's hope that the fireworks away at Pen Enez don't encourage Jerry to start looking in our direction.

Luckily the Panzers are stationed near Plouguerneau, about twelve kilometres to the west of us, and they normally only come up to Pointe de Beg Pol for gunnery practice. I'm concerned that we don't become involved in a firefight before we've got Sub-Lieutenant Tabarly and Corporal Kane safely back on board."

One hundred yards astern, Hermann Fischer's Camper and Nicholson, similarly, lay hove-to and closed up for action, weapons traversing constantly, maintaining the barely visible coastline as the primary target.

Try as they might, neither boat could remain bow-on to the shore to present a consistently minimal profile and Tremayne's hope was that, as the lead boat, his Fairmile looked most like an E-boat to anyone who might be looking out to sea from the fields above the shoreline. The darkness still made it virtually impossible to distinguish the true shape of the boats with any degree of certainty.

Meanwhile, Sub-Lieutenant Tabarly and Corporal Kane had beached their canoe, bows pointing back to the sea and paddles loosely stowed in the cockpit for rapid access.

They had both been challenged – and responded – with the correct code words on landing, and were quickly surrounded by a group of five members of the Confrèrie de Saint Michel, led by Jean-François. Underneath his alias he was Capitaine de Vaisseau, Jean-Pierre Duhamel of the French Navy.

Given the option of escaping to Britain to serve with the Free French Navy – or the Royal Navy – he had elected to stay in Brittany and run the Confrèrie.

From his pre-war service with the French Navy, based at Brest, Capitaine Duhamel knew the whole of western Brittany like the back of his hand.

To reduce the risk of reprisals against an innocent local civilian population, Duhamel – with approval from London – had decided to concentrate on the clandestine selection, training and deployment of agents throughout Brittany, west of St Malo, rather than engage in high-profile attacks with explosives and weapons. He knew, however, that sooner or later, active sabotage and the elimination of key figures would, inevitably, become part of the Confrèrie's role.

To divert the Germans' blame for sabotage away from local

civilians, Tresco had already supplied the Confrèrie with items such as badged British green berets, woollen 'cap-comforters', Woodbine, Players and RN-issue cigarette packets, Swan Vestas matchboxes, and other "incriminating" evidence to leave behind to suggest British Commando raiding parties.

Duhamel's intelligence gathering was of an exceptionally high order, and he constantly passed updated information to Tresco about German naval and troop movements; identifying ships, units and equipment, in detail, for Anglo-French Intelligence based in London.

Unfortunately, the quite ridiculous rivalry and unnecessary squabbling between SOE and SIS meant that information transmitted from France to Tresco and London was often delayed, or withheld, so losing opportunities for the most timely action where it was most needed.

Several times, he had almost been trapped by the Gestapo and Enever suspected that both British inter-service red tape, as well as French informants, rather than German agents, might well be the source of Nazi intelligence on Duhamel's activities in the role of 'Jean-François'.

In Jean-François' party was the agent code-named Muguette, a young woman who had managed to infiltrate the German OKM by working as a clerical assistant and translator in the secretariat division of the Kriegsmarine in Brest. London regarded the information that she could supply to Anglo-French Intelligence to be of exceptionally high potential value.

Like Jean-François and Muguette, all the other members of the group used code names to preserve their anonymity as otherwise ordinary French citizens. Members neither knew the true identity nor the civilian occupation of the other members of their particular 'cell' of the Confrèrie.

The party rapidly moved up the beach under cover of darkness. Corporal Kane and two members of the French group, who also carried Sten guns, maintained a mobile all-round defence as the group ran over one hundred yards to a narrow cave entrance, invisible from above and set back, well hidden, in the unwelcoming, rocky cliff face.

Looking like an irregular fissure in the rocks, the entrance – which was almost nine feet high and under two feet wide – opened into a sizeable, boulder-strewn cave.

At high tide, the cave typically filled with sea water to a depth of around three feet, but rarely more. A natural rock ledge protruded for about thirty feet – two-thirds the depth of the cave – along one wall. This provided sufficient room for at least a dozen people to sit or stand, in comfort and safety, above the high tide. Easy access was provided to the ledge by any number of the large boulders that lay on the floor of the cave. About sixteen feet wide and – at its highest point – almost fifteen feet high, the cave was an ideal refuge and had been used by generations of Breton smugglers bringing in contraband from England and elsewhere.

With the tide coming in, as a precaution, Jean-François ordered everyone onto the ledge. Flasks of hot coffee and cognac were quickly produced, along with some indeterminate but delicious soft cheese and, inevitably, bread. With several 'merci beaucoups', Corporal Kane rapidly exhausted the extent of his French vocabulary, as he and the others devoured the very welcome food and drink.

Speaking in English, both for Corporal Kane's benefit and that of Squadron Leader David Addington, a RAF Intelligence Officer in the group, Jean François began his briefing for Sub-Lieutenant Tabarly.

"It is quite clear that someone close to the centre of the Confrèrie is working for the Germans. All four agents who came across yesterday have been captured. They walked right into a well-prepared trap, which had been set by the Gestapo following the capture, interrogation and execution of the two members of the Confrèrie who were due to meet the canoeists sent by Lieutenant Commander Enever. Those four will also be brutally interrogated until they break and give the Gestapo the information they want – then they, too, will be shot," said Jean-François.

Corporal Kane's face betrayed the bitter anger he felt, as he thought about the laughter and fun that he had enjoyed with the Frenchmen during the weapons training and instruction in canoe handling techniques that he had conducted for them. Silently, he recalled the post-training evenings in the New Inn, on Tresco, where the four had attempted to teach him French songs and had roared with laughter at his attempts to pronounce the words correctly.

Short, but wiry of stature, Kane had been nicknamed 'le petit caporal' by the four who then laughingly dubbed him 'Napoleon' Kane. To think that these four, with whom he had shared so much during the last three months, were soon to be executed – if they had not already been shot – drove Kane to silent fury. Tabarly, too, felt shock – even despair – as he thought about the four agents for whom he, Enever and Emma Fraser had had such high hopes.

Loath to accept the reality, he asked Jean-François, "But are you sure – could there possibly be some mistake?"

"Mais non, mon ami. Sadly it is exactly as I say. There is no doubt that we have a traitor among us," said Jean-François, deliberately letting his gaze move slowly round the group sitting talking, while eating and drinking, on the rocky ledge.

Tabarly instinctively followed Jean-François' searching look, but neither the slightest fidgeting, nor facial expression, betrayed any discomfort – let alone guilt or fear – among those present.

"We are determined to maintain the Confrèrie de Saint Michel and to continue the gathering and transmission of intelligence information for as long as we can, and as efficiently as we can," continued Jean-François. "We will also continue to do all we are able to help Squadron Leader Addington to develop and keep open an escape network for RAF and Allied air crews who are shot down over this side of the Channel."

"And, if I may suggest," cut in Addington, "we will maintain escape routes for people *other than* downed air crew who want to get back to England."

"Oui, bien sur, David. Now I want you Daniel and you David to walk with me while we talk some more. It is still dark and we have time before you, Daniel, must return and before the Boche Panzer Lehrbattaillon wakes up and begins to practise shooting at the waves again!"

Turning to Kane, Jean François said: "Caporal, if you please, stay 'ere and get to know the rest of our little group. Muguette will introduce them all to you, but I can tell you, Louis, the ugly one, built like a gorilla, was also a fusilier-marin, so you already 'ave much in common, I think."

"You mean sir, I also look like a gorilla?" asked a grinning Kane, as he shook the huge, outstretched hand of the smiling former French Marine. The loud laughter that followed, Tabarly thought, represented, as much as anything, a welcome release from the introspective tension that had built up within the group following Jean-François' reference to a traitor.

"Bienvenue, petit caporal. My friends 'ave tell me about you when they 'ave speak by radio to us. You are very welcome 'ere," said the amiably ugly Louis.

Outside the cave, Jean François said, "We will walk quickly, gentlemen. I want to show you something that the others do not know about, other than Louis who can be completely trusted. Follow me, please."

The group rapidly made their way up a narrow winding track which led to the top of the low cliff face, across a large field and into a woodland about three hundred yards deep. Through this, the group emerged in an open area, devoid of trees — apart from a few poplars — where an old farmhouse, with a separate barn, stood barely discernible in the, as yet, still dark night.

The horizon to the south-west continued to be illuminated by flashes, and the repeated "crump," typical of British four- and six-pounders, could be heard regularly, but now without the answering "crack" of an 88.

"Sounds like maybe we have some success gentlemen," said Jean-François with a wry smile.

Stopping outside the entrance to the barn, Jean François spoke urgently, but quietly:

"David, Daniel. I am absolutely convinced that there *is* a traitor in the Confrèrie, close to its heart. Too many things have gone wrong to be merely a coincidence, or bad luck. What is more, I am sure that I now know who it is. I had my suspicions and so I set little traps, and each time this person has fallen into them. What we must find out – and quickly – is how much they know and have already told the Boche. Then I have to deal with them."

Silently and meaningfully, Jean-François drew his finger across his throat.

"You really have no doubts about this?" asked Tabarly.

"Non, mon cher Daniel, none whatsoever. Luckily, over eighty percent of our network is still unknown to this person, because I keep that knowledge to myself. This place I show you now is also unknown to them. I fear, 'owever, that because of this traitor, the Germans 'ave cracked the code we use for our radio transmissions, which is why they often know what we are planning to do. All R/T messages about tonight's meeting stated that we would meet at Pen Enez, and even those closest to me believed that until, at the last minute, I brought them here by lorry instead."

"We must then change the code," said Tabarly.

"I agree," replied Addington, "but let's keep the existing one and feed in duff information to Jerry, while we use a new code for our own purposes. That enables us to lay any false trails that we may need."

"D'accord, David," agreed Jean François. "This I also believe we must do. Daniel, I suggest you discuss this with Lieutenant Commander Enever as soon as you return. Alors, mes amis, let me show you my little secret."

With Jean François in the lead, the three went into the old barn which was a typical west Breton farmhouse, now empty. The family who owned the farm had recently fled south to join relatives in Vichy, France. Unable to live any longer under German occupation, they had decided to leave the area.

Their decision had been brought to a head when the Germans had commandeered one hundred hectares – over half their land – for Panzer gunnery training.

A farmer from the same village, who was also a trusted member of the Confrèrie, grazed his own cattle – along with those of the previous owner – on the land, and acted as a caretaker to the abandoned farm. This was a deliberate intervention, on the part of the Confrèrie, to maintain an impression that the farm was occupied and in working order. The Germans seemed happy to share the commandeered land with the cattle, so long as they had complete freedom of movement for their trainee tank crews. Apart from churning up some of the grazing land with their caterpillar tracks, they seemed to spend most of their training days, so far, firing at practice targets, with many of the shells whistling past on their way out to sea.

Once inside the barn, Jean François swung out from the wall a primitive, ancient elm Breton dresser, which served to hold the typical clutter of farm hand tools and small implements likely to be found in such a building. Behind the dresser was a low door, set in the wall. Ducking, in turn, the group quickly passed through this door into a long, narrow room, approximately fifteen feet long and seven feet wide. Inside were a large French farmhouse kitchen table, some old elm chairs and two collapsible beds. On the table stood a small but powerful radio transmitter and receiver. Beneath the table was a threadbare mat and under this were several removable floorboards, which provided a hiding place for the radio when it was not in use.

Some old, empty wine bottles, a chipped drinking glass and a selection of recent horse-racing newspapers, gave the hidden room the appearance of a "den" where the farmer might temporarily escape from his family.

Deliberately scattered stirrup-irons, bits, a head-collar and a bridle, together with an old, well-worn leading rein and an old sack of horse feed, complete with a bucket, lent a suitably equestrian feel to the room, should it ever be discovered.

On the outside of the barn, immediately adjoining and so covering this hidden room, were two loose boxes, with hay nets regularly filled by the caretaker. These added to the intended impression that this was essentially a small stable, in regular use, and nothing else.

Already, two of the younger Panzer officers had asked if they might keep their horses there, so that they could go riding in their free time. Under Jean-François' instructions, the farmer, acting as caretaker, had agreed to this, and even offered the Germans the services of a part-time groom to help them look after their horses.

With what could be a succession of German Panzer training

battalions coming into the area for field manoeuvres and gunnery practice, Jean François saw the advantages of operating right under the Germans' noses. Tabarly agreed that providing a groom and regular fresh hay was a shrewd stratagem.

"Just don't offer them free Calvados or Armagnac – that's lulling suspicion too far," he had joked, when Jean François told him of the two young Panzer officers.

"Mais non, mon ami. We show them polite, but impersonal efficiency but no unnecessary initiatives and that, I think, will keep them off our backs.

Our 'farmer-caretaker' understands that he needs to use intelligent anticipation about their obvious expectations, but nothing more," replied Jean François with a knowing smile. "With many years of learning to fool Paris bureaucracy, this farmer has become a very good Breton version of the 'Good Soldier Schwyk'," he added.

Tabarly quickly looked at his watch. "Mon Dieu! We have thirteen minutes to collect Corporal Kane, get back to our canoe and signal the MGB that we are returning. But, before I leave here, I must be clear about the information I take back to Lieutenant Commander Enever."

"Please, Daniel, tell him exactly what I have told you. Tell him I will take care of everything here around L'Aber Wrac'h, and that only this latest operation – not the Confrèrie – has been compromised. Make sure that he is aware of the important role of Squadron Leader Addington."

Back at the entrance to the cave, Tabarly collected Corporal Kane – who looked decidedly uncomfortable about Louis' enthusiastic and decidedly un-British farewell bear hug. With a quick handshake with each of the group, Tabarly, followed by Corporal Kane, moved down the beach towards their canoe.

"Au revoir, mes amis. A la prochaine," called Jean-François quietly. "Prenez garde!"

The two raced silently to their canoe, retrieved their paddles and pushed the canvas cockleshell into the water. Tabarly jumped into the bow seat while Corporal Kane held the canoe steady. Quickly, he too scrambled in and each "broke" their paddles, pushing the two halves into the seabed, each side of the canoe, in order to "walk" it into deeper water. With the keelson clear of the stony seabed, they re-joined their paddles and began pulling furiously for the MGB, standing off some five hundred yards out to sea. In the darkness, they could just make out the familiar and welcome shape of the Fairmile, with the blurred outline of Fischer's Camper and Nicholson slightly astern of her.

Tabarly flashed the agreed recognition signal and received the Yeoman's response within seconds from MGB 1315. Paddling against the tide was extremely hard work, as Enever had predicted. Icy water regularly cascaded over the canoe bow and cockpit coaming, drenching the two paddlers. Tabarly's arms ached desperately and, eventually, the wiry, muscular Kane was largely making way on behalf of both of them.

On the bridge of MGB 1315, three pairs of binoculars searched the blackness for any signs of the telltale phosphorescence from paddle-blades, or bow wave, to start tracking the approaching canoe.

"Wind's freshening, sir, so it is, and the sea's getting more than a mite choppy," muttered Irvine, addressing Tremayne.

"You're right, Cox'n. Even over that distance they'll be exhausted and soaked through."

Willoughby-Brown was the first to see the silver flashes of the churned up water as the canoeists pushed through the wind-whipped waves, paddles whirling like windmills, but no longer in unison, as the rapidly tiring Tabarly struggled in vain to match the pace and strength of the experienced Marine sitting astern of him.

"There they are sir," he said quietly to Tremayne. "One o'clock and I reckon three hundred yards away, sir."

"So they are. Well done, Number One. Let's go and meet them. Right Cox'n, slow ahead. Steady as she goes."

"Aye aye sir. Slow ahead it is sir."

Using the voice tubes, Tremayne quietly gave the order: "All gun crews keep a sharp look out. Gun crews will fire on my command."

"Yeoman, make to 1501: '*Prodigal sons returning. Please keep station, am going closer to pick them up*'." Turning to the First Lieutenant, Tremayne ordered: "Welcoming party at the scrambling nets, if you please, Number One, to pick up canoeists and cockleshell. We'll be stopped close inshore, so issue small arms and ammunition to both watches."

Willoughby-Brown looking enquiringly at Tremayne who responded: "You and I will forget our Webleys, Number One. They'd be useless at this distance, so too would the Remington. Grab a couple of Lanchesters though and put them handy on the chart table."

Slowly the MGB approached the hard-paddling pair, with engines pulsating slowly, as they ticked over at low revolutions. Within minutes, Tabarly and Kane were alongside and being dragged up the scrambling nets by helping hands and onto the MGB's deck.

The hasty but warm welcomes were followed by dry clothing and hot tea, laced with rum, as Petty Officer Irvine turned 1315 towards Tresco and home.

At just over five miles clear of the Breton coast, Tremayne gave the order: "Full speed ahead, Cox'n. Don't spare the horses."

"Yeoman, make to 1501: *'Home. Maximum revolutions'*."

The Leading Yeoman Signaller picked up the flickering Aldis response from the Camper and Nicholson, keeping station one hundred yards astern, and called to Tremayne, "Message from 1501, sir: *'Like the virgin sturgeon I need no urgin'*."

"Thank you, Yeo." Tremayne smiled as he said to Willoughby-Brown: "Lieutenant Fischer, I see, has lost none of his spontaneous wit!"

"Acknowledge please, Yeoman."

Turning to the voice tube he called, "Sparks, this is the Captain speaking."

"Sir, Leading Telegraphist Jenkins 'yere."

The lilting Rhondda accent was unmistakable.

"Thank you Jenkins. Make to 1316 and 1317 on R/T: *'Situation report, please'*."

"Aye aye, sir."

Tremayne had seen and heard the same exchange of gunfire that Tabarly had witnessed and had been wondering how his colleagues had fared. Standing with the First Lieutenant on the bridge, he had experienced the same cold feeling that he had when his boat had stood off from Pen Enez, at almost point-blank range from the lethal 88s.

The Fairmiles – as he well knew – were not the fastest of craft, neither were they as agile as some of the other, smaller MGBs and MTBs. It only needed one high-velocity 88mm shell in the wrong place, and a boat of such displacement was finished. He knew, too, that even three or four direct hits in less vital areas could create carnage and wreak havoc in so small and virtually unarmoured a vessel.

His mind drifted back to his close friend Lieutenant Bill Mitchell, who was lost when the *Portree* went down somewhere off the Kerry coast. Had Bill died when the torpedo struck, or was his death the result of the submarine's 88? Had he just simply drowned, alone, in those cold, grey, uninviting waters off south-west Ireland?

Why Bill? So wise and understanding, he had been a "Rock of Gibraltar" when Diana had been killed and he had needed a friend. Why did Bill have to die? Tremayne felt a sudden shock of surprise when he reflected that he had never once asked that often inevitable, but pointless, question when his wife had died.

"Signal from 1316 sir." The musical Welsh accent defied the attempts of the speaking tube to de-humanise the telegraphist's voice, and brought Tremayne back with a jolt.

"Message reads, sir: *'Quite a party. Beaufighters chamfered up the 88s. We both completed destruction of battery. 1317 took a hit in W/T room. Some casualties. Confirm ETA 10.00 hrs'.*"

"Thank you, Sparks. Make to 1316:" said Tremayne, "*'Well*

done. What casualties? Come home safely. Please signal message to 1317'."

Minutes later, the reply from 1316 came through and Tremayne summarised it for the First Lieutenant: "1317 lost her leading telegraphist, Number One, and had three seamen wounded, one seriously. It looks, though, as if between them, the Beaufighters and our lads have really thumped that battery. The Germans will replace it – and quickly. But, we have shown, in a small way, that we have the will and the clout to hit them, to quote our gallant Admiral, 'in their own backyard'. I'm surprised that Jerry hasn't come looking for the culprits already, Number One. Have both watches stand down from action stations and resume defence stations, please. Oh, and Number One, organise Watkins to come leaping around, like a young gazelle, with a 'wet' of kye for everyone, please."

"Aye aye, sir. Young *gazelle* sir?" The mobile eyebrow became even more parabolic. "The vision I have, sir, is somewhat more ursine." As Tremayne burst into laughter, Leading Seaman Nicholls' urgent voice called from the starboard side of the bridge. "Two 'igh speed craft – look like Fairmiles, sir – approaching. Bearing green 0-four-0, one thousand yards."

"Thank you, Nicholls," said Tremayne, bringing his binoculars back to his eyes.

"Number One, resume action stations, and better belay the kye, I'm afraid. What do you make of them Cox'n?"

"Dunno, sir, but they're not Fairmiles, so they aren't."

Tremayne studied the two rapidly approaching vessels intently. "Damn," he muttered to himself, "I can't see their bloody ensigns in this half light, at that angle."

A flash from the bow of the leading boat, followed quickly by a whoosh and a sharp bang, confirmed them, beyond any doubt, as E-boats.

Pressing the alarm button, Tremayne shouted, "Stand by all guns. Fire as you bear. Shoot, shoot, shoot."

"Yeoman, make to 1501: '*Am engaging the enemy. Independent action*'."

"Signal from 1501, sir: '*Tally-ho. The leader is yours, I'll take number two*'."

"Thank you, Yeo. Acknowledge. Hell, that was *bloody* close!"

A second shell from the leading E-boat whistled over the bridge, taking the port signal halliards with it.

Almost instantaneously, a cheer suddenly went up from Leading Seaman 'Dhobey' Young, as several shots from his forrard two-pounder hit the wheelhouse and bridge of the approaching E-boat, causing a succession of bright flashes along the superstructure.

'Lofty' Towers had also managed to get the German vessel within his angle of sight and began pouring 20mm shells into her from his twin Oerlikons from 1315's after deck. The starboard Vickers, similarly, were peppering the approaching E-boat with .50 calibre, adding to the noise – and adrenalin flow – on board the MGB. Within seconds, the deck, on either side of the wheelhouse, became increasingly littered with spent cartridge cases, as the port Vickers was similarly brought to bear and opened fire on the leading E-boat's upper works. The acrid smell of cordite hung over the MGB's deck and bridge and the din of battle was deafening.

Seconds later, 1315 was herself straddled by 40mm shells from the E-boat, and immediately both the forrard pom-pom gun-captain and his gun-layer collapsed bloodied and writhing on the deck as their two-pounder power mounting took several direct hits.

Before Tremayne could even give an order, the First Lieutenant – who had appeared on the forrard deck complete with Lanchester – grabbed Corporal Kane and yelled:

"With me, Corporal. Let's get that bloody two-pounder back in action."

More shells struck 1315, holing and splintering her wooden hull in several places, instantly killing one of the Chief's engine room crew.

Speaking into the voice tube, Tremayne shouted: "Chief, Captain here. Are you alright? What's the damage?"

The usually phlegmatic Chief sounded badly shaken.

"I'm OK, sir. Engines are fine, but oh God, McAllister's dead – he's got no face sir. He's got no bloody face." His voice suddenly broke and rose an octave to a high-pitched sob.

"Alright, Chief. Get a grip. You've got a job to do." Tremayne didn't intend to sound so harsh and uncaring and quickly added, "We're rather busy up here at the moment. I'll be with you when I can."

At the forrard two-pounder, the First Lieutenant and Corporal Kane quickly, but gently, moved the badly wounded gun-captain and his dying gun-layer.

"Corporal, I hope to heavens that you know how to work this bloody thing," said Willoughby-Brown, grabbing a fresh belt of two-pounder shells from one of the pom-pom's ammunition lockers, located around the damaged gun platform.

"I do sir," said Kane, agilely clambering over the wreckage of the shattered power mounting to take command of the pom-pom.

"What's more, sir, we can still traverse her by hand, thank God."

The E-boat rapidly slewed round to starboard, presenting her stern to Tremayne's MGB and so allowing her after 20mm to start raking the Fairmile, the shells bursting high against the boat's armoured bridge. At the same moment, Corporal Kane traversed the damaged two-pounder, with the First Lieutenant acting as loader and gun-layer.

"Shoot, man, bloody well shoot!" yelled Willoughby-Brown, as the E-boat began to accelerate away, out of her sharp turn. The pom-pom responded seconds later, hitting the E-boat's after 20mm gun magazine, which exploded in a vast sheet of bright orange flame, hurling the bodies of the two gunners overboard like limp rag dolls.

"Full ahead, Cox'n – after them," shouted Tremayne. "Let's hurt the bastards!"

"Keep firing Corporal, you've got her range," called the First Lieutenant above the din of so many automatic weapons firing at once.

Suddenly, another explosion, louder than the first, accompanied by a new huge fireball, stopped the E-boat dead in the water.

"Damn them to hell – keep shooting," yelled Willoughby-Brown, feeding more ammunition into the two-pounder. "Keep shooting. We must have hit their large-range fuel tanks."

"Main deck ammunition locker, sir" shouted Kane. "Those things are powered by diesels, sir – they don't 'brew up' as we would, sir."

Both port and starboard Vickers were still pouring rounds into the now-sinking E-boat, as the remaining members of her crew began scrambling over the rails and plunging into the water to escape the inferno that had erupted from the bridge aft, as far astern as the rear gun.

"Cease firing. All guns cease firing. Check, check, check," came Tremayne's curt command, as the German sailors took to the water.

"Well done, Number One. Please attend to the dead and wounded. Well done, Corporal Kane. Good shooting," called Tremayne.

Turning to the Vickers gunners either side of the bridge, Tremayne shouted with a broad grin: "Fine shooting lads. 'Neaters' all round, once we're clear of this lot."

Swinging round to find Fischer's Camper and Nicholson, as the confusion of battle died down, Tremayne was horrified to see a high pall of dense, black smoke issuing from the rear of the MGB. Accompanying the fire was an increasingly foul stench of burning oil, carried over the water by the wind.

"What the hell?" he began and then, immediately astern of Fischer's boat, he saw the second E-boat burning and settling in the water, well down at the bows.

"Yeoman," he called. "Make to 1501: *'Congratulations. Report please'*."

Then to his First Lieutenant: "Number One. Stand by to pick up E-boat survivors – life belts and scrambling nets, if you please."

Still collecting his thoughts and reviewing all that had happened in so short a space of time – under ten minutes since Nicholls first saw the two unidentified vessels – Tremayne suddenly realised that his left arm was throbbing and his sleeve was covered in blood. Shrapnel, most likely, from the E-boat's after 20mm gun, had badly gashed his arm just above the elbow, luckily missing the bone but creating a flesh wound about three inches long and quite deep. Quickly, taking off his duffel coat, uniform jacket and sea-duty white jersey, he pressed on a wound dressing to staunch the flow of blood.

Struggling with one hand to tie the dressing down, he was aware of another pair of hands taking over.

"Let me do that, sir. I'll have it fixed in a jiffy, so I will," said a very concerned looking Irvine.

"Thanks Cox'n. I've only just become aware of it. Must have been shrapnel, or a ricochet."

Quickly dressing again, Tremayne resumed his position on the bridge as the Yeoman of Signals called to him, "Message from 1501, sir: *'Thanks. Well done you. Damage looks far worse than it is. Our whaler hit by incendiary fire'.*"

"Acknowledge, please, Yeoman."

Meanwhile, a leading hand and three ABs had mustered at the guardrail to pick up any German survivors as they scrambled aboard and to escort them below, under armed guard.

"Number One, it's time to come into your own as a linguist," called Tremayne. "Take charge of the prisoners and escort. Get their wet gear off and onto heating pipes, and make sure they are issued with any spare towels and dry clothing, and then a good stiff tot."

"Aye aye sir. Perhaps it would be an idea to soften them up for interrogation, sir, with the threat of Watkins' kye."

"Remember, Number One, we're bound by the rules of the Geneva Convention. A war crimes tribunal wouldn't look too kindly on that!" grinned Tremayne.

Five survivors – one being supported by two of his comrades – were struggling to swim in the cold, swelling sea to the side of the MGB. Shocked, exhausted and demoralised, they drew pity, rather than hatred or contempt, from the escort party. As always, for sailors of any navy, it was the sea, not their adversaries, that was the real – and common – enemy.

"Quick," shouted Willoughby-Brown. "Lifebelts to the injured man and those helping him. Give this chap here a boathook to grab. Let's get them aboard quickly. Lively does it lads."

The First Lieutenant hung from the scrambling nets with a rating gripping his arm while he reached down with his other hand to drag a young, exhausted German officer on board.

Quickly the five – including the one whose left leg appeared to be broken – were helped on board where they dropped, completely spent, onto the MGB's wooden deck.

The officer was the first to recover. Struggling to his feet, he saluted Willoughby-Brown and said: "Leutnant-zur-See Eugen Lang. Ich danke Ihnen."

The First Lieutenant returned his salute, held out his hand – which the German grasped – and said: "Es freut mich sehr. Leutnant David Willoughby-Brown. Willkommen ambord!"

Turning to the leading hand of the escort party he said: "Sharpe. Take them below. Search them, then give them dry clothes and towels. We'll issue rum all round – including the prisoners. Let's make it 'neaters'. It's been quite a night."

Addressing the AB nearest to him, he said: "Berridge, you trained as a sick berth attendant originally. Look after the injured man as best as you can and report his condition to me."

In faultless English, the wringing wet and still shivering German officer turned to Willoughby-Brown and said, "Lieutenant, I thank you for your consideration for my men."

The prisoners were quickly ushered below, and Tremayne gave the order: "Full speed ahead Cox'n. Dawn is breaking and we still have a good way to go. The E-boats we've just destroyed may be part of a flotilla. If they are in the vicinity they cannot help but have seen or heard our firefight. Capable of forty knots against our twenty-seven, they'd rapidly catch us up, so let's move now."

Calling the Yeoman over, Tremayne said, "Yeo, make to 1501: *'Please report casualties and any prisoners'*."

Within one minute, the Yeoman reported, "Answer, sir, from 1501: *'Four wounded, one seriously. Three prisoners. PO and two ratings'*."

"Acknowledge, Yeo and make to 1501: *'All prisoners to be blindfolded before arriving off Scilly. Interrogation by Senior Naval Intelligence Officer before transfer to Helford Base'*."

Tremayne turned to Irvine: "Cox'n, take charge of the bridge please. I'm going below to see the Chief. Unfortunately Stoker-Mechanic McAllister has been killed. Call me if anything develops."

"Aye aye sir. I'll save you a mug of 'neaters', so I will, when Watkins gets up to the bridge sir."

Tremayne was conscious of the searing pain in his left arm as he went below. He quickly went to his makeshift bunk and gave himself a shot of morphine – something he'd forgotten to do in the frenzy of activity during and following the engagement with the two E-boats. Looking pale and drawn, he went to the tiny engine room.

"Chief, I'm sorry I didn't make it sooner. I've rather had my hands full. I'm very sorry, too, about young McAllister – he was a good hand. We can ill-afford to lose men like him."

At that moment, Watkins, complete with rum fanny and mugs, was passing the open door of the engine room when Tremayne stopped him.

"Watkins, a mug of your devil's brew for the Chief, if you please."

"Aye aye sir. An' beg pardon sir, but yo' look as if yo' could do wi' one yerself, sir, if yo' don't mind me saying."

"Thank you, Watkins. Your perceptiveness never fails to astound me," Tremayne smiled, reaching for the mug of neat pusser's rum offered to him.

"Thank you, sir. Some say it's a gift sir," replied the AB with a broad grin as he made his way towards the prisoners and escort sitting in the forrard mess deck.

Turning once more to Petty Officer Duncan, Tremayne said, "I'll write to McAllister's next-of-kin, Chief. Can you let me have details please?"

"Aye aye sir, I can. It'll be his young wife – she's only just nineteen sir, an' expecting their first bairn. I have their address in my locker, sir."

"Oh God, this bloody war." Tremayne's anguish broke through his customary reserve. Recovering himself, Tremayne said quietly, "Let me have the details – her first name and their address – when we get back to Godolphin."

Outside the engine room, he took a deep draught of rum. The thought of a nineteen- year-old widow, expecting her first child – one her husband would never see – moved him deeply. It was some moments before he could compose himself sufficiently to move on to see the First Lieutenant and the escort with their five prisoners.

Entering the forrard mess deck, he told the prisoners' escort party to stand easy as they sprang to attention. To Leutnant-zur-see Lang he said simply: "I'm sorry about your boat and your men. The gods of war are capricious and callous. How is your wounded crew member?"

"Thank you for your kind treatment, Lieutenant. Matrosen-Stabsgefreiter Köster is in a bad way. I would like him to have medical treatment as quickly as possible, please, when we reach our destination. Where are we going Lieutenant?"

"To answer your first request, Herr Leutnant, I assure you Leading Seaman Köster *will* receive urgent professional medical care when we land. Your second question I cannot, of course, answer." With deliberate vagueness, Tremayne added, "As we are still several hours away from our base, I must now return to the bridge, but my First Lieutenant will do what he can to make you as comfortable as possible in the circumstances." Turning to the German officer once more before leaving, Tremayne said with a smile, "I hope our rum is to your liking. It is, I know, an acquired taste and we don't carry schnapps on board!"

The German officer smiled gravely in return and saluted as

Tremayne left to resume his position on the bridge.

The high winds persisted and the seas continued to churn, with the bone-chilling spray constantly flying over the wheelhouse and bridge, soaking those exposed to the skin as 1315 pushed her way through the surging waves.

Tremayne called down the voice tube: "Sparks, Captain speaking. Make to 1316 and 1317 and relay our position, in code, to both. Make: *'RV Buoy "Y", 10 miles SSE of home. ETA 10.00 hours'.*"

Willoughby-Brown returned to the bridge as both boats acknowledged Tremayne's signal.

"Well Number One, it looks as if we shall meet up at the RV, more or less on schedule, with 1316 and 1317. They are converging on our course and we should have visual contact within the hour, so long as the weather allows."

The relief of the morphine had eased Tremayne's pain considerably and he began to review the events of the night, preparing himself for debriefing with Enever and, no doubt, Commander Rawlings. He found his thoughts constantly returning to Stoker McAllister's young widow and the obscene lottery that was war – and either life or death.

"Are you alright sir?" Willoughby-Brown asked, looking anxiously at his Captain with obvious concern.

"If I may say sir, you're looking dreadfully pale and I thought you were going to keel over a moment ago."

"Thank you Number One." Tremayne touched the First Lieutenant's shoulder. "I appreciate your thought. Lack of sleep and a combination of morphine and too much introspection are, I'm afraid, causing a temporary loss of sense of humour. By heavens though, Number One, I could kill for a bacon sarnie right now."

"Right sir, I'll ring for room service," grinned a much-relieved Willoughby-Brown moving to the voice tube: "Able Seaman Watkins, this is the First Lieutenant. Can you work the oracle for us please?"

"Ooh, I doubt that very much sir, but I could do a luvly breakfast, if that would 'elp, sir."

"Thank you Watkins, that would fit the bill perfectly," said Willoughby-Brown smiling broadly at Tremayne.

"Breakfast with musical accompaniment, I'll wager, sir — Watkins' version of *thé dansant* no less."

"You know something Number One — you've just restored my sense of humour. Thank you for that," smiled a still very pale-looking Tremayne. "Incidentally, I applaud the initiative you took with Corporal Kane when Leading Seaman Young went down on the forrard gun. Your action merits a mention in despatches — I'll see to it."

"Thank you sir, but it seems so undeserved. It all happened so quickly — a sort of mixture of adrenalin, sheer bloody-mindedness and instinct. There was no real thought there — only fury at the enemy — and it was Kane who knew how to traverse and fire the two-pounder."

"That's as maybe, but it was you who took the necessary initial action promptly and got things moving — and that's what counted in that situation as it so often does," said Tremayne.

"Well Number One — here comes the inevitable music; breakfast should follow in due course," laughed Tremayne, as the now customary combination of noises and smells arose once more from the galley below.

Three off-key verses of *Once I Was Shipwrecked on the Marylou*, plus the aroma of bacon, eggs and sausages cooking in the galley, had an immediate restorative effect – not only on the bridge but also throughout the boat – including the German prisoners.

Some time later, working his way through another of 'Pablo' Watkins' culinary wonders, Tremayne turned to Leading Seaman 'Brummie' Nicholls, who was similarly occupied and sharing the bridge.

"Nicholls, I've been to see Leading Seaman Young. He was badly wounded by shell splinters while in command of the forrard pom-pom. He's going to pull through, thank God, but it will be months, I fear, rather than weeks, before he'll be back in action. In any case, he's keen to get PO's rate and I've promised him I'll push him forward for promotion – he's earned it."

Tremayne paused as he eased his injured arm into a more comfortable position, before resuming: "Which brings me to you, Nicholls. Your idea about keeping the pom-pom properly lubricated could well have helped us sink that E-boat earlier this morning. Had that gun jammed, it might well be us who are at the bottom of the sea right now – or on our way to a prisoner-of-war camp in heaven-knows-where. I'd like you to take over as gun-captain of the forrard two-pounder. The First Lieutenant agrees with me that you're the man for the job. What do *you* say?"

"Thank you, sir. I'd like that. A 'townie' oppo of mine from Smethwick – Bill Savage – won a posthumous VC last month in the St Nazaire raid in 314 – a Fairmile 'C' like ours, sir – an' 'e was gun-captain of the forrard two-pounder. I'd like to do it for 'im sir, as much as anything."

"Thank you Nicholls. I'm very glad you've accepted, and I appreciate your reasons for doing so. Who do you want as your gun-layer?"

"It 'ud 'ave to be Able Seaman Watkins, sir. 'E's from Smethwick as well, an' 'e'd want to do it for Bill Savage too, sir."

"Right Nicholls, then it's as good as done, so long as Able Seaman Watkins agrees."

"'E'll agree sir," said Nicholls, with a meaningful grin.

At 09.45 hours, the port lookout shouted, "Two Fairmiles, line astern, on converging course sir."

"Well spotted Thompson." Tremayne swung his binoculars round to the two boats racing to join them, white water cascading off their forrard decks as they punched through the rolling waves.

"Yeoman, make to 1316 and 1317: '*Welcome back. You did a great job*'."

"Well Number One, it won't be long now. A hot bath will be very welcome."

"Absolutely sir, but you must get that arm seen to sir. You've lost quite a lot of blood."

"Don't mother me, Number One. I'm fine. Lieutenant Commander Enever will want to see us, along with Sub-Lieutenant Tabarly, as soon as we arrive in New Grimsby. Tabarly's already been in touch with Intelligence Section and let them know our ETA."

"Sir, signal from 1316: '*Nice to be back, Dad*', and 1317, sir: '*We does it to oblige dearie*'."

"Acknowledge, Yeoman and make to all boats: '*Diamond formation.*

1501 astern, 1316 and 1317 abeam, port and starboard'."

Approaching St Mary's at low tide, Tremayne spoke to Irvine, who had not left his post once since 04.00 hours – even eating his breakfast with one hand on the wheel.

"Thank you, Cox'n. Again, you've been a tower of strength."

Ill at ease with praise and not quite sure how to handle it, the Cox'n muttered awkwardly, "Thank you sir. I was just doing my job, so I was."

Tremayne smiled at the shy, yet formidable man as he continued: "It was pretty close at low tide yesterday and there'll be even less water under her keel this morning. Set your course through Great Minalto and the Ledges for Castle Bryher Neck, if you please, Cox'n. We'll go outside Black Rocks, but inside Scilly Rock, then round Shipman Head. With Gimble Point on our port beam, we'll come down New Grimsby Sound to Braiden Rock."

"Aye aye sir."

Having negotiated the jagged and dangerous Northern Rocks and left Hell Bay and the north end of Bryher behind them, 1315 was between Shipman Head and Gimble Point when Tremayne gave the order: "Hands fall in for entering harbour. Starboard watch forrard, port watch aft. Royal Marines fall in with the starboard watch."

As Corporal Kane rushed out to the forrard deck, he was given a rousing cheer by both watches, forming up, to smiles from those on the bridge. Having secured off Braiden Rock, Tremayne addressed his crew – sadly depleted by casualties:

"Thank you all for what you did last night and this morning.

I am proud to have you serving with me – every one of you."
He let his eyes seek out each face in turn.

"This was our first time in action together and it won't be
the last. When we go on our next mission, I will be glad that it's
you that I'm with. Sadly, we have had to say "goodbye" to two
of our shipmates, Able Seaman Steele and Stoker-Mechanic
McAllister, while another one, Leading Seaman Young has been
seriously wounded. I'm very glad to say, however, that he should
make a full recovery. Get some sleep now. Duty watch will
commence with the dogwatch. Carry on."

When 1501, 1316 and 1317 had each secured, Tremayne quickly
debriefed the three boat captains. Despite the casualties and largely
superficial damage to the four motor launches, the operation
had been a success with the battery at Pen Enez completely
destroyed and significant intelligence obtained for Lieutenant
Commander Enever, as well as several prisoners of war.

Tremayne took Hermann to one side.

"Hermann, we each have a group of blindfolded prisoners
to whom Lieutenant Commander Enever will wish to talk. Keep
them under guard until they can be transferred to Helford for
further interrogation and then on to a POW camp.

Helford are sending a Camper and Nicholson, with a Vosper
as guard boat, and will pick them up at 13.00 hours. Commander
Enever is coming down to interview them separately on board
our two boats, along with some character from SOE
Headquarters. You haven't told your prisoners about those I have
taken and I've not told my group about those you rescued. We'll
let them discover that later. It may also expose any inconsistencies

for Intelligence in the information the two groups provide if interrogated separately.

Incidentally, thanks for guarding my rear, Hermann. It was good to know you were watching my back."

"I'm just sorry that I wasn't able to watch your arm for you. That wound looks nasty. You need to see the MO pretty pronto Richard."

"I have to see Lieutenant Commander Enever immediately for an intelligence debriefing and then, no doubt, old "What? what? what?" will want one of his pain-in-the-arse operations briefings, what?!"

As before, they parted with laughter and Fischer returned to his boat, moored alongside 1315.

"Well Number One, another fine mess I've got you into," smiled Tremayne as they clambered onto the jetty.

"You showed a hell of a lot of initiative – and courage – and you set a damn good example of leadership to the crew. I'll make sure that Commander…"

"Richard!" Tremayne was cut short in mid-sentence by Emma Fraser scrambling down the rocky quayside path to meet him.

"What have they done to you? Your sleeve – it's soaked in blood. Daniel didn't tell us that you've been wounded."

"Och, lassie, it's nay bother," grinned Tremayne, imitating Emma's response to him at the previous evening's briefing.

"I'm fine, really. A good clean up and a fresh dressing on it and I'll be right as rain. But thank you for your concern. I'm just on my way to see Lieutenant Commander Enever. The prisoners are under guard, blindfolded, but one of them is quite badly wounded and needs urgent medical attention – and that I must attend to. Hermann Fischer is still on board 1501, and Petty Officer Irvine, my Coxswain, is in charge of my boat."

"This is why I'm here Richard. Lieutenant Commander Enever and a fellow from SOE's Department 10, who is a German national, are coming down now to interview the prisoners. Daniel Tabarly has been in contact with us and so he will spend the morning debriefing. We'd like to see you in 101 at 15.00 hours, which gives you a chance for some sleep – and to get that wound seen to."

"By the way," said Emma laughing, "for a mere Sassenach, you can muster a pretty good Scots accent when you try."

"Although my father's family are Cornish, my mother was a McIntyre and came from near Oban – so that's where it must originate," said Tremayne, smiling.

"That's much better – that only makes half of you Sassenach! Come on, I'll walk with you back to the sickbay and make sure you get that arm looked at," she said, the gentle blue eyes serious once more.

Tremayne was essentially quite a shy person, especially in the company of women, and, over the years, he'd relied on a degree of formality to create distance and so avoid familiarity and social intimacy.

Yet he found Emma was so easy to talk to. Her earnestness, alternating with a refreshing spontaneity, was almost childlike. As they walked and talked, he became caught up in her natural enthusiasm for their surroundings – the islands themselves, the many different and unusual wild flowers, the wide variety of sea birds and the intensely beautiful emerald, turquoise and aquamarine of the shallow seas between the islands.

Rather than competing with each other, they built upon one another's observations, frequently laughing at the improbability of some of the conclusions they were reaching on matters as diverse as rock formations, the names of some of the off-islands, the local surnames – and even the naval traditions that were now defining so much of their lives.

Before Tremayne realised it, he was standing outside the sickbay at HMS Godolphin with an anxious Emma Fraser saying, "I want to know how that arm is. I want diagnosis – and prognosis – please, Richard. Keep me posted."

Three

A bunch of Swiss Admirals

Tremayne spent longer with David Hegarty, the Surgeon Lieutenant, than he had expected. When he finally left Godolphin's sickbay, it was with a heavily bandaged left arm secured in a sling and a plentiful supply of painkillers. Hegarty's domain – like so much of Godolphin – was minuscule, cramped and utilitarian in the extreme. Yet, within these spartan and seemingly permanent 'temporary' facilities, the medical officer and his one sickbay attendant had already established a degree of professional caring beyond reproach. As in other functions of the base, the severely limited, but essential resources of the sickbay were the result of Admiral Hembury's scrounging, poaching and enterprising re-appropriation of Admiralty property.

Hegarty, of a similar age to Tremayne, had been another source of support in helping him to come to terms with Diana's death.

As a consequence, the two men had become close friends, with a high regard and respect for one another.

The same caring came through, once again, as Hegarty said, "That arm is going to hurt like hell for a bit – and keep you awake – Richard, so I'm giving you something to put you out for the count each night until the wound starts to heal. Keep that sling on for at least the next five days. I don't want the wound to open up again."

Feeling rather like a trussed chicken, Tremayne took his leave of Hegarty and the sickbay and made his way over to hut 101 for the debriefing with Lieutenant Commander Enever and his team of Intelligence Officers.

"My dear boy, come in – grab a pew. Richard, I had no idea about your wound until Emma told me this morning – how are you?" Enever's instant warmth was immediately apparent. "I must say, though, you make a marvellous wounded hero, doesn't he Emma?"

To his utter embarrassment, Tremayne found himself colouring up at Enever's comments and wishing that the floor would open up beneath him. He instinctively knew that understatement – which came naturally to him – would most likely sound contrived and *unnatural* and so have the opposite effect to the one he intended.

To avoid feeling even more embarrassed and awkward, he opted for a rather lame: "Thank you sir. I'll be glad when this confounded sling comes off so that I can go sailing again around these wonderful islands."

"Hmm, I seem to remember Richard, Nelson managed to

sail quite well with only one arm – and just one good eye!" replied Enever, with his eyes twinkling.

Emma was quick to sense Tremayne's acute discomfort and vulnerability and tactfully intervened: "Shall I bring Richard up to speed on the consequences of the information that Daniel brought back to us, sir?"

Enever did not miss the rescue attempt and smiled indulgently. "Please do. Then I can take up the story and tell him what we have in store for everybody before our next critical operations in Brittany with the Confrèrie."

"The most urgent and critical issue, Richard," Emma began, "is that there is a double agent close to the centre of the Confrèrie. As a result, the two agents whom you took over two nights ago have been captured, interrogated and, by now, most probably executed."

Tremayne leaned forward, listening intently.

"It took some pretty inelegant pressure," the normally gentle blue eyes reflected a toughness and resolve that surprised Tremayne, "to persuade Jean-François to disclose the name of the traitor to us. It is, in fact, Muguette, who has been acting as a double agent in the pay of the Abwehr. Because, as we now know, the Confrèrie is structured as a series of small independent "cells", her knowledge of its members and their activities is still localised and, therefore, restricted, thank goodness. But, since she operates closely with Jean-François, she is a major threat and therefore extremely dangerous. Consequently, Jean-François himself must be in considerable peril and in danger of arrest."

"And presumably that could happen at any time?" asked

Tremayne, visibly concerned at what he had just been told.

"Exactly, Richard. Let me come in here please, Emma," Enever spoke quickly. "We have finally persuaded Jean-François that he must convince Muguette that he has caught and executed the traitor – some fictitious person that she can't possibly trace and check up on. She will then assume that she is in the clear, and Jean-François will act as if he endorses that. Jean-François wanted to try – and then execute her – but frankly we see her as more use to us being kept alive and acting as a bearer of false tidings."

"Quite a *ruse-de-guerre*, sir. As a simple sailor I'm quite out of my depth here," laughed Tremayne. Increasingly, he found the Byzantine intrigues and machinations of the intelligence world a source of fascination and a spur to developing a closer understanding of something he recognised as ultimately vital to winning the war at sea.

"There's much more to come, Richard! Acting on instructions from the highest levels within both SIS and SOE – for once they agree with one another – we will now feed Muguette false information via Jean-François. By apparently preserving the existing transfer of intelligence within the Confrèrie, we will maintain what seems to be normality from Muguette's point of view."

"I'm intrigued sir. How will we pass information to Muguette that seems genuine and that will not arouse her suspicion when, in fact, it is counterfeit while, at the same time, feeding real information to Jean-François?"

"Ah, dear boy, now that's precisely where you come in." If

anything, Enever looked and sounded even more donnish as he clearly relished the intrigue that he was now becoming so deeply immersed in.

"Future transmissions will be largely W/T, Richard, but using RAF equipment and so transmitting and receiving on RAF frequencies. This will create the impression that our activities are shifting from the sea to the air and that agents are being inserted – and extracted – not by boat, but from aircraft, one way or another. We have made sure that we will use RAF radio frequencies that the Germans already know and most certainly monitor. As summer comes on, with the nights becoming shorter, we shall start to make much more use of our "fishing boats" to land agents and to bring them back to Tresco."

"Presumably, sir, the fishing boats – as well as the MGBs and MTBs – will all be fitted with RAF W/T equipment?"

"Yes, absolutely so. Yours and Fischer's, along with the phoney fishing boats, will be the first to be equipped with the new kit. We'll use both English and French, as appropriate, based upon new codes in what will be largely gobbledegook. These will allow Jean-François to pass on to Muguette plausible interpretations that will cause the Germans to respond to them and deploy forces to deal with what will turn out to be non-events. The true interpretation of the gobbledegook will be acted upon by Jean-François and the various "cells" of the Confrèrie."

"But surely, sir, sooner or later, the Abwehr will come to realise that we are pulling the wool over their eyes. Once they recognise this, then Jean-François will be living on borrowed time which could be terminated without any warning."

"True, Richard, and to delay that for as long as we can, the reasons for events not turning out as the Germans expect from their "doctored" information, will have to appear as credible and realistic as possible. We're now convinced, in any case, that the Germans are allowing Jean-François to continue to operate, in order to use him as a source of valuable intelligence – especially since they have cracked our codes. So to allay their suspicion – and keep them off Jean-François' back – we'll have to let them have some minor successes."

"As you can imagine," Emma added, "the initiative lies with the Abwehr, just as much as it does with us. We believe that they are already using Jean-François, as we intend to use Muguette. They can make their moves, at any time to suit themselves, and steal a march on us. We and the Germans are locked into a game of tactical intelligence 'chess', with each 'player' trying to outguess, out-guile and out-manoeuvre the other."

"And a pretty lethal game at that," said Tremayne, "where neither side can ever be really sure of the other's game plan."

"Precisely. And because of this, Richard, we must widen our repertoire of both initiatives and responses. The time, the place and the circumstances can all determine how we must best act to insert and extract agents in the future. Especially in the case of the rescue of Jean-François and his family, which could become a much more immediate problem."

Emma produced a photograph showing Capitaine Duhamel, an elegant lady and two young children – a boy of about eight and a girl of around five or six.

"Let me come in again Emma, please." Enever put down his

pipe again and leant forward – sure signs, Tremayne had previously noted, that the Senior Intelligence Officer was about to ratchet up the intensity and level of confidentiality of the discussion.

"We have to be ready and as fully-trained as possible to undertake such operations more professionally – and in the immediate future. The luxury of time is something that we just don't have. Right now, we're up against a well-trained, determined and very professional enemy. So, Richard," Enever's eyes twinkled again, "all boat crews, including officers, together with our friends the 'Royals', will undergo two weeks' intensive training in weapons handling, unarmed combat, rock climbing and the use of canoes and rubber dinghies. Seven hours – one per day of week two – will be devoted to acquiring a minimal, basic working vocabulary of every day phrases in French and German – with our Welsh speakers learning some Breton and dropping one of the other languages. All officers and about a dozen selected POs and ratings will attend the language training sessions."

"But, in the meantime, sir, what about Jean-François? Jerry might not wait for us to complete our training before making his move," suggested Tremayne.

"That is a strong possibility, Richard. If the balloon does go up and Jean-François' arrest looks imminent, then we will abort further training and move post-haste to bring him and his family out of Brittany. As far as we know, his hideout near Pointe de Beg Pol is still safe, but we can't be sure just how far Muguette and her masters have compromised our security. At best, it can only be a matter of time before the Germans are on to that hideout."

"If things do go 'live' suddenly sir, I imagine we will also put in diversionary rescue attempts at different bogus locations – and using aircraft – to confuse the Abwehr?" enquired Tremayne.

"Exactly, Richard," said Emma. "Hmm, not such a 'simple sailor' after all!"

Tremayne light-heartedly countered, "When the war's over, I can already foresee a brand new career opening up for me as a stiletto-toting, Breton-speaking nightclub bouncer in St Malo!"

"That's somewhat different from the barrister you intended to become, eh Richard?"

Enever smiled, benignly, as he looked at Tremayne over the top of his steel-rimmed spectacles. "With that arm of yours, I don't really see you throwing too many people over your shoulder, or abseiling down Shipman Head. Not for the next few days at least."

Commander Rawlings, who had just joined the meeting, took over at this point.

"Right on cue. What? Thank you, Enever. Now Tremayne, I want all officers and ship's company assembled on the parade ground at 16.30 hours sharp for a briefing by Admiral Hembury and Captain Mansell. They will outline the training programme for the next fourteen days. Following that briefing, Colour Sergeant McGrory will give everybody the details of today's activities before Corporal Kane takes boat crews – and all officers," he added with a snide smirk, "out onto the firing ranges on Castle Down at the north of the island. Despite what Lieutenant Commander Enever has just said, *I* don't expect some footling scratch to give you an excuse for not participating, Tremayne. What?"

"I'd no intention of ducking out, sir. That is not *my* style." Tremayne's response was icy and struck home, as intended. Rawlings, momentarily fazed, broke off eye contact, aware of the steel that lay only just below the surface in the other man.

That afternoon, after the short, inspirational addresses by the Admiral and Captain Mansell – HMS Godolphin's Commanding Officer, Colour Sergeant McGrory of the Royal Marines, a short, thickset Glaswegian with seemingly no neck, took command of the parade in the consummate style that only experienced senior NCOs can.

Watched approvingly by a nonchalant, but immaculately turned-out Captain Waring – the officer commanding HMS Godolphin's small Royal Marine detachment, McGrory quickly established his presence and credentials, initially at the expense of the unfortunate Able Seaman Watkins. Spotting the comparatively short, rotund figure of the seaman from Smethwick relaxing more than the command 'Parade – stand at ease' warranted, he barked: "That fat, sawn-off sailor, fourth from the left, front rank!" McGrory had the immediate, undivided attention of almost eighty officers and men. "Don't stand there like a stocking-full of diarrhoea, even if you are a stocking-full of diarrhoea. Straighten yourself up – or I'll put you where the seagulls can't shit on you."

A noticeable, instantaneous stiffening of backs rippled through the ranks – especially among the younger RNVR officers. The baleful gaze suddenly focused on Lieutenants Bower, Taylor and Fischer, who appeared to be enjoying some private joke among themselves.

Directing his full-volume attack onto them, McGrory boomed, with exaggerated emphasis, "Gentlemen, in the Royal Marines I am accustomed to dealing with officers and *gentlemen* – not a bunch of Swiss Admirals. Can I now have *your* full attention, please?!"

Once again, the reaction was instant and somewhat shocked compliance.

The normally poker-faced Captain Waring flashed Tremayne a barely perceptible conspiratorial grin, as a hushed air of expectancy settled over the parade.

The redoubtable Colour Sergeant intoned his way, still at full volume, through the afternoon's programme on the ranges, to the undivided attention of officers and men alike. At the end of it he came smartly to attention, saluted Commander Rawlings, and handed the assembled parade back to the obviously approving Director of Operations. Rawlings called the assembly to attention and then ordered: "Parade, right turn."

Determined to invest the two weeks' training with an appropriate sense of occasion, as well as importance, Admiral Hembury had produced – no one was quite sure from where – a small Royal Marine band to lead the ship's company along the island's perimeter road, through Dolphin Town and on to the path leading to the rifle ranges. Spirits lifted noticeably and immediately as the band struck up *Heart of Oak* and, marching three abreast, the column stepped smartly off the parade ground heading for the heights of Castle Down at the north end of Tresco.

Ten minutes later and passing St Nicholas' Church and the

collection of pretty stone and whitewashed cottages that make up Dolphin Town, the group were now marching to the tune *Three Cheers for the Red, White and Blue*, in recognition of the high number of RNVR officers and men in the group. More like a country dance than a military march, the step of the small column had become even jauntier at the change of tune.

At Old Grimsby harbour, the waiting Royal Marine weapons instructors picked up the column and marched it along the road to Norrard, to join the rocky pathway leading up onto Castle Down and to the firing ranges. As a musical farewell, the small Royal Marines band formed up on the quay and played the slowly disappearing column off to the Corps' own stirring march, *A Life on the Ocean Wave* and, finally, *Rule Britannia*.

In a world – and at a time – where patriotism and a sense of nationhood were still viewed as natural and the norm, many an eye of those marching shone with pride as the column maintained step, swinging along the road to the north of the island.

The next fourteen days were some of the most intensive, yet memorable times that Tremayne could recall – with sleep and personal time at a barely tolerable minimum. Into that comparatively short space of time, the instructors crammed in training on all the small arms used by the Royal Navy and the Royal Marines, as well as providing a working introduction to the most commonly encountered German rifles, pistols, submachine guns and heavier automatic weapons.

Corporal Kane especially was in his element, instructing officers on the handling of the Bren gun. "Mark my words, gentlemen, this weapon will still be in use well into the next century," was his reassuring introduction to the gun. He reserved his best, well-rehearsed phrases for the "preparation to fire" stages of his instruction. "When I say 'house the cocking handle', I'm not enquiring after the bastard's 'ealth. I mean, gentlemen, stow the bleedin' thing away – and be bloody sharp about it!"

"Hmm, I've not heard that one before," thought Tremayne with a wry smile as, like the rest, he tried to get to grips with the IAs – immediate actions – necessary to clear any stoppages and so continue firing the weapon.

Unarmed combat instruction followed the usual intensive pattern of break falls, defensive blocks, vicious jabs, chops and kicks, with the Royal Marines instructors unashamedly enjoying themselves at 'Jolly Jack's' expense.

A succession of throws over hip and shoulder, together with leg-sweeps designed to off-balance an enemy prior to the invariably terminal boot in the nape of the neck, completed the training in unarmed, close-quarter fighting.

An increasingly bruised and battered Nicholls and Watkins inevitably became the instructors' favourite stooges, 'volunteering' to demonstrate strangleholds and some very painful head, neck and arm locks to the guffaws of their insensitive shipmates.

"Bloody 'ell, kid," muttered a somewhat black and blue Watkins to his Brummie "townie" during a NAAFI teabreak. "This bleedin' lot must be even wus than yower old woman – an' 'er's bloody dangerous enough!"

Willoughby-Brown, brought up in a cavalry family with the fond belief that their sole raison d'etre was to lend tone to any battle that might otherwise become a mere vulgar brawl, was horrified by the raw, brutal reality of knife-fighting techniques. Much to Petty Officer Irvine's amusement, shock completely immobilised the First Lieutenant's usually very agile right eyebrow, during instruction on the commando fighting-knife. Sensing the refined and sheltered upbringing of the young Sub-Lieutenant, the Marine instructor — a veteran of the First World War — more than exaggerated the need to thrust the knife into the kidneys, rather than the heart, when dispatching an unwary sentry.

"If it goes into the kidneys, they dies without a sound sir — all nice and quiet like. If you stabs 'em through the 'eart or lungs, sir, they screams 'orribly — an' just when you don't want no bleedin' noise."

All the usually eloquent First Lieutenant could mutter by way of response was, "I say, that's a bit off isn't it?" Willoughby-Brown was not alone in his revulsion at the thought of close-quarter battle with a fighting-knife. Several of the ship's company looked similarly green about the gills and fell unusually silent during instruction on the Fairbairn and Sykes commando stiletto.

Neighbouring Bryher and St Martin's islands — as well as the north end of Tresco itself — provided enough cliff faces and rocky outcrops for training in scrambling, ascending and abseiling techniques. Rock climbing and cliff assault, similarly, proved to be somewhat alien activities to sailors who were more at home on a heaving deck than a sheer rock face.

Once again, the sailors' efforts on unfamiliar ground provided the highly trained Royal Marine instructors with ample ammunition to yell derisory comments about "Swiss Admirals" and "web-footed matelots". Officers and ratings alike came in for ribald criticism from their temporary tutors, but all appeared to take it in good part, noted Enever and Tremayne.

As is often the case, in the seemingly perpetual rivalry between "bootneck" and "matelot", there is merciless mutual ribbing and "black" humour but no real antagonism or hostility.

In the NAAFI in the evening, after training sessions, sailors and their Marine instructors alike were to be found sharing the same tables, drinking pints of scrumpy or beer together, and joining in raucous choruses of – among other songs – *The Dockyard Cavalry* led, inevitably, by 'Pablo' Watkins, complete with beatific smile and waving sombrero. The physically punishing activities of close-quarter battle training had, nevertheless, already had a somewhat restricting impact on his normally more expansive gestures. The Marines, especially, grinned knowingly at one another at the frequent and very audible "'kin' 'ells", as Watkins's battered and bruised limbs struggled painfully to fulfil the frenetic demands of a choir conductor's role.

Frequently, the more intense and demanding the shared experience, the greater the resultant camaraderie and team spirit, and Tremayne was quick to see – and feel – this as the ever more challenging fortnight ran its course. Boat crews were beginning to develop and grow as effective, close-knit teams, where mutual support and good-humoured interdependence became increasingly evident.

Lessons in rudimentary conversational French, German and

Breton were held in the same room that served as the NAAFI canteen, providing something of a cultural contrast to the evening's choral works in the same building.

The specialists from SOE and SIS were seen, variously, by the seamen and Marines as "odd bastards", "bleedin' nutters" or "soddin' sadists". These provided training in sabotage skills involving the new plastic explosives, creating ingeniously deadly booby-traps, as well as the use of silenced CO_2 pistols.

By the end of the exhausting fortnight, mock attacks, small group raids and the simulated despatch of stooges acting as "enemy" sentries, all confirmed creditable proficiency in the essential and more lethal skills of clandestine raiding.

The sailors' attempts to handle the two-man canoes in surf and choppy seas also provided their Marine instructors with enough stories to dine out on for years to come. Even so, the level of competence achieved was sufficient, both to get ashore and to paddle the return journey to a waiting submarine or motor launch, while keeping critical supplies and equipment dry and immediately usable.

Acquiring proficiency in French, German and Breton was a different matter and some teachers were reduced to near despair. As one "Y" Service language instructor was heard to exclaim to one of his colleagues in utter exasperation, "For God's sake, mother, sell the pig and buy me out."

Despite the selective, rather than universal, success of the crash course in languages compared with the rest of the two weeks' training, sufficient people emerged who were able to understand – and speak – every day terms and phrases.

As was expected, the Welsh speakers took to the Breton language quite well but, with typical Celtic pride and ingenuity, suggested that they could also use their native language, ship-to-ship, with W/T when circumstances demanded such a stratagem.

For once, beaming with uncharacteristic approval at an idea which deviated from the all-defining Admiralty Fleet Orders, Commander Rawlings' profound observation on the suggestion was: "That'll teach the Hun to break wind in church. What?"

The dutiful, but strained smiles of the Welsh members of his audience at the training course debriefing, possessed an eloquence beyond mere words...

For Tremayne — and for most of the officers attending the post-training debriefing — the most valuable contributions were those of Admiral Hembury and Lieutenant Commander Enever. Both had simple, but relevant messages to deliver, and each gave them in their differing ways.

Admiral Hembury's charismatic presence and swashbuckling disregard of Admiralty bureaucracy won him instant approval from the younger officers present, particularly those wearing the wavy stripes of the RNVR.

The major themes of his short speech were the success of the recent St Nazaire raid – denying the Germans a dock in Europe big enough to hold the *Tirpitz* and thereby virtually imprisoning her in Norwegian fjords – and the appointment of Vice Admiral Louis Mountbatten as Chief of Allied Combined Operations.

"These two factors," he said, "will give both sanction and impetus to our efforts to strike at Jerry in the territories that he has occupied. We are now much better prepared to seize the opportunities opening up for us, gentlemen. We have a clear, vital role in the wider scheme of things, as the balance slowly shifts in our favour. With Admiral Mountbatten's appointment, we now have the necessary mandate to act. Let's get on with the job – and do it well!"

The more studious Enever spoke at a tactical level about the increasing scope for initiative and action that growing experience and skill would inevitably bring. In effect, Enever gave sharper focus and definition, together with a necessary sense of immediacy, to Admiral Hembury's more strategic picture.

Intelligence Section's own debriefing of the boat crew captains – and Tremayne as the Flotilla Commander – inevitably took a more parochial and detailed turn.

Enever, opening the discussion, turned to Tremayne and said, with a broad smile, "Your recommendation for formal mention in despatches for Sub-Lieutenant Willoughby-Brown has been approved and, Richard, so too have you and Lieutenant Fischer for your parts in the last operation. So, gentlemen, my congratulations to you both – the recognition is richly deserved."

"May I add mine too, Richard, and to you Hermann," Emma held out her hand to shake those of Tremayne and the young South African officer.

"I have some more good news, Richard," added Enever. "As all four vessels were damaged, yours more severely than the others, refits have already begun on 1315, 1316, 1317 and 1501 while you were all skylarking on the ropes, rocks and rifle ranges and," the grey eyes beamed even more benignly over the spectacles, "Admiral

Hembury, with his infinite gift for procuring much-needed kit, has managed to get you a six-pounder to replace that ridiculous pom-pom of yours. What's more dear boy, it comes complete with power mounting and, to cope with the greater weight and recoil of the larger weapon, an additional reinforcing forrard bulkhead has been installed for you."

"Thank you sir – I'm delighted. Against the faster E-boats with their 40mm weapons I did feel very under-gunned. Last time we were lucky, I believe, to hit external magazines, but I could actually see our two-pounder shots striking Jerry's bridge and wheelhouse to little real effect. My new gun crew – the inseparable Brummies – will be very happy with that. I'm most grateful to Admiral Hembury, and to you sir, for your part in the productive skulduggery!"

The meeting subsequently broke up as Enever announced, "Gentlemen, it's been a bloody long and hard fortnight. I've got Captain Mansell's permission to grant a forty-eight hour leave for everyone who took part in the training. That starts with effect from midnight tonight, gentlemen. Take a good, well-earned break and enjoy yourselves. We start operations in earnest next week, assuming the Abwehr, or Gestapo, make no sudden moves against Jean-François."

A buzz of conversation immediately erupted around the table as leave options were considered and instant plans were made – then rejected as impracticable – and revived again.

"I should tell you, gentlemen," interrupted Emma, "both of the Vospers will be running liberty men – and that includes you – to Penzance, prior to onward passage to the Helford River base, if anyone is interested. The Vospers will leave New Grimsby quay at 00.30 hours sharp," the blue eyes were laughing as she added a peremptory "what?", that produced a momentary disbelieving silence followed by a huge roar of laughter from Enever and the boat captains.

"How about coming sailing Richard?" asked Fischer. "Your arm looks much better, and I can't make Cape Town and back in forty-eight hours!"

"Thank you Hermann, I would love to, but I need to go to Plymouth – and then to visit my parents who also live in Devon. I haven't seen them in months."

"I have to report to Devonport tomorrow forenoon," Emma cut in, "and I'm travelling by the air-sea rescue launch that Admiral Hembury "borrowed" from the RAF and forgot to return. It leaves at 06.00 hours tomorrow. Can we offer you a lift, Richard? It would be more convenient, I think, than going to Penzance and taking pot luck with the trains up to "Guz". It also means that you'd get a good night's sleep first. We should be arriving in Devonport at 09.30 hours. Does that fit in with your plans?"

"Thank you, Emma. It would help enormously. I'd like to take up your offer. I'll be on the quay at New Grimsby just before 06.00 hours. I take it swords and medals will not be worn?" Tremayne's normally serious grey eyes teased, rather than mocked, her air of businesslike efficiency.

"Och no, sir," she replied with exaggerated solemnity. "Not unless you've got the leading role in the local production of *HMS Pinafore*!"

"Touché! 06.00 hours it is, Emma."

The British Power Boat air-sea rescue launch taking Tremayne, Emma Fraser and two French officers to RN Devonport was small compared with MGB 1315. She was just over seventy feet long – under two-thirds the length of Tremayne's craft – and she had a curious power-operated perspex gun turret aft of the bridge. Rather like the large dorsal gun turrets of a heavy bomber, the transparent dome of the launch mounted twin .50 calibre Browning machine guns, principally for anti-aircraft defence.

With a maximum speed of thirty-two knots, she quickly cleared the Scillies, en route for Land's End and then Devonport dockyard.

Tremayne discovered that the two French officers – both sub-lieutenants – were due to attend a special training programme in W/T and R/T procedures prior to returning to Tresco for the forthcoming operations in Brittany. Paul Guillet was a lively twenty-two-year-old Breton who had spent most of his time since leaving school working with his father's fishing fleet out of Camaret. He had served as a junior lieutenant reservist with the French Navy and, like Tabarly, knew the complicated, indented Breton coast and its dangerous rocks intimately. Short of stature, dynamic and very "physical", Guillet was an engaging man with an excellent command of English, if somewhat punctuated, from time to time, with the most improbable of malapropisms. At one stage on the journey, he asked a very shocked Emma if she, too, was "ravished". Coming to her rescue, and reversing their roles of the previous day, Tremayne managed to work out, amid a lot of embarrassed laughter, that the young Breton had become confused about the meaning of the words "ravenous" and "famished", and had decided that "ravished" must be the logical compromise.

"Heavens, Paul," said a smiling Tremayne. "Carry on like that and we'll have to help out the Abwehr radio monitors with a special interpreters' phrase book so that they can still de-code our messages! I think, Emma, it's about the only time I've actually seen you fazed by something someone has said!"

"It's not the sort of question a girl with a sheltered upbringing expects to have to answer. At least not on first acquaintance," she added, laughing at Guillet's confusion and obvious embarrassment.

Pierre Quilghini, the other young French officer, was something of a contrast. Tall, good-looking with refined, aristocratic features, he was both more serious and more elegant in his movement than Guillet. Somewhat reserved, he possessed an inner strength that Tremayne sensed in conversation with him. He also spoke excellent English. His father owned a large silk weaving company near Vadencourt in Picardie and Quilghini had been learning the business with a view to ultimately taking it over. Unfortunately, the outbreak of war had put a temporary end to those plans. Like Guillet, he too had become a junior officer in the French Naval Reserve and had escaped to England via the evacuation from Dunkirk.

"Are you going to Devonport, sir, to the barracks?" Quilghini asked Tremayne.

Tremayne hesitated before replying. "Well no. Actually, I'm

going back to look at what used to be my house in Plymouth. It was destroyed – and my wife was killed – in an air raid fourteen months ago. Until now, I haven't really felt ready to revisit it."

Emma looked across at Tremayne, her face serious and concerned.

Tremayne continued, "By the way, gentlemen, my name is Richard. Let's forget rank here, please."

"John Enever told me about your circumstances, Richard. I'm so very sorry. This last year must have been terrible for you. What you're planning to do takes a lot of courage."

"Emma, thank you. I've certainly known happier days. To misquote some gallant Frenchman *'C'est la guerre, mais ce n'est pas magnifique!'* I think," he continued, "that coming to terms with the finality and trying to fill the awful void are some of the most difficult things to cope with. More in hope than with any basis of reason or logic, I'm returning to Plymouth to try to get a better hold on reality."

"For a similar reason, when this wretched war is at an end, I want to go to St Valery-en-Caux in Normandy," said Emma quietly.

"Isn't that where the Highlanders fought so bravely, and then finally surrendered, against hopeless odds, in 1940?"

"Exactly, and it's just outside St Valery that a young subaltern, to whom I was about to become engaged, fell in the rearguard action that the Highland Division fought at the time of the Dunkirk evacuation. Iain served with the Seaforth Highlanders and he had just got his first "pip." I grieve not just for his loss, but also for his innocence and vulnerability." Tears suddenly filled her eyes and, for a moment, she had difficulty in continuing.

With no words, Tremayne simply put his hand on her shoulder.

Emma began again. "He was only nineteen – a year younger than me –and, like so many of his age, he was driven by romantic idealism and had no concept of the true horror and reality of war. His idea of fighting a battle was to lead his platoon into action to the sound of the pibroch and his Regiment's Gaelic battle cry *'Cuidich 'n Righ'* – help the King. He would have been like a lamb to the slaughter."

The tears came again and Tremayne offered her his handkerchief.

"Emma," he said gently, "I'm so sorry. I had no idea. I have been so preoccupied with my own loss, I suppose I hadn't thought as much as I should about what others might be going through as a result of this damned war."

"Iain's death – and the terrible waste of it all – is what haunts me still and wakes me up in the middle of the night. Perhaps you can understand that, Richard?"

"Only too well. And I now know why you sometimes wear a McKenzie plaid skirt – the Seaforth's tartan – when you're in civvies, when I would have expected the red of Clan Fraser." He smiled, putting his handkerchief back in his uniform pocket.

"The experience we share, Emma, is not only one of losing someone you love – and that, in itself, is hard enough to bear – but the utter destruction of so much more. It is the ending of the hopes and wishes that you cherished for such a relationship which give way, at times, to a sense of overwhelming despair. I think that is what we grieve about too, and need to work through, before we can move forward and get on with life once again."

Further conversation was rudely interrupted by a sudden, prolonged burst of heavy machine gun fire from the after turret immediately above their heads.

"Emma, stay there and keep low. Paul, Pierre – with me." Tremayne immediately took command of the situation in the tiny wardroom.

He dashed aloft, with the Frenchmen at his heels, onto the rear deck, to be met by a grinning seaman carrying an empty .50 calibre ammunition belt.

"Sorry sir, just testing weapons. We're entering 'Torpedo Alley' here sir. Jerry often comes sneaking in, looking for some likely victim to let fly at with aerial torpedoes. Usually Ju88s or the occasional Arado 196, sir."

"Are these two Brownings all you have as a means of defence?" asked Tremayne.

"No sir. Since leaving Tresco, we've also rigged up port and starboard Lewis guns, on Scarff mountings, each side of the bridge sir."

"Well, they'll certainly add to the noise – and to the fire power – even if they are pretty ancient." Tremayne looked around quickly to convince himself that the duty watch, closed up at defence stations, was alert and watchful. This was an intuitive response on his part, rather than a lack of trust in the ability of the launch's youthful skipper.

As they continued their journey, having passed Land's End en route for Plymouth, Tremayne took some time to look at the fascinating coves and inlets along the south Cornish coast and the rolling waves crashing against the shoreline, before returning below to rejoin the others. A school of dolphins gracefully rising and falling alongside the launch and gannets diving for prey off the port beam as they drew close to Land's End, temporarily took his mind off what he had to face in Plymouth.

The rest of the journey was uneventful and the motor launch arrived in Devonport at 09.25 hours.

"We depart for Tresco at 18.30 hours prompt from this quay, gentlemen," called the RNVR sub-lieutenant acting as boat captain. "We'll see you then. Good luck!"

Taking a bus from the dockyard, Tremayne soon arrived in Plymouth, alighting close to the heavily bombed city centre. He felt an empty sickness in his stomach as he attempted to walk resolutely towards what was once *their* road and *their* house – the home he had shared with Diana. The extent of the devastation created by the blitz on Plymouth shocked him. The city centre that he had known when stationed in Devonport was little more than rubble and eerie, empty shells of buildings that once had been shops, public or commercial offices and private houses. The bombing raids of early 1941 had laid waste to so much of what had been the heart and residential areas of the city.

Roads close to his house that should have been so instantly familiar to him were completely unrecognisable and, for a moment, he had to check his bearings to establish exactly where he was. So much had been cleared away – including what were once day-to-day landmarks. The near-empty streets, with the tidily stacked piles of bricks and stones, and the now wide-open spaces where houses had once stood in neat rows, shocked and momentarily disorientated Tremayne.

Judging the distance from the corner of the road to where he recalled their house had once been, he stopped and gazed at the anonymous heap of carefully tidied rubble. Tremayne suddenly realised he felt nothing, just the numbness of a spectator to some cataclysmic occurrence in which he is not really involved, but merely a bystander.

This was not *their* house – it couldn't possibly be. Theirs had a burgundy door with a ship's bell, a small, neat picket fence and so many flowers. There were also two storeys – and a roof with chimneys – obviously this pile of stones was not *their* house. That must have been somewhere else – he must have made a terrible mistake. Whatever possessed him – standing staring at rubble – trying to imagine it as a house where not just *people*, but *he and Diana* had once lived – and loved.

But gradually, the emotional anaesthetic began to wear off. The insulation from the terrible, incomprehensible reality started to recede. Progressively, what took over was the reality of an inordinate void.

A once familiar sense of ownership, of intense involvement, and now, utter loss, were replacing the opiate of temporary detachment of only a few moments ago.

Tremayne became, once again, so painfully aware of where he was and the terrible reality of what had happened that night while he was away in the Atlantic, on board *HMS Portree*. For a moment he closed his eyes, hoping against hope that he had imagined everything and that, when he opened them again, there would be their house, exactly as it was when he had kissed Diana goodbye and climbed into the RN truck that took him to his ship.

The subsequent sense of desolation he felt as he walked back to the bus stop was a state of deep emptiness, beyond tears. Overwhelming loss and numbness stayed with him throughout the bus journey to his parents. He had no recollection whatsoever of anything between Plymouth and Newton Ferrers where his mother and father lived.

So as not to distress them, Richard Tremayne made a supreme effort to be their son once again, and he struggled to make sure that his responses were as genuine as possible, and not those of an automaton.

Both parents – in their differing ways – were solicitous and caring. His mother fussed over him and called him "ma bairn" two or three times. His father, who had also served as a naval officer, talked 'sea, ships and sailors', and tried assiduously to avoid any issues of feelings and coping, letting his son take the lead on the subject of his visit to his former home.

Much as Tremayne felt a deep attachment to and love for his parents, it was with a profound sense of relief that he boarded the bus that was going straight through to Devonport.

Back on board the British Power Boat air-sea rescue launch, Tremayne remained for some considerable time on the after deck, his hands on the safety rail, as he felt the cold wet foam spray whipping past his face from the surging bow wave. Alone with his feelings and thoughts, he was hardly aware of the rising and falling of the drenched deck beneath his feet.

Emma Fraser was the only other passenger for the return

journey to Tresco, apart from three able seamen who were replacements for some of the crewmen wounded in the last operation to Pointe de Beg Pol.

She had instantly recognised and understood Tremayne's need for solitude, and involved herself in paperwork from her meeting with the Intelligence Section at Royal Naval Barracks, HMS Drake, at Devonport.

One hour out from Scilly, Tremayne was still up on deck and Emma, having raided the tiny wardroom's drinks cabinet, took him a large gin and tonic. By then, it was a clear late spring evening, dark and cool, yet beautifully clear and fresh.

"Good evening, sir. The sun went down over the yardarm two hours ago, so I thought you might like a drink, sir," she said smiling, but anxiously watching his face for his reaction.

Tremayne laughed out loud as he took the drink from her. "Emma, thank you so much. Please forgive my boorish behaviour. It was inexcusable to be so unsociable – and to such a pretty serving wench!"

"I guessed you must have had a pretty dreadful day – in Plymouth at least – and you looked like someone who really needed time to himself when you came back on board. One of the duty watch ABs has produced an absolute mountain of bangers and mash. Come and have some in the wardroom if you feel up to it. Despite that duffel coat, you must be chilled to the bone, as well as hungry."

"Sounds a wonderful idea, Emma. As a matter of fact, to quote our Breton friend from this morning, I'm absolutely 'raveeshed'", joked Tremayne, as he followed Emma to the wardroom below.

Emma studied her dining companion as he opened the bottle of claret that he had discovered in the tiny wardroom's drinks cabinet.

"Sorry," he said with a boyish grin, "no time to let it breathe I'm afraid."

The pain of the morning visit still showed on his face, but he had moved beyond the excluding reserve and preoccupation that she had been so aware of when he first boarded the motor launch. Because Tremayne found conversation with her so easy, he relaxed, visibly, in her company. Within minutes, he began to be his old self again, alternately taking the lead, or responding, in conversation with her.

The next hour, over supper, was spent talking about their respective days at university, sailing – an interest they discovered they shared, Tremayne's hilarious experiences during the previous weeks' training and then, somewhat more seriously, the likely turn of events involving the flotilla during the coming months.

As the launch drew close to Scilly, they went up on deck in order to see the islands, now distinct and clearly outlined, in what was a wonderfully bright moonlit night.

"They are so unbelievably beautiful," said Tremayne, "at any time of the year and in almost any weather conditions. With the moonlight on them, they are spectacular. Just look at the shadows they cast on the water when it's calm like this."

"Whoever selected them as a base for covert operations was something of a genius," said Emma. "Especially since the Germans left the Scillies alone in the First World War, apparently out of gratitude to the islanders for their kind treatment of the survivors of the Hamburg steam packet, the *Schiller*, when she sank off the Western Rocks over sixty years ago."

"Let's hope that their gratitude remains throughout this war. The last thing we need is to have our cover blown by some snooping photo-reconnaissance Condor or Ju88."

The motor launch quickly came alongside at Braiden Rock and secured at the jetty. Tremayne and Emma walked back to HMS Godolphin's wardroom, deep in conversation all the way.

At the entrance to the Wren officers' quarters, Tremayne touched Emma's arm lightly and said, "I always seem to be thanking you lately Emma, but thank you again for the marvellous 'restoration' job. I came back on board from Plymouth feeling completely desolate – as if in some emotional vacuum. You've worked wonders in bringing me back into the here and now, and I'm grateful to you for that."

As they parted to go their separate ways, Emma sensed that for her, at least, the relationship between them was moving to a different – and deeper – level...

Four

The net closes in...

Rear Admiral Hembury looked deep in thought as he read the transcript of a W/T transmission handed to him a few moments previously by Lieutenant Commander Enever. The rapid developments in the extent to which the Confrèrie appeared to be compromised, and the degree of real danger now facing Jean-François, had become urgent priorities for action for Naval Intelligence. The primary network and infrastructure for handling and deploying agents in Brittany had suddenly appeared to be on the brink of collapse, with the risk of untold critical intelligence falling into German hands.

"Not only is Jerry beginning to sit up and take more notice of our friends in the Confrèrie – it looks as if he means business, and *soon*. What do you make of it, John?"

"I agree sir." Enever removed the empty pipe from between his teeth. "For one thing, it's an ultra-cautious message, despite being transmitted in Breton and, secondly, such caution suggests that Jean-François is operating at a suddenly increased level of risk and, therefore, probably in imminent danger of capture."

Hembury re-read the Telegraphist's transcript, his finger tracing the flow of the message, as well as the actual words, as if seeking confirmation of the apparent intended underlying message.

"The sentence translated as *'My sister would like to take a much more prominent role in running the business'* strongly suggests to me that Muguette *is* being pushed by her German masters to move closer to the top of the Confrèrie as a possible number two to Jean-François. Is that how you read it, John?"

Admiral Hembury again looked across the table at Enever, questioningly.

"It would seem so, sir. Because of her apparently key role for the Confrèrie – being employed by the OKM – she has a powerful argument for an even bigger role and the Gestapo, or Abwehr, would naturally seek to exploit that. However, Jean-François can equally put forward strong, seemingly legitimate and logical arguments for refusing her request."

"I'm sure he can manage that problem very well – at least in the short term, but what is of major concern is that the Abwehr has decided to raise its game in this fashion." Hembury paused to take the cup of coffee offered to him by Jenny, the young Communications Branch Wren.

"With Muguette in a more senior role within the Confrèrie, Jerry can remove Jean-François and gain more control over the input, the throughput – and the output – of intelligence from the network as a whole."

Enever interrupted briefly. "The big question, sir, is how long have we got before the Germans make their move and take Jean-François?"

"Quite so. Jean-François is a courageous – and formidable – man, but under threats of torture to his wife and children it would be only reasonable to expect him to give away a good deal of vital intelligence to his interrogators: intelligence which exposes and compromises our section of Naval Intelligence – *and*, more specifically, the Tresco flotilla."

Admiral Hembury looked thoughtful for a moment before continuing: "There is, of course, always the cyanide capsule option but, in Jean-François' case, that is an alternative that I want to avoid at all costs." Jean-François is too important for such a solution. What is more, he's been a good, loyal friend to us and our job is to get him out of France when the time comes. We, the SOE and the SIS all owe Jean-François a great deal and under no circumstances will we play the role of 'perfidious Albion'.

Some thirty minutes later, the two were joined by Tremayne, Emma Fraser, Daniel Tabarly and Commander Rawlings to plan and put into operation a dress rehearsal, using the converted fishing vessels, to rescue Capitaine Duhamel and his immediate family. Now officially identified as Operation Marie-Claire, the rescue attempt was to be based upon a pick-up from a location, to be agreed, and an eventual transfer from Tresco to SOE HQ in Baker Street.

Once again, Admiral Hembury led the discussion by

reviewing the recent initiative of the Abwehr and the threat it posed to Jean-François' continuing safety – and the security of the French Section of British Naval Intelligence.

He explained to the meeting that the disguised fishing boats had now been modified and repainted, and were ready for operational use. There were sufficient French or Breton officers to captain them, or to act as First Lieutenants. In some instances, such officers would serve as deckhands, in order to deal with real Breton fisherman once the disguised vessels started to mingle with the fishing fleets off the coast of Brittany.

Tremayne raised the question of armament, pointing out the practical difficulties of mounting any weapons heavier than .50 calibre Brownings, fitted to fishing gear or stanchions and loosely covered with nets.

"That is exactly what we intend to do, Tremayne."

As usual, Rawlings' response was terse and inappropriate, to the point of boorishness. "You surely didn't imagine that we'd be going in with Bofors fore and aft. What?"

Seeing the sudden tightening of his jaw muscles and sensing that Tremayne was about to respond with some cutting riposte, Enever quickly came back into the conversation. "Exactly so. There are sufficient items of equipment on board a fishing vessel that can double, with a bit of adaptive ingenuity, as a temporary mounting for either Brownings or Vickers 'K' guns. Fishermen's nets, or tarpaulins, all make ideal temporary covers that can be whipped away in an emergency."

"What Commander Holden, the Head of Coastal Forces Operations at the Helford River flotilla, calls "operations boxes" will also be stowed on board, out of sight but readily accessible for sudden use," added Emma.

"These contain personal weapons, chosen by individual officers and crew members, and typically include Bren guns, sub-machine guns, grenades, pistols, fighting-knives and even knuckle-dusters. They are usually covered in trawled fish or, again, the fishing nets."

Hoping that she had added sufficiently to Enever's diffusing of likely scathing retaliation – as well as outlining the practical realities of arming a fishing vessel – she looked across at Tremayne, relieved to see his complete concentration on what she had been saying.

"Clearly, Richard, we want to avoid confrontation and the use of weapons as much as possible. Our aim is to be accepted – by the French as well as the Germans – as bona fide members of the fishing fleet. That will make our job so much easier." Enever reached across his desk and showed the group a list of port identification numbers, fishing vessel names and paint schemes. "We constantly keep updated, via the Confrèrie, on the serial numbers and colour schemes for the particular area in which we are going to operate. For example, if we want to mingle with boats from Roscoff or Carantec, we might try to look like a fishing vessel from nearby Lannion – or vice-versa."

"What about some of the rather improbable inventions which are supposed to have come out of the Helford flotilla sir, like, for example, the 'exploding crustaceans'? We're surely not going to use these are we sir?" asked Tremayne, with a rueful smile.

For a moment, Enever thought that Rawlings looked as if *he* was about to explode.

"No, not those Richard, they were something of a disaster. The 'gadgets department' of SOE seemed ignorant of the fact that lobsters, when alive in the sea, are largely shades of dark blue. To the horror – and amusement – of the genuine fishermen among the crews, SOE's workshop produced model lobsters in various pretty shades of pink – the colour they turn when boiled!"

Enever assiduously avoided any eye contact with Rawlings and addressed his remarks principally to Tremayne and Rear Admiral Hembury as he struggled to keep his mischievous and very visual sense of humour under tight control.

"We have, however," he continued, "created, from one of the fishing vessels in our flotilla, a very passable Breton tunnyman called the *Ar Voulac'h,* which will carry cargoes of plastic explosive cleverly disguised as tunny fish. Real tunny fish will be piled up on deck, whenever possible, to give some visual authenticity to the "catch". The explosive dummies will be "landed" as a catch and then taken away by members of the Confrèrie. It sounds unbelievable, but Commander Holden and SOE, London, assure us that the ruse works. This time, I've been assured," Enever paused and beamed at the members around the table, eyes twinkling above the glasses perched on the end of his nose, "that they've got the colours absolutely spot on!" he added with a barely perceptible wink to Tremayne.

"It *is* extraordinary, but if it's a means of getting explosives ashore for sabotage that is relatively foolproof – and secure – then we *should* try it sir," Tremayne looked directly at Rawlings, waiting for the expected apoplectic disapproval. He did not have to wait for long…

"You surely cannot be serious, Tremayne? Lobsters that blow up! Tunnyfish that explode! I would remind you, Tremayne, that this is the Royal Navy – not some confounded circus or freak show! What?"

"Thank you for your views, Commander." Rear Admiral Hembury forestalled any further eruptions from Rawlings. "You're quite right. This *is* the Royal Navy and it's a Navy that I – and all of us here" – he looked meaningfully at Rawlings – "are going to make damn sure remains the world's best, by keeping up-to-date and adapting to the demands of a war like no other that any of us have experienced before." He paused for effect and looked again, directly at Rawlings. "Do I make myself clear?"

The affirmative responses from the other officers in no way diminished the Admiral's obvious attack, aimed at the unfortunate Rawlings.

"Might I suggest some coffee and a short 'biological break' sir?" tactfully suggested Enever, ready to pour some oil on the stormy waters and gathering his papers together as a signal to terminate the meeting.

After the coffee break, which came as profound relief to most of the members, Sub-Lieutenant Daniel Tabarly briefed the meeting on the finer points of sailing a fishing boat in the coastal waters of Brittany.

He confirmed the typical German stop-and-search procedures, and where to stow the operations boxes for both maximum security and optimum accessibility. He emphasised the need to be punctilious in following – and using – the current recognition signals, especially in the presence of German patrol craft or nosey, low-flying aircraft.

"I am a former fisherman and I will tell you what Breton fishermen typically do on the deck of a tunnyman, or fishing boat. Above all, gentlemen, they look busy — but *relaxed*. They look up at German vessels that pass close by, but they don't stop and stare at them; they get on with what they were doing before the Boche arrived."

He picked up a sample of the made-up Breton fisherman's blue smock, wide unfashionable trousers and traditional cap.

"When you receive these, gentlemen — even though they have already been washed — please boil them two or three times more and dry them out in the sun, which I understand you sometimes 'ave in England! Then you ask your wife — or girlfriend — to sew a patch on one knee or per'aps the elbow and — *voila* — you look like a Breton fisherman."

Tremayne was very amused at the thought of Rawlings — complete with battered smock, patched pants and Breton cap set at a jaunty angle atop the incongruously cropped iron grey hair — hauling in yard upon yard of fishing nets. He knew, however, that his image of Rawlings would remain just fanciful speculation. The Commander would be far too much of a liability in the sort of operations that were being planned.

To arouse minimum curiosity amongst the locals on Tresco, training in boat handling techniques usually took place after dark, returning before dawn broke. Some protection was provided by Albermarles and Beaufighters, which overflew the fishing boats at about five hundred feet. On both the dress rehearsal and on Operation Marie-Claire itself, it was intended that there should be intermittent air cover in case enemy E-boats, or aircraft, took too close an interest in a single apparent Breton fishing vessel, way off course, and seemingly heading to or from England rather than a port in Brittany. Once the Tresco boats mingled with the fishing fleets from Breton ports they would not stand out, and so would generate little or no suspicion and, therefore, be less vulnerable.

Tremayne was allocated the modified fishing boat *Monique*. Originally of Breton origin, above the waterline she looked the genuine article. Under Tabarly's expert eye, her hull had been painted pale blue and white, while her upperworks were mid-brown. To go with her French name, she had been given a number which identified her as being from Roscoff.

Tabarly's greatest challenge had been that of convincing Naval Stores to provide him with sufficient quantities of paint in colours which bore no relationship to standard 'battleship grey' – and enough iron filings to create the suitably 'distressed' look of a working boat. With a regulation tricolour painted each side of her bow – to conform to a ruling imposed by the Germans, her varnished masts and spars, and her brick-red sails, she looked exactly what she was intended to be. Only her powerful diesels and the underwater configuration of her hull identified her as something very different from a normal, traditional Breton fishing boat.

Disguised as supports for netting were port and starboard swivel mountings for Browning .30 calibre machine guns. Because of their ease of handling compared with the larger, heavier

.50 calibre Brownings, Tremayne decided that they were more versatile and, therefore, more useful weapons. Supplementary, automatic firepower was provided by three Bren guns, while his operations boxes contained Lanchesters, two Remington semi-auto shotguns, captured German "stick" grenades – for ease of throwing, commando fighting-knives, several CO_2 silent pistols, and Browning automatics.

For Operation Marie-Claire, Tremayne was able to retain Willoughby-Brown as his First Lieutenant and Petty Officer Irvine as Coxswain.

For his Sparks, he kept Leading Telegraphist Geraint Jenkins – 'Jenkins the Wireless', and selected Leading Stoker-Mechanic Cameron to double as deckhand and number two to Petty Officer Duncan, his 'Chief' in charge of the diesels.

The by now well-washed and weathered Breton fishermen's clothing was being worn regularly by Tremayne and his crew when training on board the *Monique*. The experience of swapping naval rig for what he clearly regarded as cast-offs from Pantomime Hire proved near-traumatic for the Ulster Coxswain. Protesting one evening to the PO's mess at large he had said, "For nearly twenty-five years, I've worn Royal Navy uniform with pride, so I have. If I'm to be killed in action, then I want it to be as a British sailor, so I do, not as something out of Mother-bloody-Goose, gentlemen!"

To which declaration of disapproval came the chorus, from those sitting near to him, "so you don't!"

For the role of Confrèrie liaison officer, Tremayne opted for Sub-Lieutenant Pierre Quilghini. Although Paul Guillet had the more intimate knowledge of the dangerous coasts of Brittany – and its fishing industry – he was inclined to be impetuous, thought Tremayne, and, therefore, liable to act less predictably in a crisis. Quilghini's quiet reserve and reflective approach suggested both more steadiness and greater reliability.

Tremayne felt, too, that the man from Picardie would fit into the crew as a team member rather than as a very independent-minded individualist, which was Guillet's style.

Tremayne recognised that he needed people of initiative who were flexible and who could respond intelligently – and, above all, effectively – in an emergency. But, he reflected, he also needed people on whom he could rely and that meant people who instinctively thought *we*, not simply *I*, when things got difficult. He saw *those* attributes in Pierre Quilghini.

Following Sub-Lieutenant Tabarly's recommendations, officers and men alike on board the *Monique* and in Lieutenant Fischer's new command, *La Chasseuse*, quickly learned the roles and detailed activities of deckhands aboard a typical fishing vessel.

Lieutenant Commander Enever called Tremayne and Fischer in for a final briefing before their dress rehearsal for the safe extraction of Jean-François and his family.

"Richard," began Enever, "Emma has a letter for you which I think you'll find intriguing."

"Let me guess, Emma," joked Tremayne, as he took the buff envelope. *"Dear Sir, my daughter tells me…"*

"Certainly not, Lieutenant Tremayne – well not yet, at least!" Emma's response was greeted with loud laughter from the others.

"Fifteen-love, Fraser serving," Enever quipped, as he removed the inevitably unlit pipe. "Read it Richard – aloud, if you please."

Tremayne read to the group with a good deal of hesitation and embarrassment:

"Dear Lieutenant Tremayne and your crew.

I want to thank you most heartily for the courtesy and kindness that you showed to me and to my men when you picked us up after our Schnellboot sank. You did so much more than the demands of the Geneva Convention and you could have left us to drown. In doing what you did, you undoubtedly saved Matrosen-Stabsgefreiter Köster's life. He and I will never forget that. I hope that we may yet meet again in happier circumstances.

Yours most sincerely,

Eugen Lang, Leutnant-zur-see, Kriegsmarine"

"Thank you, sir. I'm most touched. For my part, I hope that I can meet Eugen Lang again, sir. He's an impressive officer, but he also happens to be a very likeable fellow. It's a great pity that we have to fight people like him – he would make a marvellous colleague."

"Meeting him might be tricky, Richard – you know as well as I do how bloody tortuous our red tape is to work through. He's presently at a POW camp near Devonport, but I'll see what I can do for you," Enever quickly wrote a note in his diary before continuing. "Right, Richard, Hermann – dress rehearsal!"

Enever then presented the detailed orders and plan of action for the extraction of four agents – two to be picked up by Tremayne and the other pair by Fischer.

"This action, gentlemen, is for real. We have four agents, three men and a woman, who need to be pulled out quickly. The Gestapo is moving in closer, and it's now only a matter of very little time before they are taken. They are from different "cells" of the Confrèrie but their capture – and interrogation – would doubtless help Jerry to add more critical pieces of information to the jigsaw puzzle that counter-intelligence so often becomes. We want to see how viable fishing boat extraction – and insertion – are, before we pluck Jean-François and his family from under the Germans' noses."

"How far apart are the extraction RVs from one another sir?" asked Tremayne.

"Emma has the details, Richard. Emma, please."

Turning first to Hermann Fischer, Emma handed him his orders indicating that his task was to rendezvous at 07.00 hours the next day with a fishing boat from Roscoff, the *Kersaliou*, ten kilometres due north of the fishing port. Emma explained that there would be several fishing boats moving around at that time, so that two vessels coming close together would not attract much attention.

"You will recognise the *Kersaliou*, Hermann," she said, "by the bright orange and purple quartered pennant which she always flies from her foremast. Your passengers, who will be transferred by rubber dinghy on the blind side of the shore, are two important agents we need back here as soon as possible. No one, with the possible exception of the odd fishing boat, will be able to see the shuttling of the agents if you heave-to twenty or so yards directly opposite the *Kersaliou*, keeping her between you and the shore. Your estimated time of departure from Braiden Rock will be 24.00 hours."

The blue eyes focused on Tremayne's serious, attentive face.

"As an alternative to picking up the Duhamel family from another fishing vessel, Richard, your dress rehearsal involves anchoring close inshore, where your agents will paddle out to meet you. They too will be in a rubber dinghy, which you will need to sink once they are on board the *Monique* to destroy any evidence for the Gestapo. Your RV will be the Plage de Pors-Meur, four and a half kilometres west of the small town of Plouescat. You will anchor one hundred yards offshore and they will come out to you carrying lobster pots, to allay suspicion of anyone who happens to be around. Your ETA will again be 07.00 hours when the fishing fleets will be very much in evidence and so your activities in broad daylight will, we hope, seem perfectly normal at that time of day."

"Who am I picking up?" asked Tremayne.

Enever re-entered the discussion at this point. "Two agents, Richard. One is a member of Squadron Leader Addington's RAF escape route team – a Frenchman whom we need to pull out before the net closes and our system is compromised. The other is a woman – a Russian NKVD agent. Her name is Svetlana Semeonova and the SOE were under enormous political pressure from the Soviets to insert her into western France to see how the Confrèrie de Saint Michel functioned as a model network. I suspect that the Russians are keen to develop something similar for their many partisan units currently operating in German-occupied territory within the USSR. By all accounts, dear boy, she's stunningly beautiful, deadly with a pistol, and has a black belt in one or other of those extraordinary unarmed fighting arts like ju-jitsu. We want to get her here, to question her and find out what she's been up to in France. We then have to arrange to return her to her NKVD controller. Another woman – also an agent of the NKVD – was caught by the Germans and shot in Brittany recently, so the Soviets asked us to pull the second one out before the Jerries captured her too. ETA at your RV will be 07.15 hours."

"Although she is a member of the Intelligence Service of one of our allies, I take it, sir, that we will be fairly guarded in what we disclose to her since she is not a member of the Confrèrie."

"Absolutely. 'Handle with caution' is the cry. I believe we must assume that the NKVD had another agenda and reason for inserting two agents into Brittany. Those reasons may not be entirely compatible with our activities and those of the Confrèrie. Now here are your orders. Emma, please."

"ETD is also 24.00 hours for you, Richard. Full speed until the onset of daylight, and then seven or eight knots as you begin to mingle with the fishing fleets. We are concerned, obviously, that if captured, any of you could be shot as spies if not in uniform. Our strongest recommendation," the blue eyes showed deep concern again, "is that you simply put on your smocks over RN Coastal Forces white sweaters. In our view, naval issue working-rig trousers are neutral enough to pass muster in all but the closest encounters. Don't put yourselves at undue risk – either with the Germans or, for that matter gentlemen, with that Russian Amazon!"

Enever and the others exploded with laughter, as Fischer added to the comment with: "Let her come with me Richard. I'm not half as good looking as you and Corporal Kane told me I was a "natural" on a judo mat—whatever that may mean to Svetlana!"

Tremayne smiled, "I think you're right, Hermann, she sounds positively terrifying. Marquis of Queensberry Rules are much more my cup of tea."

"And tea and vodka don't mix well either, Richard," quipped Enever.

At 24.00 hours, the two fishing vessels quietly slipped their moorings and set off for Brittany. The smell of new paint was only too apparent, but as Godolphin's 'chippy' had told Tremayne, after a few hours at sea with the wind blowing, the freshness would soon wear off. South of St Agnes, in the open sea, they both opened up to maximum revolutions and a speed of thirty-two knots, keeping each other company.

Fifteen miles from the French coast they separated, and Tremayne's telegraphist, acting as temporary yeoman, flashed a signal by Aldis to Fischer's boat: *"Alles gute, Korvettenkapitän. Auf Wiedersehen."*

A grinning Fischer called out from his wheelhouse, "Yeo, acknowledge. Make to *Monique*: *'Best of luck with Comrade Svetlana. See you'.*"

As dawn began to break, Petty Officer Irvine—equally at home in the traditional wooden fishing boat wheelhouse of *Monique*, despite his protestations about fishermen's rig—called out: "Fishing vessels bearing red four-five-0, sir."

"Thank you Cox'n. Number One, see if you can identify their port of origin."

"Aye aye sir. According to the latest pennant numbers in Sub-Lieutenant Tabarly's list sir, they look as if they are from

Carantec," responded the First Lieutenant, looking intently at the Breton boats through his binoculars.

With the Ile-de-Batz some twelve miles off her port beam, Irvine guided *Monique* slowly and leisurely through the fishing fleet, exchanging waved greetings with the Breton crews closest to them who were gradually emerging in force from Carantec towards Plage de Pors-Meur.

"Right on time, Number One, 06.45 hours, with just under four miles to go."

Tremayne called to his crew, who were busying themselves on deck with nets, winches and all the paraphernalia that can be found on board a fishing vessel apparently at work.

"In thirty minutes we'll be one hundred yards offshore. As far as we know, there are no Jerry strong points or pillboxes, but keep weapons handy and ready for instant use. Sub-Lieutenant Quilghini take a Bren please, and Jenkins be ready with a Browning. Cover our port bow. Number One also grab a Bren, please, and Cameron take the other .30 calibre. Please cover our starboard bow. Make sure that the Lanchesters are also close at hand. Close inshore, even they will be pretty effective. Make your every shot count. Right Cox'n, take her in please. All lookouts keep your eyes open for rocks. The coast here is treacherous — especially as we get closer to the beach."

Tremayne grabbed two Lanchesters and spare magazines — for himself and for Irvine. Very much a weapon of the Royal Navy — even the Royal Marines used Sten guns — the Lanchester was, in effect, a direct copy of the 1918 vintage German Bergmann MP18. With a magazine of fifty 9mm rounds and a theoretical rate of fire of six hundred rounds per minute, it was a useful, accurate weapon – especially at ranges up to one hundred yards.

Tremayne reaffirmed the signal codes for his meeting with the French agent 'Philippe' and the NKVD operative, Svetlana Semeonova.

"Look out for the two of them at the foot of the cliffs immediately below the highest point. They will flash a green light three times in rapid succession, and will keep repeating this until we answer by hauling down our Breton pennant from the mainmast."

At 07.16 hours, one minute late, two people appeared at the foot of the cliffs and gave the correct signal to *Monique*'s challenge. Weapons were trained on the two figures and on the cliff tops behind them, ready to seize – and maintain – the fire initiative if fired upon. Quilghini rapidly hauled down the pennant and the two – now clearly identifiable as a stocky, well-built man and a slim, tall woman – pushed out a rubber dinghy into the sea and began paddling strongly towards the fishing boat, the choppy waves lapping over the bluff bows of the small, ungainly craft.

"Fishing nets for scrambling, if you please, Number One. Prepare to help our guests on board," called Tremayne from the fishing boat's wheelhouse.

Quickly, a most striking blonde woman in her mid-twenties scrambled aboard and, with a penetrating look, took in all the faces of those on deck. She was followed by a compact man with a military moustache, who ventured an enthusiastic "Bonjour! Enchanté, Messieurs", while grabbing as many outstretched hands as he could and shaking them vigorously.

Weights were quickly lashed to the rubber dinghy and it was rapidly sunk in the dark swirling waters.

"Right Cox'n, take us back to New Grimsby. Slow ahead."

Turning quickly to the Leading Telegraphist, Tremayne, conscious of their closeness to shore, spoke quietly: "Jenkins, some hot coffee and something to eat for our guests and our crew please."

Remembering protocol, however alien its form, Tremayne addressed the two agents, now sitting on lockers and taking in their new surroundings.

"Comrade" — the term sounded strange to him as he said it — "and Monsieur. You are both welcome on board. If you prefer to stay on deck please do so, but put on these smocks and keep low, behind the bulwarks. Too many people on deck will arouse suspicion."

"If we have trouble, then I will fight. Where are the weapons kept?" demanded Svetlana, the flashing almond green eyes holding Tremayne's surprised stare. "We should be armed to defend ourselves."

The challenging look and the defiant set of the head came far too soon into the journey for Tremayne, who snapped: "I am in command of this vessel and you will take your orders from me. Is that understood? If weapons are needed, they will be allocated immediately and will be fired when I give the order. Comrade, Monsieur, breakfast will be served directly."

Again, the green eyes flashed — this time in fury, but an angry Tremayne drew on a cutting edge and level of personal authority way beyond the two wavy RNVR stripes normally visible on his arm.

"Quite a paddy that one, sir, so she has," said Irvine with a broad grin, as Tremayne returned to the wheelhouse. "Even without the E-boats or Ju88s, it'll be an exciting trip back, so it will, sir."

"Hmm, 'Swain, we'll bloody well see about that. Sometimes I think it's a great pity that the Navy gave up the practice of keel-hauling people – especially those given to mutiny and insubordination!"

"I've never seen our skipper as mad as that before, so I haven't," chuckled Irvine to himself as Tremayne busied himself with the charts, checking the course back to Tresco and studiously avoiding any further contact with the Soviet agent.

Willoughby-Brown, ever the height of tact and charm, lowered the temperature significantly by personally serving coffee and bacon sandwiches to the two agents. Speaking faultless French to Philippe and surprising everyone with a passable knowledge of Russian, the First Lieutenant engaged the two in conversation which was frequently punctuated by laughter and by exclamations of delight from "Olga from the Volga", as Irvine had immediately dubbed her.

"Young Jimmy the One is charming the pants off her, so he is," stated the Coxswain, with the exaggerated air of confidentiality of one who believes his knowledge of such things is both definitive and absolute.

"Well, we can but 'ope 'Swain, and 'e won't be the first – nor the last neither, I'll wager," chuckled Jenkins, who had just brought the Coxswain his breakfast at the wheel.

As *Monique* left the comparative anonymity of the fishing fleet behind her, seemingly looking as if she were searching for new fishing grounds, Tremayne knew that the risk to them was increasing significantly. A lone French fishing vessel, heading in the direction of England and so far away from the rest of the fleet, would invite suspicion and a close look from patrolling German E-boats or marauding Ju88s and Heinkels.

Tremayne called to the First Lieutenant, who was still "unfreezing the ice maiden", as Irvine had put it. "Number One, break out the weapons please. Everyone at defence stations."

By way of an olive branch – but ready for any rebuff – Tremayne crossed the deck to where the two agents were sitting talking.

"Comrade Semeonova, may I offer you a choice of weapons?"

Conscious of how ridiculous and pompous that could sound as he said it, Tremayne became even more embarrassed as Philippe roared with laughter and said, "Mon Dieu, Capitaine, do you intend a duel with the lady? She must have annoyed you very much!"

This broke the edginess between them, as all three burst into laughter.

"Thank you Lieutenant Tremayne – I don't suppose you carry a Degtyarev 7.62mm?" The amused green eyes mocked Tremayne's earnestness.

"No Comrade, as it happens we don't, but we have a spare Bren gun, which is our equivalent, and you are welcome to try one of our Lanchesters which is similar to your PPSH-41 Shpagin sub-machine gun."

"Aha. You know our weapons well, Lieutenant. How so?"

"When I served in HMS *Fleetwood*, an anti-submarine frigate,

I made one trip, as convoy escort, to Murmansk, and there I met several Soviet sailors and members of your naval infantry – the "Black Death" so-called. It was with them that I first came across Soviet small arms and I was impressed."

"Good. Now let me see if *I* am impressed with British weapons."

Tremayne fitted a magazine to the Bren gun, which Cameron had secured in the starboard mounting. He then took Svetlana through the loading and cocking procedures and stood at her side. "In your own time, independent fire!" he called.

Pulling the gun into her shoulder and tucking her face onto her hand round the top of the butt, the Russian agent took two or three deep breaths and squeezed the trigger. With a broad grin, she squeezed off half a magazine and then rapidly emptied it, the grin growing even wider.

"Well, what do you think?" asked Tremayne.

"Otlichno! Splendid!" She grinned again enthusiastically.

"As good as the Degtyarev, Miss?" asked Cameron, who was hovering with another Bren magazine at the ready.

"No – better! I like it very much."

She turned to Tremayne. "Thank you, Lieutenant. Can I try the Lanchester now please?"

"Of course." Tremayne fitted the fifty-round box magazine and handed the weapon over.

Willoughby-Brown, who had joined the group, stood next to her – the mobile eyebrow acting as the cautionary word of command – and then yelled: "Orgon! Fire!"

Firing short bursts this time, she alternated between shoulder and hip, shooting until the magazine was empty.

Tremayne looked at her, his eyes questioning.

"Yes — it's good — very good — and it is well made. I like it, but I prefer the PPSH-41, its magazine holds seventy rounds and its rate of fire is much higher!"

"Load it on Sunday and fire it all bloody week, so you do," muttered an unimpressed Irvine to Jenkins, who had stayed with him in the wheelhouse — watching events through the open doorway.

"So, Comrade Semeonova. Will you take one of the Brens and make that position in the bow your station if we are attacked? We now have two Brens allocated to starboard and one to port, with one each of the Brownings both sides of the boat."

Tremayne had been so concerned to improve relationships with Svetlana, in such a close environment, that he had completely forgotten about Philippe.

"Would you prefer to take your chances on deck with a Lanchester, Monsieur, or do you prefer to be below if we come under attack?"

"Capitaine, I was a soldier in the army of France. Naturally I would prefer to be on deck if the Boche appear. A lesson on the Lanchester, please!"

Closed up at defence stations, *Monique* made her way, at full throttle now, heading for the Isles of Scilly. Philippe's earlier professional training immediately showed as he quickly became familiar with the Lanchester, firing from the hip and from the shoulder, with single shots and bursts. After emptying three magazines, Philippe turned to Tremayne with a satisfied smile. "Alors, Lieutenant, I am very much at 'ome with this weapon.

I like it. The balance is perfect and it is beautifully made. I look forward to using it."

There was a slight swell on the sea and the sky was clear – too clear – thought Tremayne, as he returned to the wheelhouse after the short weapon familiarisation session with the two agents.

Checking his charts on the tiny chart table next to Irvine, Tremayne calculated they had about twenty-five miles still to go. The lack of both cloud and sea mist made the *Monique* both very visible and vulnerable, felt Tremayne. Turning to Irvine, whose eyes were still fixed on the horizon ahead, he said, "Not like a Fairmile, eh Cox'n, but actually faster."

"No sir, she's..." Irvine's response was cut short by a yell from the First Lieutenant.

"Three aircraft – look like Ju88s – bearing green 0-four-five."

"Action stations! Keep all guns ready, but covered." Tremayne looked quickly round the deck. "Aircraft, green 0-four-five. Wave to the bastards!"

There was no mistaking their make and origins. They were, as Willoughby-Brown had first identified them, Ju88s.

Sweeping in low over the *Monique*, in close 'arrowhead' formation, they roared past, their engines deafening the waving figures on the deck below.

"Phew! That was close, sir." Willoughby-Brown managed a rather strained grin.

Tremayne's eyes never left the fast-diminishing aircraft as they headed for France.

"Wait! One of the bastards is turning round – he's coming back for another look. Everybody look busy. Handle the nets covering weapons, but keep all guns concealed. Quickly throw one net overboard and start obviously hauling it back in. Number One, just you and I will wave. Cox'n slow ahead! Reduce to half revolutions."

Within a matter of seconds, the inquisitive Ju88 was back overhead – this time flying even lower and more slowly.

"Number One. I'll watch him. Where are the other two?"

"Still on course, sir, and disappearing. Must be two thousand yards away by now sir."

"Stand by everybody. He's turning again for a closer look."

Before Tremayne could give the order to make net retrieval look even more obvious, a sustained burst of machine gun fire from the Ju88 churned up the sea immediately ahead, and then abeam of the *Monique*'s bow.

"That, Number One, is a shot across our bows which, I take it, means 'stop, turn about and return to Brittany'." Tremayne called to the Coxswain in the wheelhouse.

"'Swain, let's dance to his tune and see what happens. Alter course to back-bearing and head us back to France, and maintain half revolutions."

Within seconds, the Ju88 roared over them once more, as Tremayne and the First Lieutenant waved in apparent acknowledgement.

The German bomber turned, yet again, and flew back slowly over, as Tremayne waved his Breton cap at the front gunner, clearly visible in his Perspex-enclosed 'greenhouse'.

"Let's hope that keeps the bastards off our backs, Number One. Cox'n, maintain this course for five minutes at half revolutions. If Fritz doesn't come back, we'll hightail it back on our original course at full speed ahead."

"Aye aye, sir. Do you think he'll be back?"

"I'm sure he will 'Swain, but *when* is the real issue. I don't want to lose too much way complying with his bloody orders."

After five minutes, with no sign of the Ju88, Tremayne gave the order.

"Cox'n, resume our original course, if you please – maximum revolutions. Let's go home."

Tremayne looked around the deck at those still closed up at action stations.

The First Lieutenant and Stoker-Mechanic Cameron were each at an automatic weapon, covered by a fishing net, on the starboard side of the *Monique*, together with Svetlana Semeonova, whose long blonde hair was blowing in the morning breeze, making her look like a Wagnerian heroine. "All she needs," mused Tremayne, "is a horned helmet, a flowing cloak and a spear, and she'd make a magnificent Brünnhilde."

Across on the port side, Sub-Lieutenant Quilghini and Leading Telegraphist Jenkins were also at their posts, scanning the distinct horizon. Sitting on a barrel of fish, cradling a Lanchester, was Philippe – smoking what Irvine termed "an unholy Frog concoction of camel dung and tram tickets".

Cameron, who was searching the sea and sky with binoculars, suddenly shouted: "Sir, aircraft approaching. Dead astern."

All eyes turned aft to Cameron's pointing finger, "It's the Ju88 coming back sir," yelled Willoughby-Brown.

"All guns. Stand by to fire – get those nets off," called Tremayne.

The Ju88 was approaching rapidly at a height of around one hundred feet. At three hundred yards, the front gunner opened fire – sweeping the deck and starboard bulwark of the *Monique*.

In the middle of frantically tearing away the fishing net covering the Browning, Cameron gave a sharp cry and collapsed onto the deck, dead, his throat and chest suddenly so much torn red meat and his blue uniform riddled with rapidly staining holes. Tremayne shouted: "All guns, open fire. Shoot, shoot, shoot!"

Simultaneously, Brens, Brownings and Lanchesters opened up a deafening cacophony in immediate response.

The Ju88 swept overhead, now down to about eighty feet above *Monique*'s mainmast.

"He'll turn shortly for another go at us. As he comes in, starboard guns concentrate on his engines. Port guns aim at the front gunner and pilot," yelled Tremayne, adjusting the rear sight of his Lanchester. "Make that bloody 'greenhouse' your target. As he passes over us, shoot just in front of his nose, and keep your gun swinging as you fire. *Don't* stop in order to shoot, or you'll miss him at this height," called Tremayne urgently. Tremayne cocked the Lanchester as he took aim. "Here comes the bastard now. Cox'n, hard a-starboard, maximum revolutions. Stand by all guns. Aim carefully. *Fire!*"

A burst of fire from the Ju88's front gunner shredded the wooden roof of the wheelhouse and hit Svetlana, who fell to the deck with a shrill cry, before his transparent 'greenhouse', in turn, was shattered by Quilghini and Jenkins and he fell forward lifeless over his machine gun. A bomb dropped by the Ju88 whistled over the foremast and exploded in the sea only yards ahead of *Monique*'s blunt bow, drenching those on deck with sea water and peppering the hull and superstructure with steel splinters.

Swinging the Lanchester, Tremayne emptied the whole fifty-round magazine into the Ju88's starboard engine as the others raked its undersides with .30 calibre shots.

Willoughby-Brown yelled, "We've got the bastard – his starboard engine's on fire. You've got him, sir!"

"Getting better with the 'high birds', eh, Number One!" grinned Tremayne, fitting a fresh magazine to the Lanchester.

Thick black smoke was, indeed, starting to pour from the engine, which spluttered intermittently and then finally cut out.

The Brens and Brownings continued to pour bullets into the Ju88 as it began to slip lower and lower, until it finally glided into the sea about a mile and a half away.

"Well done everybody," shouted Tremayne. "Well done. After her Cox'n! Let's pick up any survivors. Number One, please see to Svet…" Tremayne stopped, as he saw Willoughby-Brown kneeling down and holding the Russian woman while he applied a wound-dressing to her arm.

The high Slavonic cheekbones accentuated her paleness and the First Lieutenant gently folded his own smock, and one given to him by Philippe, and slipped them under her head as she lay, motionless, alongside the bulwark.

"Sub-Lieutenant Quilghini, Sparks, keep that aircraft covered as we approach it."

Tremayne moved across the deck to place a tarpaulin over Cameron's body. The Stoker-Mechanic had taken a burst of machine gun fire in the upper body and must have been dead before he hit the deck.

Moving across to Svetlana, he smiled and said, "I think *your* shooting was 'otlichno', Comrade. You did well. We'll get you to our Medical Officer as soon as we land at Tresco. You're obviously in very good hands here."

Tremayne looked at Willoughby-Brown and smiled. "Number One has made a good job of that dressing and, I see, has given you a shot of morphine. Can I get you anything else?"

"No thank you Lieutenant, just leave this lovely sailor boy with me!" The green eyes sparkled despite the pain that she was obviously in.

Willoughby-Brown flushed bright scarlet and grinned self-consciously at Tremayne.

"I think I can do that, but I might have to borrow him back occasionally." Tremayne laughed, as he returned to the bullet-marked wheelhouse.

"Two Jerries standing on the port wing, sir. The Ju88 is starting to settle sir. It'll soon go under, so it will."

"Thanks 'Swain – no weapons with them, as far as I can see. Take her alongside please, as close as you can. Jenkins, lifebelts to the two Germans, but keep them covered and shoot them at the first sign of any nonsense," he addressed Quilghini and Philippe, whose automatic weapons were trained on the two shivering survivors.

The German airmen – a lieutenant and a sergeant – were quickly dragged on board, soaking wet and frightened, obviously assuming that they were in the hands of members of the French Resistance. Willoughby-Brown got up from where he'd been kneeling down, attending to Svetlana, as they came on board.

In fluent German he asked them if there were any more members of the crew. Still dazed and very wary, the more nervous of the two, the young sergeant, told the First Lieutenant that the only other member of the crew was the front gunner whose bullet-riddled body still lay in the shattered forrard gun position.

Tremayne ordered them to be given blankets and to be blindfolded to avoid them seeing that they were being taken to an island instead of the mainland. Jenkins disappeared below to produce hot kye and an issue of rum for everybody, including the two prisoners of war.

Philippe took over as their guard, his finger close to the trigger of his Lanchester.

As *Monique* resumed her course for Tresco, three Hurricanes from RAF 1449 Flight based on St Mary's, Scilly – their escort – came racing over. Flying low, they waggled their wings in recognition, before circling the now rapidly sinking Ju88 and roaring back over the fishing vessel.

" "Y" Service at Godolphin must have been monitoring Jerry's transmissions as the Ju88s reported our position to their base, Number One. It's a pity our escorts didn't get here a bit earlier," said Tremayne, with an edge of bitterness in his voice, as he looked across the deck at the lonely tarpaulin-covered mound, lying so still beside the wheelhouse. He thought of the letter that he would have to write to loved ones – about a dead son, husband or brother – so soon after the last one that he'd sent.

"That's one lesson for us, Number One. We need to co-ordinate air cover much more effectively. It means that we need Sparks at his set, maintaining radio contact with base more closely, and not on deck."

As the Isles of Scilly came into sight, Tremayne ordered Jenkins to radio ahead so that Svetlana could be transported straight to Godolphin's Medical Officer and sickbay on arrival.

He also reported the capture of the two German airmen whom Enever and his team would most likely wish to interrogate before sending them on, by motor launch and then lorry, to a POW camp on the mainland.

To reduce interest in *Monique* — and speculation about who she was and what her role might be — Tremayne opted for a route away from St Mary's, the main island and the most populous of the Scillies.

"Take her through Gorregan Neck with the Western Rocks on her port beam, Cox'n. Keep the Minaltos to starboard and we'll then set a course through Castle Bryher Neck and back to New Grimsby as before."

"Aye aye, sir. Wind's freshening, so it is, sir."

"Thank you Cox'n. You're right, it is — and we'll use it! Number One, hoist the mains'l and the white ensign. Let's go home in style!"

Daniel Tabarly's training was quickly in evidence, as the deck crew rapidly and expertly hoisted the heavy canvas sail. Under the approving eyes of Tremayne and the First Lieutenant, sheets were secured with the smooth rhythmical ease of experienced fishermen.

"Handsomely done, Number One. Tabarly did an excellent job with them – and they've learned quickly."

"Let's hope that they convince the Germans equally well, if ever we have to move under sail off Brittany, sir"

Half an hour later, *Monique* – trim in her bright characteristic Breton paintwork and with her weathered brick-red sail still set – sailed past Cromwell's Castle and, with Hangman's Island on her starboard beam, turned onto her mooring buoy, fifty feet or so off Braiden Rock.

Back once more in RN Coastal Forces uniform, the deck crew reefed the mains'l and lashed it expertly to the spar, as the First Lieutenant dropped *Monique's* kedge, eventually securing her to one of the Vospers moored alongside the temporary quay.

Svetlana was quickly transferred to Godolphin's sickbay, still demanding that her "wonderful sailor boy" accompany her.

"You've certainly scored there, Number One," grinned Tremayne. Please make sure our Comrade is comfortable and not driving 'Doc' Hegarty to distraction, then join me in the wardroom for an early lunch – I'm ravenous!"

Lieutenant Commander Enever's operational debriefing got off to a lively start immediately after lunch. Hermann Fischer began his report in fine form, recounting – with some typical embellishment and 'colour' – his encounters with Breton fisherman and the German Navy during his return visit with the two rescued agents.

"Pierre Guillet saved our bacon on both occasions. First of all, we were invited to an early morning booze-up on board a tunnyman from Concarneau, who'd come up north for what he'd hoped were going to be more profitable waters. Much to the lads' disappointment, Pierre very imaginatively extracted us from that Bacchanalian engagement."

"I'm intrigued Hermann, what on earth did he do?" asked Enever, with a broad grin.

"As the tunnyman drew near, obviously intent on contact with us, Guillet grabbed some gentian violet from the medical kit and rapidly painted some purple spots on my face. He managed to convince them that I'd just come back from French Equitorial Africa and had contracted typhus there. He'd already covered my head and shoulders in a filthy old blanket and propped me up, looking like death, against the trawl winch casing. He then spun them a yarn about taking me to a former French naval hospital for tropical medicine, situated on the Ile d'Ouessant. As we entered Breton fishing waters, an hour before, he had insisted on flying the international code signal 'W' — *'I require medical assistance'* — to add some impact to his story. Wishing us well, they took off as rapidly as they could! We continued due west, having hauled down the international code flag while I tried scrubbing the purple spots off my face!"

"What on earth happened next?" asked an incredulous Enever.

"Just as I was about to set course north-west by north for Scilly, a German R-boat, searching for a downed Heinkel crew, stopped us and asked us to keep a look out for their men who had baled out somewhere in the vicinity. This Pierre promised to do in the most fractured barely intelligible German, adding that we would send out a radio signal if we did see their airmen. We even secured alongside them so that we could pass them a box of mackerel that we'd only just trawled. With several emphatic "*dankes*" and a most impressive salute from their skipper, they then went on their way and we continued on ours. After that, sir, we were lucky. We neither saw nor heard anything, until the three escorting Hurricanes found us and overflew us a few times as we headed back, at maximum revolutions, for Tresco."

"And the agents? Anything to report there?" asked Enever.

"No sir. The pick-up and return were absolutely fine – apart from the two incidents I reported, sir."

"Good. Well thank you Hermann for bringing back two very important people to us."

Fischer left the meeting after his report to return to the *Kersaliou* to supervise the installation and testing of new mountings for the .50 calibre Brownings, which he had opted for, on the fore gallows and winch-drum casing supports.

Turning to Tremayne, Enever removed his empty pipe, placing it on the table next to his notepad and pen.

"Richard, we managed to monitor your rather dramatic encounter with the Ju88s by radio, picking up Jerry's transmissions. We heard the one you shot down radio for an R-boat, reporting that his starboard engine was on fire and that he was about to ditch. Well done – that was a splendid effort! I understand that young Cameron was killed. I'm sorry to hear that. Poor Petty Officer Duncan will begin to think that there's some sort of jinx on his engine room crew."

"Yes sir. I've already drafted a letter to his parents which I want to work on a little more before I send it," replied Tremayne.

"Your mysterious and glamorous Russian lady was also hit,

but not too seriously I gather. We want to talk to her as soon as she starts to recover. SOE think that there's quite an important story behind NKVD activities in Brittany. How much of that we'll get from her, heaven only knows."

Tremayne smiled ruefully. "I'd be very glad, sir, if someone *would* interrogate Miss Semeonova – preferably at great length. She's completely monopolising my First Lieutenant – he's totally smitten!"

"As he's never been smut before, no doubt," laughed Emma.

"I'm afraid I got off to a very bad start with her by reading the riot act within minutes of her coming on board, but young WB's charm and wit restored the situation."

"He's a man of many parts, quite clearly," said Emma.

"Right," added Enever. "Willoughby-Brown has a lot of potential as you have discovered and, I may say, is maturing and developing so well. I want him to stay with you, Richard. He's learning a lot from you, and I appreciate your caring and the guidance you give him. He's growing under your tutelage and, if he continues to develop as he is currently, he'll make a fine officer."

"You should also know," said Emma, "that WB worships the ground you walk on Richard. He told Lucy Caswell, one of my younger third officers, that you were his hero and were the sort of officer *he* wanted to become."

"That's a daunting image to live up to, and it makes me terrified that I might let him down. Thank you for telling me, I'd no idea," said Tremayne. "I hope to heaven that I don't fail young David – I think a great deal of him." Tremayne then recounted details of the rescue and return of the two agents, emphasising the need to co-ordinate air cover for such operations much more closely and effectively.

"Point taken," responded Enever. "This must certainly be guaranteed for Operation Marie-Claire, which is likely to take place within forty-eight hours, according to reports we're receiving from Jean-François about suddenly increased Abwehr interest in the Confrèrie." He looked intently at Tremayne.

"I very much regret that you were so exposed and for such a long period, but I know that the RAF is stretched beyond all reasonable limits at the moment. We have, however, already set up a joint Operations Planning Group to provide both greater and more readily accessible air cover for the rescue of Jean-François and his family."

Enever looked at his watch. "We have another meeting now with Captain Mansell, Commander Rawlings and a Squadron Leader from a Beaufighter base in Cornwall. I'm taking Emma and Lucy out for supper to the New Inn this evening, Richard. Why don't you and WB join us at 7.30 in the bar and we'll talk more – unclassified stuff, naturally," added Enever with a smile.

"Thank you sir. I'd like that very much. I'll see if I can prise my First Lieutenant away from the Russian Valkyrie! I look forward to joining you sir – and you Emma."

The evening at the New Inn developed as one of the most relaxed and enjoyable that Tremayne could remember in a long time. With everyone having changed into 'civvies', the occasion immediately became less formal and 'naval' – more like a gathering of friends who were meeting one another because they *wanted* to.

When Tremayne and Willoughby-Brown entered the bar, Enever and the two Wren officers were already there. Enever's naturally warm, avuncular style put the others at ease from the start.

In a white sleeveless blouse, wearing a Fraser tartan skirt and with her dark, softly waved hair, Emma looked quite lovely, thought Tremayne.

"I hope that you approve, sir," said Emma, with a mock curtsy and eyes laughing at Tremayne's obvious discomfort, his admiring look exposed to everyone's amusement.

"Emma, you look absolutely stunning. I do apologise – I was staring. It was so rude of me. It's just that I'm so used to seeing you as Second Officer Fraser, in uniform and..."

"And not as a beautiful young woman, eh Richard!" Enever, with his customary perceptiveness and directness, deflected the others' attention from Tremayne and onto himself. "Join the club, dear boy. I confess I do exactly the same – even at my age!"

Lucy Caswell and David Willoughby-Brown quickly established two sources of common ground and shared interest. Lucy, a linguist working in the Intelligence Section at Godolphin was, like Tremayne's First Lieutenant, fluent in both French and German. Within minutes, they were exchanging multilingual jokes, exploring one another's knowledge of the more arcane dialects of low German and the French of Provence.

Their second common thread was that both their fathers had served in the light cavalry – in different, but closely related, hussar regiments.

"I'll ask my father if he knew a Captain Caswell," said Willoughby-Brown with characteristic earnestness. "He served with the regiment for what must be at least a hundred years!"

"My father resigned his commission to join the family business, shortly after he became captain. Anyway," said Lucy, "he always used to quote some Frenchman or other who is alleged to have declared that anyone still alive in the hussars over the age of thirty must surely be a blackguard!"

"But it would be fascinating to see if they did actually know one another – blackguards or not," laughed Willoughby-Brown.

"Well, we hope that the same rules don't apply to sailors," said a smiling Tremayne. "David is thinking of applying for a regular commission and making the Navy his career!"

"Somehow, David doesn't strike me as the blackguard type – whatever that might be," replied Lucy, her large brown eyes suddenly serious.

As the evening progressed, Lieutenant Commander Enever then revealed something of the pre-war – other – side of his life. A chartered surveyor by profession, he had joined the Civil Service following the great slump in the early Thirties. Serving as a young petty officer in the First World War, Enever had subsequently joined the RNVR in 1923, gaining a commission some two years later. Married, with two sons, both of whom were now in the Royal Navy as young ratings, Enever impressed Tremayne, who listened intently as the older man described his life with both the Civil Service and the Royal Navy.

It seemed, reflected Tremayne, that little ever fazed Enever – not because he was indifferent or superficial but rather the reverse in that he positively refused to be marginalised or defeated by the "system".

Enever gave the impression of someone who always rose above the trite, the restrictive and the over-regulated. This was not by arrogance, self-importance or vanity, but rather, it seemed to Tremayne, an unrelenting refusal to allow creative resourcefulness, common sense and goodwill to be subordinated to bureaucracy. For that, he admired Enever and his balanced, sane outlook on life.

Supper itself – despite rationing and wartime restrictions – was a fine affair, consisting of delicious locally-caught fish and fresh vegetables from the landlord's own private source of supply on the island.

When Emma commented on the excellent food, all Dick Oyler, the landlord, would say, with an exaggeratedly conspirational wink, was: "Ask me no questions my dear – and you know the rest of that…!"

John Enever had brought two bottles of an excellent Chassagne Montrachet that Admiral Hembury had given him from *his* equally vague and un-named source of supply. Such fine white Burgundy added immeasurably to both the dinner and to the flow of conversation between the five officers who were so obviously at ease and enjoying one another's company.

At the end of supper, Enever excused himself to attend a late evening meeting with Admiral Hembury, leaving the four young officers to make their way back to Godolphin.

Comparing notes on nineteenth century French authors – much to Tremayne's amusement – Willoughby-Brown and Lucy wandered off round the cluster of small stone cottages of Palace Row towards New Grimsby quay, leaving him and Emma to walk back to Godolphin together. In a rare moment of silence between them, Emma, sensing a slight withdrawal on Tremayne's part, said quietly, "A penny for them, Richard."

Caught off guard, Tremayne said, rather too quickly, "Oh, nothing really. I was just thinking about the evening we've had. My apologies, Emma, for seeming so preoccupied."

"And you're feeling guilty about the evening — is that it?"

Surprised at her directness, Tremayne said, "In a way, yes. I suppose I am. I've enjoyed tonight so much, and yet it just doesn't seem right to do so. And I know that must sound ridiculous to you. I was so clear about the ground rules as a married man; I think I knew exactly what the boundaries were and how to keep within them. As a widower, I haven't even identified, let alone come to terms with, the rules. I think that's partly what the guilt is about Emma. Does that make sense?"

"In answer to your question, Richard, yes — it does make sense — I understand that. I've been down the same road myself, about a year after Iain was killed, when I started to go out in mixed company again. For a long time I felt enormous guilt. I think that guilt is probably the hardest emotion of all to get rid of. It seems to have a disturbing recurring quality, and sometimes the most odd or unexpected things can trigger it. And what is the rest of the guilt about, Richard? Do you know?"

Tremayne and Emma were leaning on the harbour wall, both watching the dark sea gently lapping along the shore. Above, the cloudless, starry sky seemed to add an intensity and sense of occasion to their conversation.

Turning towards her, Tremayne said quite simply, "It's

about you, Emma. In your company I experience both an unbelievable feeling of peace, but also a great sense of joy. That is what I feel so guilty about. It seems wrong, somehow, to feel so happy again."

"I've felt something similar and I've also been trying to come to terms with it. For me, Richard, it started at our second meeting and I've been struggling with my feelings ever since. I'd told myself that I'm just not ready to have such a relationship with anyone else – and especially in a situation where either, or both, of us could be killed or, worse, horribly maimed."

Tremayne paused for a moment before responding. "Perhaps, irresponsibly, I hadn't really considered the war, but I had told myself that, with Diana's death, there never could be another close relationship. And now I'm at a point where all my values and…"

"And ground rules?" Emma smiled as she looked at him.

"Yes. And my ground rules are all up in the air, and I don't know where the hell I am right now."

"Do you want to stop the relationship before it really starts?" asked Emma quietly, her eyes fixed on Tremayne's.

"No Emma, that is something I *don't* want. But I need some time to get things straight in my mind."

"It's a matter of heart, not head, Richard, and that's why it is so hard to work through. Let's go on as we are," she said, taking his hand, "and keep it at this level until we both feel more sure."

"But how will we…"

"We'll know, Richard. Until then, let's just enjoy each other's company. Let's laugh together – and not feel guilty about that. But let's not love – that can come later. When we're both ready, and when there's no guilt – only happiness – in each other's company." Tears filled her eyes and the rising and falling of her breasts belied the calmness with which she had spoken to Tremayne.

"Thank you Emma. There are times when I so need your sense of perspective." He kissed her lightly on her cheek and, taking her hand, said with a gentle smile, "Come on, young Second Officer Fraser, let me escort you back to the wardroom – it's time we had some shut-eye. I think we might be in for a pretty busy day tomorrow."

Five

Operation Marie-Claire

T he following night, at 24.00 hours precisely, MFV 3028 – the *Monique* – quietly slipped her moorings off Braiden Rock and quickly made her way through New Grimsby Sound. From there, she set course through Tresco Flats, past Great Rag Ledge and, taking advantage of the high tide, sailed south, keeping Samson Island on the starboard beam, into the deeper water of St Mary's Sound.

Having cleared St Agnes, with the jagged Western Rocks well to starboard, Tremayne ordered course to be set for Pointe de Corsen, on the west coast of Brittany, some thirteen miles east of the Ile d'Ouessant and fourteen miles west of the naval port of Brest. Operation Marie-Claire had begun…

The day had started for Tremayne with an urgent summons to attend a meeting with Lieutenant Commander Enever and a senior member of SOE's French Section from Baker Street HQ.

After the briefest of introductions, an unusually businesslike Enever told Tremayne: "At 02.30 hours this morning, we received a radio transmission from the Confrèrie – checked as authentic by "Y" Service operators – that the Gestapo had made a sudden move against Jean-François."

Tremayne watched Enever intently, conscious that he, in turn, was being closely observed by the still anonymous SOE agent.

Enever continued his report. "The message we received stated that two leading members of the Confrèrie – including the redoubtable Louis, sadly – had been seized by SS troops and immediately handed over to the Gestapo. Jean-François and his family at once moved to their hideout, at the farm at Pointe de Beg Pol, to lie up there pending our rescue operation."

"Is that where we pick up Jean-François from sir?" asked Tremayne.

At this point, the SOE agent responded to Tremayne's question.

"No, unfortunately not." He removed his spectacles and leaned forward, almost confidentially, towards Tremayne.

"Jean-François and his family, together with three other members of the Confrèrie, arrived at the farm by lorry to be met by the two Panzer officers who stable their horses there. They, it appears, had decided to spend the night at the farm following a range firing exercise, in order to ride their horses before re-joining their regiment for breakfast later that morning. Apparently, they were awakened by the sound of the lorry and several French voices outside the stable at two o'clock in the morning. They rushed out, pistols in hand, only to be cut down by several bursts from the Confrèrie agents' Sten guns."

"That's unfortunate. What happened next?" asked Tremayne.

"As we understand it, the firing alerted several SS and Wehrmacht patrols who were out and about in the area looking for curfew breakers. It was one of the SS patrols that reached the farm within about twenty minutes and discovered the two Panzer officers. Before he died, one of these was able to give an accurate description, we believe, of Jean-François and his group to the SS patrol. They, in turn, radioed the Gestapo who were already holding Louis and his colleagues prisoners in Brest. They, we presume, were then questioned further about Jean-François and the Confrèrie. We know that Jean-François and his party left the farm rapidly before the SS arrived, but where they fled to we have no idea, as yet."

Lieutenant Commander Enever, who had been dictating orders to his secretary, came back into the discussion at this point.

"Richard, we are obviously still in the dark at this stage, but as soon as we receive a pick-up rendezvous from the Confrèrie for Jean-François, we will let you know immediately so that you can get over to Brittany with all haste. In the meantime, please make ready. You will be taking *Monique,* unless you hear to the contrary, and please make sure that your operations boxes have all the kit you will need to enable you to sustain a firefight, should any develop. Ensure, too, that you have enough Brownings and Brens to cope with any low-flying aircraft that interfere beyond mere inquisitiveness. Operation Marie-Claire, I'm afraid, will not be a pushover, Richard. Jerry is now fully alerted — and extremely annoyed. North-west Brittany and its coastal waters will be swarming with Germans – both Wehrmacht and the SS. Apparently, when the balloon went up, Jean-François summarily executed Muguette and, as a result, the Abwehr and Gestapo are both hopping mad and out for blood. That act also put paid to our plans to use Muguette as a stooge, feeding false information into German intelligence. More I cannot tell you at the moment, but I'll keep you posted, Richard, as soon as I hear anything further…"

=====O=====

Meanwhile, at around one o'clock that morning, Jean-François had been suddenly awoken from an already troubled, fitful sleep, by an urgent telephone call, warning him that an operation was underway to seize him and destroy the Confrèrie.

The speaker – a trusted agent, using the new code and speaking in Breton – also told him that the Germans had taken Louis and another agent, 'Fernande'. The speaker went on to say that before he was taken, Louis managed to transmit a brief message, in the same code, stating that Muguette had given critical information to the Abwehr. It was this that had prompted the Germans' sudden move.

Jean-François and his family quickly dressed, grabbed their already packed suitcases and rucksacks and immediately set off for an intermediate RV – a disused barn, close to the church, in the small village of Brendaouez, near Guissény.

He summoned three trusted senior members of the Confrèrie to meet him there in twenty minutes and then telephoned Muguette to join him for an urgent meeting at the RV in thirty minutes, knowing full well that she would inform her masters of the planned rendezvous.

Prior to Muguette's arrival, Jean-François told the three agents of the events of the last few hours and how he intended to deal with the situation that had developed so dramatically that night.

Just in case the Germans did arrive, Jean-François and the three agents organised themselves in all-around defence in the stoutly built stone barn. Their lorry was parked by the church, but well hidden from view behind a tall hedge. It was readily accessible by means of a small door at the rear of the barn, screened from view by a very high stone wall which gave about thirty yards of cover, before a quick dash through trees to the waiting lorry.

As Muguette entered the barn, asking why the hurried meeting in a rendezvous new to the Confrèrie, Jean-François drew his pistol, complete with silencer, and ordered her to kneel.

Her complexion turned chalk-white as she protested, demanding to know what Jean-François was doing – and why.

"Muguette, it is time to make your peace with God. Your collaboration with the Germans has led to the deaths of too many of our members. The information leading to the arrest of Louis and Fernande – a young mother and widow of a soldier killed in action near Dunkirk, we know came from you. Even as we speak, both agents may already be dead – murdered by the Gestapo."

Raising a pistol to her forehead, he asked the now shaking, terrified double agent: "Do you have anything to say before sentence is carried out? You have proved yourself a traitor to France and have betrayed your countrymen to the enemy. You know the penalty and you know the code of the Confrèrie. We have all the evidence we need – and more. No doubt your friends, the Germans, are already on their way here, thanks to your treachery."

Looking up, her fearful eyes pleading with him, she said, in little more than a hoarse whisper, "Please, Jean-François, please don't do this. I was wrong, but you don't understand. Please. No. Oh God, NO. DON'T…"

The silenced automatic coughed twice.

A sudden expression of disbelief momentarily crossed her face before she fell dead at Jean-François' feet, the back of her skull blown away.

"Quickly," he said to the three others who stood immobilised, shocked, staring at the now still body, "into the lorry, as fast as you can, before the Boche get here. Move!"

The group ran the short distance to the lorry and drove off rapidly in the direction of Pointe de Beg Pol and the farm, with its carefully prepared hideout.

Still visibly shaken by the ruthlessly quick and efficient dispatch of Muguette, the three agents sat in stunned silence in the back of the lorry, each with his own private thoughts. With them, wrapped in blankets and now fast asleep, were Jean-François' two young children, mercifully unaware of what had happened minutes before.

Francine, Jean-François' wife, sat in the cab with him, cradling a Sten gun with full magazine in her lap. She interpreted his silence as preoccupation with the hazards of driving quickly, with only sidelights on, along treacherous narrow lanes and with the possibility of pursuing Germans somewhere behind them in the dark.

After what seemed an eternity, but which was actually less than thirty minutes, Jean-François finally turned the lorry into the cobbled farmyard and parked it with a squeal of brakes, close to the old barn and its adjoining stables.

Together with the three Confrèrie agents, he moved towards the barn door – leaving Francine to stay with their children in case they woke up not knowing where they were.

By now, the three agents were starting to recover from the shock of Muguette's merciless and clinical execution and began talking loudly about the likely fate of their comrades, Louis and Fernande.

Suddenly, unexpectedly, from around the corner of the loose boxes that served as stables, the two Panzer officers appeared who kept their horses at livery there.

Both were brandishing pistols and the leading one, now pointing his gun at Jean-François, called out sharply, the tension obvious in his voice: "Halt! Wer da?"

"Merde! The Boche are already here," exclaimed Jean-François. Before he could reach into his pocket to retrieve his own pistol – which would probably have proved a fatal move – the three agents carrying Sten guns fired several bursts, almost as one, into the two Germans.

Obviously awakened by the noise of the group's arrival, but now suspicious and frightened, the two officers were caught unawares by the speed of Jean-François' reaction.

With an unnerving scream, one collapsed as the heavy 9mm bullets tore his chest apart at point-blank range. The second one groaned and fell to his knees before pitching forward, face first.

"Quick, grab those pistols – they're Walthers. They could come in useful," ordered Jean-François, the first to recover. "The noise of that shooting will bring all hell down on our ears. Let's get out of here as fast as possible."

"But where the devil do we go now?" asked the eldest agent, a baker from Roscoff, who used the code name 'Jerome'.

"The coast is our best bet now and we must hope that Tresco can send a boat across to pick us up and take us back to England," said Jean-François.

"There is a good potential pick-up place close to Pointe de Corsen, about ten kilometres north of Pointe de St Mathieu. There will be plenty of traffic around the sea there – French and German – and so one of Tresco's new modified fishing boats could be ideal. The north Brittany coast is far too dangerous. The Germans will expect us to try to escape from there, so we're going to move further south. Pointe de Corsen is virtually on the route of German naval craft travelling in and out of Brest and we'll try to pass off as fishermen from southern Brittany looking for new fishing grounds. One of the Tresco boats should blend in perfectly in those busy waters."

With his foot hard on the accelerator, Jean-François hurled the ancient Renault lorry and its occupants out along the narrow road leading towards Plouguerneau.

"We'll keep to the lanes east of the town," he said, "and we'll avoid all main roads until we've got at least as far as St Renan. From there, we'll drive due east along the back roads to Pointe de Corsen."

Turning to his colleague, who was still shocked and alone with his thoughts after the rapid slaughter of the two Panzer officers, he said, "Jerome, using the new RAF frequency, please let Tresco know where we're heading. Use the latest code which is still secure and transmit in the Breton language, naturally," he added with a rueful smile.

"Let them know that the exact ETA will be given in a later transmission."

=====O=====

At about the same time, in the still calm sea, many miles to the north, *Monique's* specially transformed hull and two 500 h.p. Hall-Scott engines pushed her south, toward Brittany, at a steady twenty-eight knots.

Glistening silver phosphorescence crowned the churning black waves, giving the only relief to the otherwise total darkness.

Recently repainted, with a light blue and white hull and with brown upperworks, in daylight she looked every inch what she was intended to represent. The earlier damage to her wheelhouse and hull had been carefully repaired in New Grimsby and she was fully restored for duty.

A little over sixty-five feet long, *Monique* was bigger than many of the Breton fishing boats, but compared well in size and form with a typical, large Concarneau tunnyman.

In rougher seas, or in a heavy swell, *Monique*'s speed had to be reduced because of her tendency to ship water forward, despite her redesigned hull. Special pumps had been fitted on deck to get rid of the constantly invading sea water.

Whenever she was operational in enemy waters, the pumps had to be removed and stowed below to avoid inviting suspicion and awkward questions.

Posing as a fishing vessel and when close to fishing fleets, she was forced to keep her speed down, typically, to between seven and ten knots.

At the dimly lit, simple teak chart table in the cramped wheelhouse, Tremayne pored over the details of the small islands and rocks scattered across his approach to Pointe de Corsen.

By his side, Petty Officer Irvine stood silently, hands on the wheel and eyes constantly scanning the blackness abeam and ahead.

For Operation Marie-Claire, Tremayne's crew consisted of Sub-Lieutenants Willoughby-Brown as First Lieutenant, who spoke fluent French, and Pierre Quilghini who, as a native French and Breton speaker, would bluff his way through any close contacts with either Breton fishermen, or gendarme inshore patrols. Petty Officer Irvine, Tremayne's declared "Rock of Gibraltar" was in his inevitable role of Coxswain. The rest of the hand-picked crew consisted of Leading Telegraphist 'Taff' Jenkins, Leading Motor Mechanic Jock Campbell and – as deckhands – Leading Seaman 'Brummie' Nichols together with Able Seamen 'Pablo' Watkins and Jean-Marie Lebrun, the Frenchman who spoke fluent, convincing Breton, as well as French.

Sacrificing portability and compactness for significantly more "punch", Tremayne had exchanged the mounted Bren guns for .30 calibre Brownings and replaced the original .30 calibre weapons with two heavy .50 calibre guns. A demonstration on Castle Down, during the two weeks' training, had convinced Tremayne of the .50 calibre Browning's awesome fire power, particularly when in a sustained firing role. Hidden under nets, the Brownings were all ready to fit onto their ingeniously adapted mountings within seconds.

The Brens were consigned to the operations boxes, along with the rifles, shotguns and short-range automatic weapons, ready for use in any close-quarter firefights that might develop.

With a full complement of nine officers and men, Tremayne knew that whether as a launching party, or as a shipboard crew, with the weaponry they possessed they could give a good account of themselves.

Emerging from the tall, narrow, painted wheelhouse on to the deck, Willoughby-Brown walked aft to join Sub-Lieutenant Quilghini who was sitting on a herring box, sheltered from the cold breeze by the net winch. Within seconds, the two were deep in conversation, speaking in French. Dressed in faded blue caps and smocks they looked – and sounded – for all the world like two young Breton fishermen who had grown up together in Roscoff, Camaret or Concarneau.

'Brummie' Nichols, the duty watch killick, was perched on the forrard derrick table, one arm around the mast while he held his binoculars in his other hand, keeping a constant lookout, straining to see anything in the inky blackness.

In the wheelhouse, Tremayne checked his watch and, turning to Irvine, said: "I make it about forty minutes to go, Cox'n, until we have the Ile d'Ouessant on our starboard beam. It's over ten minutes since our Beaufighter escort left us to return to base so, from now on, we won't have their radar to warn us of enemy aircraft or naval vessels in the area."

Conscious of the numbing effect of watchkeeping in the small hours – and without waiting for a reply from his as ever taciturn Coxswain – Tremayne called up Able Seaman Watkins to the wheelhouse.

"Watkins. I think a mug of kye for everyone is called for. We may be in for a long and busy night so we'll save the rum for the run home!"

"Aye aye, sir." The stocky, rounded figure of Able Seaman Watkins disappeared below to the primitive galley to prepare the first "wet" of the watch.

As Tremayne returned to his charts, a rapid tapping on the wheelhouse door was followed almost instantaneously by Leading Telegraphist Jenkins' anxious entrance.

"Urgent signal from Godolphin, sir."

Tremayne glanced quickly at the contents, swore softly to himself and said, "Thank you, Jenkins. My compliments to the First Lieutenant and Sub-Lieutenant Quilghini. Please ask them to join me in the wheelhouse immediately."

Seconds later, Tremayne began his briefing of his two officers. Turning to Petty Officer Irvine he said, "Listen in if you will, please, Cox'n — you'll be taking us to where we now have to go."

"Aye aye, sir."

Tremayne addressed the group, crammed cheek-by-jowl in the wheelhouse.

"Gentlemen, a pick-up at Pointe de Corsen is no longer possible." Tremayne looked at Willoughby-Brown and Quilghini.

"Jerry is just about turning north-west Brittany inside out, trying to find Jean-François and his party. The countryside is swarming with motorised patrols and checkpoints are being set up on all major routes — especially those leading to the coast."

"Can we expect increased activity from the Germans at sea as well sir?" asked Willoughby-Brown.

"I'm afraid so, Number One. Out at sea, we can expect to see a lot more E-boats and aircraft too, and closer to the shore, we may have visitations from both the Kriegsmarine and gendarme harbour patrol boats.

"Lebrun and I can take care of the gendarmerie. With your permission, sir, I will act as skipper and Lebrun can be the deckhand who speaks to them in either Breton or French while the rest of you — apart from the First Lieutenant — remain silent," said Quilghini.

"Thank you Pierre. Let's keep them off our backs and convince them that we're harmless fishermen simply trying to make a living," said Tremayne.

"I'll do the same with Jerry, sir," added Willoughby-Brown, "and Pierre can also speak German, while obviously sounding genuinely French."

"Perfect. Thank you, gentlemen. Now to the matter of our new rendezvous with Jean-François — and I need you to listen to this please Cox'n."

"Aye aye, sir." As before, the Coxswain's attention remained on the instruments in front of him and the interminable velvet blackness ahead.

Tremayne continued. "From intelligence picked up from the Confrèrie — and other sources — Godolphin tells me that, for some reason, the Germans are only concentrating their search on north-west Brittany. South of Brest, everything appears to be normal with only the routine patrols active and the usual random 'stop-and-search' procedures."

Tremayne paused momentarily, focusing on each face in turn.

"The new plan is this, gentlemen. The Confrèrie will mobilise a succession of vehicle changes, along relatively safe routes, for Jean-François and his family to travel south, as fast as possible, to somewhere near to Concarneau."

"That's a major fishing port on the south coast, west of Lorient," interjected Quilghini. "From there, Jean-François could take a fishing boat almost anywhere further east, or south, away from his usual territory."

"Absolutely so – and it's a big enough town in which to remain relatively anonymous, Pierre." Tremayne resumed his briefing.

"The intention is that he will take a Concarneau herring drifter or tunnyman due south to the Glénan Isles, where we are to rendezvous with him in just over fifteen hours time at 17.00 hours. He and his family will transfer to the *Monique*. Our exact rendezvous will be the La-Jument buoy, which indicates the seaward entrance to the channel into the archipelago formed by the Glénan Isles. That is here gentlemen," said Tremayne, tapping the chart with his pencil, "some ten miles south of Concarneau. Jean-François' fishing boat will bear a small green and gold striped pennant which she will haul down as she approaches us to confirm her identity."

"I know these islands well," Quilghini spoke again. "They are quite low and very rocky – a little like the smaller Scillies. In places, they are similar to the Western Rocks and are very dangerous." Looking at Irvine, he added, "I offer you my 'elp, Coxswain, with the navigation when we reach the Glénans."

"Thank you sir, I'll need it, so I will."

"What about fuel sir? Have we enough to reach the Glénans and then return to Tresco?" asked Willoughby-Brown.

"Luckily, we have just about enough. There are still those extra fuel tanks below from our last voyage which, thankfully, I forgot to have returned to the main store tank at Godolphin," replied Tremayne.

"We now have a hell of a long journey through enemy waters," he continued.

"Please ensure that the operations boxes and their weapons are readily available. We cannot mount the Brownings until late in our return journey – that would be too obvious – unless there's a major emergency."

Turning to Willoughby-Brown, he said, "Number One, with Sub-Lieutenant Quilghini's help, please make the deck look as authentic as possible, with nets out and ready to cast overboard. We'll start trawling as soon as the Roches de Portsall appear on our port beam. We have three boxes of fresh mackerel in ice from the sea off Bryher. Open these up, please, and make them look like our own catch.

Officers, and you too please 'Swain, will keep pistols, safety catches off, in your pocket ready for immediate use. Everyone of us has been trained in the use of a fighting-knife, so make sure that fish gutting knives are lying around, ready for instant use should things get to really close quarters. So, Cox'n, set your course due south from here please. Already the first signs of dawn are in the sky and…"

"Mon Dieu! What is *that*?!" suddenly exclaimed a startled Quilghini.

"Ah, Pierre, that is the redoubtable Able Seaman Watkins serenading us. An unaccompanied nautical oratorio you might say," laughed Willoughby-Brown, "and overture to a rare epicurean experience."

The adenoidal lament grew louder as 'Pablo' Watkins lurched his way towards the wheelhouse, a tray of spilling mugs in his hands: *"This is my story, this is my song, I've been in the Andrew too 'bleedin' long. So roll on the Nelson, the Rodney, Renown…* Oh, sod it. This bloody 'eaving deck."

"Thank you Watkins. For kye like this, even the Coxswain is prepared to put up with your dreadful caterwauling," said Tremayne with mock seriousness, as he took the steaming mug from the Able Seaman.

"Caterwauling, sir? I'll 'ave two-bob, each way, on that sir," said Watkins with a broad grin, as he winked at Petty Officer Irvine.

"Will it be extra sausages for you, sir, for breakfast?" he asked Willoughby-Brown, an expression of bland innocence on his face.

"I shall hold you to that Watkins and thanks for the kye," said the First Lieutenant, his left eyebrow assuming its characteristic trajectory.

"The assets definitely outweigh the liabilities," laughed Tremayne, as Watkins disappeared below to return to what he termed his 'kye caboose'.

Dawn began breaking as *Monique* appeared off the north Brittany coast. She immediately dropped her speed to around eight knots and gradually edged her way towards a small fleet of herring drifters and another group which looked like crabbers, moving west, Quilghini guessed, from Roscoff or Camaret.

At reduced revolutions on both engines, *Monique* was inclined to pay off to starboard and to relieve the consequent strain on Petty Officer Irvine, Tremayne reverted to a system of watch on and watch off for all hands, with Leading Seaman Nicholls sharing the Coxswain's role with the Petty Officer. In this form of watchkeeping, at least one officer, one engineer and one deckhand were on duty at all times.

Watkins, an Able Mechanical Engineer, took over from Leading

Motor Mechanic Jock Campbell while 'Taff' Jenkins stood down but left the small transmitter receiver on, ready to be called back on demand.

With nets cast, *Monique* mingled in with other fishing boats, making her way south at around four knots.

It was Willoughby-Brown who suddenly saw smoke appearing on the horizon, on the starboard beam, as *Monique* was approaching the Pointe de St Mathieu at the entrance to the major inlet leading to the huge naval base at Brest.

Through his binoculars, he was able to make out a German destroyer flotilla approaching at speed from the west. He counted four and, as they drew closer, thick smoke belching from their raked funnels, he was able to read their pennant numbers, identifying them as vessels from Kapitän Erdmenger's 8th Destroyer Flotilla.

Willoughby-Brown found himself admiring their powerful, businesslike lines and aggressively flared bows, as they steamed rapidly across *Monique*'s bow towards their base at Brest, their scarlet, white and black Kriegsmarine ensigns fluttering from their after masts.

Launched between 1940 and 1942, the twelve destroyers of the Z23 class had previously served in Norwegian waters before moving to Brest and, as a consequence, were popularly known as the 'Narviks'. Heavily armed for their size, they were proving to be a menace in the Channel and other British waters – despite their poor sea-keeping characteristics, laying mines that accounted for many Royal Navy and Merchant Marine vessels.

Assuming that, as lead fishing boat, *Monique* would be under close observation from several pairs of binoculars, Willoughby-Brown and Able Seaman Lebrun waved their caps – the Frenchman muttering several obscene oaths about 'Les Boches', much to the First Lieutenant's amusement.

=====O=====

Thirty or so miles away, at about the same time that Erdmenger's destroyers were crossing *Monique's* bow, Jean-François and his family had reached the small town of Daoulas, almost eight miles east of Brest.

They had travelled there by farm cart, a lorry carrying supplies for the Kriegsmarine and, most recently, a Kubewagen – the German army's equivalent of the jeep. Dressed in the uniform of a senior NCO of the Belgian volunteer Waffen SS regiment 'Legion Flandern', he had succeeded in bluffing his way through two checkpoints by sheer arrogance.

With his wife and children hidden under camouflage netting and sections of canvas military tents in the distinctive SS splinter-pattern in the back of the Kubewagen, Jean-François' story had proved watertight so far.

His well-rehearsed story was that he was taking the equipment to his newly arrived regiment's training area, close to the coast south of Brest. Forged SS papers supplied by the Confrèrie had convinced sentries up until the moment he had cleared Daoulas.

His first heart-stopping moment occurred at a checkpoint barrier just outside the town, on the road to Le Faou.

Two very young and obviously keen German sailors, dressed in pea-jackets and wearing forage caps, stopped him and demanded his papers.

As he handed them over to the elder of the two, the younger one began prodding the netting and tent covers with his rifle and bayonet.

Alarmed that one of his children or his wife might be badly injured and call out, Jean-François stood up, threateningly, in the well of the driver's seat and screamed at the sailor, pointing to the sinister death's head insignia on his cap and threatening dire retribution from SS headquarters at Brest.

"Your name, rank and number and the name of your ship." The sailor, badly shaken, responded to order, whereupon Jean-François – dropping his voice an octave lower and speaking in a quieter, menacing tone – said: "Well, Matrose Stein, you will find yourself protecting some God-forsaken naval base on the Baltic from partisans before the month is out." Raising his voice to a scream once more, he shrieked, "and stand to attention and salute when you speak to a superior officer. Now raise that damned barrier and get out of my way."

Standing to attention, but obviously trembling, the two young sailors stared ashen-faced as Jean-François put his foot down and the Kubewagen roared off south.

Jean-François was wringing wet from perspiration as he reflected on how lucky he had been and how different it would have been had the Feldgendarmerie – the German military police

– stopped him, rather than two over-keen, but inexperienced, naval conscripts.

Most ordinary service personnel remained bemused by the idiosyncratic system of SS ranks and were never sure whom to defer to, or salute, when confronted by the spontaneous arrogance of such supremely confident, hectoring louts. On this occasion, ignorance, confusion and fear had saved the lives of the agent, his wife and his two children.

At the next prescribed rendezvous, a remote farm outside Le Faou, Jean-François handed over the Kubewagen and the SS-Oberscharführer uniform to the local members of the Confrèrie de Saint Michel. In exchange, he was given a suit, shirt, shoes and underwear, plus spare clothing, all with Swiss manufacturers' labels sewn into them. A Swiss passport, identifying him as a banker from Geneva, together with passports for his wife and children and a cover story were also handed to him. For transport, he was provided with a Citroën Traction-Avant car with a full tank of fuel, principally siphoned from German military vehicles and those of the French gendarmerie. Obtaining the petrol had itself been an operation conducted with great ingenuity and panache, bordering on the sublime, by Confrèrie agents.

Jean-François retained his pistol, with silencer, three spare clips of 9mm ammunition and the British commando fighting-knife so proudly presented to him by Corporal Kane when the two had met at Pointe de Beg Pol.

He set off south, with the good wishes of the members of the Confrèrie, who then rapidly dispersed – leaving no trace of the rendezvous and the transaction.

He drove without incident through several small towns, keeping his speed down to avoid attracting attention and to give the impression that, like the few Frenchmen lucky enough to obtain some of the increasingly scarce petrol, he too was trying to conserve his precious and diminishing supply of fuel.

Jean-François' luck held until he reached a small town just north of Quimper. Two German soldiers with a motorcycle and sidecar manned a checkpoint barrier closing the road to traffic. As they turned to face him, he saw what he had dreaded most – the aluminium gorgets of the Feldgendarmerie, which hung on chains around their necks. Slowing down in response to their peremptory raised arms, he could see from their confident faces and arrogant stance that they were a very different proposition from the two sailors near Daoulas. They wore grey-green leather overcoats and steel helmets and looked as if they meant business.

While the one covered Jean-François and the car with a machine pistol, the other thrust his hand belligerently through the now open window of the car and demanded: "Your papers".

Jean-François handed over the passports and some letters of introduction to various German-controlled French businesses, given to him by the Confrèrie.

"You are *Swiss?*" – the word was said with a sneer which was insulting and obviously intended to be demeaning.

"Yes I am. So are my wife and children," responded Jean-François with studied calm, as he unobtrusively and slowly moved the pistol to a position for ease of sudden use.

"So, where are you going?" The tone of the Feldgendarmerie

NCO was still offensively arrogant.

"To Lorient, to the German-controlled ship builders, Chantiers Maritime de Bretagne – they make small, fast patrol boats," responded Jean-François, his heart pounding and his forehead beginning to sweat.

"Do you sell yourself to the British, as well as to us? Isn't Swiss so-called neutrality about exploiting the many commercial opportunities of this war? While we fight, self-satisfied pigs like you sit around making fat profits."

Jean-François' response was swift and simple.

"No, I do not do that. Any other questions?"

"No. Here is your passport, you Swiss arsehole. You may go."

Without any thanks, Jean-François drove forward, changing gear as the car slowly gathered speed.

"Halt!" the curt command cut short his sigh of relief.

"Get out of the car – you, the driver," ordered the sergeant.

"Come over here. Quickly!"

Jean-François only just had time to slip the pistol into his inside pocket as he stepped out of the car and moved cautiously towards the two military policemen.

"Quickly, you lazy Swiss bastard," shouted the sergeant.

"We're going to check you out properly. It is the easiest thing in the world for some swine of a French terrorist to pretend to be a Swiss citizen. Get over here."

Both Germans were now staring intently at Jean-François and covering him with their machine pistols.

Instantly, a desperate plan began to form in his mind.

He appeared to stumble, clutching under his open jacket at

his chest as he gasped: "For God's sake… it's my heart. I can't cope with shock like this. My tablets please…"

"What are you talking about, you blockhead?"

"Help me please. My tablets are in the car in the glove box. I need them *please*…"

Both Germans looked towards the car and momentarily lowered their guns.

Jean-François' hand came out from under his 'pocket', holding his silenced pistol.

The sergeant was first to react, swearing obscenely, as he brought the MP38 up ready to shoot the Frenchman. He was a fraction of a second too late and his brutal, contorted face disintegrated as three heavy 9mm slugs tore it apart.

His colleague, slower on the uptake, stared horrified and shouted, "Gott in Himmel. Was mach…" He never finished the sentence, as two rounds from the Browning High Power in Jean-François' hand cut him down, shot twice through the heart.

He quickly ran over to the two inert figures and, feeling feeble signs of a pulse in the sergeant, put a further round through his forehead between the eyes. "Dead men tell no tales, my friend." Jean-François' voice was totally unemotional as he squeezed the trigger. The other military policeman must have been dead before he hit the ground. There was no sign of a pulse at all.

Jean-François quickly dragged the two bodies to the side of the road and rolled them into the ditch alongside, covering them with foliage, twigs and the ferns growing along its edge.

He rapidly lifted the barrier with its counterweight, ran back to the car and drove off, at speed.

He slowed down to drive through Quimper and then headed east, south-east for Concarneau and the coastal rendezvous arranged by the Confrèrie.

Turning to his wife, he murmured, "I'm sorry about that. I hope the children didn't see."

"No. I covered their faces by holding them close to me. I thought you were going to be shot and I did not want them to see that. I closed my own eyes too. I was shaking so much, I was terrified."

=====O=====

By contrast, *Monique's* passage south to rescue Jean-François and his family, was proving to be somewhat less eventful.

Able Seaman Lebrun and the First Lieutenant had exchanged greetings and banter with the crews of two fishing boats which had come within hailing distance, apparently without arousing suspicion.

A patrol boat of the local gendarmerie had come within about fifty yards of the *Monique*. After maintaining station for about a quarter of an hour, during which time she kept the fishing vessel under close observation through binoculars, she turned away to scrutinise other fishing boats in the vicinity.

Once again, Willoughby-Brown and Lebrun paused to wave nonchalantly to their observers and then continued to busy themselves with various items of gear on deck to preserve their seeming authenticity as fishermen.

Their next encounter with a visitor wishing to satisfy his curiosity occurred as they were passing the vast entrance to the Baie de Douarnenez.

Now mingling with several other fishing boats but obviously looking somewhat larger, an Arado 196 reconnaissance floatplane, on coastal patrol, flew over them very slowly and then returned for a second look. Passing over at a height of around one hundred and fifty feet, the small rudders on each float were clearly visible, as was its Staffel insignia on the green fuselage – a white seahorse on a red shield.

Even from that height, the closest, most meticulous observation would have merely revealed men in typical Breton sea-going rig carrying out legitimate and necessary tasks as a fishing boat crew.

As Willoughby-Brown looked up briefly at the departing aircraft, his private thoughts about her functional yet elegant, well-proportioned lines were rudely shattered by Watkins' eloquent farewell – "Sod off, Arseface."

"Quite so, Watkins. My sentiments, too," he said, stifling a laugh at the incongruity of their different reactions to the intruder.

As *Monique* continued her passage south, with the Ile de Sein off her starboard beam, Leading Telegraphist Jenkins came up on deck, rubbing the sleep from his eyes.

"Sir," he said, addressing the First Lieutenant. "A signal from Godolphin, sir. Can't make head nor tail of it sir," he added, handing the written transmission to the First Lieutenant.

"Thank you Jenkins. Sorry the beauty sleep was disturbed."

Lebrun took the proffered message from Willoughby-Brown and said, "It is in Breton, sir. They confirm the rendezvous and the time. We are to meet a transfer boat and its cargo. The name of the boat, a Concarneau tunnyman, is *Penmarc'h*."

Shortly afterwards, Willoughby-Brown's watch stood down and Tremayne took over with his duty watch, with Petty Officer Irvine back at the wheel and Sub-Lieutenant Quilghini around to speak French or Breton when needed.

Monique continued to steam south, ploughing her way slowly through the now heavy, rolling Atlantic swell in the Baie d'Audierne. Ahead lay the giant lighthouse on the Pointe de Penmarc'h, before a turn to port and a further twenty miles to the Glénan Isles.

"A hell of a 'wet' boat sir, so she is," said Irvine, as the heaving seas poured over her blunt bow and rolled the length of her deck.

"You're right Cox'n," replied Tremayne, "and even with those pumps, I'd hate to be in her in Biscay in a force nine. I'm glad we've got the two Frenchmen with us. Sub-Lieutenant Quilghini made sure that everything on deck that could move was locked down and secured before we left Braiden Rock."

Further conversation was interrupted by a steady roar of aircraft, flying low, approaching from the starboard beam.

Tremayne left the wheelhouse just as two giant Focke-Wulf Condors passed over *Monique* at about five hundred feet, their eight engines deafening those on deck.

Watching the graceful, yet sinister aircraft, Tremayne's thoughts immediately returned to his last encounter with

Condors when he was Gunnery Officer on board *HMS Portree*. A burst from the leading Condor's forrard 20mm cannon had wrecked much of *Portree*'s bridge wing, killing the port machine gunner. Tremayne heard again the terrible noise of the Condor's gun and the screams of the young AB as he had died in a hail of cannon shells.

As if in slow motion, he vividly remembered, too, seizing the undamaged twin Lewis guns, traversing them, and emptying their magazines into the duck-egg blue underside of the aircraft when it slowly flew over *Portree*.

As the two flew over *Monique* – no doubt returning from an Atlantic patrol, looking for potential targets for the submarine "wolf packs", thought Tremayne – his mind turned to his close friend Bill Mitchell, who had later been lost at sea when *Portree* had been sunk by a U-boat.

He recalled Bill's calm, steadiness and the genuine concern he had shown which had saved Tremayne's sanity after Diana had been killed.

"You, Bill," reflected Tremayne, silently, "were the greatest friend a man could have had. I was privileged to have known you. Christ! How I miss your company and your great sense of humour. I wonder what you would have thought of this phoney fishing boat and this sneaky sort of warfare?"

As he returned to the wheelhouse he thought, "And you, too, Bill Irvine, are a bloody good hand and I'm damn glad I've got you as my Cox'n." Like Bill Mitchell, Petty Officer Irvine was rock-steady under fire and had that wry, dry sense of humour that appealed so much to Tremayne. The two had much in common it seemed, and not simply their first names, thought Tremayne, as he moved next to the Cox'n.

"Scourge of the Atlantic sir, those bastards," said Irvine nodding after the now disappearing Condors.

"Aye, Cox'n and especially the Western Approaches," replied Tremayne.

About thirty minutes after the Condors had flown over *Monique*, Irvine said quietly, "Lighthouse coming up sir, on the port beam so it is."

"Thank you Cox'n. We'll clear that and then set course east, south-east for the Glénans."

Returning to the deck, Tremayne called out to Quilghini: "Haul in the nets if you please, Sub. Let's see what we've caught for supper. Perhaps we can trade some of our catch for a bottle or two of Commander Rawlings' claret when we get back!"

Reckoned to be the highest lighthouse in the world, the one at Penmarc'h looked truly impressive with the midday sun shining on it. Close by, Tremayne could clearly see the awesome rocks along the inhospitable and dangerous shoreline, which was capped with the scattered white villas, the churches and other buildings of the villages of St Guénolé, Guilrinec and Penmarc'h itself.

Everyone on deck, including Tremayne, had stripped to the waist to enjoy the glorious weather. The sea, so often dull, monotonous grey was, for once, a deep, translucent green with white crests constantly foaming and breaking on the waves. Several curious seabirds, accustomed to following the many fishing boats that operated in the area, flew over them looking for signs of their catch.

The early morning heavy swell had given way to smaller waves, which no longer cascaded over *Monique*'s bow but merely created a sparkling bow wave and wake. Winching the nets in via the wooden 'gallows', Tremayne and the crews shared an almost childlike delight in their morning's catch, with Quilghini and Lebrun able to identify the different types of fish for them.

Mixed in with the many varieties of fish were enough langoustines and crabs for, as Tremayne put it, "a pretty major feast for supper on board tonight!"

As the Glénan Isles came into sight, Willoughby-Brown, who had come back on watch, and Tremayne, began searching them for any signs of the Concarneau tunnyman carrying Jean-François and his family.

At about three miles distant, with still no sign of the transfer boat, the two officers were horrified to see the sleek, purposeful shapes of three E-boats emerge from behind Lach, the southernmost of the islands, heading west, south-west.

"Sir, they're changing course. They're heading this way," said Willoughby-Brown.

"And making maximum revolutions," added Tremayne, as the three boats lifted their bows in unison, with the waves hurling spray up over their flared, purposeful looking hulls.

"Put your binoculars away, Number One. Have both watches at defence stations and have the operations boxes open – but well concealed."

Turning to Quilghini, Tremayne ordered: "Sub, start sorting our catch into boxes please – we've got plenty of empty ones. Make sure that there's a good mix of fish and crabs for our gallant friends from the Kriegsmarine just in case they do come calling."

Tremayne could clearly see the officers on the bridge of the three E-boats, now in 'arrowhead' formation, looking at his boat through their binoculars.

Then, as one, the three very businesslike vessels reduced their speed, quickly re-forming into line-astern formation, and slowly passed by – their captains saluting and waving as they resumed their original course.

"Quickly, Number One, smile and wave back at the bastards."

"Phew," exclaimed Willoughby-Brown. "For a moment there, I thought we'd been rumbled, sir."

"So did I, Number One. My guess is that they used us as an opportunity to exercise their pre-search approach procedure."

"A close one, Cox'n," said Tremayne, putting his head round the wheelhouse door, "but we can breathe again."

"Aye, aye sir." The steady response and expressionless face gave no hint whatsoever of what the redoubtable Coxswain may have thought – or felt – as the E-boats had approached *Monique* so purposefully."

"Look, there sir. There she is," called Willoughby-Brown from the bow, "off the port beam coming out of the islands, bright blue and white hull – and a dark red sail."

Tremayne nodded to his First Lieutenant and then said, "Right everyone. Take your weapons out of the operations boxes just in case it isn't our guests. Keep them behind the bulwarks but ready for instant use. Make all weapons ready."

Looking aft, to the travel winch and 'gallows', Tremayne called,

"Watkins, Nicholls, pull the fishing net around you so that you can't be seen. Have your Lanchesters ready to shoot if anything goes wrong. Shoot on my command and make your shots count."

The fishing boat approaching – a Concarneau tunnyman – was now about four hundred yards away, the sun shining on her paintwork. Fluttering from her main mast was a green and gold pennant.

Through their binoculars, the three officers on *Monique*'s deck could clearly make out a group of six people – all adults – dressed similarly to themselves in fishermen's smocks and caps. There were no children to be seen anywhere.

At around three hundred yards, two figures on the tunnyman began waving to those on the deck of the *Monique* and a third hauled down the green and gold pennant.

"That's the signal," called Tremayne, "wave back to them. I can read her name now – it is the *Penmarc'h.*" She was as Tremayne had imagined her. Broad beamed with a bluff bow and transom stern, sturdily built and yet beautiful in her own unadorned, primitive way. *Penmarc'h* was largely blue and white with light brown upperworks and a traditional brick red sail at her mizzen mast. She had a long bowsprit and her masts and spars were all gleaming with varnish.

Within minutes, the tunnyman was alongside and, from a hatch in her forrard deck, two laughing, excited children appeared.

A stocky, straight-backed man with a goatee beard and the most piercing blue eyes that Tremayne had ever seen, stepped forward, introducing himself as Jean-François.

"May I present my wife, Françine, and my children, Jean-Pierre

210

and Céline. We are all so happy to meet you," he said, grabbing Tremayne's outstretched hand.

Quickly, Jean-François, his family and a tall, very military-looking man, whom he introduced as Colonel Harberer, were helped over the bulwarks and guard rails and onto the deck of the *Monique*.

"Monsieur, Madame, Colonel. Welcome aboard! We must get underway promptly as we have a long journey ahead, but may I first offer you a glass of champagne to celebrate what I hope will be the start of your new life," said a smiling Tremayne.

As *Monique* rapidly pulled away from the tunnyman, Tremayne proposed the toast: "To freedom."

At this point, the two children burst into peals of laughter as Nicholls and Watkins emerged, somewhat sheepishly, from their temporary shroud of soaking wet and foul-smelling fishing nets.

"Bloody 'ell, Brum. Thank God I don't 'ave to sleep with yo'. Yo'm 'ardly a bed of bleedin' roses," said Watkins, forcing a somewhat strained grin across his well lived-in features.

"What I lack in personal 'ygene, my son, I mek up for with technique and personality," said Nicholls sagely, deadpan as ever.

"Ah, I know. That's wot yo'r missus is always a-tellin' me," countered a grinning Watkins.

"What ever language was that, is it *English?* — I simply do not understand them," said a very bewildered Madame Duhamel.

"No, Madame, neither do we," laughed Tremayne, re-filling her glass with champagne, "but if there is ever any trouble, they are marvellous people to have on your side."

After the brief welcoming celebration, Jean-François, his family and the Colonel who, Tremayne learned, was a leading military strategist and the principal military advisor to the Confrère, disappeared below.

Their living and sleeping quarters, for the long journey to the Isles of Scilly, was the tiny cabin which Tremayne and his two officers had temporarily vacated.

Already, they wore appropriate clothing in which to appear on deck, but Quilghini had warned Tremayne that more than about five or six people on view would arouse suspicion and invite inspection from any German or French gendarme who happened to see them from the many aircraft and coastal patrol vessels in the area.

"The children, especially," he added, "must remain below until we are close to Scilly."

By mid-evening, *Monique* had passed the Pointe de Raz and the Ile de Sein and Tremayne ordered her course to be set north, north-east, through the narrow Passage du Fromveur, keeping the Ile d'Ouessant on the port beam.

Joining in with a small fleet of crabbers returning to Camaret, *Monique* ploughed slowly through the still calm sea.

Ahead of them lay the treacherously rocky waters between the Ile d'Ouessant and the Pointe de St Mathieu. Having been glad of Quilghini's navigational experience in the tricky archipelago of the Glénans, the Coxswain readily accepted the French officer's offer to assist with a night-time passage through the jagged, tearing rocks between them and the Passage du Fromveur.

"It will be very dark by the time we reach the rocks and islands west of St Mathieu and if you don't know these waters well, sir," he said, addressing Tremayne, "you can quickly find yourself in serious danger."

"Right Sub, thank you for the offer to help – we'll take it gratefully! It will be even more risky, however, to travel close to the coast with so many patrol boats out looking for Jean-François."

Just beyond the Pointe de Penhir, the accompanying crabbers with their dark red sails turned east to return to Camaret, leaving *Monique* to continue her way north, alone.

Approaching the Pierres Noires lighthouse, Quilghini took over the wheel as temporary Coxswain, allowing Irvine to stand down, off watch, for a much-needed rest. Bearing north-east, *Monique* pushed on with the scattered rocks and islands, fine on her starboard bow, towards the Passage du Fromveur.

The dark mass of the Ile d'Ouessant came into view as a blurred outline to port. Tremayne ordered, "Slow ahead, both, Sub," to reduce the sound of her movements and to cut down the silvery phosphorescence which showed up brightly whenever the moon appeared in gaps in the clouds. He had previously ordered *Monique* closed up at defence stations, with the Brownings uncovered and ready to fix to the disguised mountings, fore and aft.

They had just gained the north end of the Passage du Fromveur and were about to move into the open Atlantic again, when Nicholls, the port lookout, suddenly called to Tremayne, who had been joined on the foredeck by the First Lieutenant.

"Sir, vessel approaching on the port beam at high speed. I picked up her bow wave with the binoculars."

"Thank you Nicholls. Well done."

Turning to those standing near him, Tremayne said: "Number One, Sub, grab Able Seaman Lebrun and stand by to act as spokesmen with our visitors. Do all you can to keep them from boarding us. Spin them a yarn about our steering malfunctioning and tell them that we've only just managed to repair it. Tell them, too, that we're on our way back to Carantec. Our pennant numbers will fit in with boats from there as well as Concarneau – unless they check up on us. Make the story convincing, gentlemen, we're relying on you."

Tremayne ordered the operations boxes to be opened up and both he and the rest of the duty watch grabbed Lanchesters as personal weapons. Quickly, he laid out rows of hand grenades on the deck, close to the bulwarks.

"Nicholls, Watkins, Jenkins. Load and cock the Brownings and make ready for firing." He touched Quilghini's arm. "Sub, use the loudhailer to respond to them if they signal us – and the best of luck."

Tremayne quickly went below to warn Jean-François, his wife and Colonel Harberer and to hand them each a Lanchester.

Returning on deck, he ordered everyone to remain below the sheerline of the bulwarks except for Quilghini, Lebrun and the First Lieutenant. Almost on cue with his order, the rapidly approaching boat turned on a powerful searchlight, holding *Monique* in its glare and temporarily blinding those on deck.

It was an E-boat, its menacing 40mm bow gun trained, at

point-blank range, on *Monique*'s fragile wheelhouse.

In heavily accented French the E-boat captain, using a loudhailer, ordered *Monique* to stop immediately. The echoing voice continued, "What boat are you? Where are you from? Where are going to?"

Quilghini responded, also by loudhailer, giving the story that Tremayne had hurriedly instructed.

"How many people are on board?"

"Tell him a total of seven, Sub, and that you're the skipper," whispered Tremayne urgently from below the top of the bulwarks.

"Your name," continued the harsh voice.

"Pierre Hentic, from Roscoff," replied Quilghini, rapidly thinking up a convincing Breton surname.

"We are going to board you. Prepare to receive a search party."

"Oh, shit. That's the last thing we need," muttered Willoughby-Brown, as a group of six German seamen, led by an Oberleutnant zur See, rapidly formed up at the guard rails of the E-boat.

"We are coming alongside. Secure our lines fore and aft," ordered the voice behind the loudhailer.

Two of the landing party took up lines ready to throw across, as the E-boat manoeuvred slowly alongside *Monique*, her massive, purposeful bulk towering over the fishing vessel.

"Right," whispered Tremayne, "as soon as the lines are secure, shoot everyone on deck. Jenkins, Watkins, cover that bridge and wheelhouse in grenades. Smother the bastards with explosives."

As the Oberleutnant gingerly started to clamber from the E-boat on to the bobbing deck of the *Monique*, Tremayne and

Nicholls opened fire, killing him instantly and putting down four of his boarding party following close behind him.

Grenades thrown by Jenkins and Watkins removed the three figures watching from the bridge.

On Tremayne's shouted command, Quilghini and Lebrun seized the Brownings and began sweeping the E-boat's deck from bow to stern. Unable to traverse either their 40mm forrard gun or the 20mm Oerlikon aft, the E-boat was rendered virtually helpless.

The two seamen not killed in the first bursts of shots from Tremayne and Nicholls, valiantly began returning fire before being cut down by the Brownings, now secured on their mountings. Still lashed to the *Monique,* and with no one now obviously in command, the E-boat had been temporarily immobilised by the swift, co-ordinated reaction of *Monique's* crew.

Capitalising on their early initiative, Tremayne yelled to those on deck, "Close on me, lads. Let's chamfer the bastards up."

Following him on to the deck of the E-boat, Willoughby-Brown, Quilghini and Lebrun, closely followed by the inseparable Brummies and Jenkins, stormed on board the stationary German vessel, firing as they charged and hurling grenades through open doors, down ventilators and into companion ways.

"Deck cleared fore and aft," shouted Tremayne above the mayhem, "let's get below, lads."

The first sign of resistance came from a mess deck amidships, as five German ratings and a Senior Warrant Officer barricaded themselves behind overturned tables and chairs and opened fire with pistols.

There was a sudden sharp cry as Nicholls fell, clutching at his chest, and then, almost immediately afterwards, a succession of unearthly screams as Watkins emptied his Lanchester into the group trying to defend their mess deck.

Tremayne shot a Warrant Officer who appeared at the entrance to the engine room and then dropped two grenades down the stairwell leading to the E-boat's machinery. As the engine room exploded, with flames and smoke blasting vertically up the stairwell, those still alive attempted to stagger, or rush – according to their wounds – for the upper deck.

An Engineer Officer who lurched forward through the rapidly spreading smoke, pistol in hand, was quickly dispatched by Quilghini, while Willoughby-Brown, wielding one of the two Lanchesters, cut down the already blood-covered diesel engine mechanics coming up behind their Chief.

Quickly checking the shattered bridge, Tremayne found both officers and the E-boat's coxswain dead, or dying, from grenade shrapnel.

Astern, Quilghini and the others had taken prisoner the six remaining crew members who had surrendered and were standing dazed by the sudden shock and ferocity of the short, sharp engagement.

"Sir, Nicholls's been hit. Can I go to him?" asked Watkins anxiously.

"Of course, Watkins. I'll ask the First Lieutenant to help you."

Willoughby-Brown and Able Seaman Watkins rushed to where Nicholls lay in a pool of rapidly spreading blood, his face contorted with pain.

"What took yo' so bleedin' long, Pablo?" he gasped, his voice faint and indistinct.

"Sorry mate, I was a bit busy. Am yo' alright, Brummie?"

Willoughby-Brown pushed forward and quickly jabbed a hypodermic with morphine into Leading Seaman Nicholls' arm.

"Rest easy, Nicholls. We'll get you to the MO as fast as possible," he said, catching the distress in Watkins' eyes.

"Will he be alright sir?"

"We'll do our best Watkins," said the First Lieutenant, "but that wound in his chest looks nasty. Help me get him back on board *Monique*, the E-boat's beginning to settle. All those grenades we used must have holed her hull badly."

Meanwhile, Tremayne stopped to take a quick stock of the situation. It was utter carnage and chaos, with bodies seemingly everywhere, lying around the E-boat's deck and shattered wheelhouse. Although the firefight had lasted less than ten minutes, such was its ferocity that thirteen officers and men – including Nicholls – lay either dead or severely wounded.

The E-boat was damaged beyond their ability and capacity to save her and she was already down by the bow, to the point where immediate evacuation was essential.

"Return to *Monique*," Tremayne shouted. "Look lively lads, the E-boat is going down rapidly." He quickly sought out the stretcher party, carrying the badly wounded Leading Seaman.

"Careful there, lads, with Nicholls. Keep him as still as you can. Take him down to the after flat and stay with him, Watkins. Sub, get those prisoners onto our deck and keep your gun trained on them please. When they recover from the shock of what's happened, they might become difficult."

In the brief time that the engagement lasted, Tremayne had felt nothing except an overwhelming drive to destroy the E-boat as a threat to his crew and the *Monique*. All his adrenalin, energy and focus had been directed towards destruction of the enemy and anything that got in his way.

Now, after the intensity of the firefight, when a whole rapid succession of people and events had appeared in such sharp relief, he felt completely drained of emotion and energy.

He turned to Willoughby-Brown and Quilghini and said quietly, "Thank you, gentlemen. You did exactly what was expected of you – and so much more besides. We fought as a team and, between us, we've sunk a bloody E-boat – as well as defeating an enemy at least three times our number. The trouble is," he continued, a smile crossing his face, "no one will believe us at Godolphin."

"Well, actually they will, sir. I grabbed the E-boat's ensign as she began to settle," said an exuberant Willoughby-Brown, producing the neatly folded Kriegsmarine flag from beneath his fisherman's smock.

"God help us, Number One. There's a hell of a lot more to you than meets the eye," laughed Tremayne.

Back aboard *Monique*, Tremayne briefed his passengers on the engagement and then went below to see Leading Seaman Nicholls.

The bullet had entered Nicholls' chest, high up on the right hand side. The absence of any exit hole indicated the bullet was still lodged somewhere in Nicholls' body.

"Stay with him Watkins until the morphine takes effect and he starts to drowse, then come back up on deck. I will ask Madame Duhamel, who was a nurse, to visit him regularly until we get him back to Godolphin."

"Aye aye sir — and thank you sir."

Tremayne called Willoughby-Brown over and together they went aft to the huddled group of frightened looking prisoners.

"Names, ranks and numbers as a matter of formality please, Number One, and then I want to know which flotilla they belong to, how many E-boats it consists of, where they are based, and what they were doing around the Ile d'Ouessant. Start off with the one who seems most nervous or frightened, then check information individually with each of the others."

"Aye aye sir. I take it, sir, that we strictly observe the rules of the Geneva Convention?"

"Exactly, Number One — apart from asking them those questions. But if they refuse to answer, you can tell them that when they reach our base — refer to it as "the mainland" — SIS will take a very different approach from ours. We've so little space on this tub, but we'll keep them under lock and key with Jean-François and the Colonel taking it in turns to guard them."

"Will I blindfold them as we did before sir?" asked the First Lieutenant.

"Absolutely, Number One. Fifteen miles out from Scilly."

Sub-Lieutenant Quilghini resumed his role as temporary Coxswain and Tremayne ordered: "Full revolutions, both engines, Sub. Let's get home as quickly as we can."

Dawn found *Monique* in waters that were forbidden to any

French fishing vessel. This, Tremayne knew, was where they were at their most vulnerable.

Calling his Leading Telegraphist to the wheelhouse he said, "Jenkins, make to Godolphin, please: '*Would welcome the umbrella. Have sunk an E-boat. Bringing six POWs and deliveries*'."

"Deliveries, sir?" asked a puzzled Willoughby-Brown.

"Yes, Number One. An unflattering description, I'm afraid, but that's the code name for Jean-François and his family."

Some minutes later, Jenkins reappeared at the wheelhouse, wearing a broad grin.

"Signal from Godolphin sir."

"Number One, Sub. From Lieutenant Commander Enever, called Tremayne: '*Congratulations, but make it the Tirpitz next time. Umbrella imminent*'."

"What's that about doing miracles, but the impossible taking a little longer?" laughed Willoughby-Brown.

Shortly after receiving the signal, Watkins as starboard lookout shouted: "Aircraft dead ahead. Two of them sir. And three more behind them."

"Action stations, everyone. Stand by to open fire," shouted Tremayne.

In seconds, all four Brownings were manned and turned onto the rapidly approaching aircraft. The leading pair were twin-engined planes and the following trio were clearly single-engined fighters. Those on the Brownings were lining up their sights with the oncoming aircraft, their thumbs hovering over the firing buttons.

Petty Officer Irvine, who had come back on deck to resume

duty as Coxswain, called out: "Beaufighters, followed by Hurricanes, sir, so they are."

"Thank you Cox'n. Stand down gun crews." Turning to the First Lieutenant, Tremayne said, "Am I glad to see them, Number One. Please call Monsieur and Madame Duhamel and the Colonel up on deck. They will be much in need of fresh air. Let them enjoy our 'umbrella' too. Please tell them to bring the children up if they're awake. They'll enjoy this too."

As the five aircraft roared overhead, those on deck waved furiously, their yelling and cheering reflecting the strong sense of relief at being once again in the company of their protective escort.

Two hours later, the Isles of Scilly appeared on the horizon and Tremayne ordered the six German prisoners to be blindfolded and brought up on deck from their cramped quarters.

Throughout the final stages of their return journey, the three Hurricanes from Flight RAF St Mary's and the Beaufighters from Cornwall had constantly circled and traversed the tiny fishing boat.

Approaching St Mary's, Tremayne checked his charts in the wheelhouse and said, "The tide's in Cox'n. Take us in, half revolutions, through The Road, with Samson to port and directly up to Braiden Rock."

"Aye aye sir. Been quite a trip sir, so it has."

"By God, you can say that again, Cox'n," grinned Tremayne.

Moving through Tresco Flats with first Appletree Point and then HMS Godolphin to starboard, Tremayne ordered: "Hands fall in for entering harbour."

Seeing the broad grin still on Willoughby-Brown's face, he said, "Number One, fall in the prisoners as well. Let's do this in style, with 'bags of swank' as the Royal Marines would say. Oh, and Number One, you and Sub can hold up the Kriegsmarine flag on display as we pass Godolphin!"

Moments later, the First Lieutenant called the hands, lined up on deck, to attention.

Then, turning to the line of six blindfolded prisoners ordered: "Kriegsgefängener! Habt's Acht. Stillgestanden!" As one, the Germans came smartly to attention alongside their captors.

As they passed close to Godolphin, their trophies proudly displayed, they heard Enever's unmistakable voice call for: "Three cheers for the *Monique*."

Tremayne returned the salute of some half a dozen officers and over thirty POs, ratings and Wrens who had turned out to welcome them back.

He searched the line of figures now waving and cheering and then, among the excited faces, he saw her.

Tremayne raised his hat, with a broad grin, and Emma, smiling, waved back.

Operation Marie-Claire was over. Mission accomplished.

Six

Some leave due

Monique's homecoming was memorable. Tremayne felt a great sense of elation, despite his lack of sleep, as the small fishing boat sailed into New Grimsby harbour. Taking Emma, and about half a dozen of their colleagues, Lieutenant Commander Enever rushed down the steep track to Braiden Rock to meet Tremayne, his crew and his guests, as they secured alongside the rocky makeshift jetty.

Like an enthusiastic schoolboy, Enever could scarcely contain himself as he pumped Tremayne's hand.

"My dear boy, you actually *sank* an E-boat with an unarmed fishing vessel. This is surely naval history!" Tremayne grinned back, somewhat overwhelmed by Enever's effusive welcome, yet overjoyed to be back home after the savagery of the firefight aboard the German E-boat.

"And you brought us these guests, despite a journey that makes the voyage of the Argonaut look positively uneventful in comparison!" Enever turned to welcome the Duhamels and Colonel Harberer. Speaking in fluent, animated French, he guided them up the rocky track from the anchorage to the pathway and an escort party, detailed to take their luggage and guide them to Godolphin.

Returning to Tremayne, he beamed as he said, "Splendid, Richard, absolutely splendid!"

"Thank you sir. It wasn't that spectacular, really. We did have some luck on our side," responded Tremayne, looking somewhat bemused by Enever's enthusiasm as the latter took his arm and walked the cluttered deck of the fishing vessel, still talking excitedly.

"The E-boat captain's fatal mistake was to secure alongside us, sir. Had he continued to stand off while he put a boarding party onto us from one of his dinghies, his forrard armament alone could have blown us right out of the water at the first sign of trouble. All we did, sir, was to take advantage of his bad decision and exploit the consequences before he could recover the situation."

"Richard, you're too modest, but thank you for what you and your crew have achieved. It was an impressive performance. Well done, too, for bringing in those prisoners – they are a real bonus." Enever stopped and turned to face Tremayne, his voice more concerned and serious.

"We are very interested to know just what *is* going on, on the Ile d'Ouessant.

Something is certainly afoot there, I'm absolutely convinced, which could explain why the E-boat intercepted you so quickly while you were making your way through the Passage du Fromveur. Both SIS and SOE want to question these chaps you brought back to see just what they know. My guess is, Richard, that we'll be called upon to mount an operation to the island sooner rather than later.

"What reports we do have from members of the Confrèrie about the Ile d'Ouessant have been rather vague and mostly supposition, I feel, and generally lacking in worthwhile detail. They've been generally conjectural, rather than factual, but building up the jigsaw puzzle, from seemingly unrelated scraps of information, suggests that a major reconnaissance operation must be on the cards."

"Will that be undertaken by MGBs rather than fishing boats to give us the necessary firepower, sir?" asked Tremayne.

"Possibly, but until we know the form, I'm going to keep my options open. In either case, adequate support from the RAF will be crucial."

"That *is* a critical issue, sir." Tremayne hesitated, before continuing. "In my second signal to you, sir, I indicated that we had a badly wounded crew member, Leading Seaman Nicholls and, as a matter of urgency, sir, I should like to. . ." Enever cut in, smiling.

"It's all in hand, Richard. That harbour defence launch behind you is taking him to St Mary's hospital for immediate treatment and then he will be flown to RNB Devonport, to our own hospital, where he will receive the best of care.

I will personally maintain tabs on his progress for you and keep you in the picture."

A discreet cough behind him made Enever turn around. "Oh. Good Lord, yes. Thank you, Emma. Yes, I want to hold an officers' debriefing with you, your First Lieutenant and young Quilghini as soon as possible, today, on Operation Marie-Claire. Commander Rawlings will also be present."

Enever's eyes moved heavenwards in mock despair, as Tremayne smiled in response.

"He wants to know how the operational aspects of the rescue went, so be prepared to give him chapter and verse on the logistics, routines and procedures. It's now 10.40 hours. Debriefing will be at 14.00 hours and will take place, as usual, in room 101."

As if on cue, Emma stepped forward. "Richard, you and I need to spend about an hour before the debriefing, checking the sequence of events and particularly the timings. Commander Rawlings, as you know, is a stickler for detail." Her eyes similarly rolled upwards in mock dismay.

"Absolutely, Emma," said Enever, joining in the laughter, "and I'll leave you two to go through things so that, hopefully, the debriefing will run smoothly. Incidentally Richard, the Duhamels and Colonel Harberer will be taken by the motor launch to meet Rear Admiral Hembury at the Helford Base and thence, by car, to London for detailed debriefing with our friends from SIS and SOE and an update on the latest state of the Confrèrie and the extent to which it has been infiltrated by the Abwehr. You and your crew have done a first class job. Operation Marie-Claire has been an unqualified success. I will send my report to that effect to the Admiral. He will be absolutely delighted, I know."

Returning Tremayne's salute, Enever strode off back to

Godolphin, taking his team with him – apart from Emma Fraser.

Touching Tremayne's arm, she said softly, "I'm so glad you're back safely, Richard. We were all so relieved to receive your signal after what seemed an interminable radio silence. Hermann Fischer was with us when the message came through about the E-boat. He let out one almighty 'fanbloodytastic' and slapped a shocked Commander Rawlings on the back!"

Tremayne roared with laughter. "If Hermann is court-marshalled, I hope I shall be called upon to be his defending officer – we'll have a whale of a time, in front of all those stuffed shirts. Tell me, Emma, whatever did Rawlings do?"

"Well, first there was a stunned silence and the Commander went very white. Then he turned a bright red. What we thought would be an uncontrolled explosion dissolved into spluttering incoherence, punctuated by several 'whats?', before he stormed out of the room!"

"Wonderful stuff – worth a guinea a minute," said Tremayne, still beside himself with laughter. "Poor Rawlings. He sounds like a candidate for Apoplectics Anonymous."

"Well, at least he will have calmed down and reverted to his usual petulant self by the time you go to see him. All of which reminds me Richard, when may *I* have my wicked way with you?"

The blue eyes teased him gently and, for a moment, Tremayne found himself lost for words.

"How can I possibly resist such a request?" He laughed, then in a more serious mood, replied, "I feel rather like a walking compost heap at the moment. Let me go back to the wardroom, shower and change and then let's go up to the New Inn and discuss the operation over some coffee."

"Sounds good to me Richard, and we can talk now as we walk back to Godolphin together."

Deep in conversation with Emma, Tremayne began to realise just what impact the events of the previous night had had on him.

Quick to pick up on his overriding concern for Nicholls, Emma let him talk through his impressions of the operation and the range of feelings that he had experienced with their changing fortunes throughout 'Marie-Claire'.

She recognised that if he talked out his experiences so soon after the operation, he would find it easier to focus on the operational data and intelligence that Rawlings and Enever would expect from him later in the day.

Arriving back at HMS Godolphin, Tremayne suddenly said, "Heavens, Emma, I've been so selfish demanding your attention, and not once have I asked you how you are and what you've been doing for your part in the operation. I'm becoming so damned self-centred as to be downright boring; I apologise."

"Richard, I've not had to face E-boats, Condors or German destroyers. I've not been in a firefight looking death in the face. For goodness sake, listening to you *is* part of my job. Anyway, I care about you and if talking together helps at all, then I want to do that. I hope that you realise that you also help me when you listen to my concerns. So, stop being difficult, go and have your shower and I'll see you in the entrance lobby in twenty minutes sharp. Don't be adrift Tremayne. What?"

Tremayne laughed as he exaggeratedly came to attention and saluted, "Aye, aye, Ma'am!"

Opening his cabin door, he was given a rapturous welcome by Bertie who brought him his Number One cap, carrying it in his mouth and wagging his tail furiously.

"Bertie old fellow, what *would* I do without you and Emma. You two are becoming my sheet anchors." As he said that, the thought suddenly hit him that throughout Operation Marie-Claire – even during the quiet moments in the small hours – Diana had hardly crossed his thoughts. He could not recall touching her photograph in his duffel coat pocket when he had put it on, over his fisherman's clothes, for the return to Tresco.

"What the hell is happening, Bertie? Am I forgetting my wife after only fifteen months? Well old fellow, at least you are keeping me focused on the here and now… and so, too, is she, thank God." Tremayne smiled to himself as he thought of Emma's gentle practicality and sensitivity. He reflected on how glad he had been to see her – the one face he had really wanted to see – as *Monique* glided past the cheering crowd outside Godolphin.

Changed out of his makeshift Breton rig and back in uniform, Tremayne met Emma in the lobby and they began their walk to the New Inn for their preparation for the afternoon's debriefing meeting.

They were greeted at the door by Dick Oyler's wife, Aileen; a large, welcoming woman of instant warmth and friendliness. While Dick's family had lived on Tresco for generations, Aileen came from the village of Kilmoganny in the rolling hill country and farmland of County Kilkenny, close to the border with County

Tipperary, and had settled on the island some fifteen years earlier when she and Dick married.

"Sure, and you're looking fine, the both of you. Sit down and we'll have coffee for you in two shakes." She quickly found Tremayne and Emma a quiet corner in the bar where they began working immediately. Emma skilfully identified and then drew together the key threads of Operation Marie-Claire from Tremayne's responses to her questions, gradually building up a coherent sequence of events from start to finish.

Essentially a rehearsal for his forthcoming debriefing with Rawlings, Enever and, it now transpired, senior representatives from SOE and SIS, Tremayne already began to feel better prepared for the afternoon meeting.

While some things stood out in sharp relief in his memory – because of the intensity and vividness of the particular experience – other aspects of 'Marie-Claire' were almost a blur.

"Both recency and the sheer violence of some of your experiences can get in the way of perspective and context," said Emma. "It'll take some time for the operation to fall into place in your mind, which is precisely why we wanted to work through things before you face what could be a pretty rigorous interrogation – especially from our two senior visitors. Both are Colonels. The SIS officer is primarily an Intelligence Corps Specialist who has served, under cover, in France and elsewhere in occupied Europe – more or less since the early days of the 'phoney war' in 1940. The Colonel from the SOE was evacuated at Dunkirk and, after operating for some time behind enemy lines during the retreat, he began to build up contacts with French

Resistance groups which he subsequently extended after he returned to England."

"Emma, that's been immensely helpful; thank you for your time and patience. Some of my responses must have sounded like those of a drunken sleepwalker." Tremayne smiled as he looked up from the copious notes he had been taking.

"You're absolutely right about the need to untangle my thoughts and recall of events. The most vivid recollections are not just exploding grenades, or ill-intentioned hot metal flying past my ears, but also some of the things that people said to me, or did, in the heat of action. Now, they would seem utterly inconsequential to Rawlings and the Colonels but, at the time, they were so very significant and completely relevant. Lack of sleep, too, I think has distorted some memories and lent out-of-context importance to others."

"I'm sure, Richard, that after a good night's sleep, a lot of things will begin to fall into place for you. I do know that Hermann, Mike Taylor and Bob Bower are planning some pretty alcoholic celebrations in the wardroom tonight for you, WB and Pierre Quilghini, so be warned and have a good excuse for an early exit."

"Oh Lord!" Tremayne's rueful smile said it all.

"Pretty well the whole wardroom will be there – apart from those on duty watch. You're Godolphin's star hero, Richard."

"Right now, 'zombie' would be a far better description, but if they have to carry me out tonight, you'll know I did my best," laughed Tremayne.

The debriefing began promptly at 14.00 hours with, Tremayne was relieved to see, Enever in the chair. Clearly master of the situation, it was a different Enever from the usually gentle, empathetic "professor" that Tremayne was becoming accustomed to working with.

For once, Rawlings was relatively civil, obviously conscious of the two Army officers who matched him, rank for rank.

Colonel Jobling, the SIS officer, was, like Enever, a rather donnish academic who cleverly phrased his questions in such a way as to draw out the maximum relevant information from Tremayne.

Though softly spoken, Jobling possessed a razor sharp mind with the trained ability to probe, question and check, until he had the information he needed. Tall, grey-haired and slimly built, Tremayne saw him as a possible former professor of law, or jurisprudence, or perhaps a barrister, who had moved into military intelligence for the duration of the war.

By contrast, Colonel Farrell, the SOE officer, was much more an obvious professional soldier. Similarly tall, like Jobling, Farrell was of athletic build, balding, with a trim military moustache. His uniform insignia identified him as an officer from the Rifle Brigade and he wore the ribbon of the Military Cross.

The rapport between Farrell and Tremayne was instantaneous, born of instinctive mutual respect, without either really knowing much about the other.

The debriefing went well, the focus being not only on what had just occurred with Operation Marie-Claire, but also on the activities that were believed to be taking place on the Ile d'Ouessant.

Both Jobling and Farrell had more to add to the jigsaw, though each had only the most fragmentary information, apart from two critical observations.

The most significant facts to emerge were that RAF photographic reconnaissance had identified new buildings and large radio aerials, although the majority appeared to have been designed for receiving rather than transmitting.

Colonel Farrell's principal contribution was of equal concern. Two SOE agents, who had managed to drop by parachute onto the island, had noted a number of British MTBs and MGBs which, it was assumed, had been captured after Dunkirk.

The agents had reported that all of the vessels were of comparatively new appearance and no attempt had been made by the Germans to change their insignia, paintwork and pennant numbers to those of the Kriegsmarine Schnellboot flotillas.

"Hmm," said Enever. "Do we have a German Godolphin, gentlemen?"

"That is how we are beginning to read the situation," replied Colonel Jobling.

"Obviously Jerry monitors us, as we monitor his radio transmissions, but the size and number of aerials does suggest to us that they have built a major listening post on the Ile d'Ouessant. The few transmission aerials are quite enormous and could be used for sending signals to the many U-boat 'wolf packs' operating in the Western Approaches."

"It looks, then," said Farrell, "as if Jerry has not only built himself a major intelligence gathering unit there, but also a base for offensive and maybe clandestine operations."

"Presumably gentlemen, neither E-boats nor U-boats have been seen there in great numbers – only those acting as watchdogs?"

"Absolutely so, but a few Arado reconnaissance floatplanes have been spotted close to the new radio station." It was Jobling who answered Enever's question first.

"At this point," Tremayne asked, "what is the nature of the defences around not only the base, but the island as a whole, sir?"

"Good question, Tremayne," Farrell's response was crisp and to the point. "Finding the answer to that is, I believe, most likely going to be your next mission."

"Well, Richard, you joined us for the challenge and variety of operations I seem to recall," said Enever, his eyes twinkling over his spectacles.

"Getting a grip of the situation and finding out exactly what the Germans are up to on the Ile d'Ouessant should certainly meet some of your reasons for transferring to Special Forces, Tremayne," added Farrell with a smile. "Such an operation will be no walkover. Jerry is clearly on constant alert, covering every approach to the island with customary Teutonic thoroughness. We have to out-guile him in order to retain the initiative and element of surprise which are so critical in this operation."

At this juncture, Enever cut in: "We know that German radio traffic in the region has increased significantly during the last few days – and is continuing to do so. They are using a new code system, which our radio intercept cryptographers are in the process of breaking down and are already beginning to make some sense of. Once we receive a clearer picture from those communications boffins, we should then have a better idea of the purpose of the base and what our primary objectives are."

Enever removed his pipe and, leaning forward, paused to engage each person's attention before he continued.

"It seems to me gentlemen that, at this stage, our possible options are these. One, we land a large commando force sufficiently strong to fight its way through – and out of – any resistance offered by the garrison. Even under cover of darkness, such a sizeable force would be easily picked up by German radar. Given that we could put their radar out of action by air attack, prior to any assault, Jerry would soon get wind of an intended raid by a force of this size because of the difficult approaches to the island. An operation on this scale poses major exit, as well as entry, problems and constant full air cover would be absolutely vital."

Tremayne and the two Colonels nodded in agreement and Tremayne confirmed the strong sense of relief that he and his crew had felt when their air 'umbrella' made its appearance on their way home from Operation Marie-Claire.

"Secondly, and once again using cover of darkness appropriately, we could infiltrate a small, highly-trained team of specialists, say ten at the most, to undertake detailed surveillance of installations and defences. Such a group could also selectively destroy targets by delayed explosions. Well-armed, a team of this size stands a good chance of fighting its way out of local trouble and making its escape." Enever slowly and meticulously cleaned out his pipe, to let this particular option sink in, before continuing.

"Primarily, gentlemen, we're after vital information – not a major set-piece battle, although destruction of such a location is a very attractive option, especially if in so doing we can substantially delay likely reconstruction. A third option is to mount a major air raid and blow the base and its installations to smithereens."

Enever looked expectantly at both Colonels as he quietly filled his pipe with studied concentration and then asked, "What do you think, gentlemen? Which strategy, in your opinion, has the greatest chance of success?"

"Well, I know which option I'd go for John," Farrell responded in his characteristically clipped manner, "but I'm intrigued to hear what young Tremayne thinks. He's the only one who has seen the Ile d'Ouessant and the adjacent islands at close quarters. What do you think, Leslie?"

Jobling glanced briefly at Tremayne and then turned back to Farrell.

"I take your point, Charles. Lieutenant Tremayne has actually been there and no doubt has developed a sailor's eye for the sea, the coast and the general lie of the land. I agree with you. Let's hear his view, before we make our decision and recommendation to Rear Admiral Hembury."

"Right, Richard, the floor is yours." Enever smiled encouragingly and clamped the as yet unlit pipe firmly between his teeth, while Rawlings cleared his throat somewhat theatrically and glared at Tremayne, annoyed that his opinion, as senior naval officer present, had not been sought.

Tremayne began. "My impression of the area is that it is swarming with Germans. French Resistance, I imagine, has therefore had little opportunity to set up anything for us, so we will be starting from scratch. The fear of reprisals may also have inhibited them somewhat, because punitive measures could so easily be taken against villagers there without the actions becoming general public knowledge for some considerable time. I assume, sir," Tremayne looked directly at Enever, "that your options will also have been based on that premise?"

"Quite so, Richard. Whichever course of action we decide upon must make it clear, beyond doubt, to the German authorities that it was an entirely British operation."

Tremayne continued, "Then, gentlemen, the option which I believe has the best chance of success is number two – a raid by a small group of well-led, highly-trained specialists. It is far easier to conceal and extract small teams. It is also much simpler to mobilise and co-ordinate the activities of such a group, especially at night, in terms of timing and sequence of actions."

Farrell responded immediately. "Thank you, Tremayne, that is largely how I would see such an operation being conducted with the greatest chances of success. What say you, Leslie? Do you think that Tremayne and I have read the situation correctly?"

"Yes, Charles, option two fits in closely with current SIS thinking and is probably the best way to obtain the information we so urgently need about German intentions and activities on the Ile d'Ouessant.

"I am very wary of going for option one especially, as has already been said, in view of the high risk of large numbers of Allied casualties. We still need far more experience of combined operations and inter-service collaboration, before we are able to mount a large-scale commando assault with any reasonable assurance of success.

"Option three concerns me greatly because of the likelihood of heavy casualties among French civilian workers on the base, as well as among innocent people living in the villages close to the installations. In any case, an air raid of such proportions may destroy everything, but we are still left with supposition about Jerry's intentions – not detailed field intelligence."

"So, gentlemen, option two is the one we propose, with the strongest of recommendations, to Rear Admiral Hembury."

With Farrell's customary brief conclusion, the meeting broke up – after Enever's welcome news that, apart from the duty watch, Godolphin was about to enjoy a seventy-two hour long weekend leave.

Tremayne turned to Willoughby-Brown and Quilghini. "Number One, Sub, as soon as I receive orders, or further news, from Lieutenant Commander Enever, I will brief you both. We will then work out, together, the necessary operational details for whatever our role is to be. Until we meet for breakfast on Monday morning, I wish you both a very enjoyable and well-deserved leave."

Tremayne returned to his cabin, dreading the thought of the wardroom revelries planned in his honour for that evening.

The next morning, after a dining-in night which was not nearly as awful as he had anticipated, Tremayne, together with his dog, boarded one of the inter-island launches, acting as 'liberty-boats', for the neighbouring island of St Martin's.

Because of the state of the tide, the boatman landed Tremayne – and the six ratings accompanying him as fellow passengers – at Higher Town quay, close to Cruther's Point and with the spectacular expanse of Parr Beach stretching away as far as English Island Point.

"We'll be returning from Lower Town quay – not from here – at four o'clock sharp. If you miss it, you'll be swimming back lads," called the boatman as Tremayne and the others stepped ashore and began to go their separate ways. With Cruther's Hill and its Bronze Age graves on his left, Tremayne climbed the steep hill road leading from the harbour, passing the old cottages of Signal Row on his way to Higher Town. Principally consisting of a tiny Post Office, a collection of old stone houses and cottages, and a small tearoom, Higher Town was what Enever irreverently termed the 'Metrollops' of St Martin's.

Pausing at the top of Signal Row, Tremayne gazed out over the stunningly beautiful panorama before him. Encompassing the long golden sweep of Parr Beach, the turquoise sea and the cluster of small, rocky, bracken-covered islands which make up the Eastern Isles group – home to hundreds of grey seals – the breathtaking view held Tremayne's attention completely.

The gloriously clear air, the spectacular scenery with its rich variety of colours and tones, and the enveloping sense of peace, stopped Tremayne in his tracks and he simply let the beauty of the scene wash over him. Ruffling his dog's thick black fur, Tremayne said quietly, "This is certainly some place, Bertie, the like of which I've never seen elsewhere."

Then suddenly, as if to mock his new-found sense of wonder, another, terrible, image flashed across Tremayne's mind. It was the picture, partly buried in his subconscious, of a road destroyed beyond recognition, a pile of rubble and stacked bricks where a house once stood – and of hopes and plans shattered beyond repair. Momentarily, his composure gone, Tremayne felt again the grievous sense of loss that he had experienced four weeks before in Plymouth. Most distressing of all, when he tried to recall Diana's face in detail, he found that he was uncertain about exactly how some of her features looked. "Dear God, is this to haunt me and hound me for the rest of my life?"

Suddenly aware that he had spoken out loud and that a very anxious Bertie was licking his hand and looking up at him, Tremayne focused his attention once more on the beauty of the scene before him.

"Sorry, old fellow. Let's go and call on that tearoom and see what they can come up with for both of us."

The owner, Mary Bond, a mine of information on the history of the islands, soon restored Tremayne's sense of the present and its immediate realities with her easy, informed conversation and observations on the Isles of Scilly and their recent history. She described in amusing detail the trials of running a catering business with wartime rationing and how simple barter had become a practical islander antidote to what she saw as the 'unpatriotic' black market commerce on the mainland.

After his welcome break, he took his leave of Mary Bond and her tearoom and set off again. Tremayne made his way northwards across the island to the curious red and white conical stone Daymark – a seventeenth-century structure which had served as a warning marker for countless seafarers of earlier generations.

Close by, Tremayne explored the remains of the signal station from the Napoleonic period and found himself reflecting on a different era of seamanship and naval warfare – and yet one with comparable dangers to those that he had just experienced.

The rest of his visit was spent wandering over the small paths that intersect the island and which took him over contrasting heather-covered heathland and the more cultivated flower growing areas which make up the south of St Martin's with its views towards neighbouring Tresco and St Mary's.

Eventually, he made his way onto the road – with its charming cottages and pretty gardens filled with brightly coloured lilies, agapanthus, fuschias, Livingstone daisies and so many other flowers – leading down to Lower Town quay and the launch for Tresco.

The tides favoured a return to Old Grimsby quay and, after landing, Tremayne walked across the island, through Dolphin Town and back to the naval base.

On the tiny polished wooden table in his cabin was a sealed OHMS envelope with his name typewritten across the front.

"Hmm, Bertie, I hope this doesn't mean that our precious leave together has been cancelled," murmured Tremayne, as he turned over the envelope and lifted the flap. Anticipating the worst, he opened the enclosed folded letter.

"It's an invitation to a picnic and you're invited, too, old fellow." Tremayne smiled as he read the hand-written note:

My dear Richard,

With much questionable wheedling and cajoling, Lucy Caswell and I have extracted some rare delicacies from the ship's cook and Lieut Commander Enever has donated a couple of bottles of Admiral Hembury's splendid wine.

On the strength of this, we've planned a picnic lunch on Gun Hill for tomorrow.

WB has accepted Lucy's invitation with his customary unbridled enthusiasm for the good life and I do hope that you (and, of course, Bertie!) are able to come too.

Suggest we meet at 19.00 hours in the bar at the New Inn this evening to discuss — if you are free.

Ever yours,

Emma

Tremayne occupied himself with some necessary administrative work, changing into casual civilian clothes and enjoying the luxury of a hot bath before he left HMS Godolphin for his invitation to supper.

Emma, Lucy and WB were already at the New Inn, chatting to Aileen and Dick Oyler when Tremayne arrived. He ordered a round of drinks and joined his colleagues.

"What a lovely idea, Emma. Thank you for inviting me — a picnic on this lovely island sounds marvellous. Please count me in."

"I'm so pleased that you've said yes, otherwise WB would have ended up carrying two rucksacks full of groundsheets, plates, cups, food, wine and cutlery! I managed to persuade the 'Royals' to part with two of their rucksacks temporarily, but it does mean a bit of a forced march to the other end of the island."

"Ah ha, now I see why you wanted me to come along. It was nothing to do with my charm, scintillating conversation and unbelievably dashing good looks — you just needed another packhorse," laughed Tremayne.

"Well, since you put it like that — then, yes!" responded Emma, as the four of them started to make their selections from the Oylers' supper menu.

The following morning, shortly after ten o'clock, Emma Fraser's picnic party set out from Godolphin, following the rocky coastal path via Braiden Rock and Frenchman's Point, up as far as the forbidding stony sentinel of Cromwell's Castle — the cleverly sited Civil War guardian of New Grimsby Sound.

Lively conversation, punctuated by frequent bursts of laughter, set the happy tone of the quartet's trek, as they moved up the heather-covered hill to Castle Down and on to King Charles' Castle. This earlier and badly situated custodian of the channel between Tresco and its neighbour, Bryher, was, as Willoughby-Brown eloquently described it, "a somewhat useless, if dominating old ruin".

"Hmm, that's a rather apt description of Commander Rawlings," giggled Lucy amid laughter from the others.

Walking up past Gimble Point, over the dense, springy heather, the group stopped every so often to take in the 360-degree panorama. To their right lay the impressive rock formation of Men-a-Vaur, bursting intrusively out of the sea. Home to puffins, as well as many other seabirds, the huge rock was known to the locals as 'Men-o'-war' and, from certain angles, it did look like a ship in full sail. In front of the group, as they followed the meandering path, lay Round Island, with its lighthouse, and St Helen's, while further to their right, they could see St Martin's and as far as Great Ganinick, the most westerly of the Eastern Isles.

"To port, to use nautical parlance, we have Bryher and the Norrard Rocks and beyond, Mincarlo, Samson and, if I'm not mistaken, the bird sanctuary of Annet," intoned Willoughby-Brown with mock pomposity.

"Well done, David," said Tremayne. "Your knowledge of local geography, if not your respect for old relics, has improved beyond all hope!"

"Please put in a good word for me with our formidable Cox'n, if you would Richard. He's convinced I couldn't navigate my way out of a paper bag – *so he is!*"

In a happy mood, the group reached Gun Hill and its weathered granite, set among a sea of heather, interspersed with tiny potentilla, gold, orange-flushed gorse and pink common centaury. Here and there, scattered among the seaward facing rocks, were clumps of pink thrift rosettes and stonecrop.

"You've picked a delightful spot for our picnic, Emma. It reaches all the senses, with the sun, the crashing waves below, the scent of flowers and that amazing spongy heather to walk over."

"Tregarthen Hill just over there," replied Emma pointing, "is the favourite picnic spot of so many, but this hill gives us an even more dramatic panorama, which is why Lucy and I chose it."

"It's just about as removed as it could be from the dismal, spray-drenched bridge of an MTB and standing freezing cold, hoping for a mug of 'Pablo' Watkins' steaming 'torpedo propellant'. I think that this is the closest to paradise that I've been for a long time," said Willoughby-Brown, as he unshouldered the rucksack and began laying out groundsheets, plates and glasses. "You and Lucy have done a marvellous job, organising this for us."

"Amen to that, David," added Tremayne, as he too emptied the rucksack that he had carried from Godolphin.

After lunch and more light-hearted banter, Willoughby-Brown and Lucy went off down the steep heather-covered slope to explore Cromwell's Castle and the jagged rocky foreshore, leaving Tremayne and Emma sitting, scanning the islands' seascape through a pair of RN binoculars.

"It's hard to believe that there is a war going on and that we are so involved in it, as we sit here surrounded by such peace and beauty," said Emma.

"It is. Yet over there," replied Tremayne, pointing, "just beyond the Western Rocks and that beautiful horizon, lie the U-boats' killing grounds. *HMS Portree*, my last ship, went down with dear Bill Mitchell somewhere out beyond that skyline. Before the *Portree,* Bill and I also served together, for a short time, in her sister ship *HMS Fleetwood* – 'the happiest ship in the Royal Navy' as she was called – and we became close friends. He was almost an elder brother to me, guiding me through the complexities of being an on-board naval officer, protecting me mostly from my own inexperience. I still feel his loss terribly.

"When you're caught up in events, as we are, the danger is that you come to see those as 'normality' and forget that there's so much more to life, beyond what we're experiencing right now. But I know now that what I once regarded as 'permanence' is not so and that, some day, I have to build a new normality – and that would certainly need to include a lot of days like this. This has been a real tonic." Tremayne suddenly stopped, aware of the seriousness registering in Emma's face as he talked.

"Forgive me, Emma, I'm becoming inexcusably 'heavy' and tedious. Let's have some more of that excellent coffee you poured before the others left."

"You're *not* tedious. Just remember that, in less than three years of this war, you've already experienced more tragedy, terror – and triumphs – than most people do in a whole lifetime. We both know, too, that there will be many more of all three of these before the war ends. But I'll take you up on your wish for more days like this, Richard! Let's raise our coffee cups and drink to another day here in another, better time and a return to this very same, beautiful spot!"

"That's a date Emma and, as a marker to show that the two of us were once here, give me a coin to go with this old sixpenny piece and we'll bury them together under that weathered, curious looking triangular rock just there."

"Och, and here's ma aine wee crookit bawbie, sir," laughed Emma as she handed Tremayne a well-worn and battered old penny, with a piece gouged out of its edge. For a moment, Tremayne stopped and looked at Emma.

"Good heavens! My mother used to sing a very beautiful old Scottish song about a 'crookit bawbie' when I was a child. I remember the words were very moving and the melody was lovely."

"Yes, it *is* a beautiful song," said Emma. "I know it well. It's about a love that develops between two very young people, but becomes lost when they move apart, and is then re-kindled when they meet up, by chance, in later years. Perhaps, Richard, some day you might, to quote that song – 'gang wi' me tae bonny Glen Shee' – who knows?"

Emma paused, conscious that Tremayne was regarding her intently. "I believe, Emma, that one day I will."

In this latest exchange, both were noticeably more relaxed and at ease with the growing closeness between them.

A sudden burst of laughter announced the return of Willoughby-Brown and Lucy from the castle and shore below.

"With a bit of imagination y'know, Richard, we could transform Cromwell's Castle into a very passable 'stone frigate'. There's so much potential storage space there for boats' kit, fuel, ammunition and spares and it would also make a wonderful flak tower to warn off any snooping Ju88s or Heinkels. We really ought to make the old building earn its keep!"

Tremayne laughed. "I can just see the newspaper headlines, David: ' *RNVR Officer succeeds where van Tromp and the Dutch fleet failed. Utter desecration of a treasured English monument*'."

They then set about clearing away the remains of their picnic and, afterwards, slowly walked back to HMS Godolphin over Castle Down, talking animatedly and laughing together all the way.

That night they dined as a foursome at the New Inn but then, as before, split into two couples after their supper together. Willoughby-Brown and Lucy left to wander along the many sandy beaches on the east of the island. Even by ten o'clock, the cloudless June sky still provided enough light to see for miles and Emma and Tremayne strolled down to Appletree Bay and the long stretch of beach there.

Sitting beside Emma on the sand, Tremayne took her hand and said, "This has been a marvellous and memorable day – I've enjoyed it beyond measure. Thank you Emma."

"In such uncertain times, days like this – and the memories they can create – represent something of the sanity that we all need in the midst of all the madness that comes with war." Emma paused as she began to reflect upon what she had just said.

"Richard, we both love these wonderful islands and, like me, you also enjoy sailing from what you've told me. Sid Christopher has lent me his dinghy for tomorrow, the last twenty-four hours of our leave. I was planning to sail around and explore the Eastern Isles and then, if time and the weather allow, go on to look at St Helen's and the puffins on Men-a-Vaur. Why don't you come with me? Monday and the damned war will come round again soon enough. Why don't we just make the most of the time we still have?"

Conscious of the momentary hesitation before he said, "Yes Emma. I'd love to – and thank you," she asked, "No feelings of guilt Richard?"

"No," he answered, "this is something I really would like to do."

Emma reached out and touched Tremayne's arm. "The pain and sadness *will* take time to come to terms with – for both of us. But we have to move on. We're still young and we have lives to be lived – and we can help one another to cope with the terrible sense of loss that we each sometimes feel. So many things can unexpectedly trigger both painful and happy memories – that's only natural – but you and I can build some happy and unforgettable memories of our own. I would like to do that for us – but you must want to do that, too, Richard. I am conscious that there is a part of you which, understandably, is intensely private and where any intrusion would be unforgivable trespassing." The gentle blue eyes held his own as she talked. "Am I in forbidden territory already?" she asked.

Tremayne took both her hands in his. "No, dearest Emma. You never intrude, but you do help me a lot – and yours is help that I need; really need. I sometimes hesitate, or hold back, because I often feel that you do all the giving and I do all the taking. I want to spend the day with you tomorrow – that would be a privilege." Tremayne smiled and, conscious of a need to lighten the mood of their conversation, said enthusiastically, "Tell me about the boat you've managed to find here. What will we be sailing tomorrow?"

"She's not a class boat, as far as I can tell, and she was built here on Bryher. She is clinker-built, about twelve feet long and schooner-rigged – and we have her for the whole day."

"She sounds just right for these waters," said Tremayne. "This will be one leave I won't forget – or ever want to forget."

Aware of the gathering darkness, Tremayne glanced at his watch.

"Good 'eavens! It's long past the time when it's just not right and proper for a young lady to be keeping a sailor company what she 'ardly knows." With mock solemnity, Tremayne put on his 'strangled chief petty officer voice' with its 'irritable vowel condition', as he termed it.

Turning to Emma, he smiled. "Right, Cox'n, take us home.

Half revolutions – both engines. It's a beautiful night, let's not rush!"

Holding hands, they slowly walked back to Godolphin, conscious of the waves softly lapping the shore and the elusive fragrance of the island at night. At the entrance to the wardroom, Tremayne stopped and kissed Emma lightly on her cheek, sensitive to the spontaneity with which she had turned to him.

"Goodnight, dearest Emma. Let's meet for breakfast at half past eight and plan our day's sailing then."

Tremayne went to his cabin but found sleep difficult, his emotions in turmoil. Eventually, he did drop off but it was a disturbed, fitful sleep, with a confusion of dreams alternating with periods of wakefulness. Morning's arrival was something of a mixed blessing and Tremayne went to breakfast, guessing that Emma would be there already. She was and so, too, were a few other duty watch RNVR officers.

Mick Taylor's friendly reserve provided the quiet, socially undemanding start to the day that Tremayne needed.

After checking the map that Emma had brought to breakfast, they slipped out of the wardroom and made their way down to the quay, where Sid Christopher had moored his dinghy.

"Oh, she is a little beauty! Her varnish and rigging look almost brand new. She looks to be a pretty sea-kindly boat, too," said Tremayne. "Let's try her out and see how she handles."

With life jackets on and provisions stowed in the tiny forrard locker, they hoisted the brick-red sails and quickly pushed off from the quay.

With St Martin's off the port bow they eventually reached

Great Ganinick, the nearest of the Eastern Isles. They skirted Little Ganinick and then sailed round to Great Arthur. Tremayne was entranced by the beautiful small sandy bays and little rocky coves, where so many grey seals lay basking in the morning sun. Tacking around Ragged Island, they set course for the dramatic rock of Menawethan at the outer edge of the Eastern Isles.

"They are beautiful islands and these are ideal waters – given the weather – for small boat sailing," said Tremayne. "Theirs is a very different beauty from that of the Hebrides, where the islands are much bigger. Have you sailed there too, Emma?"

"I've sailed around Coll and Tiree and also Colonsay with its glorious Kiloran Bay, but I've yet to sail among the beautiful Outer Hebrides. That, I think, would really be a fantastic experience. What about you?"

"I've sailed the waters around Eigg, Muck and Rhum, and they can be pretty terrifying in bad weather, but – given the right conditions – I'd also love to try the outer islands. Is that another date, Emma?"

"I think it could be! Oh, look, Richard, we have company!" Excitedly, Emma pointed to two sleek porpoises, which were snaking through the water close to their dinghy. "Aren't they a wonderful sight?"

"Something of a rare privilege," said Tremayne, "and what a benign, companionable presence they seem to have. It's as if they really want to make contact with us."

Having rounded Menawethan and the Innisvouls they headed for the empty and pretty sandy beach on Great Ganilly for lunch. In the bright midday sun, the shallow sea between the islands had taken on dramatic hues of turquoise and sapphire and – in other places – more intense shades of blue. Sailing through the many waving fronds of dark olive seaweed reaching up from among the rocks on the seabed, they beached the dinghy and stretched out on the warm sand.

"These islands are absolute gems and what I think we ought to do is persuade the 'Royals' to lend us one of their two-man cockleshells and come canoeing round here when we next have some leave. How about that for another date, Emma!"

"Have a sandwich – and stop making improper suggestions to a young lady," laughed Emma. "But yes, paddling to somewhere like Little Ganilly or Nonour with their pretty little beaches would be great fun. It's a date, Richard!"

"You know, Emma, looking out over the Hanjague and those other little islands over there – and in this glorious sun – we could be castaways on some remote Pacific island. Even cook's bully-beef sandwiches are something of an exotic experience in these surroundings."

"Just wait and see what we have to follow – a couple of real 'Nelson slices' from the NAAFI!"

"Oh Lord," said Tremayne in mock horror, "I've managed to escape those glutinous wedges ever since I was a cadet – until now. How could you?!"

Their happy and relaxed lunch over, they made ready to set sail again.

"Richard, John Enever wants to see me at eight o'clock this evening to confirm my promotion and to discuss a letter he has for me."

"My warmest congratulations, Emma." Tremayne kissed her on her cheek. "This is great news and so well deserved. Let's raise a glass to that, tonight at the New Inn!"

"That would be lovely. Look, the weather's holding. Let's go for Men-a-Vaur, St Helen's and —". Tremayne interrupted, laughing, "…and any other islands that happen to get in the way!"

They pushed off from the beach into the incoming tide and set off for the north coast of St Martin's. Sailing past St Martin's Head they reached White Island and then headed for Round Island with its Victorian lighthouse. With St Helen's to port, they sailed close to the imposing rocky mass of Men-a-Vaur and it was an excited Emma who was first to see the nesting puffins, perched on the steep rock face towering over them. By early evening they were back at Tresco, tying up Sid Christopher's dinghy at New Grimsby's jetty.

"Let's hear about your promotion, Emma and see what John Enever has to tell you. I think I'm as excited about it as you are!"

As they entered Godolphin's main door, an unusually serious Enever came over to them and handed Emma an official-looking Admiralty envelope.

"Emma, you've earned this promotion and, in my opinion, it is long overdue. My congratulations! You have worked so hard for us and deserve this. There is a letter for you, too. Please read it now."

He looked at Tremayne and said, almost inaudibly, "I'm so sorry, dear boy. This infernal, damned war — it beggars belief."

A puzzled Tremayne looked questioningly at Enever and then at Emma as she carefully opened the envelope.

He saw her suddenly turn white as she looked up at him, her eyes full of tears.

"Oh! No! Richard, I've been seconded to SIS in London, on promotion, as Naval Intelligence Liaison Officer – with effect from tomorrow. I have to leave by motor launch for Penzance at 05.00"...

Seven

Reconnaissance or raid?

For a moment, Tremayne and Emma stood in shocked silence. Enever, sensitive as ever to the situation, said quietly, "I'll leave you both – you probably have a lot to talk about. If you do need to discuss your new appointment Emma, I'll be in my office until nine o'clock, but a thorough briefing has been planned for you in London tomorrow night. Goodnight to both of you and good luck, Emma, we will all miss you terribly – you've been a marvellous colleague."

"Goodnight sir and thank you." Tremayne was the first to react, aware that he was thanking Enever on behalf of Emma, who was trying to fight back her tears. The significance of Tremayne's immediate response was not lost on someone as aware of others and their reactions as Enever.

"I think," said Tremayne gently, "that we both need that drink we promised ourselves. Let's slip up to the New Inn but not stay too long – you need time for yourself tonight. I will though – unless you tell me otherwise – come down to the quay with you tomorrow, Emma."

With the ship's company still away making the most of their leave, the bar at the inn was deserted, apart from two locals who nodded briefly as Tremayne and Emma walked in.

Preoccupied with their own thoughts and feelings, each found it difficult to speak. Once again, it was Tremayne who reacted first. Taking Emma's hands in his, he said, "This is *not* the end Emma. We *will* see each other again, I promise you. As soon as I have leave again, I'll come up to London – or we'll meet somewhere else, away from town. This wonderful weekend makes a separation – however temporary – even more painful. I ..."

Emma interrupted him. "My head told me that such a weekend couldn't last for ever, but my heart wanted it to. I was so happy. It's as simple as that – however unrealistic and childish that might seem. I think I might say things to you, Richard, which I don't believe you are ready to hear just yet if we sit together much longer. So let's please just drink up and go back. I have a lot of packing to do and some thoughts to get straightened out before five o'clock tomorrow. Please don't come to the quay with me in the morning – I just couldn't handle it. Please try to understand that."

"Emma, I do understand and I believe I would probably feel the same. I'm going to miss you desperately. In the last three months you've come to mean so much to me. You're part of my life now." Seeing her tears beginning to start again, he gave her his clean handkerchief and said softly, "Come on, we'll go back now."

Tremayne found it hard to believe that only an hour ago they had been so happy in each other's company, relaxed and laughing – and now this...

They reached Godolphin having hardly said a word – each engulfed in their own feelings.

In the deep shadows created by what served as the Master-at-Arms' gatehouse, Emma stopped and quickly turned. "Richard, hold me. Hold me close." Tremayne felt her shaking as the tears poured down her face. Suddenly she stopped as Tremayne gently stroked her soft hair and, lifting her face to him, she kissed him on the lips. "Please don't forget me Richard." And then she was gone.

"Dearest Emma, I can never forget you. I've passed the point of no return. There's no going back now," murmured Tremayne, but he was probably the only one who heard the words...

The next day began with a boat captains' briefing which first lieutenants also attended. Commander Rawlings took the floor, ready as ever to assert his authority and position of command. As self-important and unsubtle as ever, he opened the meeting with customary pomposity: "A major operation is imminent, but I'm not yet at liberty to disclose details of it to you. It is still top secret and therefore restricted to senior officers only."

"Puffed up old fart. He wouldn't know a bloody secret if one fell on him," whispered Hermann Fischer to Tremayne. The baleful, humourless pale eyes swung round to Hermann. "Fischer, is there something that you wish to share with the rest of us? Although I hardly think that you, of all people, would have anything significant to contribute to this briefing."

"Thank you for the invitation, sir. That was most kind. But no sir, I've mislaid my pencil and wondered if Lieutenant Tremayne had a spare, sir. I was very keen to take some notes, sir."

"As we say in the pukkah Navy, Fischer, ' Really Never Very Ready'. What?"

Rawlings positively beamed at what he assumed was an outburst of appreciative laughter from the meeting for his laboured humour, but which, in reality, was spontaneous, universal and amused approval for Hermann's irreverent sarcasm. Most of the officers present held RNVR — not RN — commissions and resented Rawlings' frequently expressed insult about the naval volunteer reserve.

Rawlings droned on for what seemed an interminable period before, thankfully, he handed over to Lieutenant Commander Enever.

"Gentlemen, to summarise Commander Rawlings' debrief, our preparation and training programme will last four weeks, based here, in the Isles of Scilly. One: we will undergo intensive seagoing exercises in infiltration, and also escape and evasion. Two: we will develop a far higher capability in aggressive close engagement of enemy coastal forces and aircraft. Three: we will significantly improve our coastal surveillance capability. Four: we will develop far closer and more effective co-ordination between the various participating armed services — I don't need to remind you that Rear Admiral Lord Louis Mountbatten's recent appointment, as Chief of Combined Operations, underscores that critical need. Five: we will further develop our ability to operate under cover and clandestinely *on land* in support of surveillance, reconnaissance and demolition teams.

"Since the forthcoming operation is still being planned and, as yet, no final decision has been made as to which vessels will be used on the day, training will involve both MGBs and converted Breton fishing boats. This will ensure that everyone has the maximum opportunity possible to gain much-needed experience – and the necessary specialist boat-handling skills.

"Success in operations of the kind we are planning depends upon physical fitness, skill, determination and high self-belief. Those are the qualities we shall be developing, along with teamwork and inter-team co-ordination over the next four weeks."

Pre-empting any interruption from Rawlings, Enever quickly asked, "Are there any questions, gentlemen?" The audience was grateful for the clear succinct summary that Enever had provided after Rawlings' rambling and frequently self-promoting rant. What questions there were, tended to be mostly boat-specific and so were quickly dealt with by Enever.

Rawlings, anxious to regain central prominence, stepped in to take command once again. "All boat captains and crews will report to their vessels at Braiden Rock anchorage at 12.00 hours, ready to sail by 12.20 hours. Sealed orders will be given to boat captains at 12.00 hours, on board. Is that clear?" The general response of indifferent, eye-avoiding silence, prompted Rawlings to repeat the question in a more provocative and personal form: "Have I made myself plain – even to you, Fischer? What?"

"Oh most certainly sir – very plain. Lieutenant Commander Enever made it all abundantly clear, thank you sir." Laughter erupted once again at Hermann's refusal to be publicly bullied or belittled by Rawlings. Unsure as to why people should laugh at this point, Rawlings exited the room in as noisily a self-important manner as he could muster. As Rawlings left, Tremayne muttered to Fischer, "Hmm, Hermann, every village has one!"

Enever assumed command of the briefing once more and relaxed attentiveness took over immediately from fidgety boredom.

"Your praise was far too generous, Lieutenant Fischer – I'm flattered," he began, among more laughter. "You will need the rest of the forenoon watch, gentlemen, to brief your crews and get everyone on board – in several senses of the term. I cannot stress highly enough the importance of building self-belief and self-confidence – as the bedrock of both determination and capability – in what we shall be undertaking. Work on those issues as much as you can – you're going to have to depend upon them. And remember gentlemen, your crew's self-confidence rises to the level of *your* demonstrated belief in them. You lead – they follow. But most of all, they follow the example *you* set and that applies as much to training as it does to action. You've heard it before, no doubt, but remember Marshal Suvorov's dictum on preparation for war – 'Hard on the parade ground – easy in battle'. Now, before you escape back to your boat crews and today's exercise, I have two important announcements. First, gentlemen, I should like to introduce you to Second Officer Jane Topping."

At this point, a young, smartly turned out Wren officer stepped forward from where she had been sitting at the back of the room.

"Jane is taking over as an Intelligence Officer from Emma Fraser." An audible buzz went round the room. "So, welcome aboard Jane. Glad to have you with us. Any difficulties with this rough, uncouth lot, do let me know and they'll be clapped in irons."

This was greeted by laughter and cheering before the assembly settled down again.

"Second Officer Fraser has been seconded, on promotion, to SIS London as a naval liaison officer, which is an enormous – and richly deserved – feather in her cap. I shall miss her terribly," the sympathetic eyes held Tremayne's for a fleeting moment, "we all will. She has done an excellent job here. Her new appointment has been under wraps for some time and, for reasons of confidentiality, I was only allowed to disclose the details to her last night. Let us all wish her well in her new role."

Enever paused, a benign avuncular figure, looking around at the faces before him.

"Right, gentlemen, that is all. Thank you for you patience. To your boats – go!"

Tremayne, like the others, dashed off to collect his sea-going kit from his cabin and then quickly made his way to Braiden Rock and MGB 1315.

Tremayne's critical eye approvingly took in her freshly-painted hull and upper works, scrubbed decking and, most impressive of all, the new forrard six-pounder on its power mounting, as she gently rose and fell with the swell of the tide. Aft were new twin 20mm Oerlikons, while amidships, to the rear of the wheelhouse, were the port and starboard new twin 0.5" calibre Brownings in adapted Mark V armoured power mountings. Supplementing these, twin 0.303" Vickers machine guns had also been added to each side of the small armoured upper bridge.

The boat's refit had been thorough and Tremayne felt a fresh sense of pride in her as he stepped on board, to be greeted by a saluting Willoughby-Brown, as First Lieutenant, and Petty Officer Bill Irvine, his redoubtable Cox'n. After returning their 'pusser' parade ground salutes, Tremayne warmly shook hands with both.

"Number One, Cox'n, it's so good to be serving with you both again and it'll be interesting to see how much more we can develop as a crew over the next four weeks. I haven't seen our sealed orders yet, but my guess is that we're in for a pretty busy time."

Turning to Willoughby-Brown, he said, "Number One, take me through the new crew list, please, after the Cox'n and I have checked on his priorities."

To Irvine he simply asked, "As a start, are you happy with what you've seen so far, after her refurbishment?"

"Aye sir. She's looking very trim and smart as paint, sir, so she is. They've tidied up the wheelhouse a wee bit and there seems to be more space in there, sir. She looks just fine, sir, so she does. Er, if that's all, sir, I'll get things ready for the off."

"Yes, thank you Cox'n – of course. Carry on please."

Tremayne knew from experience how uncomfortable the taciturn Irvine was with conversations that extended beyond a few short sentences and he had quickly learned to be brief and respect the Cox'n's need for curtailed and relevant exchanges. In common with many from Northern Ireland, Petty Officer Irvine had a sharp and ready wit and his often unexpected, yet so very apt, turns of phrase would leave those around him helpless with laughter, frequently without even the trace of a smile on his own face. For his part, Irvine respected his boat captain's gentle courtesy and he was only too aware of the 'steel' that Tremayne's politeness masked. He'd smiled to himself, recalling one occasion when Tremayne had been reviewing his young, rather 'green' First Lieutenant's difficult encounter with an aggressive, insubordinate rating, with the words: "Remember, Number One, the most important lesson a gentleman learns is to know when to stop being one. Stay calm, be polite, but hit home – very hard – with few words. Watch your body movements as well, they can give away a lot about how confident – or otherwise – you may be feeling. Don't move back – either stand where you already are, or move forward *towards* the other person"…

As Tremayne and Willoughby-Brown began discussing preparations for the imminent exercise, Irvine noticed how closely they worked together and how, increasingly, the First Lieutenant was taking the initiative with suggestions and solutions.

Tremayne was glad to see so many of his former crew back with him and he had a personal word for each as they began to muster on board. Welcoming Leading Seaman Robson, a tall, lanky rating from Tyneside, as the replacement for 'Brummie' Nicholls, he then spoke to Able Seaman Watkins to find out how Nicholls was progressing.

"Fine, thank you sir. 'E's now safely in sickbay at Devonport, sir, moaning 'is 'ed off – which is a sure sign 'e's getting better sir."

"So, we should be seeing him soon, Watkins, I hope."

"As soon as 'e starts mekking a grab for Sister, they'll kick 'im out, sir, and *we'll* 'ave 'im back again!"

The First Lieutenant dismissed the assembled crew, after Tremayne's short welcoming address, in order to stow their kit and change into Number 8s – their working rig – with orders to return and fall in for briefing at 12.10 hours.

Tremayne, with the First Lieutenant, opened up his orders as soon as they arrived.

"Well Number One, today and tomorrow we're to defend ourselves against 'sudden attacks by low-flying aircraft'. They, Heaven help us, will be attacking us by dropping bags of flour, so that a measure of our anti-aircraft defensive strategy can be gauged by the number of white splodges on our boat!"

"Self-raising or plain, I wonder, sir?" queried Willoughby-Brown, his eyebrow expressively quizzical.

"That, Number One, is Commander Rawlings' top secret strategem. Apparently, we are to get our own back tomorrow when we shoot at target drogues, towed by aircraft coming in at varying heights above sea-level. Just in case you're thinking that revenge is sweet, I'll remind you, Number One, that firing on our own is a court-marshal offence – and Lieutenant Fischer would not make the best defending officer!"

Tremayne continued, on a less flippant note.

"For today's exercise there will be no Flotilla Commander,

so it's going to be a matter of independent action by individual boats. Tomorrow is different. I'm to resume as acting Flotilla Commander and the object of the exercise is to see how we can successfully mass and co-ordinate firepower, to destroy as many drogues as possible with minimal hits to ourselves. All four boats today are to assemble at 12.35 hours, two thousand yards due north of White Island. Lunch is ad hoc and alfresco and ration packs have been placed on board. I'll brief the crew and we slip moorings at 12.20 hours precisely."

As Irvine left the bridge to check charts in the wheelhouse, Tremayne turned to his First Lieutenant.

"David, unbelievably, this is the first opportunity we've had to discuss our leave and that marvellous picnic that Emma and Lucy organised for us. Did you enjoy the day too?"

"Absolutely, it was a great day. And the next day, while you and Emma went sailing, Lucy and I hired a small boat with an outboard and just enough rationed petrol to make the return trip to St Agnes, which is a marvellous place with wonderful views over the dreaded Western Rocks and Bishop Rock lighthouse. Lucy and I were just astounded by the news of Emma's sudden departure. It seems so grossly unfair to both of you."

"I think that what has happened just harshly emphasises the point, David, that all's fair in war, if not so in love. For both of us, the immediate answer seems to be to plunge ourselves into whatever the job on hand happens to be and to see one another at every possible opportunity. Ah, here they come. David. Call them to attention please, abaft the whaler, and I'll brief them in two minutes."

Tremayne swung himself down into the wheelhouse and said, "Cox'n. I'm just going to brief everyone on today's exercise. You know the score, but listen in please from the bridge."

Standing next to Willoughby-Brown, Tremayne spelled out the day's programme, amused by the number of audible "'kin'ells" that his briefing produced when he reached the point of mentioning the flour bombs.

At 12.20 hours precisely, all four motor gunboats slipped their moorings and headed up New Grimsby Sound, with crews stood to at defence stations. After passing the outlying rocks of Kettle Bottom, just north of Tresco, the flotilla set course to starboard for its appointed RV, two thousand yards due north of White Island. Already hove-to when they arrived, was an RAF air-sea rescue launch, her after perspex machine gun turret reflecting the glare of the early afternoon sun, in intermittent blinding flashes of light, as she swung slowly on her mooring line in the calm turquoise sea, the foam lapping gently round her elegant bow.

Standing on her forrard decking, a RAF sergeant, dressed in sea-boots and a cream, sea-going, polo neck jersey, addressed the MGBs as they closed on him.

"Heave to alongside, please, and secure, to receive RAF liaison officers, one per boat. MGB 1501, followed in sequence by boat numbers 1315, 1316 and 1317."

"Hmm, Number One, an addition to sealed orders. I wonder if they have any more little surprises up their sleeves."

After Fischer's rapid pick-up, Tremayne secured alongside the launch and a stocky, fair-haired, youthful RAF officer leapt on board, grabbing the guard rail as he did so.

"Hello, I'm Squadron Leader Tim Stanley. Are you Lieutenant Richard Tremayne?"

"Yes sir and welcome aboard. This is my First Lieutenant, David Willoughby-Brown. Please join us on the bridge sir."

Stanley scrambled nimbly up alongside Tremayne and the First Lieutenant, shaking each warmly by the hand.

"My God, you've got some armament on this thing – enough to sink the bloody *Scharnhorst*, I shouldn't wonder!"

Tremayne found himself already taking a liking to the purposeful, energetic RAF officer and his uncomplicated, boyish approach.

"I imagine you're wondering just what the hell I'm doing, fouling up your plans and schedules and lowering the tone by leaping onto your very smart boat – and, by heaven, she is smart. She puts our ASR launch to shame."

"Thank you, sir. We're rather proud of her. Well, as this RV was different in substance from our brief and we weren't expecting so distinguished a guest," Tremayne smiled, "I did wonder, sir, what -"

Stanley cut across Tremayne.

"Look Richard, it's critical that we get on with one another closely and as soon as possible, so please cut out the 'sir' – my name's Tim. Ostensibly, the other liaison officers and I are going to be with you to act as guides, giving the boat captains a pilot's perspective on attacks on small boats as the exercise progresses, today and tomorrow. Of far more importance, however, is the relationship we build together in preparation for the intended necessary teamwork when the balloon goes up later in the summer

– we're going to be relying upon one another."

Tremayne responded in a more relaxed way to match the informal approach of the RAF officer, "Thank you Tim. That helps a lot. We are certainly going to need to work hand in glove with you if we are to be successful when exercises become real warfare. From what we hear, this year seems to be turning into the raiding season and therefore a central part of Churchill's declared intention to start a conflagration throughout Europe."

At this point, the RAF motor launch moved off eastwards in the direction of St Mary's.

"She's off back home – we, of course, are stationed on St Mary's and I command a Hurricane squadron there." Looking skywards, in the intended direction of the imminent aerial attack, Stanley said, "Right Richard, you can expect flour bombs any moment now!"

"Cox'n, full ahead and prepare to zigzag like hell. I want to keep this boat free from flour."

"Aye aye, sir," then inaudibly, "like pat-a-bloody-cake baker's man, so it is."

"Yeoman, make to all boats: *'Flour is on its way'.*"

"Aye, aye, sir." 'Taff' Jenkins' unmistakable Valleys' lilt was evident in just those three words.

"Number One, scour the horizon for our friends, please. You, too, Yeo and let me know the minute you see anything."

"Aye, aye, sir. Oh sir, 1501 and 1317 acknowledging – and 1316, sir.

From 1501, sir: *'The flour in your hair only makes you more beautiful'.*"

A shout from their westward-facing stern directed the

attention of all on the bridge rearwards. It was 'Geordie' Robson, manning the after Oerlikons.

"Five aircraft, sir, one thousand yards, coming in low – and fast."

"Stand by, all guns. Track them as they come in and follow through as they come past, or over us. Simulated fire aimed just in front of them."

"Steady, lads. NOW, fire as you bear. Shoot, shoot, shoot!"

Irvine hurled the MGB through a series of rapid, exaggerated zigzags, as the various gunners frenetically swung and counter-swung their weapons to home in on the aircraft, coming in at well over three hundred and fifty miles per hour.

The aircraft quickly passed over 1315, their speed unduly emphasised by their ultra-low altitude, which was estimated at only fifty feet as they flew by.

"All guns cease firing! Check, check, check," yelled Tremayne. "Simulate ammunition checks and reloading, IMMEDIATELY."

"Cox'n, gun crews, well done everybody. No hits!" called Tremayne.

"Well done Richard," echoed Stanley. "That was impressive. What excellent drill."

Four more mock bombing runs were made against the flotilla, which remained split up, to operate as individual units, in order to dissipate the force of the "enemy" attack.

On the third run, 1315 took a hit on the corner of her stern, as two of the "bombers" combined cleverly to straddle her with flour bombs.

At the day's end, back at Godolphin in room 101, Enever and

the four RAF officers conducted the post-exercise debriefing. Relatively few hits had been made, but Enever and his airforce colleagues skilfully drew out the major lessons learned from the day, before briefing the boat captains for the following day's airborne target practice.

The next morning, as acting Flotilla Commander, Tremayne ordered 'diamond' formation, so that the incoming aircraft would be forced to tow their orange canvas drogues into the maximum concentration of defensive fire, as they, in turn, attempted to attack the MGBs.

The day went well, with gun crews learning the critical importance of both accurate anticipation and unhesitating reaction when firing live ammunition at swiftly moving targets, from high-speed, zigzagging boats.

For two more days, the target practice – and testing variations of it – continued until, as Tremayne was able to confirm with the other boat captains, gun crew reactions and gunnery skills had both reached requisite battle levels. What he was also able to report back to Rawlings and Enever was that co-ordination and rapid, unified response between boats were of an impressively high order.

In the weeks that followed, the skills learned in the previous training programme were revisited and further honed to prepare officers, ratings and Marines for likely close-quarter battle and hand-to-hand fighting. Developing what the formidable Colour Sergeant McGrory termed 'the Commando Spirit' was an essential part of the training, in order to imbue those taking part with the mental – and emotional – cutting edge and single-minded determination so vital in raiding and aggressive reconnaissance.

Necessary patient stealth was developed by learning to crawl, unnoticed, through undergrowth – and other singularly unpleasant obstacles devised by the Royal Marine instructors – for one hundred yards and taking not less than a full hour to do it. Anyone who completed the distance under the stipulated time was sent back to do it again.

Silent approach landings on both rocky and sandy beaches, from two-man canoes and rubber dinghies, were practised at night and in the very early dawn, as was beach reconnaissance from the sea, wearing swim fins and rubber 'pilotage party drysuits'.

After the intensive and frequently exhausting training, the flotilla had undoubtedly become a well-knit, skilled and toughened fighting force – mentally and physically fit for purpose.

Lieutenant Commander Enever called a training review meeting for the morning following the completion of the programme. All participating officers, including those of the RAF and some shadowy figures – assumed to be from SOE or SIS but never officially identified – attended the review.

After about forty-five minutes of evaluation and debrief, Enever, who was in the chair, announced: "As you must doubtless realise, Commander Rawlings and I are pleased with the results of the programme." He looked directly at Rawlings, in a manner that implied 'contradict me at your peril'. In the absence of any challenge from his superior to his assertion, Enever continued, "and so too are our friends from the Royal Air Force and our colleagues from Government Intelligence. The time to put your training to the test has unexpectedly arrived. The Met boys have given the all clear to use canoes or rubber dinghies in open water for the next four days, after which time rough seas will make such passages impossible for several more days. So tonight's the night, so to speak, and the target is – as many of you correctly assumed – the radio and radar station on the Ile d'Ouessant."

At this point, Enever unrolled a large-scale wall map of the target area. "Currently, we are suffering catastrophic shipping losses – both among merchant ships and convoy escort vessels – and clearly radioed intelligence is a key aspect of the Germans' success. The objective is to establish exactly what equipment the Germans have – and are using – on the island and, subject to approval by radio from here, to destroy those key installations likely to have the most destructive, long-term impact on their radio warfare effort in the Channel and the Western Approaches. That's the *what*, gentlemen. Now this is *how* we will do it.

"We will use all four MGBs for the safe delivery of the reconnaissance party. Richard, you will command the flotilla and 1315 will carry five two-man canoes, plus the reconnaissance party consisting of seven Royal Marines, Squadron Leader Stanley and two of our guests from Intelligence – Captain West from SOE and Captain Thomas from SIS. Both Intelligence Officers are specialists in radio intercept warfare and are also experts in the design, as well as the use, of both transmitting and receiving equipment. They must be brought back safely, with their information, at all costs.

"The island is very small, we estimate three and a half miles by one and three-quarters at the most, so there are few places to hide and post-operation survival time will be no more than about two or three days. Retrieval of the party will be a matter of extreme urgency.

"Your immediate backup will be Lieutenant Fischer in the Camper and Nicholson and he will have an RAF liaison officer and a captain from SIS on board. Lieutenants Taylor and Bower will also each have an RAF liaison officer and a member of either SOE or SIS on board and all boats will carry one native French speaker. OK, so far?" Enever looked around the room and, in response to the affirmative nods, he continued: "The insertion of the reconnaissance party must take place in darkness and tonight there is no moon. Richard, you and Hermann will pass by the Côte Sauvage to the west of the Ile d'Ouessant, which – so French Resistance tells us – is the less patrolled and guarded coast. You will then make your way south, past Pointe de Pern and around into the entrance to the 'horseshoe' that is the south-western end of the island.

"How far in you go to drop the 'recce' party will depend upon local sea and weather conditions, as well as the risk of visibility. Hermann will be in close attendance throughout. There will be only two Confrèrie members on Ouessant as reception committee and guides – 'Philippe' and 'Nadine' – but the very size of the masts will indicate the party's landmark. You and Hermann will hightail it out of there once you receive the signal confirming landing and RV with Mick and Bob, to return home at maximum revolutions.

"Retrieval of the party will be arranged by coded radio message and will be at night, using MGBs or, according to timing and circumstances, our fishing boats, already painted up and numbered as if they were from Roscoff. This immediately legitimises the initial stage of their passage northwards toward Scilly, in daylight, after the pick-up.

"Lieutenants Bower and Taylor will, in effect, be 'riding shotgun'. More specifically, they will be your 'eyes and ears' and added firepower on the journeys in and out. The RAF will provide necessary air cover, via the liaison officers. Estimated time of departure will be 21.30 hours tonight from Braiden Rock, gentlemen. Maintain maximum radio silence, consistent with the progress of events."

Enever dealt with questions and the meeting dispersed at 18.20 hours.

Prior to setting off, Tremayne convened a short final briefing for boat captains, first lieutenants, Lieutenant John Litherland – the subaltern in charge of the Royal Marine party, and the intelligence and liaison officers.

At 21.30 hours precisely, with exhausts bursting into life and a rumble of engines, the flotilla moved off from its anchorage, heading for the open sea beyond St Mary's, its course set for the Ile d'Ouessant. Clear of the islands, Tremayne signalled: *'Diamond formation – speed twenty-seven knots. Maintain defence stations'*.

With the deepening dusk, the four boats held formation, with subdued lights and the inevitable telltale phosphorescence of bow waves and wakes.

The passage south was uneventful and, at five miles due north of the Ile d'Ouessant, Tremayne ordered "half revolutions" to reduce noise as the flotilla began to bear off to starboard, approaching the north-west Côte Sauvage of the island.

Tension and concentration were evident on every wheelhouse bridge and at every gun. Adding to the atmosphere of tense preoccupation, both orders and conversation were confined to brief whispers. In the stillness of the night, even the smallest sound was magnified alarmingly, increasing the tension and edginess on each boat. With the Pointe de Creac'h abeam to port, the guard boats of Taylor and Bower turned slowly to starboard to take up station and wait at the appointed RV, four miles due west, for the two MGBs of Tremayne and Fischer, when they returned from dropping off their canoeists.

Tremayne took MGB 1315 past Pointe de Pern at a little over seven knots, her engines running almost silently. Gun crews constantly traversed their weapons, their eyes straining in the dark to pick up possible targets, while on the bridge the tension mounted again as the boat glided noiselessly into the deep U-shaped bay of the canoeists' drop zone.

Dead ahead, approximately one thousand yards away, lay the village of Lampaul while five hundred yards away, to starboard, somewhere in the pitch black, was the small rocky bay where Philippe and Nadine, their guides, should be waiting.

Quickly, Lieutenant Litherland and his well-drilled Marines assembled their canoes, equipment and weapons bags, expertly organising the other members of the reconnaissance party in hushed voices. The canoes were silently lowered into the water and the paddlers began to scramble down into them, as Willoughby-Brown and two ratings secured and stabilised the cockleshells bobbing in the sea, gently lapping against the gunboat's hull.

Tremayne turned to the Yeoman of Signals and said quietly,

"Yeo, recognition signal, please. Three short white flashes."

"Aye, aye, sir." The Aldis lamp stabbed the otherwise impenetrable blackness of the night.

"Here it is, Number One, four white in reply plus one green for 'go ahead'. We'd better…"

Suddenly, Litherland let out a sharp, stifled cry of agony when, with a sickeningly audible crack, his ankle snapped as he violently twisted it, scrambling over the gunboat's side with fifty pounds of equipment in the rucksack he was carrying on his back.

Tremayne whispered urgently to the two ratings, "Look lively! Help Mr Litherland back on deck. Careful there! Robson, grab that rucksack and get it off his back. Number One, keep the canoe stable please – there's only the stern paddler in at the moment."

Tremayne whispered urgently to the single canoeist below.

"Paddler, hold fast and keep the others close by. Mr Litherland looks as if he's broken his ankle." Litherland, clearly in extreme agony, muttered his thanks to Tremayne and the two seamen.

"Yes, sir. It's Corporal Kane, sir. I'll hold things together down here, sir." The calm, authoritative and audible whisper reached those on the gunboat's deck.

"Good man. We'll be with you as quickly as possible."

Willoughby-Brown quickly injected a phial of morphine into Litherland's injured leg and temporarily made him as comfortable as he could on the deck. Tremayne picked up Litherland's rucksack.

"Number One, I'm taking over the recce party from Mr Litherland. Cox'n, the First Lieutenant will assume command of the boat from now on. I think I'm going to be fairly busy for a few days. Stick to the plan, Number One. I'll be in touch as soon as I can – and good luck!"

"Good luck to you, sir."

Tremayne quickly shook Willoughby-Brown's hand and, with Litherland's rucksack over his shoulder, he scrambled down into the waiting canoe as Kane's bow paddler.

"Number One, pass me down a Lanchester, bayonet and eight magazines please. I can't stand those bloody 'gas-pipe' Sten guns."

Tremayne and Kane pushed off, paddling rapidly – almost instantaneously establishing a unified rhythm as they passed through the other canoeists and took the lead, heading for the distant beach.

Minutes later, they were guided in through the surf by the shielded torches of the two French Resistance members. Exchanging rapid and muffled coded greetings with Philippe and Nadine, Tremayne then quickly briefed the others on his role as group leader, in place of the injured Litherland. The canoes and paddles were stowed in a small cave, set in the rocky shoreline and not obvious to anyone unfamiliar with the detail of this stretch of the island's coast. The party moved off quickly, inland, led by the two agents. Each member carried weapons, rucksacks containing rations for three days, a lightweight sleeping bag, explosives and various items of what Willoughby-Brown termed 'burglars' kit'.

The RV turned out to be one of several old farm cottages close to Lampaul. While Philippe stood guard outside, Nadine led the party into the large farmhouse kitchen for hot coffee laced with cognac.

Moving aside the old table, she rolled back the ancient well-worn carpet to reveal a trapdoor, leading to a cavernous underground cellar.

"Where you may sleep, gentlemen. I don't think you will be disturbed. But first, when you are ready, we will take you to see the radio station. It is less than two kilometres from here." Collecting Philippe and led by Nadine, the group set off to reconnoitre their target. Avoiding the roads and crossing fields, following the boundary hedges or old stone walls, the group eventually came up to the perimeter fence surrounding a group of large buildings, barely visible in the dark, and the huge, dominating masts.

West and Thomas, the two radio intercept warfare specialists, moved to the front of the group, next to Tremayne. "They're bloody big – absolutely enormous from what I can see in the darkness," muttered West, "but Don and I must get much closer to see them in detail."

"Agreed," whispered Thomas. Turning to Tremayne, he added, "There were two sentries close to the main entrance, but I've seen no one this side. Let's cut the wire and Andrew and I will slip in to look at the beasts at close quarters."

Tremayne signalled to Corporal Kane to join him and the two Captains.

"Corporal, we're going to go through the wire to look at the masts. Check first that it's not electrified then, if OK, cut a way through for us. Deploy your Marines to cover us and our exit."

Crawling over to Squadron Leader Stanley, Tremayne said, "Tim. Come and join us – we're going in to inspect the masts."

He then signalled to Nadine and Philippe to join the reconnaissance group.

"You will need to report back to your colleagues in the Confrèrie on what we discover here."

The wire turned out to be inert and Kane cut open a man-sized flap. The group slipped through, leaving the Marines to take up positions of all-round defence outside the perimeter fence. West and Thomas worked together carefully, examining each of the masts in turn – a task that took over a tense, nerve-racking and watchful hour. With the sky beginning to lighten perceptibly, the two radio specialists, along with Tremayne, Stanley and the two French agents, crawled back towards the gap in the wire and the protection of the covering party.

"What's the verdict, gentlemen?" whispered Tremayne.

"Bloody dummies the lot of them – with just one exception, which superficially preserves the location as a transmission station for anyone radio monitoring the place."

"Are you really telling us that all these huge masts are phoneys – except for just one? Is this some decoy to lure bombers – and idiots like us – into some sort of trap?" asked an incredulous Stanley.

"My guess, sir," responded Thomas, is that this is an elaborate – and very convincing – cover for a real transmission and listening station somewhere damned close. But on the mainland, most likely just in from the coast."

" I agree," said West. "It's a very clever ploy. The positive outcome of this reconnaissance is that we now have a better idea of what Jerry's up to and we can play along with that, just as long as it suits us."

"There are masts a-plenty on the Ile de Sein, but that's thirty miles south of here and too far away to pass this station off as that one," added Tremayne, "but having come so far, I'd like to know just where the real station is. Certainly Lieutenant Commander Enever and Intelligence will want to locate the real one."

"Let's get out of here and signal Willoughby-Brown and the others to come back for us," whispered Stanley. "I'll organise an 'umbrella' of air cover for ..." Further discussion was abruptly terminated by a tense German voice nervously shouting "Halt! Wer da?"

"Oh shit!" muttered Tremayne urgently. "Nadine, tell him that you and your brother were walking your dog last night and she disappeared. Tell him that you think she must have found her way through a hole in the fence that you discovered. Philippe, quick, go with Nadine, NOW! Corporal Kane, fast as you like, please. Deal with him silently."

Nadine approached the sentry, her hands up, playing her part to perfection. Looking suitably terrified and speaking schoolgirl German, she walked tentatively towards the sentry who shone a torch into her face while cradling a machine pistol in his other hand. Philippe placed both hands on his head and kept mumbling, "Pardon, monsieur, pardon." Then, simulating a yapping dog, he whined in an appropriately pleading tone, "Mein Hund, mein Hund, wo ist er?"

The sentry shifted his torch onto Philippe's face and raised his machine pistol to the Frenchman's chest. "Halt, du Schei..." Suddenly, with a loud gasp, he arched his back in agony as Kane's fighting-knife went in, up to the hilt, in the region of his kidneys.

"Mon Dieu!" Visibly unnerved by the sudden turn of events, Nadine stood still for a moment, shocked and confused. Quickly recovering herself, she seized the dropped machine pistol and torch and, turning to Kane who emerged from the dark by her side, said shakily, "Thank you, Corporal, I don't think he believed either of us. I think he was going to shoot us."

Tremayne stepped forward, motioning the others to follow him.

"Well done, Corporal Kane – you saved the situation. We'll take him through the wire and then we'll replace the flap and cover it in weeds. I want to hide the body so that the Germans will assume that he's deserted and not even be aware of our intrusion. Nadine, leave his machine pistol in the undergrowth so that when it is eventually found, it won't look as if he was killed by the locals for his weapon."

Clear of the compound, Tremayne asked Philippe where they might quickly dispose of the sentry's body. The Frenchman hesitated for a moment and then said, clearly in a moment of inspiration, "Ah, tomorrow, there is a funeral in Lampaul. They have already dug the grave. All we do, monsieur, is dig a little deeper, bury our friend and tomorrow the curé, in all innocence, will lower the late Madame Jeuvell on top of him. Quelle delicatesse, monsieur!" Philippe grinned wolfishly at the prospect, but even more so at Tremayne's fleeting expression of undisguised horror.

The churchyard lay about three hundred yards to the west of the base and, as luck would have it, the grave diggers had left their spades propped up against a nearby headstone. Within half an hour, the job was done and Tremayne ordered a return to the farm and its cellar.

By now the summer dawn was transforming night into a cloudless day and the risk of discovery had increased proportionately.

Tremayne was leading the group, crouching in single file along a tall hedge, when a burst of automatic fire and a scream of pain from the collapsing Marine immediately behind him, caused everyone to throw themselves flat on the ground, dropping into the ditch running along the hedge.

Tremayne called out, "Anyone see where the shots came from?" Kane responded first, "Small copse, sir, one hundred and fifty yards, two o'clock. Two fingers right of the big chestnut tree. MG mounted on someone's shoulder." The Marines were already looking after their own, but their faces told the others that the wounds were fatal. Another burst came in, churning up the ground around them, just as Tremayne took control of the situation.

"They can't have got on to us yet — it must be regular standing patrol and just our bloody bad luck."

"I think, yes," said Nadine, "but then they often go for shooting practice along the coast."

"That's useful," replied Tremayne, "a firefight will sound as if that's exactly what they're doing."

Turning to the Intelligence Officers, he said, "You two must get back safely. Keep low and stay down. I'm going to right-flank them. We can't extricate ourselves from this by running — they've effectively pinned us down. We've got to fight our way out of it."

He ordered Skeldon, the Royal Marine Bren gunner and Stanley, acting as the gun's feeder, to "keep the bastards' heads down" while he, Kane and the remaining Marines attacked the German patrol in the small copse from the flank.

Addressing the quickly-appointed assault group he said, "We'll 'pepper-pot' forward, using fire and movement, and keep bloody low. We've four smoke grenades between us and we'll throw them, on my command, and assault through the smoke from the flank while Skeldon maintains fire on them with the Bren."

He then ordered "Fix bayonets" — the heart-stopping command that concentrates any fighting man's mind.

Rapidly the group moved off to the right, half crawling, half ducking and weaving, making use of whatever ground cover they could find.

Skeldon continued to lace the German position with his Bren and — when not passing fresh magazines to the Marine — Stanley was adding single, carefully aimed shots from his Lee-Enfield. Already he had accounted for one German, but there were at least another five, plus the MG 34, making return fire life-threatening in the extreme, pumping out nine hundred rounds per minute, with an awesome noise like loudly tearing calico.

At forty yards from the copse, Tremayne ordered "Smoke!" and the four grenades exploded about ten yards from the Germans, quickly generating a blanket of thick, swirling dark grey smoke between them and the assault party.

At the appearance of the smoke cloud, Skeldon continued to fire but lifted his sights to allow Tremayne's assault group to rush in from the right and complete the job.

Tremayne next ordered the Marines to prime their high explosive grenades and then yelled "Grenades!" Five well-drilled arms came up and over and, seconds later, the explosions – sounding detached and eerie from beyond the smoke – ripped the German patrol apart. The momentary sense of detachment was replaced by a terrifyingly personal involvement in events, as the screams of the wounded and dying rent the air.

Tremayne yelled, "At 'em, lads. CHARGE!" Seconds later, they were in among the Germans, screaming oaths, shooting, bayoneting and clubbing.

Then, just as suddenly, it was all over. The butcher's toll was six dead and wounded Germans and another wounded Marine. Tremayne took in the scene, visibly shocked by it. No longer was his heart racing with alternating fear and elation. He felt completely drained and numb. Seeing Kane tending to the wounded Marine he said quietly, "Thank you Corporal. Like 'Swain, you were another 'Rock of Gibraltar'. I won't forget your part in today's scrap. It was no picnic. How is Fox?"

The wounded Marine grinned back at him, pale beneath his camouflage cream. "I'll live, sir. Thank you."

Even before Tremayne thought to order it, the Marines were already dressing the two surviving Germans' wounds, handing them lighted cigarettes and sharing their water bottles with them.

Quickly the party regrouped and moved back to join the others.

Tremayne thanked Skeldon for his handling of the Bren gun and then addressed the rest of the group. "We'd better get moving before the rest of the garrison is around our ears. Sadly, we have to leave Prothero behind. We can't take him with us. We looked after them. They, I believe, will take care of him."

Reluctantly leaving the young, dead Marine where he had fallen, the group quickly moved off to return to the farm.

Within a few minutes, which tension and the shock of close-quarter battle turned into a near-eternity, the group reached their hideout unseen.

In the cellar, Tremayne said, "Fritz will soon be crawling all over the place and all potential escape routes will be covered by aircraft, E-boats and anything else that he can throw at us.

They will expect us to try to escape by sea and the beaches will be guarded twenty-four hours. We have to find a more secure way back to the canoes. Turning to the two French agents, he said, "Nadine and Philippe, we all thank you for your courage and resourcefulness. You've done more than we could have expected of you. Would you prefer to disappear now or do you want to come back with us?"

"Thank you monsieur, but our place is here, in France. We will stay with you to show a better way to your canoes, then we will go."

Tremayne posted two sentries to keep a lookout for the inevitable German search parties, while he, Stanley and the two agents decided on their escape options.

"We have to wait for MGBs or fishing boats to pick us up from our canoes to take us back," said Stanley, "and that means lying low until dark, hoping that neither we nor our canoes are discovered."

"That certainly seems the obvious way, I agree", said

Tremayne, "but tell me Philippe, where is the German E-boat base on the island? There must be one somewhere. We were very swiftly pounced upon by an E-boat when we came this way a few weeks ago."

"There is, yes. It is in a small bay, one kilometre west of Penn Arlan, but there are usually only two or three such boats and also what the Boche call a Räumboot but I don't know what this is in English language."

Captain West, who had been on the fringe of the discussion, interjected: "That's an air-sea rescue launch, Richard."

Tremayne paused for a moment and then a broad grin crossed his normally serious youthful face. "You know, gentlemen, I'm inclined to travel home in style. Why don't we 'borrow' an E-boat? Nothing could out-run us — except aircraft — and your colleagues would doubtless deal with them for us, Tim?"

"Absolutely. It's a risky option, but to quote the learned von Clausewitz, escape from here *is* an option of risks — whatever we do. I'm in favour of this idea. It has an enormous appeal to my sense of the outlandish!"

Consensus followed quickly and the group, with the help of Nadine and Philippe, worked out the details of the least exposed route to the tiny German naval anchorage on the north-east coast of the island.

"Because of the risks of being spotted, I suggest we travel as two groups, five minutes apart exactly. I'll take one group of five and Tim, would you lead the other four?"

"Most certainly."

"Because we have to get Andrew and/or Don back — and

preferably both of them, I suggest that there should be one in each group."

"Agreed."

Further discussion was cut short by urgent tapping on the kitchen door. It was Marine Howe.

"'Scuse me, sir, Jerry looks as if he might pay us a visit. There's a patrol of eight Germans about two hundred yards along the road and coming this way."

"Thank you, Howe. Call Tandy in and get you both down into the cellar. Nadine, Philippe, please do your well-rehearsed caretaker and wife act. The rest, down below please and take everything with you."

The carpet and table were drawn across the trapdoor and Nadine busied herself with peeling potatoes, while Philippe resumed painting the door of one of the outbuildings – another job that he'd already prepared as a 'cover'. Sudden loud banging on the door announced the patrol's arrival.

A composed but suitably anxious Nadine opened the door, to be immediately pushed to one side as the Germans forced their way into the kitchen.

"W- would you like some coffee, gentlemen?" she asked.

"Yes and be quick," replied a middle-aged captain. He barked orders at his troops who immediately began a search of the house and the outbuildings.

"What are you looking for? Can we help you, sir?" The air of compliant innocence was worthy of the best drama school training.

"We are looking for British commandos who have murdered

several of our soldiers. If we find them here, you and your man will be shot – and so will they."

Below, in the cellar, Tremayne and the others sat tensely waiting, gripping rifles and sub-machine guns. The sudden movement of the table being dragged across the kitchen floor above their heads made Tremayne start, and he aimed the Lanchester directly at the trapdoor, easing the safety catch to 'Off'. Just as quickly as it had begun, the dragging stopped, to be replaced by a succession of scraping chairs as the Germans sat down to coffee and home-baked bread in the kitchen.

After what seemed to Tremayne and the others an interminable, tense time, hoarse orders, followed by more scraping chairs, announced the Germans' noisy departure.

The table was pushed back and Nadine's welcome friendly face appeared at the trapdoor opening.

"Gentlemen, you can come out now," she laughed.

Tremayne and the others were forced to continue lying low until dusk began to fall in the late evening. Leading the first group, Tremayne, accompanied by Nadine, took Captain Thomas, Corporal Kane and two Marines, including the wounded Fox, who stoically refused any assistance with what was now a worsening wound. Exactly five minutes later, together with Philippe, Stanley led the others out of the farmhouse, following Tremayne's route.

Several times, in the advancing darkness, Tremayne was forced to stop, in silence, as German search parties out looking for them passed close by.

Shortly after midnight, Tremayne's small group reached a

point where they could observe the tiny improvised Kriegsmarine base. Watching the patterns of sentry deployment and movement, Tremayne and Corporal Kane identified the optimum timing for eliminating the guards on duty watch.

While they were finalising their boarding strategy, Stanley's party silently joined them.

Tremayne briefed Stanley and then gathered the others around him, huddled behind the shelter of a low wall.

"All weapons except the two SOE silent pistols to have safety catches *on*.

"Don and Andrew, you will use your CO2 pistols to shoot any sentries whom we haven't eliminated with fighting-knives and, gentlemen, remember these are single-shot weapons, so don't bloody well miss. Get in close and aim for the head. I want any engineers on board the E-boat that we select to be kept alive. We'll need them to get us home."

"If push comes to shove, Richard, I can probably help," said Thomas. "I own a large diesel launch and can probably find my way around their engine room, so long as I can call on Fritz for initial assistance at least."

"Thank you, Don – that's a great help."

Tremayne called over Marine Howe, who carried their portable radio.

"Is the radio still working Howe? We're going to need it soon."

"Yes sir, but we'll get better reception if we persuade Jerry to let us use his, sir."

"Howe. That's a stroke of genius. Let's do that once we're on board. Right, Tim, Corporal, Howe and Maguire, let's get ourselves an E-boat. We'll take the one moored on the right of the jetty. Come on!"

The group crouched down and moved silently down to the jetty, using whatever cover they could. The sentry on the after deck stood with his back to them. Maguire crept along the jetty, hidden from the sentry by the E-boat's raised canvas sea-going dodgers, and then silently climbed on board. He approached the unguarded back of the sentry, who never heard a sound, until Maguire locked his arm round the seaman's throat from behind and thrust the knife low down into his back. He collapsed silently into the arms of the Marine who lowered him to the deck.

Maguire put the sailor's beribboned cap on his head to give himself the right superficially familiar profile in the dark. Howe and Kane, meanwhile, crept along the after deck towards the sentry pacing the forrard deck, hidden from him by the wheelhouse and bridge. Both froze as a petty officer appeared on the bridge and called to the bow watchkeeper. As the petty officer disappeared below again, Maguire, still in his German navy cap, moved forward along the side of the bridge and grunted at the rating on the bow deck who moved closer to him.

"Was sagst du?" Maguire, a powerfully built man, hit the sentry hard in the solar plexus and, with his left hand over the man's mouth, jammed his knife into the doubled-up rating's heart.

He was dead before Maguire could lower him quietly to the deck. Tremayne then waved the others onto the E-boat's deck, motioning them to be silent. Detailing the others to lie low on deck behind the canvas spray dodgers, Tremayne sent Stanley and three Marines, with one CO_2 pistol, to take control of the rear half of the boat via the after hatch. He, Kane and Maguire, with the other silent pistol, entered the boat through the forrard hatch in front of the unmanned wheelhouse.

Tremayne heard laughter and loud conversation coming from below. He burst into the small, crowded, noisy wardroom – pointing the silent pistol at the captain's head. "Sit still – *everybody*! We will shoot anyone who moves." Shouting, followed by a scream, suggested that Stanley's party had encountered trouble – but dealt with it – when he heard the Squadron Leader call "Stern secured."

Tremayne turned to the E-boat captain: "I want your engineer and your radio operator – now."

The German officer told Tremayne to go to hell, at which point the Englishman turned to Maguire.

"I will count to three and if the captain does not do as I say, shoot these two petty officers here."

Wishing that he'd never given such a barbaric ultimatum, Tremayne began to count slowly, "One, two, thr…" The Sten gun barrel came up to the first ashen-faced German's eyes, Maguire's finger curled purposefully round the trigger.

"STOP. Stop." The captain called forward a middle-aged officer and a young senior rate. "Your engineer and your radio operator."

Tremayne called forward Thomas and Marine Howe who both appeared from the after half of the boat. "Here's your engineer Don. Get us on our way."

Tremayne then addressed Skeldon, the tough, stocky section Bren gunner, "Keep Captain Thomas company and make sure the engineer does what Captain Thomas tells him to do."

Tremayne turned to Stanley. "Tim, let 'Mother' know we're on our way — ETA 0.500 hours. Organise continuous air cover please. Better let them know that we are in an E-boat, flying a Kriegsmarine ensign! There are at least three Arado floatplanes here and once Jerry realises what's happened, he'll come looking for us. Once you've got through, please join me on the bridge. At best, we may have a twenty-minute head start — and, most likely, a lot less — before the hunt for us begins in earnest."

Tremayne motioned to the Marine guarding the German telegraphist: "Any nonsense with our young radio operator here and you know what to do." Tremayne's eyes held those of the German captain.

"Corporal Kane, Howe, Maguire, take our hosts and lock them in the ratings' quarters aft and secure the after deck hatch. Corporal, see to Fox's wound, please, make him comfortable and leave him on guard outside the door of the prisoners' quarters. When they are secure, Corporal, join us on the bridge."

Tremayne raised his Lanchester meaningfully. "Captain, you and your crew will now move aft."

As the Germans moved off under guard, the captain turned to Tremayne. "I don't know who you are, but would you have shot my crew?"

"I am a British naval officer. No, I would not shoot unarmed prisoners, but," Tremayne smiled ruefully, "I needed your co-operation, captain."

"It was a gamble, then, for both of us."

"Exactly."

Tremayne went to the bridge, taking Captain West with him, to familiarise himself with the E-boat's steering and controls. Within minutes, he quietly ordered "Slip" and lines, fore and aft, were cast off, having called "Slow ahead" to Thomas via the connecting voice tubes.

The three immaculately cared for Daimler Benz 16-cylinder diesel engines responded effortlessly with a deep, low rumble and the graceful E-boat moved away with minimum fuss from the small jetty.

A figure on the bridge of the E-boat moored on the opposite side of the jetty shouted, but Tremayne merely waved in response. In the darkness it was impossible to recognise people, but subdued lighting near the jetty at least showed the distinguishing boat captain's white-topped naval cap that Tremayne had 'borrowed' from his reluctant prisoner.

After three minutes of near-silent running, Tremayne called down to Thomas: "Let's go home, maximum revolutions!"

The sharply chined bows lifted out of the water as the E-boat surged forward in response to the full throttle and spray whipped over the narrow forrard deck and the low, elegantly sculptured armoured bridge. Compared with the bulky, slower British Fairmiles, she was a greyhound – long, lean and very fast.

Stanley and Kane appeared on the cramped bridge, alongside Tremayne and West.

"Aircraft cover will commence in forty minutes. There'll be four Beaufighters from Cornwall and, as we get closer to Scilly, Hurricanes from my squadron on St Mary's will take us home. Corporal Kane and I took the very unwilling Sparks to join the others after I'd got out of him what I needed to make the radio work. We also put the engineer away – Don's as happy as a pig in muck down there in the engine room. He's treating those bloody great throbbing diesels as if they were his own new-born babes!"

Tremayne turned to Kane, "Corporal, please ensure that all your 'Royals' – apart from Fox – can handle the 20mm guns, fore and aft, the 3.7cm flak gun amidships and the two foc'sl-mounted MG 38s. Check ammunition availability and test-fire all weapons when I give the order." Then, speaking though a megaphone left on the narrow perimeter rim of the bridge, he called: "All gun crews will stand to at 'action stations'."

Addressing West, Tremayne said, "Andrew, please check that the two bow torpedoes are ready to fire. Any problems – drag a crewman out of the prison quarters. One of the 'Royals' will be only too glad to help you!"

Tremayne felt excited, like a child with a new toy. The E-boat handled more responsively and felt more manoeuvrable than the equivalent British boats. With her length of one hundred and fifteen feet and her weight of over one hundred tons, she ploughed purposefully through the waves at a maximum speed of thirty-eight knots. Her low wheelhouse and bridge suggested, however, that she was most likely to be every bit as 'wet' as the Fairmiles in rough seas, mused Tremayne.

After a further twenty minutes, Tremayne ordered "Test all weapons" and the still, empty night was suddenly filled with a harsh, staccato cacophony as the Royal Marines blazed away with the new, unfamiliar armament.

The gun crews stood to at action stations on the command

"Cease fire!", Stanley taking over from Howe who went off to explore the mysteries of the E-boat's galley and the means of making hot drinks for the prize crew and prisoners. Pusser's kye just did not figure in the German boat's drinks list and rather strong ersatz coffee was the only drink that Howe was able to produce for the entire crew on duty watch. He did find some schnapps in the wardroom, which he added rather liberally to the hot, black, indeterminate liquid.

He had just finished serving drinks to the rather surprised and somewhat bemused prisoners, when Tremayne sounded the deafening klaxon, calling: "Stand by to fire, all guns. Aircraft astern."

Tracking the E-boat's phosphorescent wake were two aircraft, roaring in from astern at about eighty feet above sea level, anonymous and unrecognisable in the still black, but clear, starry night. Stanley and the Marines, manning the guns, traversed and elevated the weapons, lining them up on the deafening roar of engines as much as on line of sight. Standing next to Tremayne, West seized the starboard Spandau MG 38 and swung it round, aiming it in the general direction of the ever-increasing noise.

Seconds later, a sustained burst of machine gun fire, accompanied by a sharp, shocked cry of pain from the gun crew amidships and the randomly patterned splintering of the wooden deck, confirmed they were not RAF Beaufighters.

Almost simultaneously, guns astern, amidships and on the foc'sl opened up at what was, for a brief moment overhead, recognisable as an Arado 196 reconnaissance floatplane.

The second one roared over the E-boat dropping a small bomb, which exploded in the sea close to the port bow, drenching the bridge and the forrard gun crew who were still firing at the rapidly vanishing first aircraft.

"All gun crews. Check ammunition, the bastards will be back." Tremayne spun the wheel to starboard and then began violently zigzagging the big boat.

"Here they come again," muttered West. "All guns. Stand by to fire!" yelled Tremayne. "Fire as you bear. Shoot, shoot, shoot!"

Kane, calm as ever under pressure, inched the 3.7cm flak gun round, with Maguire as his gun-layer, and then opened fire at point-blank range — shredding the leading Arado's stubby radial engine. Moments later, it exploded and dived down into the sea. All other guns homed in on the second Arado, as Tremayne twisted and turned the E-boat in a tight zigzag to avoid another bomb which fell almost as close as the first, exploding in the sea and showering the decks and foc'sl with shrapnel and spray.

A sudden deeper, throatier roar coming in from almost dead ahead, heralded the arrival of four powerful Beaufighters in 'arrowhead' formation.

A great cheer went up from Stanley and the Marines, while Tremayne and West pumped each other's hands like long-lost friends meeting up after years apart, as the second, unfortunate Arado rapidly succumbed to the deadly combined firepower of at least two of the heavily armed Beaufighters.

"Take the wheel, Andrew — I must thank our gallant Squadron Leader and check who was wounded back there."

Tremayne and Stanley shook hands, "Thanks, Tim, much

appreciated." Tremayne then turned to see Kane bending over Maguire, his normally impassive face contorted in grief. "He's just died, sir. Hit in the first burst and he continued as gun-layer, with half his chest shot away."

Tremayne briefly touched Kane's shoulder. "I'm so sorry. I know he and you were mates. I lost a great friend too, Corporal, when my last ship, the *Portree*, was sunk. I'll give you a hand getting him down onto the deck." Carefully, Tremayne and the Marine lifted Maguire off the gun-layer's seat and laid him gently on the wooden deck, next to the gun he had served so courageously. "Once a Marine – always a Marine, Corporal," said Tremayne quietly.

Tremayne called to Marine Howe. "I think we could all do with another cup of that lethal brew of yours, Howe, please."

"Right away, sir." And then to Kane, " I'm bloody sorry, Corp, I really am, Mick was one of the best."

Deeply moved by what he had just seen, Tremayne returned to the bridge to relieve West at the wheel.

He maintained maximum revolutions and, as they drew closer to the Isles of Scilly, Stanley's Hurricanes came out to meet them, waggling their wings in recognition to the waving crew members lining the deck. It was the dawn of what looked like being a glorious, clear summer day and soon, one by one – and then in groups, the beautiful islands began to appear on the horizon and gradually take on their distinctive and familiar shapes.

Tremayne's heart lifted as he steered the boat through St Mary's Road and northwards to Tresco and New Grimsby. He was looking forward to getting "home", but what made homecoming less than perfect was that Emma would not be there to meet him this time.

Enever, as always, was there to greet them — waving enthusiastically, along with Litherland on crutches and with his foot encased in plaster, Jane Topping, and a new, tall RNVR sub-lieutenant.

With the E-boat moored at Braiden Rock, and the German prisoners already blindfolded and paraded on deck, Tremayne scrambled off the boat and climbed the steep rocky path to salute and then shake hands with Enever and greet the others.

"Dear boy, for once, just fail at something and prove to us that you're human, too!"

"If it hadn't been for John's 'Royals', sir — especially Corporal Kane — and, of course, Tim Stanley, I most certainly would have failed." Tremayne addressed Litherland: "I'm so sorry, John, I lost two of your Marines — Prothero and Maguire — and young Fox was wounded and needs proper treatment urgently."

"We heard all about it by radio. Tim and Marine Howe have kept us well informed about events. Communications have been excellent from your end," said Enever.

"Tell me, Richard, what *is* that sleek, menacing thing like to handle — she looks very impressive close to."

"Like a dream, sir. I wish we had a few of those!"

"Well, dear boy, it's one hell of a present that you've brought Admiral Hembury — he'll be absolutely delighted, as I am — *and* more prisoners for him. Well done!

"Now, Richard, you must be completely exhausted. I will talk with Tim and our friends from the Army. John here will take charge of his Marines on one leg – which I really must see – and you get off back to the wardroom and a bath. Oh, by the way, there's some mail for you!" Enever's eyes twinkled over his glasses.

"Debriefing at 14.00 hours, so get your head down for a few hours – that's an order!"

A blissfully happy Bertie – who was looked after by the Oylers whenever Tremayne was away – greeted him ecstatically as he entered his cabin, rushing to bring him a present.

"Bless you, Bertie, for the normality that you bring to my life," laughed Tremayne, as he ruffled the black fur and stroked his dog's head. "Now, old fellow, who's written to me – I just hope...!"

Tremayne saw an Admiralty envelope with his name and address written in the now familiar, sensitive, round hand and, underneath it, a colourful postcard.

"Thank you, dearest Emma, thank you," murmured Tremayne and then he opened and read the letter. It was happy, almost chatty, and full of lighthearted and amusing memories of the wonderful weekend they had shared so recently, yet, in other ways, so long ago. It was signed, he was delighted to see, *'With my love, Emma'.*

"Now, Bertie, who on earth has sent me a postcard from Spain?"

Tremayne, puzzled, looked at the photograph of a pretty old mill somewhere in Andalucia, turned the card over and began to read...

My dear Richard,

I hope this finds you happy and well!

The "old firm" – Portree – foundered, sadly, as you must have heard.

All at sea for a while, I was picked up by the competition, but didn't like
the food, "accommodation" and lack of freedom. So, I decided
I needed a break, as it were, and legged it as soon as I was able.
Am hitching lifts through Spain at the moment with the "Rock" in mind.
See you soon, I hope. Take care!
Yours aye,
Bill (Mitchell)

"Bill! Thank God, you're alive, old friend, thank God," said Tremayne out loud. And, as emotion took over, the tears of joy just flowed…

Eight

A postcard from Spain

Despite remaining awake throughout the previous night, bringing back the reconnaissance party from the Ile d'Ouessant, Tremayne found sleep impossible. Emma's sensitive, yet lighthearted letter had reaffirmed both the growing closeness and continuity of their relationship. In that, Tremayne was finding the security and deep affection that he now recognised he needed – and wanted, despite his otherwise high independence and self-sufficiency.

The unbelievable and joyful news from Spain had restored the emotional sheet anchor and close bond that he had shared with Bill, his trusted friend and mentor, which he had long believed he'd lost forever.

From Bill's handwritten date, the card had already taken well over four weeks to reach Godolphin via Gibraltar – redirected from the Royal Naval Barracks, Devonport – and Tremayne wondered just where his friend might be now.

Unable to fall asleep, Tremayne finally got up, shaved, soaked in a hot bath, dressed and walked up to the New Inn for coffee and an early breakfast.

Aileen Oyler stood in the doorway enjoying the warm morning sun, smiling as always.

"And how's yourself, Mr Tremayne?" she asked. "Sure, but you're looking a bit tired. Now don't tell me it's that lovely girl I've seen you with?"

"Good morning Aileen – and how's Herself?" laughed Tremayne. "No, unfortunately, this is not Emma's fault – I rather wish it were," he added somewhat diffidently. "I've just been busy on a little job."

"A little job, is it? I often wonder what you sailor lads get up to in those mystery boats of yours. You disappear and then come home – thank God – and I think, now where on earth could they have been to? So, would it be bacon and eggs that you'd be wanting – and some good strong coffee?"

"It would indeed, Aileen, thank you – that sounds like heaven to me."

"Me ould Da' has just sent me over some real 'tater bread from Kilmoganny. Would you not like a couple of slices of that, fried with your bacon?"

"Sheer bliss! Thank you, Aileen. Did your mother bake the potato bread?"

"Sadly no. She was killed in 1921, when I was a just a girl."

"I'm so sorry, Aileen. Was it an accident?"

"No, Mr Tremayne, it was no accident. Now, sit you down. Sure and I'll get your breakfast."

Tremayne, conscious that he must have touched on some raw, personal nerve, gratefully accepted the newspaper that Aileen had offered him and began trawling through the latest news. "Tactical withdrawals" by the British army – mostly retreating from Rommel's seemingly unstoppable Afrika Korps in North Africa and against the equally relentless Japanese in Burma – appeared to be the most optimistic items that he could find. However, his spirits had already been lifted by Emma's letter as well as by the wonderful news from Bill Mitchell, which he was still trying to take fully on board. Aileen Oyler's superb 'Irish' breakfast exceeded his expectations. All traces of weariness and strain gone, Tremayne settled up and set off to walk round Tresco. Before leaving he did, however, say to Aileen: "Aileen, if I inadvertently raised something that I should not have done, then I do apologise. Forgive me."

"Of course not, Mr Tremayne. Sure I just get very upset when I think of Mam and how she died all those years ago. Now, off you go for your walk and blow the cobwebs away. Dick and I will see you soon – and your lovely young lady, I hope!"

Reflecting on the happy turn of events in his own life, Tremayne walked up to Castle Down and over Gun Hill where, but a few days ago, he and Emma had held their picnic and had each buried their 'crookit bawbies'. He smiled at himself for checking that the triangular rock was exactly where he and Emma had placed it. He had brought with him an empty official issue RN cigarette tin – a 'Blue Liner' – in which he had placed a piece of paper on which he'd drawn the customary heart pierced by an arrow with the words 'Richard loves Emma, July 1942'. He raised the stone again, scraped some more soil away, and placed the tin under the two coins before pushing the stone back into place and standing on it to bed it back into the earth. Smiling to himself a second time, he said, "Tremayne, you idiot, you're like a besotted, romantic fourteen-year-old schoolboy! At some distant future date, someone's going to be wondering 'Who the hell are Richard and Emma – and whatever happened to them?'"

He crossed over to Tregarthen Hill, stopping to take in the glorious panorama of the islands, before passing the ancient cairns and walking down into Old Grimsby and, eventually, back to HMS Godolphin.

Back in his cabin, he began to write up a report on the sequence of events of the Ile d'Ouessant reconnaissance and the significant implications of them. Three questions were constantly at the back of his mind when he reviewed an operation. Why – and why not? What could and should we do *differently* if we were to do that again? What are the main lessons that we need to learn from the experience?

He then took time to write to Emma, only referring to the operation in passing. Just to amuse her, he mentioned that he'd checked the stone to make sure it was still in place, but made no reference to the cigarette tin and his note. Like Emma, he kept his letter lighthearted but personal and signed it with his love – something he found to be a very significant step to take.

After a light lunch in the wardroom, Tremayne made his way to room 101 and the operation debriefing.

Enever had lost none of the boyish enthusiasm and infectious energy that he had shown at five o'clock in the morning when Tremayne had secured at Braiden Rock anchorage.

"Gentlemen," he began, the inevitable unlit pipe between his teeth, "that E-boat you brought back for us is a sensation! 'Jolly Jack' and most of our officers have been swarming all over her, green with envy. One could make a small fortune, I'll wager, just by taking them out in her at a shilling a time on trips round the bay! Apparently, she's a modified Type 38, which means she is very similar – if not identical – to the E-boats that have been wreaking such havoc in the Channel these last twelve months, including the sinking of one of our destroyers which is no mean achievement. She is part of Kapitänleutnant Niels Bätge's 4th Schnellboot Flotilla, based in Ostend but operating regularly in these waters."

The twinkling mild grey eyes switched to Tremayne, "To say the least, Richard, he must be pretty choked with you for relieving him of one of his expensive toys. I have it on good authority though, that the captain of the E-boat that you took– Leutnant von Mirbach – is even more miffed about having his best cap nicked than he is about the seizure of his beloved Schnellboot! Somehow, Richard, you just don't fit his description of you as a 'Verdammter Seeräuber' – a damnable pirate!"

Placing his pipe on the table in front of him amidst the others' laughter, Enever continued, "Our engineers confirm that she is capable of close to forty knots – and could sustain that for about seven hundred miles with her fuel tank capacity. By comparison, our Fairmiles look – and feel – positively elephantine. With Admiral

Hembury's permission, I can see enormous potential for her use in this flotilla.

We already know the different German flotilla insignias, as well as most of their various camouflage paint schemes; so, if we *are* allowed to keep her, we can ring the changes on different disguises for her and her roles in our little flotilla."

Enever and Captain Waring, together with Tim Stanley as senior RAF officer, led the debriefing of the operation itself.

Enever had already spent half the morning debriefing Thomas and West, the two Intelligence Officers, and so he fed into the meeting summaries of their verbatim, but detailed reports of the operation.

The discovery that the masts on the Ile d'Ouessant were cleverly disguised fakes had come as a major surprise to everyone – especially to Enever. Opinions about the motives behind such an elaborate *ruse de guerre* still varied, but there was complete agreement that the real ones must be located, their purpose confirmed beyond all doubt, and action to deal with them agreed and implemented as soon as possible.

Waring, for his part, had nothing but praise for Tremayne's handling of his Marines in action. He was clearly impressed by the fact that a sailor had been able to move out of his own environment and both lead and act, with consummate skill and confidence, in a battle arena that was both different and unfamiliar. Enever had received similar reports on Tremayne's operational leadership from Stanley, West and Thomas. He beamed with obvious personal pleasure as he said, "What I am pleased to announce, Richard, is that your name is being put forward formally through official channels for the award of a Distinguished Service Cross. This time, we'll do our damnedest to make sure the application sticks."

For a moment, Tremayne was caught off guard, too taken aback to speak, but he recovered quickly to express his thanks and characteristically say, "But there are others who deserve formal recognition, sir, especially Corporal Kane, Marine Maguire and Squadron Leader Stanley."

"They – and others – will be considered in the light of today's reports and also further reviews of the operation at higher level," replied Enever.

The debriefing concluded about two hours later, with the confirmation that further reconnaissance – and continued collaborative action with the Confrèrie – would take place during the coming months. Future action of this nature would depend, in the light of this experience, upon a thorough examination of the lessons to be learned from the Ile d'Ouessant operation, at senior inter-service levels involving SOE and SIS.

"In the meantime, gentlemen, we keep the sea lanes open for our agents in Brittany and members of the Confrèrie, which is where I do see a role for our new acquisition, as well as that already established for our fishing boats and MGBs."

As the meeting broke up, Enever called Tremayne back and indicated a seat opposite his own.

"Richard, for the next couple of days, I'd like you and your crew from 1315 to take the E-boat out on trials in the waters around here for a radius of about twenty miles. I want your crew to become completely familiar with her, so that they can handle her competently and confidently in any kind of emergency. Take the other boat captains along so that they, too, can take her out and use her if you're on ops elsewhere.

"If Admiral Hembury lets us keep her, instead of grabbing her for Devonport, we can get a hell of a lot of use out of her. Our proven ability to handle her could be a determining factor in who should keep her. We've enough diesel here already, which I've organised from St Mary's, and there's still ammunition a-plenty on board. So, dear boy, enjoy your ill-gotten gains – and get her crew up to scratch!"

Enever paused to light his pipe. "By the way, to avoid having you shot up by some returning, trigger-happy Beaufighter or Mosquito, we've rigged up a white ensign for you and stowed the Kriegsmarine ensign in the Bunting Tosser's locker, for possible future use. We have painted on her the number S53 and her cover story, on operations, will be that she is part of an S-boot training flotilla and has taken the same pennant number of an E-boat that was sunk by a mine in British waters in March of this year. We'll also make the number difficult to read by making it look worn and weather-beaten – and genuine enough. The technical boys have put in one of our radios alongside the German set so, as the situation demands, you can use either – or both."

Tremayne saluted Enever and returned to his cabin to prepare a briefing for the other boat captains and a sequence of induction and familiarisation for his crew.

Next morning at 08.30 hours, Schnellboot S53, complete with her trainee complement and three extra boat captains, set course due north for sea-trials and induction training for her new crew.

Taking the wheel in turn after a detailed inspection of the boat, Bower, Fischer, Taylor and Willoughby-Brown were all as impressed as Tremayne by the E-boat's exhilarating acceleration, high top speed and handling.

At maximum revolutions, her businesslike bow thrust clear of the water, exposing the black anti-fouling paint which covered her keel and lower hull below the overall light grey of her upper works and the remainder of her sleek hull above the waterline.

Crew members and officers alike tested her various weapons in turn, generally being most astounded by the phenomenal rate of fire of nine hundred rounds per minute each from her two MG 38 machine guns. In the absence of targets, the devastating impact of such firepower could only be imagined, but drew more than one astounded and admiring "'kin'ell" from Tremayne's crew.

Tremayne, interested to have Irvine's considered opinion about the E-boat, asked, "Well, Cox'n, what's the verdict, or is the jury still out?"

"Never seen anything like her, sir. Never handled anything like her before, sir, so I haven't."

The craggy, strong face relaxed for a moment as Irvine clearly savoured his recollection of standing on the bridge, minutes ago, with her wheel in his capable, experienced hands.

"But I think she's a little cracker, sir, so she is."

Praise indeed from this consummate seaman and remarkable man, thought Tremayne.

Addressing his fellow boat captains – and First Lieutenant

—Tremayne said, "Right, gentlemen, let's take her south — now you've a feel for her in open waters — and play hide-and-seek among the Western Rocks. Take her down to the Bishop, Bob, and then we'll see what she's like at manoeuvring at speed in that graveyard of so many fine ships."

With Irvine by his side on the wheelhouse bridge, Bower took command and raced due south at thirty-eight knots, her bow wave cascading continuous white spray over the forrard deck and foc'sl, the sheer force of her speed transmitted as continuous vibration through her entire hull and upper works.

As Bower closed on Bishop Rock lighthouse, he turned sharply to port and, with green water surging over her starboard gunwale, S53 hurled herself at the Crebawethans, holding her course for the neck separating them from Jacky's Rock and the fearsome, jagged peaks jutting out of the churning water.

"Thank heavens you kept the spray dodgers up, Richard," Hermann laughed. "That drenching turn of Bowers could have ruined my 'perm'!"

The awesome Western Rocks are about as testing an experience for a navigator and captain as any — especially at such high speed. Tremayne spent almost two hours there, giving his colleagues the opportunity to gain confidence and skill in navigating competently, in what could turn out to be E-boat temporary hideouts were they ever to come snooping — or hunting — around the Isles of Scilly.

Taylor, Fischer and Willoughby-Brown then took it in turns to navigate through the dangerous, tricky rocks between Melledgan and Annet, the largest uninhabited island after

Samson, before Irvine eventually took S53 back to Braiden Rock anchorage.

Tremayne set his crew about cleaning up the E-boat, while he debriefed the officers on the day's sea-trials and navigation and handling of the formidable craft. Two similarly intensive days of gaining experience in handling the E-boat followed before a gleeful Enever announced at dinner in the wardroom, "Gentlemen, we've got her! Admiral Hembury has agreed that we should keep S53 and he's coming down to Godolphin to see her for himself sometime next week. Well done on your handling of her these last few days and thank you all. You've done an excellent job."

Increasingly aware of the extent to which he was missing Emma, Tremayne wrote to her again and found himself eagerly looking forward to the mail each day. Then, at the end of the week, Emma managed to telephone him. Clearly so happy in one another's company, the telephone call – lasting almost twenty minutes – seemed to fly by. They laughed, reminisced and discussed hopes and dreams, rather than plans.

Unfortunately, both were on duty watch over the weekend as Emma's new role involved her in managing a small team responsible for monitoring German radio traffic at all hours of the day and night. However, they promised to meet at the earliest opportunity.

The following week arrived with the confirmation of Rear Admiral Hembury's intended visit.

Rawlings excelled himself, making the most of his role as chief organiser of the impending, auspicious occasion. Hectoring, threatening and browbeating without let up, he bullied many of those junior to him into grudging compliance.

Jane Topping, Enever's PA and replacement for Emma, together with Sub-Lieutenant Maurice Simmonds, the tall, young new addition to Enever's team, took the brunt of Rawlings' ill-tempered, choleric outbursts against the Intelligence Section. Both, with creditable maturity and commendable calm for their years, got things done – despite the irascible and intolerant senior officer.

The day before the Admiral's visit, Enever took Tremayne aside. "Best bib and tucker tomorrow, dear boy, the Admiral wants to talk with you."

Other than their inevitable conspiratorial twinkle, Enever's eyes gave nothing away.

In a tiny naval station like Godolphin, it was hard to contrive the sense of occasion that is so easy – and natural – at the main bases like Devonport, Portsmouth and Chatham, with their tradition, potential for pomp and their long history.

Duly, Admiral Hembury arrived with his aide-de-camp and addressed the assembled ship's company and Royal Marines on what served as the base's temporary parade ground.

He was fulsome in his praise for Godolphin's achievements and the measure of the sincerity – and authenticity – of his public recognition, noted Tremayne, was that he talked about *specific* events and accomplishments, in detail, quoting chapter and verse.

From Hembury, there were none of the customary generalisations and blandishments so often churned out by armchair admirals and generals, but rather genuine appreciation of the courage, determination and disregard for personal safety shown by members of the both the Royal Navy and Royal Marines. He spoke as if he had been in the situations he described and with the people whose achievements he applauded, because, mentally and emotionally, he *had* been there. His anguish when he spoke of casualties was palpable and the losses suffered in recent operations clearly moved him personally.

At the conclusion of his address, Rear Admiral Hembury announced: "I now have three extremely gratifying duties to perform." At this point his aide-de-camp, wearing a gold, ceremonial aiguillette, moved alongside Hembury.

"Will Lieutenant Tremayne and Captain Waring step forward?"

Both officers marched seven paces forward, halted in front of the Admiral, saluted and stood at attention.

"Lieutenant Richard Tremayne, RNVR, is awarded, by order of His Majesty King George VI, for extreme courage in the face of the enemy and gallantry in action, the Distinguished Service Cross. My warmest congratulations, Tremayne and well done!"

Tremayne stood in disbelief as Hembury took the medal from the velvet cushion held out by the aide-de-camp and pinned it over his left breast.

Almost mechanically, he replied, "Thank you, sir," saluted, turned about and marched back to rejoin his brother officers.

Waring was presented with a posthumous Military Medal for Marine Maguire, with the citation: "For bravery and extreme devotion to duty in the face of the enemy, Marine Maguire remained at his post though mortally wounded."

The citation brought Tremayne back into the world again as he saw, once more, in his mind's eye, the vision of a distraught, yet controlled Corporal Kane, cradling the dead Marine Maguire in his arms.

Next, it was Corporal Kane's name being called. And then, suddenly, there *was* Corporal Kane's tough, compact figure, head held proudly high, as he marched up, ramrod straight, past Tremayne to receive a bar — a second MM to his existing Military Medal — from Rear Admiral Hembury. As the Corporal returned, marching back to his section, Tremayne thought how much that phrase known to generations of Royal Marines — and which he had quoted to Kane — applied so aptly to men like them: *'Once a Marine — always a Marine'*.

That night, the wardroom was a place of celebration and, much to Tremayne's utter discomfort, he was at the centre of it. Essentially a shy man who needed more than average space and privacy, Tremayne had to gear himself up into what Wade termed his 'mental executive mode'.

To his relief, temporary escape came when a steward called him to the telephone outside the wardroom.

It was a very excited and happy Emma who had seen a signal of the notice of Tremayne's citation and award in the Naval Intelligence Section at SIS.

This time, they were only able to talk for three minutes because Emma was on duty watch, but that was enough to help Tremayne through the next two hours, before he was able to escape once more.

The following evening, after a day of combined exercises with

Squadron Leader Stanley's Hurricanes, Tremayne retired to his cabin to spend time writing a long-overdue letter to his parents, to let them know of his DSC before it appeared in any newspapers. This was still a time when successes were something of a rarity for the British, and journalists seized upon any good news as if it were gold dust. He had just finished the letter when the ship's tannoy system requested his presence in the wardroom bar to meet a visitor. Tremayne hastily put on his uniform jacket, grabbed his cap and walked over to the tiny bar.

An officer, in the uniform of a RN Lieutenant Commander, stood with his back to Tremayne, chatting to the bar steward. Something about him was immediately familiar – apart from the new, additional gold half ring on his sleeve – and Tremayne instantly felt a sense of overwhelming joy. As he entered the bar, the officer turned round, smiling warmly, his hand outstretched, "Hello, young Richard. How are you – it's been a long time!"...

Nine

Hoist battle ensign

For two men who each had more than an average measure of reflective reserve in their make-up, their uncharacteristic, insatiable need to talk simply reflected the joy of a happy reunion of two people who clearly took great delight in each other's company.

When Tremayne had first heard the devastating news of what was presumed to be Bill Mitchell's death at sea, it was as if he'd lost a close, elder brother. The term 'guide, philosopher and friend', though sometimes hackneyed, described exactly how Tremayne, as a young, inexperienced officer, had quickly come to regard the older man. In Bill Mitchell, he had found a friend and brother officer who was honest, authentic and selfless and who emerged as a source of sanity and strength at a time when Tremayne had desperately needed both.

Mitchell, for his part, saw in the younger man an earnestness and sincerity, coupled with a drive to excel at whatever job he was given to do. This he had seen at first hand, in action against the enemy, while he and Tremayne had first served together in *Portree*'s sister ship, the corvette *HMS Fleetwood*.

Mitchell, an experienced naval officer, found that Tremayne already possessed the sense of duty and personal commitment to others – the hallmarks of the dependability that the crew had the right to expect of those who led them. Their close relationship had therefore developed from mutual respect, a natural affection and a shared, situational sense of humour that was irreverent and, at times, bordered on the outrageous.

After what must have been at least an hour of mutual catching up – but which seemed to fly by like a few minutes – Tremayne suggested that they went to the New Inn for supper and the convivial atmosphere of the island's 'local'.

Mitchell spoke with manifest feeling of the sinking of the *Portree* and the sadness he still felt about the loss of so many good friends. In most navies, the last ship is always 'the best' and the associated memories remain vivid for a long time. Mitchell described how, on the order "Abandon ship", he had leapt into the desperately cold water in his life jacket, swimming with two others until they were spotted by the captain of the U-boat that had just sunk their corvette. Picked up – and well treated – by the U-boat crew, they had been taken first to the naval base at Lorient and then, from there, to a prisoner-of-war camp for naval personnel, close to Nantes.

He had no idea why his rescue had not been reported, while that of his shipmates had been.

Mitchell said that the conditions there were not good and he and several others decided to make a break for it. After many weeks of digging and tunnelling, five of them – two British, two French and a Norwegian – escaped. He and the other British POW headed south for Spain and, after nearly two months of lying up by day and travelling by night, made it to Gibraltar – and safety…

They then talked about Tremayne's transfer to Naval Special Forces and both the intense training and the operations that he had been involved in since joining HMS Godolphin. Amid a lot of laughter, Tremayne described too, in graphic terms, the colourful characters that he operated with – especially his fellow boat captains, the crew of his motor gunboat and the Royal Marine instructors.

After dinner, drinking a glass of Dick Oyler's 'reserved-for-special-occasions-only' brandy, Bill Mitchell asked Tremayne quietly, "So, Richard, how's life now? It does sound to me as if it *is* getting better. Is that right?"

"At first, it was pretty desperate sometimes – especially on watch at sea and at night, staring at nothing but blackness and alone on the bridge with some unbearably painful thoughts. This place, with its unique beauty and encompassing sense of peace, has been a great help as, too, have some of the unbelievable characters I told you about." Tremayne paused thoughtfully and took a sip of brandy. "About three months ago, I met a Wren officer – Emma Fraser – a gentle, caring and sensitive girl, yet one who, like you, can quickly put the most bloody awful events into a more sane and positive perspective. Her sense of what normality should be is almost instinctive. We've worked together a good deal and, over time, have become very close. Of all the desperately bad luck, she's just been transferred to SIS in London."

"Tell me about her, Richard."

"I must admit that I went through hell at first, with feelings of guilt and a terrible sense of disloyalty towards Diana. At the same time, I felt an unnerving sense of confusion in my feelings towards Emma. I felt guilty about even sharing a good conversation and simply being able to laugh with another woman again – especially when just the two of us were together. I now know that she has become such an important part of my life that I want to spend the rest of it with her, Bill."

"If you really feel that, Richard, and if she feels the same about you," said Mitchell gently, "I don't think you need any advice from me. I think you already know what you need to say to her. Am I right?"

"Yes, as you usually are! But thank you. The guilt and confusion have just taken a long time to fade."

"Of course they will. That's natural – and inevitable. Many memories will remain – and it's OK that they do. You have to decide *how* you want your present and your future to be in terms of your relationship with Emma. That present and that future are something that only you and she can create and build *together*."

For a moment, the shadow of thought crossed Tremayne's face and then he smiled, "Thanks a lot. That helps a great deal, Bill."

"There's something else I need to talk to you about, Richard. On return from 'Gib' I was seconded to the Special Investigations Branch and, with a bit of conniving skulduggery, I was able to make HMS Godolphin my first assignment."

"Good heavens, what are we supposed to have been up to?"

"This station is largely Rear Admiral Hembury's brainchild — it's also his pride and joy and he naturally takes a close, personal interest in it and its role. He and John Enever have become aware that comparatively low-level classified information about Godolphin has been passed to the Germans. At the moment, as far as we know, nothing serious and nothing that throws any light onto what really goes on here has been let out. But, it's only a matter of time before information which *is* top secret might fall into the Germans' hands." Mitchell had Tremayne's undivided attention as he continued.

"My job, Richard, is to identify the source of the leak and to stop it, long before Tresco's crucial role is compromised in any way. I start in the morning and the first stage of my investigations is to try to establish exactly who has been seeking information from the ship's company — asking too many questions, for example — or stealing written information from the base. And then to identify who the immediate recipients of that information are. Any first thoughts, Richard?"

"My first thought is one of absolute surprise and my first reaction is 'no one that I know'. Against that, if the Admiral and John Enever both agree there is a leak, then I would treat their concern most seriously and give all the help I can. May I ask, Bill, is anyone in particular under suspicion at the moment?"

"Unfortunately, I can't discuss that issue and I'm sorry if that sounds stuffy, but just think of anyone who has quizzed you recently about Godolphin's role and what goes on here – and then let's talk about it. As you know, so much of counter-intelligence work is a matter of piecing together seemingly unconnected snippets of information, which slowly – or sometimes suddenly – produce a definite pattern of activity. And that's what I'm attempting to establish here.

"It may turn out to be a storm in a teacup – but that's what I have to establish. I have to get back now to talk with John Enever but thanks for a great evening – it's been bloody marvellous to see you again, Richard. I'm so pleased that things have worked out so well for you here. John, I know, thinks a great deal of you. So goodnight, sleep well and I'll see you in the morning!"

Later, back in his cabin, Tremayne thought about how good it was to be in Bill Mitchell's company again. For over a year, since *HMS Portree* went down in the swirling cold grey waters off the south of Ireland, Tremayne had believed for certain that Bill Mitchell had died along with his ship. It was, reflected Tremayne, as if he had returned from the grave.

He thought about what Bill had said about a leak of confidential information and tried to recall anyone who had attempted to question him. He could think of absolutely no one. Except, perhaps…but no, that was being plain paranoid. "Bertie," he said out loud to his ever-attentive Labrador, "I'll be seeing bloody snakes under the bed next. It's time I took a bath and went to bed!"

He saw Bill Mitchell briefly at breakfast and then Tremayne

was called by tannoy, along with the other boat captains, first lieutenants and all officers, to attend a meeting with Enever in room 101 at 08.30 hours.

Enever introduced Bill Mitchell to the group, stating that he was on temporary secondment to Godolphin for a short period and that he would welcome an opportunity to talk with officers, NCOs and senior rates over the next few days. After this short announcement, Mitchell and all officers who were not boat crews left the meeting.

Used to receiving confidential information, without explanation, until it was believed the time was right, no one queried Enever's brief introduction of Mitchell and merely took his presence as just one more of many new faces that came and went as a matter of course in a Special Forces base such as Godolphin.

Enever released a large rolled up wall-map of the English Channel and south coast and, using a pointer, began: "Gentlemen, we have an urgent order from Admiral Hembury." Enever moved his pipe onto the table in front of him. "From Lowestoft to Land's End, Jerry is being a pain-in-the-arse — principally with those damned E-boats of his. In just the last few days alone, German coastal surface craft — and that includes a few R-boats too — have sunk thousands of tons of Allied shipping in the Channel, with the loss of hundreds of Merchant Navy personnel. Losses in Lyme Bay, for example, have been particularly heavy including an armed trawler and a Flower-class corvette, *HMS Agapanthus*. With E-boat flotillas brought down from Norway and round from the Mediterranean to reinforce the local units, we reckon that upwards of fifty E-boats have been roaming our waters, doing enormous damage with apparent impunity." Looking slowly round the room as he filled, then lit, his pipe, Enever continued, "So gentlemen, working in collaboration with MGBs and MTBs from Helford River base, Dartmouth and Devonport, our orders are to clear the Channel of German coastal surface craft, from Lyme Bay to Scilly, by inflicting such heavy losses that Jerry won't be inclined to try his hand again for a long time. East of Lyme Bay, the Channel will be swept clean by our combined flotillas located from Pompey, right round to Lowestoft."

Enever took questions and, just before the meeting broke up, he said, "Richard will act as Flotilla Commander and will use the E-boat. She is being fitted, as I speak, with a Bofors 40mm as her bow gun to replace the puny 20mm already there. All boats are being victualled with food, water and screening smoke, as well as maximum possible ammunition and fuel."

Enever carefully rolled up the wall-map, placing the pointer on the table in front of him.

"Sub-Lieutenant Quilghini, with Sub-Lieutenant Tabarly as his Number One, will command MGB 1315, Richard's boat, which gives us a Tresco flotilla of five vessels – all of them with guns heavier than, or at least equal to, the Germans' maximum calibre weapons. What we can't match yet, is their high top speed. We will work most closely with Commander Holden's flotilla from Helford, giving us a joint group of ten boats – two of theirs being MTBs which, with a top speed of forty knots, *will* give the E-boats a run for their money. The Jerries have been operating mostly after dark and Admiral Hembury wants us to be out there, ready and waiting for them, when they appear. ETD is 16.00 hours and RV with the Helford flotilla will be 18.00 hours."

Enever paused again, looking at each of those in his audience.

"Boat captains' operational briefing will be at 14.30 hours, when both Richard and I will give you your final orders. Thank you gentlemen."

The briefing broke up with an animated buzz of conversation, as the officers began to disperse. Tremayne and Willoughby-Brown went together to see the progress of the installation of S53's new Bofors over at Braiden Rock.

Godolphin's engineers were hard at work in the bow gun-pit of Tremayne's new command, when he and his First Lieutenant reached the anchorage. In charge of the working party was Engineer Chief Petty Officer Eyles, a large, capable, rosy-cheeked man who hailed from the depths of rural Wiltshire. Standing on the rocks that made up the base of the improvised jetty, Tremayne looked up at the disproportionately large Bofors whose long barrel completely dominated the short sweep of the E-boat's forrard deck.

"Good morning Chief. How is it going – any problems?"

"No sir. We've more or less secured 'im and 'e'll be ready later this forenoon, sir. Jerry 'ad already put in a mounting big enough for one o' them flak 3.7s, sir, and all we done was to firtle around a bit to make 'im fit, sir."

"Thank you Chief and *well done*." Tremayne put a note of personal, genuine gratitude into that often trite expression of officer approval. "Please make sure that ammunition lockers are ready to hand for the gun-layer before we sail – and carry on firtling, Chief, please," grinned Tremayne.

"That thing should give us decidedly more clout up forrard, but we must have a good gun-layer, able to keep feeding the ammunition clips at a pace to maintain the rate of fire we're going to need." Tremayne addressed his comments to Willoughby-Brown, who had been similarly amused by the Chief's capacity to grace the inanimate with both gender and life so readily and easily.

"When we sank Lang's E-boat, in our first encounter with this particular type of beast, luck was very much on our side," continued Tremayne. "Seizing an opportunity that presents itself like that, often does decide who wins and who loses, David. In the next engagement, seamanship and gunnery will be the crucial factors. We will need to outmanoeuvre and outshoot them and we must get this message home at the briefing this afternoon, because, for sure, we won't outrun them – they have the legs of us every time."

Willoughby-Brown's expression of earnest concentration brought Tremayne up with a start. "Forgive the sermon, David, but the Germans' record in recent Channel engagements has been impressive to say the least, and I want to make sure that we give *them* a bloody nose and reverse the score."

At the pre-operational following Enever's typically sage and perceptive input, Tremayne reiterated the points he had emphasised with his First Lieutenant, adding, "There will be times when independent action will be vital to success." Tremayne deliberately avoided the word 'survival'. "Take it, gentlemen, but never forget we are a flotilla and there are times in battle when unity is strength, so regroup please, on command, as fast as possible. Carry battle ensigns with you – we're going to thump those bastards in style! Good luck!"

At 16.00 hours the flotilla slipped moorings and set course for the rendezvous with Commander Holden's Helford flotilla, proceeding northwards through New Grimsby Sound at half revolutions until they passed Kettle Bottom Rocks. Then, at maximum speed and fifteen miles east, north-east of Scilly, Tremayne made to all boats: *'Test weapons'*. He was quickly reassured by his new Bofors' steady "thump, thump, thump", as Watkins and Robson – his new gun-layer replacement for 'Brummie' Nicholls – let fly with several clips of 40 mm shells.

"Bloody 'ell, Robbo, this bugger's so long, if we run out of ammo we can always ram the bleeders with it," was Acting Leading Seaman Watkins' imaginative assessment of his new gun's potential.

The RV with Holden's flotilla went smoothly and, under the overall command of Lieutenant Commander Paul Draisey from the Cornish base, the two flotillas set course east for Lyme Bay to meet up with the flotilla from Dartmouth.

Draisey signalled: *'Each flotilla – 'arrowhead' formation. Tresco to starboard, please.'*

"Acknowledge, please, Yeo," said Tremayne to the ever ready Yeoman of Signals standing beside him on the bridge.

Under two hours later, the two flotillas met up with their opposite numbers from Dartmouth, who formed up as the port 'arrowhead' with Draisey's five boats as the central inverted 'vee'.

Draisey made to all boats: *'This is 'E-boat alley'. Keep your eyes open. Good hunting everybody'.*

Tremayne and his First Lieutenant were already scanning the horizon through their binoculars, as were their gun crews amidships and astern. Even by nine o'clock, the clear light of the warm summer evening still gave sharp visibility over many miles across the wide expanse of Lyme Bay to the south and to the east, the predicted, most likely direction of E-boat attacks. Tremayne, however, frequently favoured the unorthodox and unexpected. As a consequence – and as a matter of course – he credited his enemy with comparable resourceful guile, hence his insistence on all-round watchkeeping when at sea.

At full revolutions, the combined flotilla of fifteen boats began carrying out a succession of large sweeps over the bay, ever moving southwards, out of sight of the Devon and Dorset coastline.

Just before ten o'clock, with dusk beginning to gather, the leading boat in the Dartmouth flotilla signalled, her Aldis lamp flickering urgently from her bridge.

"Sir, boat on our port beam signalling. Message reads: *'Large group of small surface craft moving across our course, port to starboard'.*"

"Thank you. Yeo. Make to: *'WAIT, the skipper's seen it'.*"

Seconds later, Draisey's boat signalled: *'Action stations. We've got company. Let's go and meet them. Maintain formation'.*

Tremayne repeated the order for action stations, adding, "Stand by, all guns."

As always, the rapidly rising tension was relieved by repeated routine actions and equipment checks.

Both Tremayne and the First Lieutenant had the approaching vessels in their binoculars.

"Sir, signal from Flotilla Commander." The Leading Yeoman's voice had a distinct urgency to the Valleys' lilt. "*'Engage the enemy closely. Good luck'.*"

As the whole flotilla began to swing five degrees to port, almost as one boat, on course to bring the enemy craft dead ahead, Tremayne quickly turned to his signaller, "Thank you Yeo. Make to all our boats: *'We're engaging the enemy. Hoist battle ensigns!'*"

Seconds later, the large white ensigns broke out from the masts of the five Tresco boats.

Now clearly identified as a force of twenty German E-boats, the enemy craft swung round to meet the British flotilla head on.

"Signal from commander, sir: *'Watch out for torpedoes'.*"

At just over fifteen hundred yards, flashes from the E-boats' bow guns signalled the commencement of the battle. Watching for the telltale trails of incoming torpedoes through his binoculars, Tremayne yelled, "Bow gun. Open fire – shoot, shoot, shoot! All guns, both torpedo tubes – fire as you bear."

For several heart-stopping minutes, the opposing flotillas raced headlong towards each other, seemingly on a course of mutual, suicidal annihilation. Alert to the destructive power of torpedoes, Irvine, at the wheel, hurled the boat forward at full throttle in a succession of sharp zigzags in response to Tremayne's urgent commands: "Hard a-starboard, Cox'n – NOW! Quickly – HARD A-PORT!"

Briefly on a straight course, S53's torpedo-man released the starboard 'tin fish', only to see it pass harmlessly by an oncoming

E-boat. Seconds later, to a great cheer from all on the deck, his port torpedo struck home with a blinding flash and huge explosion, as a frantically manoeuvring E-boat struggled desperately to avoid it, but left its escape a fraction too late. The doomed vessel vanished in seconds, leaving a huge pall of dense, spreading black smoke, with curling bright orange flames at its base, over a collection of shattered, unrecognisable flotsam on the oily surface of the sea.

Several E-boat 20mm shells had already struck Tremayne's boat – mostly in the hull – and in the terrifying noise of such close, heated engagement, he was aware of other explosions ahead and to port as more vessels from both sides either exploded or 'brewed up'. The initial orderly 'charge' had degenerated into the bewildering – and now deafening – confusion of a savage mêlée as the opposing boats swept by, raking one another's decks and foc'sls with cannon and machine gun fire. Standing close by on the bridge, Willoughby-Brown gave a sharp cry as, with blood pouring down his face, he collapsed at Tremayne's feet.

"Yeoman, a wound dressing. Quickly man!" Tremayne knelt down to staunch the flow of blood and to check the First Lieutenant's pulse. Willoughby-Brown was still alive, but the wound to the side of his head was deep and blood was pumping from it. He had lost consciousness and Tremayne quickly applied the Yeoman's dressing, giving the badly wounded officer a shot of morphine and making him as comfortable as the cramped bridge would allow.

Irvine, still at the wheel, was standing with his bloodied left arm hanging limply at his side, his right hand steering the boat away from the immediate mind-numbing cacophony and chaos.

"'Swain, I'm sorry — I didn't see you were wounded."

"Yeo. Another wound dressing."

"You were busy, sir, with the First Lieutenant, so you were. It was shell shrapnel, sir, the same as hit Sub-Lieutenant Willoughby-Brown, sir."

"Sit down here on the flag locker 'Swain and the Yeoman will dress your wound."

"No, sir, I'm fine sir, so I am. I'll stay at the wheel sir."

"That's an order 'Swain. As soon as the wound is dressed, go below and bloody well stay there. I'm taking over the wheel!"

"Aye aye, sir."

Tremayne suddenly became aware that in the time he had been tending the wounded, S53's guns had not stopped firing once and the weapons aft of the wheelhouse were still shooting at the enemy boats now astern of him. Empty shell-cases of various calibres littered the decking around the boat's weapons — and were continuing to fall and collect as the automatic weapons fired without stopping, other than to reload.

Although it could only be three minutes at the most since he had last looked around, the scene on the sea close to his boat had changed dramatically. Several E-boats, British MTBs and motor gunboats were on fire with thick, billowing black smoke pouring from them, while others were gradually settling in the water, to slip slowly beneath the waves. Sailors in lifejackets, from both navies, were struggling in the water — swimming around and calling for help. Others were paddling rubber dinghies and

Carley floats, grabbing whomsoever they could – irrespective of nationality – and dragging them exhausted on board. To Tremayne, it was like a scene from some waterborne hell, with silhouettes and shadows distorted by the dancing flames lighting up the now dark night.

The remaining six E-boats were departing from the engagement, heading south for France at top speed and, apart from his own boat and the two British MTBs that were still seaworthy, there were no vessels that were fast enough to catch them.

Tremayne ordered "Stop engines" and then, "Stand by to pick up survivors. Scrambling nets down."

From what Tremayne could see from the chaos and carnage around him, nine British boats appeared to be more or less intact and capable of returning to their bases. Quickly looking around his own boat, he saw extensive cannon fire and shrapnel damage to the hull and upper-works, but she was not taking in water and her engines appeared to be in full working order. Smiling somewhat ruefully, he looked up at the now shredded, but still proudly flying battle ensign fluttering defiantly in the glow of flames from a burning E-boat, dead in the water about fifty feet away. He checked the forrard Bofors and thanked Watkins and Robson for the unrelenting fire they had poured into any E-boats that came within their sights. He was closely followed by a stoker-mechanic from the engine room, ladling out liberal rations of neat rum into enamel mugs for the whole boat's company.

Tremayne then moved aft to check the guns amidships and astern and to congratulate the gun crews for their outstanding display of gunnery. It was when he finally reached the after 20mm that he discovered the two gun crew members lying still on the deck beside the weapon's pedestal mounting. One, Able Seaman Trotter, was dead from a severe head wound and the other, Leading Seaman Morrison, the gunner, had been wounded in the shoulder and upper arm. Two members of the crew were tending to him as Tremayne came up to speak with him.

Tremayne then returned to the bridge, followed by the Yeoman who had taken over distribution of a tot to everybody in the wheelhouse and below, forrard, except to his captain.

"'Yer, sir, 'ave a tot – it's 'neaters', sir." The Rhondda lilt was like a breath of fresh air and normality to Tremayne. "Bless you Yeo. Thanks."

Looking back at the shambles on the sea around them, he called to the retreating figure of the signaller, "Yeo. Make to Tresco boats: *'Well done. Report casualties and damage. Regroup on me'.*"

He then bent down to look more closely at the deathly pale face of Willoughby-Brown who had still not regained consciousness. His breathing was laboured, but the flow of blood had stopped and his pulse, though slow, felt regular. He detailed two seamen to carry the First Lieutenant down to the bunk in the tiny wardroom, while he went to see the Cox'n, sitting in the crew's forrard mess deck, surrounded by wreckage caused by shells which had penetrated the E-boat's wooden hull.

It was Irvine who spoke first as Tremayne entered. "How's the First Lieutenant, sir. Is he going to be alright, sir?"

"I hope so, 'Swain, but it's a nasty wound and we won't know for certain until he's seen the Doc, but thank you for asking."

Turning to the Cox'n he asked, "So, what about you, 'Swain? How is your arm?"

"Oh, just fine, sir —and it'll be much better when it can lift a pint of Guinness again, so it will, sir."

"We're clearing up and taking stock and then we'll be on our way home, 'Swain."

An urgent call from the Leading Yeoman of Signals brought Tremayne back up onto the bridge.

"Message from Flotilla Commander's boat, sir: *'Commander down. Have assumed command. Please report damage and casualties'.*"

"Thanks Yeo, acknowledge and make: *'Damage and casualties to follow'.*"

"Aye aye, sir." The Aldis flickered again in response.

"What news from our boats, Yeo?"

"All have replied, sir, except 1317, Lieutenant Bower's boat. I'm afraid she blew up and sank, sir, about 'alf way through the engagement. Confirmed by 1316's Yeoman, sir." As if anticipating Tremayne's urgent question, Jenkins added, more softly, "There were no survivors, sir."

"Thank you, Yeo," said Tremayne quietly, struggling to keep his feelings under control.

"Make to captain's boat: *'Listing casualties and damage for Tresco boats'* and add *'1317 sunk — no survivors'.*"

Two minutes later, the Aldis flickered from the captain's boat: *'All boats. Well done. Start engines. Dartmouth — ETA 05.00. Follow the leader'.*

The three Daimler-Benz diesels rumbled into life and then took on a steady roar as S53, along with the other boats, set course for Dartmouth.

On the bridge, with the E-boat's wheel in his hands, Tremayne felt a sense of disorientation and divorce from reality. The inevitable shock of battle, the elation of undoubted victory and the surge of pure adrenalin that they bring, had given way to the numbing sensation of the loss of close friends and deep concern over the severe injuries of others. He allowed his thoughts to wander to Emma, her gentle blue eyes and her quiet voice with its soft, western Highland cadence, and then to the weekend they had shared on Tresco before her sudden and cruel departure to London. In his mind's eye, Tremayne saw her again as she bent to look at a wild flower with an expression of childlike wonder that crossed her beautiful face at the sight of something so simple. He saw again how concerned and caring she had looked when he had just returned from Plymouth and he recalled the sensitive understanding that she had shown him, so many times, since they had first met one another. How he wished that she would be there when he eventually returned to Tresco.

Tremayne grudgingly dragged himself back to the present and, calling to the Yeoman to take the wheel, he slipped down below to see the two wounded men. When he reached the wardroom, he was relieved to see Irvine sitting with Willoughby-Brown and he could hear the First Lieutenant speaking intermittently to the Cox'n.

"How are you, David? Is there anything you need?"

"A new head would help – this one feels a bit sore – but thank you. 'Swain has been his usual sterling self, plying me with water and changing my dressing."

"We're on our way to Darmouth to RV with the remainder

of the flotilla and there we'll get the MO to look at that wound of yours, David. And yours too, 'Swain."

Tremayne spent another few minutes with them and then returned to take over the wheel from Jenkins.

"Thanks, Yeo. How did you find she handles?"

"A bloody sight easier to turn than the Pontypridd front row, beggin' your pardon, sir," grinned the Welshman.

Tremayne laughed, "Well Yeo, she *is* built more like a wing three-quarter than a front row forward. The Germans call them 'greyhounds of the seas', by the way."

"That must make a Fairmile seem like an 'ippopotamus to them, sir."

Tremayne smiled to himself in the dark. He had never before heard such musical quality injected into the word 'hippopotamus' as that added, so naturally, by the Yeoman.

It was people like 'Taff' Jenkins, 'Pablo' Watkins and the Cox'n who so often unconsciously created an imperturbable and reassuring atmosphere around the place, as they went about the most mundane tasks and duties. "Thank God for such people", mused Tremayne.

As dawn began to break behind them in their race westwards, the south Devon coast progressively took shape and assumed a sharper, more detailed definition way off to starboard.

By the time the flotilla reached its anchorage, close to Warfleet in the Dart estuary, the early morning sun was low in the sky and creating a complete contrast with the hellish, Dantesque inferno of just a few hours ago.

Secured alongside Fischer's Camper and Nicholson and the Fairmiles of Taylor and Quilghini, Tremayne made sure that his wounded were immediately collected and taken to the naval base hospital for attention. He then scrambled over decks, clutter and wreckage to meet each of his fellow Tresco boat captains, who were gathering on Fischer's forrard deck to greet him.

"A 14 – 6 win," said Mick Taylor, "but Bob's loss makes it almost a Pyrrhic victory." Tremayne sensed that the others felt the same and even the normally irrepressible Hermann was quiet and subdued, despite the impressive disparity in vessels sunk by the two sides.

Lieutenant John Merry, the badly wounded Draisey's deputy, had organised early hot breakfasts for both officers and men and, sensing the inevitable 'balance sheet' reckoning of lives lost weighed against victories gained, ushered everyone along to their respective dining rooms.

He turned to Tremayne saying, "Our skipper here at Dartmouth, plus Lieutenant Commander Black, our Intelligence Officer, will run the operation debrief and I understand that Lieutenant Enever from HMS Godolphin will join us, Richard. That will be in two hours at 07.30. We're all a bit frayed around the edges, so let's go and eat and we can organise showers for everyone to freshen up afterwards."

"May I suggest," said Tremayne, "that we deliberately mix together officers from the different flotillas to encourage them to make new acquaintances and to break up the concentration on lost friends and colleagues. I think that we should do it for the others too. It might open up the gloomy atmosphere a bit – misery loves miserable companions and I want to break the connections for a while. "

"Good idea, I'll play host and fix it."

Out of real concern – not curiosity – Tremayne saw the ploy work well over breakfast, as the ice was broken by people getting to know others who had fought anonymously – and furiously – alongside them just seven or eight hours ago. Gradually, the combined effects of bacon, sausages, eggs and hot, fresh tea and coffee – together with new friendships developing out of shared experiences – lightened the atmosphere and the noise level rose significantly as the buzz of conversation began to dominate the room.

Tremayne found that, though tired through lack of sleep and the stress of dramatically close action, breakfast, new faces to talk to and a hot shower had invigorated him considerably. He realised too that he was actually looking forward to the debriefing and the senior officers' strategic interpretation of the battle's impact. He would certainly welcome John Enever's calm presence and professional approach at the meeting.

Captain Vaughan, the Commanding Officer of Coastal Forces at Dartmouth, Lieutenant Commander Black, his Intelligence Officer, and Lieutenant Commander Enever constituted the executive debriefing group.

Vaughan, short, stocky and strongly built, with greying wavy hair above a determined, yet finely-boned face, identified the importance of so convincing a 'trouncing of the scourge of the English Channel'. He emphasised the point that one good thrashing would not completely rid British and Allied shipping in the Channel of the E-boat menace for good.

"But," he said, "it will send the Germans back to the drawing board and force them to rethink their strategy and that, in itself, will provide a lull in the concentrated attacks upon vital sea-borne supplies to Great Britain. It will also give us some much-needed time to draw the necessary lessons from the experience and consolidate our own counter-measures."

He made a further a point that last night's battle represented the first significant victory by British Coastal Forces over their German counterparts. Too often, the Germans had won decisively – or, at best, the outcome had been inconclusive. The consequent boost to morale and confidence, he believed, was incalculable.

Lieutenant Commander Black, a lean man with piercing dark eyes and a neat black beard, offered a more detailed and piecemeal analysis, typical of the Intelligence Services' 'jigsaw' approach. What he saw to be a critical tactic for the future, was to lure out the E-boats in force – with suitable decoys – and destroy them by a combination of dominating air-power and surface craft, with heavier armament than that possessed by the E-boats.

"My guess, gentlemen," he said, "is that your superior weaponry contributed hugely to the kill-ratio of British to German boats." He looked quickly around the room at the assenting nods.

"I believe, too, that the high aggressive spirit of your attack probably caught them off-guard, having been accustomed to seizing victory themselves by speed and ruthless daring."

Enever then took over, in order to draw together the key

lessons to be learned as a basis for new tactics and strategies to keep at least one step ahead of the Germans. Over coffee break, Enever made it a priority to spend time with Tremayne and the other Tresco boat captains and, as he put it, "to hitch a lift back with you, dear boy, in that new speed boat of yours."

Tremayne made a point of visiting the sickbay to talk with Leading Seaman Morrison, the Cox'n and his First Lieutenant whose wound was diagnosed as 'serious, but not life-threatening'. "I'll put Lucy in the picture and we'll get her over here as fast as we are able," promised Tremayne.

Irvine had been classified as 'walking wounded' and, as he was very quick to tell Tremayne, could 'return to base for continued treatment'.

An amused Tremayne saw through the hidden agenda behind the Cox'n's strongly expressed wish to return to Tresco which was, in fact, only too transparent. Irvine, clearly, had more than met his match in the formidable, no-nonsense ward sister who, to quote the Cox'n, "is built like a brick ale-house and makes the commandos look like a troop of Brownies, so she does".

Shortly before noon, with Tremayne leading, in line ahead, the Tresco flotilla slipped moorings and headed out towards the open sea on course to the Isles of Scilly.

Enever, with his inexhaustible schoolboy enthusiasm for all things mechanical and nautical, was given a personal tour of S53 by Tremayne, while Irvine temporarily took the wheel. The immaculate and shining engine room impressed him immensely and he was delighted when Tremayne invited him to fire the after 20mm, having first signalled to all boats – to Enever's amusement:

'*Intelligence Officer testing weapons. Keep your heads down*'. Enever's tour ended, as delight turned to near-ecstasy, when Tremayne offered him the wheel – much to the one-armed Cox'n's thinly veiled expression of disapproval.

"Dear boy, at last I feel that I'm a real sailor! Now, while I 'aim and fire' this marvellous piece of kit, tell me about last night's scrap with Jerry."

Standing next to Enever on the bridge and regularly scanning the horizon with his binoculars, Tremayne recounted, in detail, the sequence of events of the battle in Lyme Bay.

Enever was appalled by the losses suffered, in men and boats, and by the sheer destructive mayhem of fast moving, close-quarter battle at sea. His conclusion was that it had been an outstanding victory over a determined and skilful enemy and that, in such circumstances, there was inevitably a high price to pay.

Close to Scilly, an anxious-looking, but very relieved Cox'n, took the wheel back and eventually guided S53 south, through the Sound separating Tresco and Bryher, down to Braiden Rock.

Enever and Tremayne exchanged salutes as the Intelligence Officer went ashore with the words, "Thank you for the trip of a lifetime! Secure, then bed, Richard. Let's meet in my office at 15.00 hours. Bill Mitchell would also like to see you then."

Tremayne spoke to each member of his crew, before leaving the boat to take a still protesting Cox'n to Surgeon Lieutenant Hegarty for treatment. He followed Enever's advice and went to his cabin to catch up on some desperately needed sleep. Before he fell asleep he wrote a letter to Emma, describing the night's action in no more than general terms, knowing full well that she would read about it in Admiralty intelligence reports as well as in the daily newspapers.

Rested and refreshed, he went to Enever's office at 15.00 hours, having first sought out Lucy Caswell to tell her of Willoughby-Brown's wound, but in such a way as to reassure rather than to alarm her. He promised her that he would do what he could, on her behalf, to get her over to Dartmouth to see the First Lieutenant.

Saluting Enever and Mitchell, he was greeted warmly by both men and ushered into one of the Intelligence Officer's indulgently comfortable leather club chairs – more trophies from Rear Admiral Hembury's many supplies safaris.

Enever began by confirming Mitchell's real role at Godolphin as a counter-intelligence investigator, prompted by a suspicion that confidential information about the base – and its personnel – was being passed on to the enemy.

Mitchell immediately turned to Tremayne. "Richard, you'll recall that I asked you about people here on Tresco who might have quizzed you about what you do here."

"Absolutely and, at the time, I was staggered. The only, quite innocuous conversation that I could recall where some vague interest was expressed in what goes on here was with Aileen Oyler."

"Please, Richard, try to remember exactly what you were asked. Take your time," said Enever.

Tremayne tried to remember exactly what had been said but most of it was blurred and now beyond recall, largely because of what had happened in the meantime. Then, suddenly, the change in Aileen's expression and the uncharacteristic coldness of her voice when she had referred to her mother's death – "No, Mr Tremayne, it was no accident" – flashed across his mind. When he recounted that incident, Mitchell stopped him.

"Thereby hangs a tale, Richard. From about 1919 to 1922, Aileen's father, Pat Hogan, served in the 7th Battalion of the Kilkenny Brigade of the IRA as the leader of one of their 'Flying Columns'. He and his colleagues quickly became marked men and went on the run. The notorious Auxiliaries – the Auxiliary Police – and the Black and Tans frequently called at his house to try to catch him. One day, after a Flying Column attack in which several British were killed and wounded, the enraged Auxiliaries arrived at his home at dawn, dragged everybody out of bed and interrogated them pretty brutally. Aileen's mother refused to tell them where her husband was and so the furious Auxiliaries took her outside and shot her in front of her children – including Aileen who would have been about thirteen at the time."

"My God, how dreadful for her," murmured Tremayne, "then, very understandably, she will be no lover of the British military."

"From what we've managed to unearth so far, she has asked several crew members about what goes on here. What bits of information she has gathered, we understand, have been given to a cousin whose husband is still a member of the IRA in County Kilkenny. 'Once in – never out' and 'You're only as good as your next job' are their operational philosophies. It is he, we believe, who has been passing intelligence on to the Germans.

So far, it is all low-level stuff, but any disclosure of our undercover activities here could have disastrous results – on both sides of the English Channel." Mitchell paused, searching Tremayne's face for a reaction. As if on cue, Tremayne asked, "So what has happened to Aileen? What are you planning to do about her?"

"Although technically born a British citizen in 1908 in Ireland, she took Irish citizenship in 1938, after Ireland became a Republic, and she holds an Irish passport – and that, we believe, would save her if we were to press charges. Legally this is a tricky one and we, for our part, would in no way associate ourselves with the brutal attitudes and inexcusable behaviour of the Auxiliaries."

"Naval law, in print at least, looks equally draconian," responded Tremayne, "especially the sentence – '…and shall suffer death, or any other punishment hereinafter mentioned'."

"To begin to answer your question, Richard, none of those whom we have questioned gave any indication that they had been *interrogated* by local people – and that includes Aileen, obviously. What we suspect, is that in response to the questions posed by her cousin – sinister or otherwise – Aileen has simply responded with general, conversational information and that the justifiable bitterness that she must feel over her mother's death is a separate issue. So, since Aileen knows nothing of our investigation at the base, we intend to do nothing about her, for the moment."

"Presumably, then," cut in Tremayne, "you will continue to monitor things at the other end in Ireland and, possibly, deliberately feed in misinformation from here, via Aileen?"

"Exactly so. Had we picked up a leak of real intelligence, she wouldn't be still on Tresco, I assure you. What we intend to do is to keep a close, but discreet eye on her and see what develops," said Mitchell.

"Which, dear boy, is where you come in. I received a signal this morning of your promotion, with effect from today, to Lieutenant Commander, so my heartiest congratulations!" added a beaming Enever, shaking a very dumbfounded Tremayne's hand.

"And mine, too, Richard – welcome to the club!" declared Mitchell. "The drinks are on you, tonight!"

"You're going to be distraught, I know, but Commander Rawlings is being posted to Devonport, as 'captain of a desk' at Royal Naval Barracks." The eyes twinkled over the top of the glasses.

"Your new post takes over his role, but with the title of Flotilla Commander. Internal security at Godolphin will also come under you, which is why we needed to bring you up-to-date on the information leak. You and I will be working pretty closely on this issue, but primarily you will be formally in command of the flotilla – reporting, as I will, directly to Captain Mansell."

Still trying to take in the sudden surprise, Tremayne, somewhat overwhelmed by events, managed to say, "I'm absolutely delighted – and thank you. This is something I can get my teeth into, I –"

Enever cut in, pipe in hand, "Somebody will arrive today from Naval Intelligence in London to update both of us on new strategic proposals for the developing use of our flotilla in taking covert operations further along the coast of France. The recent costly catastrophe at Dieppe shows all-too-painfully that we are not yet ready to mount the inevitable invasion of France. That is still some way off – but it will happen. Meanwhile, there is so much more that we can do with small, selective raids and detailed reconnaissance as necessary preliminaries to invasion."

"I look forward to that. Please let me know when they arrive."

"Oh – and here are your Lieutenant Commander's new rings. I'll get some young Wren to sew them on for you some time today," Enever added.

"And, young Richard, don't you dare forget that drink I've promised us on your behalf," laughed Mitchell.

His mind still in a whirl, Tremayne returned to his cabin – and the ever-faithful Bertie.

Later that afternoon, he spent time with Sub-Lieutenant Maurice Simmonds who, though part of the ration-strength of Intelligence Section, had, with Enever's approval, put in a request to serve as a First Lieutenant on one of the boats. In what was essentially an informal selection interview, Tremayne found that he liked the tall, young, highly intelligent officer and agreed to put into effect his transfer to operations. Simmonds had been trained as an executive officer and primarily as a navigator and Tremayne found him to be an engaging, personable man with a wry sense of humour similar to his own.

His thoughts then turned to his own First Lieutenant and reports from Dartmouth confirmed 'slow and steady progress – now out of danger'. In his new Service role as Flotilla Commander, he smiled to himself that his very first task, after accepting Simmonds as the new Sub, was to organise a return lift to Dartmouth for Second Officer Lucy Caswell to visit WB in hospital. Armed with the latest encouraging medical report on his improving condition, she was in buoyant mood as she left that evening on the despatch launch.

After the celebratory drink in the wardroom – which made his mess bill look positively sick – and a rather swift early dinner, Tremayne returned to his cabin with two box files full of operational papers, which Enever had passed to him to "inwardly digest, dear boy".

He was in the process of trying to make sense of these, when there was a gentle knock on his door and a rather indistinct feminine voice called, "Sir, I've come to sew your new rings on your uniform."

Tremayne picked up his uniform jacket from the back of his chair and opened the door to the young Wren he saw standing there.

The light from the wardroom corridor shone on her face and his heart leapt for sheer joy as recognition struck home.

"Emma!"

"Oh, and I suppose *Lieutenant Commander*, that I'll now have to call you 'Sir'!"

For a moment, a thoughtful but gentle expression crossed his face as Tremayne looked at her. Then it broke into a broad, welcoming smile as he said, "Dearest Emma, I'd prefer you to call me 'husband'."

A second later, she was in his arms…

Ten

Farewell to the past.
A new beginning...

Tremayne awoke to the late summer sun streaming through the window and raised himself up to look at the clock. Emma lay fast asleep by his side. The sense of sheer wonder was almost overwhelming as he looked down at her, seeing the radiant beauty of her face and her soft, dark hair fanning the ivory pillows.

Surprised, but delighted, by the late night arrival of their guests, the Oylers had promised morning tea for seven-thirty and breakfast at eight.

Aileen Oyler's spontaneous and obvious joy at the couple's unexpected appearance made Tremayne feel even more guilty that she was to be the one of the main subjects of his security surveillance on Tresco.

"Sure Dick and I have the very room for you," she had said, and – enfolding Emma in her arms – added, "Emma, alannah, you're a very special lady. I hope you'll be very happy." Turning to Tremayne, with an air of mock fierceness, she had said, "Now, Mr Tremayne, mind you look after her, or sure you'll be answering to me!"

Right on time, a knock on the bedroom door and a murmured, "Tea for you both. It's half-past seven," announced the start of the day. Emma, tousle-haired and sleepy, reached out and took Tremayne's hand. " I just can't believe this is happening. I'm terrified I'll wake up and find that it was all a dream."

Tremayne, smiling, turned to her, "It had better not be, or I'll be forever wondering who the gorgeous woman was who I've just spent such a wonderful night with!"

Knowing that they had meetings with Enever and Mitchell, starting at nine o'clock, they went down to the hotel dining room on time where again, despite the limiting restrictions of wartime rationing, Aileen Oyler had managed to produce – as she put it – "a real Irish breakfast." Alone again, briefly, their love for one another was only too apparent.

Having now become lovers, each was determined not to let that show and to preserve a professional front in the presence of others, particularly so when "on parade." Off duty was another matter although then, too, they knew that while the social 'closeness' of colleagues was acceptable, the social intimacy of lovers was not.

They arrived at Godolphin together, minutes before nine o'clock.

Enever began the meeting by explaining that the reason for Emma's visit was to establish a closer, working liaison between SIS and Godolphin, which could now become a reality with the appointment of the new Flotilla Commander – Tremayne.

Colonel Farrell of SOE was present, as was Colonel Jobling of SIS, while Mitchell and Emma represented London-based Naval Intelligence and security interests at the meeting.

A major reason for Tremayne's promotion and appointment had been not only his competence and success in sea-going operations, but the personal, as well as professional, closeness of his relationship with John Enever.

Their collaborative and collegial relationship had been one of the cornerstones of Godolphin's undoubted effectiveness in keeping the agents' sea lanes open and in undertaking necessary reconnaissance operations. As Enever put it to the meeting, "With rampant megalomania now out of the way, we'll be able to move things along a damn sight quicker. Obstruction, ignorance and disregard for the essentials have been holding us back for too bloody long." Eyes twinkling over his glasses as he looked at each of his audience in turn, Enever clearly relished his reference to the now departing Rawlings. Clearly, too, they shared his relief at the recent turn of events at Godolphin.

In both SIS and SOE circles, Tremayne was regarded as a safe pair of capable and well-disposed hands. As Farrell had once put it in Baker Street HQ, "Tremayne is a 'thinking man' who is not afraid to take necessary action. He does the right things – and he does things right."

Because of the scare over the information leak and the paramount need for secrecy to be maintained about Godolphin's true role, it was equally vital that both day-to-day security and strategic counter-intelligence be co-ordinated – and implemented – in the most efficient and effective ways. Discussions at the meeting confirmed that the closest professional contact and liaison between Godolphin and SIS, as well as with SOE, were essential.

"Real, productive synergy comes best from well-managed diversity – not unimaginative uniformity," declared Enever, "and that's what we are ultimately about."

Identifying and 'shaping' the necessary complementary roles and accountabilities of the six officers present, took up most of the rest of the day's meeting, leaving sufficient time to review, in some detail, the case of Aileen Oyler.

The general verdict on her was "a free spirit", impulsive and anxious to please people – not malicious or vengeful – and, most likely, not really politically motivated. None of the latter characteristics appeared to have any obvious connection to her personality, demeanour and observed behaviour, although, as all agreed, the former three attributes fitted Aileen to a tee.

Farrell cautioned against the naivety of too benign a view and insisted that she be kept under close, near-invisible surveillance, which the others agreed to.

The initial 'cover' under which Godolphin had been set up and had begun to operate was that of an 'Inshore Patrol Base', whose duties included guarding the Isles of Scilly and the protection of fishing vessels and their precious hauls in and around local waters.

It was agreed at the meeting that this cover was both appropriate and adequate, but that it needed to be reaffirmed from time to time in a subtle and low-key way, so as not to arouse or escalate interest in the base and the nature of its activities. Officers, POs and selected ratings would, it was agreed, occasionally make reference to routine patrol activity to reaffirm Godolphin's overt, mundane role – within Aileen's hearing – in the bar of the New Inn.

In the guise of apparent casual conversation and 'shop talk' they would also, from time to time, drop in the odd item of misinformation.

Acting as a counter-intelligence radio 'tracer', such specific and recognisable false details would be picked up by those monitoring transmissions from the Irish Republic to the Abwehr and to other enemy radio reception stations. In that way, the source of leaks – sinister and calculated, or careless and thoughtless – could, with patience, be established beyond doubt and the most appropriate action be taken.

Whatever the outcome with Aileen Oyler, she had at least – albeit unwittingly – reminded everyone of the need to maintain strict security at a base like Godolphin.

Over an informal lunch, Farrell and Jobling both warmly congratulated Tremayne on his appointment and each offered him visits to their respective headquarters to see, at first hand, what they were currently engaged in as part of the process of bringing about closer, productive collaboration.

At the end of what had been seen, collectively, as a worthwhile day, with clear outcomes and follow-up objectives, Farrell and Jobling left to share the launch taking them back to Penzance and to their rail journey together up to London.

Enever was pleased about the opportunity that so many hours in each other's company gave them to build their own relationship and to co-operate and share essential intelligence.

After they had left, Enever summarised the meeting, from his point of view, with the words, "Today I really think that we covered essential ground effectively. What I believe is most important is that, on these issues at least, we all seem to be on song and in agreement about where we go from here. I'll get Jane Topping to type up my notes and these will be circulated to all who attended the meeting."

Following a further fifteen minutes of combined shop talk and social conversation, the group broke up and began to disperse.

As he and Emma left, Tremayne said, "It looks as if it's going to be a glorious evening and sunset. Let's have supper at the New Inn and then go for a walk across the island over to Pentle Bay and along the beach. Sadly, you've got to go back tomorrow, so let's make the very most of what time we still have together. Or would you like to spend it differently?"

The smiling blue eyes teased him as she said, "Hmm. Let's just wait until we get back to the hotel — and perhaps I'll tell you then!"

At the New Inn, Dick and Aileen welcomed them back and, once alone with her, Tremayne hardly needed convincing that Emma's choice of first priority was the right one.

Afterwards, as they went downstairs for a much delayed supper, Tremayne said, "One of the wonderful things about this place — and Aileen in particular — is that you can turn up late, for a pretty obvious reason, without the customary disapproving or, worse, prurient comments. It's all so very normal and natural here."

So very aware of each other, they ate a light supper and then, in the gathering dusk, walked back past Godolphin, raising a grinning salute from the duty leading hand outside the gate, complete with his slung gas-mask container and pickaxe handle.

"For one dreadful moment, I thought he was going to salute us with that terrifying pickaxe handle at the 'present arms'," laughingly whispered Tremayne as he returned the sentry's salute.

With their arms around each other, they walked on past the impressive Tresco Abbey and its beautiful gardens, home of Major Dorrien-Smith and his family, who leased the island from the Duchy of Cornwall and whose own losses in the war had already been grievous.

Taking the sandy path between Abbey Pool and the Great Pool, the island's two freshwater lakes, they walked on towards the slowly lapping waves which they could hear clearly on such a still night as they drew close to the shore.

Eventually, with a new moon casting its silvery light on the now black sea, they reached the long, gently curving sweep of Pentle Bay, its wide stretch of sand punctuated here and there with limpet-studded, seaweed-festooned rocks.

"I still feel that I need to pinch myself every so often, to convince myself that all this *is* real and that you and I really have reached this stage in our relationship, Richard."

Taking her hands in his, Tremayne kissed her tenderly and asked quietly, "Dearest Emma, will you marry me? I meant it last night, when I said that I wanted you to call me 'husband'."

For a moment, Emma searched his face in the moonlight's reflection off the water and then said, "Yes, Richard, I will. I want to be your wife."

They stood for a moment, holding each other's hands, and then embraced silently, lingering, aware of the little time left to them to share before the morning, when Emma had to return to London. After a while, they turned to climb back over the dunes and slowly began to retrace their steps to the New Inn.

There, they asked Dick Oyler for a morning call and breakfast as before, in time for Emma to catch a motor launch at nine o'clock to take her back to Penzance and on to a succession of trains up to London.

At breakfast, Tremayne said, "I'll take up Colonel Jobling's offer to come up to town to visit SIS which, apart from leave, gives us another chance to be together. I love you so much, Emma, and I want to be with you."

Emma could feel the tears welling up and struggled to fight them back. "This time, please come with me to the boat – it's leaving from New Grimsby quay. I just need every minute with you."

Aileen, coming out of the kitchen to clear away their breakfast dishes, saw the tear-reddened eyes and went straight up to Emma and put her arms around her as she was about to leave with Tremayne.

"You'll be back with your young man again soon, alannah, and sure Dick and I will keep that same lovely room for you both."

Thanking Aileen – and Dick, who had just joined them – Tremayne picked up Emma's bag and walked with her to the quay. As the crew busied themselves stowing kit and luggage on board, they embraced and Emma walked down the quay steps, through the boat's guard rail and into the launch. Quite formally, she saluted Tremayne and, unseen by the launch's crew, mouthed, "I love you."

Tremayne returned her salute and responded with the same message, waving to her as the launch drew away, heading round into the Sound and eastwards for Cornwall.

He returned to the New Inn to collect his kit and Aileen stopped him, just as he was leaving to go down to HMS Godolphin.

"Mr Tremayne, I think I know how you both must feel. My Mam and Da' were often parted in our war in the 1920s, especially when Da' went on the run and the 'Auxies' were out looking for him. And then just after he'd been home to see Mam one night and had slipped away again at dawn, they came and shot her because she wouldn't let on where he was hiding. So, take all the time you can to be with her, Mr Tremayne, as you two make a lovely couple, if you don't mind me saying so."

"I don't mind at all, Aileen, in fact I'm delighted – and I believe Emma will be too when I tell her!"

He touched Aileen's arm gently.

"I'm so sorry to hear about your mother, Aileen, I truly am. You must hate us."

"Sure I don't – not at all. But, as they say, 'the Irish should forget their history – but the English should always remember it'!"

Looking directly at Tremayne, she added, with a smile, "I love being here in Scilly. My home is here now – and has been for these last fifteen years. Dick is my man and my place is here with him on Tresco. I don't live in – or want to be involved with – the past, but I can't just forget it. I miss my family, too – and I'm always telephoning them and writing to them. If I bore grudges, sure I would never have married an Englishman! Now, I've got work to do, but Dick and I will be seeing you again soon – and that lovely young lady of yours. Just you take good care of her!" Her words sounded severe, but her eyes said otherwise, as she bade farewell to Tremayne and began sweeping up in front of the inn door.

Her natural warmth and genuine concern certainly didn't fit with the burgeoning image of 'spy' that she had recently acquired in intelligence circles, mused Tremayne, as he made his way back to HMS Godolphin and duty watch.

At the morning briefing, the duty boat captains were given their respective sea areas to patrol. Tremayne's was the area between St Mary's and Land's End. He was warned that monitored radio traffic indicated that snooping Focke-Wulf Condors were expected on increased reconnaissance missions over Scilly during the forenoon. The radio monitors reported that they appeared to be escorted by twin-engined Messerschmitt 110 fighters, which possessed hefty firepower combined with a useful turn of speed. Tremayne and the other boat captains were also briefed that the squadron of Hurricanes based on St Mary's would be operating as air cover and in collaboration with the MGBs.

Tremayne, allocated S53, looked at his crew list for the watch. Most of the familiar crew members' names were there, except for Petty Officer Irvine as his Cox'n and, of course, his First Lieutenant. Sub-Lieutenant Quilghini had taken over Willoughby-Brown's role following the impressive part he had played in the battle of Lyme Bay. In the Ulsterman's place was one of the Breton non-commissioned officers, Jacques Domenech, who, for security purposes, had been given a British 'cover' name and a POs rate in the RNVR.

Tremayne joined his boat at Braiden Rock anchorage to see that Quilghini had organised 'clean ship' parties and, despite the shell fire damage, S53 was looking immaculate.

Returning the Frenchman's salute, Tremayne climbed on board and thanked his new First Lieutenant for his initiative and for the already crisp, workmanlike impression created on the boat.

"Glad to have you on board as my Number One, Sub. And, by the way, you are to be mentioned in despatches – deservedly so – for your conduct as skipper of 1315 in our recent affair with the E-boats in Lyme Bay.

My congratulations, Pierre," said Tremayne, shaking the Frenchman's hand.

Checking that all was clear ahead and around his boat, Tremayne ordered: "Right, Number One, let's get her underway."

Quilghini called "Start engines. Slip. Half-speed ahead" and the E-boat drew smoothly and effortlessly away from Braiden Rock, heading south for St Mary's and beyond – her course set towards the mainland, her powerful diesels turning over with a steady throb.

The weather was foul. A penetrating drizzle and a grey mist, which clung to everything, set the scene for their journey east through Crow Bar and then Great English Island Neck, the stretch of water separating St Martin's from the Eastern Isles. How very different the islands looked now, mused Tremayne, damp and indistinct – their shorelines diffused by the slowly swirling, shifting mists. Just a few short weeks ago, he and Emma had sailed these same waters in glorious weather with the sunlight playing on the white-crested emerald waves, creating an idyllic scene so typical of the Scillies when at their best.

With the imposing rocky mass of the Hanjague fine on their starboard beam, Tremayne ordered "Full speed ahead" and, as the powerful, responsive diesels were opened up to maximum revolutions, S53 surged forward, lifting her bows clear of the choppy waves.

Some forty minutes later, approaching the Cornish coast near Land's End, the mist began to lift and visibility increased considerably despite the persisting rain. Tremayne and Quilghini both began to search sea and sky alike with their binoculars. "We'll start our sweep to port now, Number One. Order half revolutions and new course, if you please."

S53 was five minutes into her first sweep when the Leading Telegraphist called to the bridge: "Message from base, sir. Two Condors, escorted by two Me 110s, approaching our area, bearing red one-four-five."

"Thank you Sparks. Acknowledge, please."

Tremayne called, "Action stations. Stand by all guns. High elevation. Keep your eyes open for enemy aircraft bearing red one-four-five."

Forrard, amidships and aft, weapons were elevated and traversed in anticipation as gun crews and those on the bridge alike, anxiously scanned the slowly lifting cloud base.

Moments later, an urgent call from Watkins, gun-captain of the forrard Bofors, directed all eyes to the port bow. There, just over one thousand yards away, were four aircraft, moving slowly, out on predatory reconnaissance. Their visual contact with S53 must have been almost simultaneous and they swung round to investigate the unexpected sight of an E-boat so close to the Cornish coast.

"Full speed ahead, Cox'n. Hard a-starboard." The long, graceful boat accelerated and slewed round, presenting her after and amidships gun barrels to the four aircraft.

"Shall we take advantage of our cover as an E-boat and wave, sir?" asked Quilghini.

"No Sub, we're here to destroy them and deter them from coming into this end of the Channel. Whatever element of surprise we do have, we'll use to gain the fire initiative and shoot first."

Tremayne yelled through the loudhailer: "Engage the enemy! All guns, fire as you bear."

First to open up was the 3.7cm flak gun, rapidly followed by the 40mm.

At that moment, the telegraphist called the bridge, "Sir, message from Flight 1449 on St Mary's, three Hurricanes airborne and heading for us."

"Thanks, Sparks – acknowledge and make: '*Welcome to the party*'."

The leading aircraft, a heavily armed Me 110, began returning fire – destroying S53's rubber dinghy with its first burst of cannon shells. Seconds later, it hit and severely wounded the able seaman manning the starboard bridge-mounted MG. Tremayne called for a medic and, without waiting for an order, the First Lieutenant raced across the bridge. Seizing the unmanned MG, he began pouring round after round into the oncoming other three aircraft. As they flew rapidly and low over the E-boat, Watkins and Robson, manning the forrard Bofors, laced their retreating rear ends with clip after clip of 40mm shells. Tremayne ordered the Cox'n to zigzag at full speed, giving each gunner the opportunity to fire in rapid succession. On the second strafing pass over the boat, a shout went up from the after gun crews. "He's hit, sir. We've hit the bastard!" Tremayne looked up to see smoke pouring from the rear of the Condor's port engines. Seconds later she exploded, at about two hundred feet above the sea, three hundreds yards almost dead ahead of S53.

Watkins called out from the bow gun, "They're coming back – moving round on the port beam, 'bout two thousand yards, sir."

Tremayne knew that all his weapons were capable of destroying targets at one thousand yards and he wanted the enemy to come within range to effect maximum destructive damage. He called out fore and aft, "Stand by, all guns. Fire on my command." The rising anticipatory tension of the next few seconds was suddenly broken by a yell behind him. "The Hurricanes, sir, they're here!" Flying three abreast, the green and brown camouflaged fighters swept in at well over three hundred miles per hour, firing as they came. The two Me 110s turned to take them on in order to let the huge, slower and more vulnerable Condor make its getaway. One Hurricane peeled off from the others and went for the Condor, leaving his colleagues to fight it out with the Me 110s, which were matched in speed and firepower – although the twin-engined German fighters were less manoeuvrable than their British counterparts.

The unfortunate Condor was quickly despatched and plunged into the sea, despite the obvious gallantry of her crew. Only too obviously, they knew that they did not stand a chance against the faster, eight-gunned Hurricane, yet they put up a courageous and desperate fight. The Hurricanes were mixing it with the German fighters in an aerial mêlée, twisting and turning, firing as a target momentarily presented itself within someone's gun-sights.

Suddenly, one of the Me 110s exploded in mid-air, to be followed, moments later, by the other one breaking off the engagement in order to make a run for home, with smoke issuing from its port engine. Sensing an easy victory, the three Hurricanes gave chase – firing until it too blew up about two hundred feet above the sea. The triumphant Hurricanes flew over S53 in a succession of victory rolls.

"Look sir, one of those has smoke coming from it. Will it get home do you think, sir?"

"I'm not sure Number One, but he will, at least, have company on his way back. Let's look and see if there are any German survivors to be picked up. Because all planes exploded before they crashed, I doubt if anyone is still alive, unfortunately, and there are no figures that I can see in the water.

For fifteen minutes, S53 cruised slowly around but found no

one alive, downed from the dogfights that the crew had so recently witnessed.

All that could be seen on the sea's surface was the usual flotsam and jetsam – fragments of the aircraft torn apart by exploding fuel, some personal effects, an empty life jacket – but neither survivors, nor bodies.

Reluctantly, Tremayne called off the search and began another sweep in the opposite direction.

They had been underway for about ten minutes when the telegraphist called out, "Mayday call sir. One of the Hurricanes is down in the 'oggin', about eighteen miles west, south-west of here, sir." He paused for a moment. Grid reference as follows, sir –"

He spelled out the figures slowly, as Quilghini took them down and began plotting the course on the tiny chartroom table.

"Thanks, Number One, we're probably one of the nearest vessels to the poor fellow. Set the course for the Cox'n, if you please, and maximum revolutions. Let's go and find him. Having just stood the crew down from action stations to defence stations, Tremayne put everyone on deck on lookout. Every pair of binoculars on board was in immediate use, searching near and far for an airman in his Mae West life jacket. The day was now much clearer, finally free from the earlier all-enveloping chilly, damp mist. Nevertheless, Tremayne and the others knew that, even in late August, the sea off Cornwall could be extremely cold and limbs became numbed after prolonged exposure.

"Number One, organise towels and any spare dry clothes

please. Scrambling nets and lifebuoys at the ready."

The search continued for nearly twenty minutes before Quilghini spotted a frantically waving figure in the water, about five hundred yards off the starboard beam.

The Cox'n spun the wheel round and pointed S53's nose at the distant figure.

Tremayne called out, "Watkins, some of your life-saving 'torpedo propellant' if you please for our guest."

"Aye aye, sir. It'll be a couple of shakes, sir."

The Cox'n reduced speed to 'slow ahead' as the E-boat drew alongside the airman and then to 'stop'. "Help him on board. Carefully does it," said Tremayne, moving forward himself to take hold of the apparently injured pilot. As Tremayne grasped the airman's wrist, mutual recognition dawned and each grinned in relief at the other.

"Tim! Here, give me your hand and let's get you dry and warm."

Through chattering teeth, Stanley gratefully let Tremayne and the others ease him through the guard rail and onto the E-boat's deck amidships. "Heavens Richard, am I bloody glad to see you. In that damned cold water, my brain was beginning to go numb – let alone my body." As he was gently lifted on board, he grimaced with pain. "My right leg was hit, fairly low down below the knee. By shell splinters, I think. While the Hurricane may not be as fast nor as beautiful to look at as a Spitfire, they are hellish tough and can absorb a lot of punishment."

"Rather like their pilots," smiled Tremayne. "Let's get you below, Tim, and find some dry clothes for you and we'll have that leg of yours seen to."

Stanley, warm and dry and, as he put it, "almost human, again", was presented with his "greatest challenge of the day", as he later jokingly admitted to Tremayne, when Temporary Leading Seaman Watkins presented him with a mug of hot tea, well laced with pusser's neat rum. "Heavens, Richard, I could run my bloody Hurricanes on that stuff!"

Tremayne sent a message through by radio to Godolphin and to RAF St Mary's, to let them know that he had picked up Squadron Leader Stanley and would take him directly to Hugh Town harbour, to be collected by ambulance on arrival and transported to the island hospital. He also reported the wounding of the AB manning the machine gun on the bridge, and the fact that he too would be taken to St Mary's.

On return to Tresco and Godolphin, Tremayne wrote both to Emma – to recount his dramatic meeting with Tim – and to his parents to let them know of his intention to marry again. He described her to them in ways that he knew would help them to relate to her on their first meeting. His mother would be completely won over by Emma's gentle Highland courtesy and her knowledge of the Gaelic, which his mother shared with her future daughter-in-law. His father, he thought, would just simply be captivated by Emma as *he* was.

During the following week, Tremayne once again went to the coast of Brittany to retrieve a compromised French agent, at the urgent request of John Farrell of SOE.

Code named 'Joelle', the agent had been parachuted into Brittany some six weeks before, only to discover that the particular 'cell' of the Confrèrie to which she had been assigned was already under close surveillance by the local Gestapo. In a pre-dawn raid, they had captured one of Joelle's colleagues and seized the cell radio and documents. Joelle had only just managed to escape, grabbing a bicycle and pedalling off in the dark. Eventually, she had made her way to Quiberon and from there, by fishing boat, to Port St Gildas on the small island of Ile d'Houat, east of Belle-Ile.

In Carnac, at the northern end of the Quiberon isthmus, she had managed to contact another member of the cell, who had immediately radioed SOE in London to let them know that the cell had been penetrated and that Joelle was in immediate and grave danger. Her contact, a fisherman from the sea town of Carnac, had sailed her across to the Ile d'Houat where she was hiding out in the cottage of another family who earned their livelihood from the sea.

Taking *Monique,* with Quilghini and Domenech in place of the now rapidly recovering Willoughby-Brown and Irvine, Tremayne had also included Watkins and Robson as deckhands and necessary firepower. Operations boxes, containing small arms and grenades, were to hand – ready to be quickly hidden under fishing nets, and convincing barrels of fresh fish, caught off St Martin's earlier the same day, were on deck.

Now painted in the fashion of a fishing boat from Carantec on the north Brittany coast, *Monique* had slipped her moorings at 22.30 hours in order to be off Quiberon by early morning. Travelling at maximum speed until dawn, when Tremayne had ordered "slow ahead both engines", *Monique* resumed her covert role as a Breton fishing boat and began trawling the choppy grey waters.

"Nets out — let's start looking like the fishermen we're supposed to be."

The hastily conceived rescue plan involved the boat-to-boat transfer of Joelle among the tiny islands — each little more than large rock formations — which lay approximately half a mile to the north-west of Huoat. Pick-up time had been arranged for 07.00 hours.

By 06.30 hours, *Monique* had passed the southernmost tip of Quiberon and the Pointe du Conguel, on course south-east for the islets forming the rendezvous with Joelle.

Just after they had passed the first of the rocky outcrops, Robson, standing on *Monique*'s foredeck, called to Tremayne, "Small fishing boat, sir, two o'clock, three hundred yards."

"Well spotted Robson. Automatic weapons and grenades at the ready but out of sight, everyone. We'll start waving in another hundred yards." Turning to Quilghini, Tremayne said, "Sub, I want you and the Cox'n to do the talking, to verify that they are who we hope they are."

Calling to the others, he told Watkins to take over the wheel while the Cox'n and the First Lieutenant spoke to the other boat's skipper and crew. "Robson, stand by to shoot on my command."

Now waving to one another, the boat crews manoeuvred their two fishing vessels alongside one another. Joelle emerged from the wheelhouse with a broad smile, as Quilghini and Domenech first spoke rapidly in French and then switched to Breton in response to the greeting of the skipper of the Ile d'Houat boat. She quickly scrambled on board the *Monique,* to be welcomed by Tremayne and the others. Moving off, after the exuberant Breton crew's noisy and very vocal farewells, Tremayne set a north-westerly course to take *Monique* into the first of several Breton fishing fleets that were emerging off the Brittany coast.

Joelle's relief to be on board was only too obvious, as she described to the others the harrowing details of the Gestapo raid and subsequent torture and execution of her co-agent; all of which had been told to her by the Confrèrie contact in Carnac.

Enever, thoughtful as ever, had provided Tremayne with a celebratory bottle of Admiral Hembury's dubiously acquired champagne for Joelle's rescue, placed deep in a barrel of ice normally used for preserving the fishing boat's catch. A very wary Robson and Watkins politely declined the offer of a glass of one of Roederer's best vintages, with Watkins saying, "If it's all the same to you miss, begging yer pardon, me an' old Robbo 'ere will drink yer 'ealth with a drop of pusser's 'neaters'." Wide-eyed, she looked at Tremayne and asked, somewhat bewildered, "Whatever is *that*?"

"Well, for a start Joelle, it doesn't come from anywhere near either Rheims or Epernay! It's Navy issue rum and today they will take it neat – and so not diluted with water – to drink a toast to you and your safe future!"

Monique steadily made her way north-west, slowly and unobtrusively working her way through tunnymen and countless other fishing boats until, eventually, she was off Ushant and the familiar Ile d'Ouessant once more.

Tremayne knew that after a few more miles on the same course, prowling German surface vessels and aircraft would begin to take an inquisitive – and potentially disastrous – interest in *Monique*.

Quilghini agreed that the only real tactical option open to them was to travel to the northernmost limits permitted by the Germans and very slowly proceed under sail, trailing her nets behind her, in a generally eastwards direction until darkness fell. When night came she would then open up to maximum revolutions and head back to Tresco post-haste.

To avoid the inevitable radio traffic monitors, so as not to initiate any searches, Tremayne had agreed with Enever and Farrell beforehand that there would also be no radio transmissions from *Monique*, until they were able to move northwards under the cover of darkness.

During the day's drifting and apparent fishing, Tremayne and his crew had seen several German surface vessels, but none had altered course to take a closer look, or come alongside to investigate *Monique*. At considerable altitude, they had also seen both German reconnaissance aircraft – heading out to the Western Approaches as scouts for the lurking U-boat 'wolf packs', and Heinkels and Dorniers returning from bombing raids on southern England – whose crews were doubtless more interested in getting back home than they were in examining the activities of a Breton fishing boat.

Dusk was beginning to take over from daylight when Quilghini shouted urgently to Tremayne, "Sir, on the port bow, small boat approaching at high speed."

"Thank you Sub. Action stations, everybody. Watkins, take our guest below into the space forrard of the engine and secure the hatch after her. Spread some loose fish over it and look as if you're in the middle of hosing them down." Dragging a spare net over the operations box, Tremayne said, "Everyone, pistols in your smock pockets and one grenade apiece. Quickly!"

As the approaching vessel came closer, she was now recognisable as an R-boat, probably out on routine patrol or even looking for a downed aircraft's surviving crew. She switched on her blinding searchlight to illuminate *Monique*'s deck and disorientate her crew. Speaking in passable — but heavily accented — French, the captain called to *Monique* through his loudhailer to heave to, with everyone standing on her deck. Quilghini announced that they were the fishing boat *Monique* of Carantec, completing their day's catch.

Even in the increasing dusk, Tremayne could clearly see the machine gun on the R-boat's bridge, pointed directly at himself and his crew. Just one burst from such an awesome weapon would clear *Monique's* deck of human life in three seconds flat. Additionally, three of the crew stood near the bow with rifles levelled at Quilghini and Domenech as they responded to the R-boat captain.

Still speaking in French, the German officer motioned to Tremayne, Watkins and Robson.

"You — all of you — come forward. I want to see you. NOW!"

Tremayne said under his breath, a note of urgency in is voice, "Watkins, Robson, step forward with me."

The German captain stared at them for a few seconds and

then announced, "We are going to come aboard to search your boat. Secure this line," as one of his seamen threw a hemp rope towards Tremayne. "Oh shit!" muttered Tremayne, as he bent down to the forrard bollard, with the pretence of securing the German boat's mooring line.

"When the bastard goes into our wheelhouse, Robson, shoot the machine gunner. Aim well and keep shooting him until he falls. He could still fire that MG, even when wounded. Watkins, shoot out that bloody light and I'll kill the officer and his three stooges."

As the German officer stepped down onto *Monique*'s deck, pistol in hand, he was suddenly called by a rating from the low bridge of the R-boat. "Ach. Du lieber Gott," and then he switched back to French, "untie the line immediately. My Funker," — he struggled for the word in French — "my telegraphist — has picked up a mayday call from a crashed German aircraft. We are leaving. No doubt we shall meet again." He saluted Quilghini perfunctorily and quickly rejoined his boat.

As the R-boat pulled away, turning to the west, Tremayne became aware that he had broken out in a cold sweat. Perspiration was running down his face and body and he shivered as he said, "My God, Sub, that was a close call."

Quilghini gave a rather forced smile as he said, "We had absolutely no plan at all to deal with them, except for the pistols we all had in our pockets."

Tremayne realised that in letting Quilghini take the lead in talking to the Germans, he had temporarily relinquished command of the situation. Almost as an aside to himself, he murmured, "That will never bloody well happen again. There's a powerful lesson for you there, Tremayne."

He ordered "rum all round" from Watkins and asked Quilghini to radio through for air cover for their return across the open sea. Joelle came back on deck, smiling broadly once more. Her palpable sense of relief at her escape and rescue made such operations worthwhile – let alone their obvious value to Intelligence – felt Tremayne, as she began talking animatedly in her native French to Quilghini and Domenech.

Within thirty minutes, Tremayne heard the now familiar note of a Hurricane's Rolls Royce Merlin engines, growing louder by the second, and he gave a flashed 'vee' signal repeated three times. By way of response, three Hurricanes, approaching in line, abreast, banked to their left and swung round over *Monique* and her crew. Tremayne repeated the signal twice more and then radioed Godolphin to tell them of his escort's arrival. The responding acknowledgement signal added, "Tim is leading them. Greater love hath no man than this, that a man leaves his bed at 01.00 hours for his friend!"

Tremayne smiled at the response from Godolphin, which had John Enever's hallmark stamped all over it.

At 02.55 hours, *Monique* slipped quietly into Braiden Rock anchorage. Enever, beaming happily but looking somewhat dishevelled and sleepy, came down to welcome the group home and to take Joelle to her temporary accommodation at Godolphin. As he escorted her to the base, he called over his shoulder, "Richard, debrief room 101, 11.00 hours. Now that you're the same rank, I can no longer *order* you to get some sleep but goodnight, dear boy, see you anon."

On the matter of sleep, Tremayne felt like the subject of one of 'Pablo' Watkins' more salubrious songs – *The Virgin Sturgeon Needs No Urgin'*. After thanking the members of his crew in turn and paying due recognition to the part each had played in the Ile d'Houat operation, he retired to his cabin and to welcome, long overdue sleep.

Captain Mansell, HMS Godolphin's Commanding Officer, joined Enever at the debriefing to thank Tremayne and Quilghini for bringing Joelle out of Brittany and safely home, stressing the importance to SOE of her timely rescue. Mansell stated, "She has apparently garnered a great deal of vital field-intelligence, which Colonel Farrell is over the moon about. As a result of Operation Marie-Claire, you will remember, Capitaine Duhamel brought us vital information about the Germans' coastal defences in Brittany and Normandy." Mansell picked up a sheaf of well-thumbed documents from the table. "Joelle has brought us more detailed information about those defences – especially those along the Normandy coast – which is also likely to prove crucial as and when the time comes to make plans to invade France. Had she been taken by the Gestapo, that would have been lost to us and turned to SOE's serious disadvantage as material for German counter-intelligence."

Mansell left the meeting after about twenty minutes to let Enever concentrate upon intelligence priorities in France from SOE's unique perspective. Towards the close of the debriefing, Enever announced that Colonel Jobling of SIS wanted Tremayne to call on him in London, to develop ideas to capitalise further upon the opportunities offered by the sea lanes to and from Brittany. "I don't suppose that there will be too much pain for you in a trip up to London, Richard!" said Enever smiling and tapping the bowl of his pipe empty against the heel of his shoe. "Transport to take you up to town has been laid on for you in the morning and your first meeting with Colonel Jobling is at 17.00 hours tomorrow. He wants you to spend time with him and key members of the French Section for most of the following day and then you will come back to us. You're highly regarded in SIS circles and I'm sure you'll find the trip worthwhile. By the way, dear boy, when you see Emma, do please give her my best regards." The grey eyes twinkled benignly above the half-moon glasses.

Tremayne left Enever in high spirits as he returned to Braiden Rock to carry out a post-operational check on *Monique.*

Later that night he managed to make a call to Emma, who obviously already knew all about Tremayne's visit.

"Colonel Jobling and my chief, Commander Beresford, both want to talk with you tomorrow. And then, Richard, if you're not too busy, I want to spend some time with you – unless, of course, you have other plans while you're up in London!" Tremayne smiled at the teasing laughter in her voice.

"Och, lassie, I'll do my best to find the odd wee minute with ye."

"You'd better – or that drubbing we gave the English at Bannockburn will seem like a vicar's garden party if you don't!"

Their call ended with the humour and laughter that each had come to find such a natural and fundamental part of their relationship.

The following late afternoon, Tremayne arrived at SIS HQ in London and was shown directly to Jobling's office. He was greeted warmly by the Colonel who spent just under an hour setting the scene for the next day's major meeting on Intelligence strategy.

"As we said to you at our last meeting, we see the invasion of Europe by the Allies as an inevitability, but the recent costly failure of Dieppe has served to show us just how unprepared we are to mount a successful large-scale invasion of Europe. It is still, I believe, probably a couple of hard-fought years off but we will do it when we are ready – and we will succeed. Incidentally, the good news from Dieppe is that Lord 'Shimi' Lovat and several other key commando leaders made it back safely, I'm delighted to say." Jobling paused to ring for tea for Tremayne and himself.

"Much of the success of our preparation and, therefore, its outcomes in Europe, will depend upon strategic and tactical intelligence of the highest order. It is here, Richard, that we see a significant role for you, working closely with us, with SIS – when we can get them to come to the table – and, of course, with dear John Enever. Tomorrow, you will meet Commander Beresford, our newly-appointed Head of Naval Intelligence here, who acts as our senior liaison officer with both the Royal Navy and SOE on matters maritime."

Tremayne raised several points for clarification, clearly intrigued and delighted by the prospect of a role more closely engaged with Naval Intelligence and at a level beyond cross-channel operations, although he recognised that these would continue to be an essential aspect of his work.

It was the shift in his new, evolving role from the

predominantly tactical 'how' to a more strategic 'what, when and why' in which he saw major personal challenges and fresh opportunities.

Tea arrived and their discussion continued for another half-hour, when Jobling announced: "Let's draw stumps at this stage and make it close of play, Richard. We'll meet here again tomorrow at 09.00 hours when the Commander and I will build upon our ideas much further. Accommodation has been arranged for you for a couple of nights and we've organised your transport back to Penzance, and then Tresco, for the day after tomorrow. I hope that you find tomorrow's meeting worthwhile. It is my belief that you will."

"I've no doubt about that whatsoever, sir. I already feel very involved."

"One of our naval colleagues will give you details of the small hotel that we use nearby and so I'll bid you good evening and see you tomorrow."

"Thank you sir – and good evening."

Jobling's secretary took Tremayne along the narrow corridor to an office marked 'French Section – Naval', opened the door for him and there stood Emma, smiling.

"Good evening sir and welcome aboard. We'll do all we can to make your stay with us a pleasant one, sir."

As the secretary disappeared, Tremayne grinned and said, "I'll bet you say that to all the sailors."

"Naturally, sir, but I don't tell them – well, not *all* of them – that if they don't object, I'll be staying with them at the same hotel!"

Tremayne burst out laughing. For a moment, they held one another close and then Emma, collecting her overnight bag, led the way out of the empty office to the stairs and out into the street.

The hotel was less than five minutes' walk away and though, by no stretch of the imagination, a miniature Savoy, it was clean and comfortable and their room was pretty in a fresh, almost rural English style.

At dinner, Tremayne said, "Tomorrow, I have some time free in the afternoon, Emma. Can you grab a couple of hours?"

"I'm sure I can. We'll meet up at one o'clock where you met me today."

Over dinner they talked and laughed a great deal with Tremayne recounting stories of mutual colleagues, including the tale of Watkins and Robson drinking the bewildered French heroine's health in pusser's rum.

The next day, Tremayne's meeting with Jobling and Beresford proved to be fruitful and exciting from his point of view. Although a vision, at that stage, the projected invasion of Europe – and the evolving role of the Intelligence Services in its preparation – provided the focus and thrust of the meeting. Tremayne felt both flattered and gratified to be party to such discussions and planning at this still quite early stage in his wartime naval career.

The meeting broke up at 13.00 hours, with the agreement to meet with a senior representative from SOE for further discussion at 16.00 hours.

Tremayne took Emma for lunch in a little restaurant across

town near Covent Garden which, despite wartime restrictions, put on a simple, but delicious lunch.

"I picked this particular place," said Tremayne, "because Bill told me that it was good and that it would be ideal for us and, secondly, because there's a shop close by that I really have to call in to."

"Now you've got me intrigued. Is there some secret, dubious hobby that you've taken up and were too embarrassed to tell me about before?"

" Emma, you've guessed it," said Tremayne laughing. "This is something that you also have to be involved in. Come with me and you'll see for yourself!"

When they finished lunch, Tremayne led a mystified Emma to a rather fine, but unpretentious jeweller's shop, about a quarter of a mile from the restaurant.

As they entered, hand in hand, the shop manager smiled and said, "Ah, it's good to see the Navy. Good afternoon, how can I help you, sir?"

"We should like to see some engagement rings please and to order a wedding ring."

For a moment, Emma was completely taken by surprise and, for once, was speechless.

"For goodness sake, get a hold of yourself Fraser. It's high time someone made an honest woman of you – and don't keep this poor gentleman waiting!"

Amid laughter – and some tears of joy – Emma took her time to choose.

As a smiling Tremayne slipped the chosen sapphire ring on her finger, he said quietly, "Dearest Emma, it's farewell to the past and a new beginning – for both of us."

Four weeks later, with a much recovered Willoughby–Brown as best man and Lucy Caswell as bridesmaid, Tremayne and Emma were married in the little parish church of St Nicholas in Dolphin Town, Tresco...

EPILOGUE

2nd JULY 2000

An important piece of naval history was commemorated with the unveiling of a plaque, at a moving ceremony at Braiden Rock anchorage on 2nd July 2000.

Dedicated to the officers and crews of the vessels that made up the Tresco secret flotilla, the ceremony was attended by several elderly veterans who took part in the many Special Forces operations from almost sixty years before. Some had proud members of their families with them. The youngest of the officers and crews present were in their mid-seventies, while many of them were well into their eighties.

Yachts in New Grimsby harbour, flying bunting from their masts, were dressed overall to salute the achievements and courage of the veterans and add colour to the otherwise quietly dignified ceremony.

Former RNVR Sub-Lieutenant Paul O'Brien, who took part in many of the operations from Tresco to Brittany, paid moving tribute to his former colleagues, including Lieutenant Daniel Lomenech, the intrepid French officer who pioneered the original sea lanes to France from the Isles of Scilly. Attending the ceremony were Lomenech's son, Jean-François, and families of members of French Resistance, rescued from Brittany by the Tresco boats all those years ago.

Also present were General Sir Michael Rose, former Director of British Special Forces, Sir Brooks Richards, a former SOE member and author of the definitive HMSO book Secret Flotillas, and Robert Crawford, Director General of the Imperial War Museum.

The party had gathered in the days preceding the ceremony and stayed together, reliving their many memories, at the Island Hotel on Tresco, which did not exist during their service days in Scilly.

The commemorative plaque, made of stainless steel, was bolted onto Braiden Rock itself, immediately above the flotilla boats' former moorings.

Approachable by the steep narrow path leading down to the former anchorage, it states:

THIS ANCHORAGE OF
NEW GRIMSBY SOUND

SERVED AS A BASE FOR A SECRET NAVAL FLOTILLA FROM APRIL 1942 TO OCTOBER 1943. BRITISH VESSELS, DISGUISED AS FRENCH FISHING BOATS, PENETRATED DEEP INTO ENEMY WATERS OFF THE BRITTANY COAST TO CONTACT THE CONFRÈRIE-NOTRE-DAME, THE MOST PRODUCTIVE OF THE INTELLIGENCE NETWORKS IN GERMAN-OCCUPIED FRANCE.

IN THIS SECLUDED CHANNEL, THE VESSELS EXCHANGED THEIR GREY NAVAL PAINTWORK FOR THE CHARACTERISTIC BRILLIANT COLOURS OF SOUTH BRETON FISHING BOATS, TAKING CARE TO AVOID A FRESHLY-PAINTED APPEARANCE.

THIS SEA-LINE OF COMMUNICATION WAS DEVISED BY DANIEL LOMENECH, A 21-YEAR-OLD BRETON INTELLIGENCE AGENT WITH EXCELLENT KNOWLEDGE OF THE SOUTH BRETON FISHING INDUSTRY. IN JUNE 1942 COLONEL RÉNAULT, HEAD OF THE CONFRÈRIE AND HIS FAMILY, WHO WERE IN EXTREME DANGER, WERE RESCUED BY THE VESSEL N51 'LE DINAN'.

THIS EXPEDITION, COMMANDED BY LT. STEVEN MACKENZIE RNVR, WITH S/LTS. RICHARD TOWNSEND RNVR AND DANIEL LOMENECH RNVR, ALSO BROUGHT BACK A DETAILED PLAN OF THE COASTAL DEFENCES THAT THE GERMANS WERE CONSTRUCTING ALONG THE NORMANDY COAST.
THIS INFORMATION BECAME THE BASIS OF THE D-DAY LANDINGS OF 1944 AND ENSURED MINIMAL LOSS OF MEN AND MATERIALS IN THAT OPERATION.

HOLDSWORTH SPECIAL FORCES TRUST 2 JULY 2000

After the touching ceremony, the group made its way back to the Bryher island motor launch Firethorne *to return to the Island Hotel.*

=====O=====

One elderly couple from the group of veterans left the hotel later that afternoon and walked slowly over towards Castle Down. Pausing every so often to take in the mind-blowing panorama and, perhaps, to catch their breath, they walked past Tregarthen Hill and on to Gun Hill.

In his hand, the man carried a small trowel. On the flat, granite summit he bent down and began to move clumps of heather around gently, as if searching for something.

"Got it!" he suddenly exclaimed. "Here, Emma, look! That's the peculiar triangle-shaped rock, with those little yellow potentillas growing round it."

"Och and ye mean, kind sir, I can have ma wee crookit bawbee back after a' these fifty-eight years!"

Laughing like excited children, Tremayne and Emma carefully eased the compacted soil away from around the rock and gradually lifted the stone.

Emma was first to see the now corroded RN cigarette tin with her heavily gouged penny and Tremayne's battered sixpenny piece on top of it. "Richard, look! Somebody's been before us and stuck a 'Blue Liner' tin in *our* secret hidey-hole."

"Good Lord. Is nothing sacred! Open it up, darling. Perhaps they left us a ten-bob note!"

"It's rusted over — it's well and truly stuck. Aha, wait a minute — the lid's moving now."

Tremayne, feigning an air of confusion and disbelief, muttered a rather perfunctory, "How extraordinary, darling."

All at once, the tin sprang open. Emma looked in amazement and then her eyes welled up with tears as she saw the hand-drawn heart with an arrow and the words *'Richard loves Emma, July 1942'.*

"And so you loved me, Richard, *before* we stayed together at the New Inn?"

"Yes, dearest Emma — and I still do."

Tremayne took her in his arms and then said gently, "Take us home, Cox'n. Dinner and packing tonight and then, tomorrow morning, the ten o'clock boat to St Martin's and 'Pablo' Watkins' daughter's guest house for a few days!"

On the way back to the Island Hotel, they met another elderly couple strolling across the heather-covered hill. "David, Lucy!" called Tremayne. "Meet us in the bar around seven and we'll sort out what we're going to do on St Martin's."...

Glossary of naval and Royal Marine terms

====================================

AB Abbreviation for Able Seaman

Abaft Nearer to the stern, than…

Abeam At right angles to the line of the ship, or boat

Abwehr German Military Intelligence

Adrift Naval term for late

After Behind, or rear, e.g. – the after (rear) deck

Aldis Signalling lamp

Ammo Ammunition

Beam The side of a ship or boat, e.g. port (left) or starboard (right) beam

Blue Liners RN-issue cigarettes and tobacco (tins were marked with a blue line, denoting official issue and not for sale to the general public)

Bofors A high-angle automatic gun of Swedish origin that fires 40mm shells

BSA The Birmingham Small Arms Company – manufacturers of military and sporting firearms

Cox'n Abbreviation of coxswain – the petty officer/rating who steers the boat

Ensign Naval flag usually indicating nationality

ETA Estimated time of arrival

ETD Estimated time of departure

Folboat Folding canvas-covered canoe

Forrard Forward, towards the bow of the ship, or boat

Gun-layer Crew member who feeds the weapon with ammunition

Guz Naval slang for Plymouth/Devonport

Halyard Rope or tackle for raising sails or flags

Jack Ship's flag, usually indicating nationality

Jack Naval slang for a sailor, e.g 'Jolly Jack'

'Make to…' The command to send a signal to someone

Matelot A sailor

MG 34, MG 38, MG 42 German machine guns, of 1934, 1938 and 1942 vintage

Neaters Popular naval term for an issue of neat rum

Nelson slice A very solid, glutinous 'wedge' of pastry and indeterminate fruit, topped with icing

NKVD The People's Commissariat for Internal Affairs (former Soviet Government Intelligence Services)

Oerlikon An automatic gun of Swiss origin that fires 20mm shells

'On parade' In circumstances which demand that protocols of rank are maintained. By contrast, 'off parade' means that titles and rank differentiation are less important and that less formality is acceptable

Pusser Slang for 'purser', in the sense of 'officially' or 'properly' naval

Rate Rank

Rating Non-commissioned sailor

RNB Royal Naval Barracks, e.g. RNB Devonport

R/T Radio telegraphy – messages relayed by voice

Royal A Royal Marine term for one of their own, i.e. a fellow Royal Marine

SBA Sick berth attendant (male nurse in a naval hospital)

SIS British Secret Intelligence Service

SOE Strategic Operations Executive – British wartime Intelligence Service

Shake Naval term for an early morning call

Slip The command to let go mooring lines and move off

SNIO Senior Naval Intelligence Officer

Sparks The ship's radio operator

Stone frigate Naval shore establishment

'Swain Another abbreviation for coxswain – often used as a form of address

'Up spirits!' Call over the ship's tannoy system to announce the serving of the daily rum ration

Wardroom Room in a ship/shore establishment reserved for commissioned officers

W/T Wireless telegraphy – messages relayed by Morse code

Yeoman The ship's signaller (often abbreviated to Yeo in addressing the Yeoman directly)

=====O=====

Acknowledgements

==============================

I am indebted to many people for the help, support and encouragement that they have given me in the preparation and writing of this book.

First, the infectious and gratifying enthusiasm of Neil Thomas, Chairman of Thorogood Publishing, which has been a great source of stimulus – and confidence – to me to complete the book.

His colleagues, Neill Ross, Managing Director and Angela Spall, Editorial Director at Thorogood have provided constant guidance and invaluable advice, upon which I shamelessly and regularly draw. They and Neil Thomas make working together enormous joy – and fun.

On the island of Tresco, people have generously given their time so freely, to answer my questions and to provide much helpful information to add historical authenticity and local context to the story. *The Secret Channel* is a fictionalised account, but it has its roots in real Scillonian and Special Forces history.

People on Tresco include:

Richard Barber, author of *The Last Piece of England* and Editor of the *Tresco Times*, who has been such a helpful source of information about Tresco's wartime history from his own extensive study.

Alasdair Moore of Tresco Estate, author of *La Mortola – In the Footsteps of Thomas Hanbury,* for his patient help in identifying so many of the beautiful wild flowers that grow on Tresco and are referred to in this book.

Robin Lawson, Manager of the New Inn Hotel, for his invaluable information about the New Inn during the Second World War.

Eddie 'the Toast Man' Birch of the Island Hotel, Tresco, who lived on the island as a young boy when the flotilla was operational.

Dora Fearnley (née Andrews) who was born at Valhalla on Tresco and, likewise, remembers the 'mystery boats' of the flotilla when she was a little girl.

On the island of St Agnes, thanks are due to Robert Anderson, landlord of the Turk's Head public house, for his help on the history and original location of the pub during the Second World War.

To Mark Critchley, who formerly served with the Royal Navy and is now a senior police officer, I owe my sincere thanks for his most helpful advice and guidance on important naval details and historical context.

To the late Sir Brooks Richards, author of *Secret Flotillas*, the HMSO definitive account of clandestine small boat operations between 1940 and 1944, I owe an inestimable debt for the time he kindly gave to answer my many questions.

Being a spectator in July 2000 at the moving unveiling of the commemorative plaque to the Naval Special Forces based on Tresco during the war – and meeting Sir Brooks – was an unforgettable experience and the inspiration for this book.

To the Naval Club, Mayfair, of which I am a member – and to Commander John Pritchard RN, the Chief Executive – I express my gratitude for the Club journal *WAVE*. This has regularly proved to be a source of relevant information on wartime Coastal Forces operations and the role of former Royal Naval Volunteer Reserve (RNVR) officers in particular.

Eight years of full-time and volunteer reserve service in first the Royal Navy (Intelligence) and secondly the Royal Marines (Special Boat Service and Commando) have provided me with a rich source of experience and material, from which I have drawn extensively for the story.

Finally, to Brenda, my wife, I owe so much for the benefit of her extensive experience as a writer and her perceptiveness in refining my own fictional written style.

She and I first canoed around the Isles of Scilly together in 1959 and were still canoeing in those beautiful emerald and turquoise seas as recently as 2007, in our seventies. Her knowledge of Tresco especially has been a great help in developing the story of *The Secret Channel*.

Mike Williams